Misrule

Misrule

BOOK 2 OF MALICE

Heather Walter

DEL REY

NEW YORK

Copyright © 2022 by Heather Walter

All rights reserved.

Published in the United States by Del Rey, an imprint of Random House, a division of Penguin Random House LLC, New York.

DEL REY and the CIRCLE colophon are registered trademarks of Penguin Random House LLC.

Library of Congress Cataloging-in-Publication Data
Names: Walter, Heather, author.
Title: Misrule / Heather Walter.
Description: First edition. | New York : Del Rey, [2022] | Series: Malice duology ; book 2
Identifiers: LCCN 2021057106 (print) | LCCN 2021057107 (ebook) | ISBN 9781984818683 (hardcover ; acid-free paper) | ISBN 9781984818690 (ebook)
Subjects: LCGFT: Novels.
Classification: LCC PS3623.A44683 M57 2022 (print) | LCC PS3623.A44683 (ebook) | DDC 813/.6—dc23/eng/20211206
LC record available at https://lccn.loc.gov/2021057106
LC ebook record available at https://lccn.loc.gov/2021057107

International edition ISBN 978-0-593-49914-6

Printed in Canada on acid-free paper

randomhousebooks.com

2 4 6 8 9 7 5 3 1

First Edition

Book design by Elizabeth A. D. Eno

For every reader who made space in their hearts for these books. I wrote Alyce for you.

And for Lindsey, always, who taught me that true love isn't just for fairy tales.

Misrule

Father,

I am waylaid in Cardon, as my ship cannot manage the remainder of the voyage home.

Briar is sacked.

My crew and I barely escaped the harbor with our lives. The Briar King is dead. The realm aflame. I heard that Princess Aurora was cursed to sleep or to die, I do not know which is true. But she cannot have survived. There was a . . . a creature. Winged and ravenous and brutal. I saw it rip a man in two with its claws, like something from a nightmare. But the monster is real.

And the beast rules Briar.

—Missive from Prince Elias to the king of Ryna. Age of the Rose, 976

PROLOGUE

A wispy plume of golden smoke curls up from the mash of ingredients in the mortar, tinged with the honey-sweet scent of Grace blood. I flex my fingers, stiff after gripping the pestle for so long, and roll away the tension in my neck.

"I found this book in Willow House," I say. Or what was left of it. "You remember how strong those healing Graces were. One almost ascended to be a Royal Grace. There was that courtier— I forget her name now—she was rumored to be over a hundred years old because of their elixirs."

I take the mortar and a spoon and go to the bed, still encased in bramble. Callow, my kestrel, warbles from her perch on a nearby stack of books.

"You see? Even Callow agrees. This must be the one."

At my touch, the intertwined vines slither apart, revealing the sleeper inside. Even after all this time, my heart still flutters at the sight of her.

Aurora.

It's been nearly a year since that terrible night in the black tower when her hand met the spindle. But her bronze-kissed cheeks still carry their healthy glow. Her eyelashes flutter as she dreams, and her lips are slightly parted, as if she might wake up at any moment and end the nightmare of the last months. Day after miserable day of failed attempts to break her curse.

"Please wake up," I whisper to her, tipping a small amount of elixir past her lips.

The golden liquid slides over her tongue and into her throat. I hold my breath, clutching her hand. The seconds drag on. And then—her pulse might be beating faster, stronger. The movement beneath her eyelids is more pronounced. I know—*I know*—that she inhales a deeper breath. Yes. This is it. She'll wake, and then we can—

Aurora's body abruptly goes slack. The heartbeat in her wrist slows until it is as faint as it ever was. Tears sting against my eyelids. One rolls down my cheek and splashes onto Aurora's coverlet, staining the embroidered line of dragons in flight. Damn everything to the bottom of the sea and back. I hurl the mortar across the room. Its crash echoes in the tomblike chamber.

"We'll try again." I swipe my sleeve over my nose, attempting to convince myself as much as Aurora. "I found two more Graces in the ruins of the Common District yesterday. Maybe their blood is capable of what we need. I'll go to the dungeons and—"

A muffled *thunk* sounds in the distance, drawing me away from the bed and to the craggy gap in the wall. The wreckage of Briar sprawls toward the sea. Smoke curls in long green tendrils from the husks of buildings and empty streets. Sometimes a shadow scurries from one hiding place to the next, likely a surviving citizen thinking I care which rank hole they choose to burrow into and live out their miserable days. It makes no difference to me so long as they don't trouble us. At least they've stopped trying to breach the palace.

Another explosion reverberates on the wind. Beyond the districts, a fleet is cutting across the waves, closing in on the scraps of wood that used to be the harbor. More humans from across the sea, announcing their presence with cannon fire. I assume the arrogant fools seek to stake their claim on Briar and its Etherium, like all the rest who have sailed to these shores. They would do better to turn around and go home. But none ever do. I sigh and prepare to Shift.

Wait, a shadowy voice in my head instructs, both mine and not mine. *Let us greet them from here.*

Here? The harbor is miles away, and I'm so high up that the ships appear as small as my fingernail. There's no way I could possibly—

Anything is possible with us, pet.

A shiver of delight trills down my spine. I dive within myself and find that den where my power lives. But it's not just mine anymore—not since that fateful night in the black tower, when Mortania's magic was released from her medallion prison and melded with my own, creating the most formidable Vila power in existence. At a mere thought, the tether of magic unfurls. It races across the districts at impossible speed, and I'm hit with the competing scents of charred earth and iron-laced stone—all bits of magic I could grasp with mine and control, the same way I did when I took this realm. But I do not linger on such petty hearts of magic, amazed that the limb of my power does not strain in the slightest. I've been testing its limits over the last months—using it to mend holes in the palace walls and summoning giant waves to block encroaching fleets. Mortania's power has bolstered my own abilities to levels I'd never dreamed possible. Even so, I've never done *this*.

My magic slams into the hull of a ship. The shock of it vibrates in my bones. Shifting my eyesight, I can just glimpse the massive vessel teetering like a child's toy. I sense the fear of the drowning sailors through the cord of my power. Hear the faint crunch of a mast snapping. An instant later, the sea claims the ship, swallowing it down in one gulp. My magic moves on to the next. And the next. Power sings across every nerve and raises the roots of my hair.

Yes, pet. This is what you were made for.

I draw myself up, savoring her praise.

But I wasn't always so receptive to the voice of Mortania. When I was the Dark Grace, her spirit haunted my nightmares. I'd been terrified of becoming as wicked as the stories rumored her to have been. By all accounts, I was. Shortly after my siege, the full weight of what I'd done to Briar settled over me. As I watched the realm burn, I thought of the citizens in the Common District, many of whom might have hated the nobles as much as I did. The children. Even Hilde, the apothecary, who treated me almost as a friend. But she'd fled like all the rest, horror-struck by the winged beast unleashing its wrath on Briar.

Take care you do not become the monster they believe you to be, she'd said.

But a monster was what I needed to be all along.

Mortania taught me that, and so much more in the last months. Her presence now is like a missing piece put back into place. One I do not intend to lose again.

"It's you."

Callow screeches a warning, and my concentration shatters. I whirl around. The barrier of oil-skinned trees that blocked the door against Tarkin's army yawns wide, and there is a stranger standing at the entrance to the library.

"Who are—" But my voice falls flat as my eyes travel over her. The long, lean-muscled limbs. Jet hair threaded with russet. A gash just below a spike of bone on her forehead is scabbed with green—*green*—blood. More bone spikes travel down her rich brown forearms, along her collarbones, and across her forehead like a crown. Her eyes sparkle like emeralds. Deep in the place where my magic lives, Mortania's presence undulates.

I have to peel my tongue from the roof of my mouth. "You're . . ." I almost cannot say it. "Vila. Like me."

She shakes her head, slowly. "I don't think anyone is like you." The stranger steps farther into the library. Glass crunches under her boots as she crosses to the gap in the wall. I'm stunned into stillness. Callow flaps to a nearer perch, protective, but the stranger is too focused to notice her. "Did you really just sink that fleet from all the way back here? It took me half a day to travel to the palace from the harbor."

A breeze gusts in through the gap. The last ship surrenders to the sea. Angry waves crash against the slick red rock of the Crimson Cliffs. I must have pushed back dozens of others in the last months. Their bones litter the seabed. "I . . . yes."

"Then all the stories are true. The Vila who seized the realm responsible for the blight on Malterre. One of *us*."

One of us. The words brush a chamber in my heart I didn't know existed. Callow screeches again, at last capturing the stranger's attention.

"Is that your bird?" she asks. "It looks like it might want to eat me."

The kestrel mutters in reply and clacks her beak.

"You don't need to worry about that," I assure the stranger. "Her name is Callow." The kestrel flares her wings, showing off.

"Hello, Callow. I'm Regan." She reaches a tentative hand toward the kestrel, who allows herself to be stroked. My suspicion ebbs. If Callow approves of her, then so do I. Mortania's presence ripples in something that might be agreement. "And you?"

"Al—" No, that name is from another time. "Nimara. Call me Nimara."

"Nimara." She draws it out, like she's tasting it. Her dark lips curve into a soft smile. And wings flap in my belly. "After the first Vila?"

"You know about her?"

"We Vila may be exiled, but we take pride in our history." She tilts her head, studying me. "Nimara is the perfect name for you."

Kinship sears through me. And there are a hundred things I want to say, to ask. But then a growl interrupts the quiet—Regan's stomach. Until now, I hadn't fully registered the ragged state of her clothes. The scrapes and cuts crisscrossing her limbs, and the salt crusting her unraveling braid. "What happened to you?"

She looks down at herself and grins. "You did. I sailed here in the cargo hold of a ship bound for Briar. It didn't exactly receive a warm reception."

Because I blasted it apart with my power, like I'd done to all the others. Wonderful. I've welcomed the first other Vila to Briar by nearly drowning her. "I didn't know. I wouldn't have—"

"Don't apologize. This"—she indicates the smoking wreckage of Briar—"is glorious. And so are you."

My flush deepens. I tug at the sleeves of my gown. "You need to eat something." Besides today, the last fleet I remember spotting was weeks ago. Dragon knows what Regan has been surviving on since she pulled herself out of the sea. I hurry to a table, where my half-eaten breakfast sits on a plate. The bricklike scone and dried meat isn't exactly appetizing. "You'll have to forgive me. The fresh things spoiled ages ago, and I've no particular skill in the kitchen."

The food is one of the only things I miss about former Briar. Fruit-filled pastries and decadent cakes and buttery cheeses— delicacies I'll likely never taste again. Maybe one of the cooks is still alive. I should have checked. Regan accepts the plate and bites off a piece of scone with effort. "This is a feast."

"I can do something about those cuts as well." I busy myself at a table, where I have some leftover ingredients from my attempts at waking Aurora.

The various powders and leaves are nothing compared to what would have been available in my Lair at Lavender House, but it will have to suffice. I pick through jars and inspect vials of multi-colored oils, calculating which would be best to—

"Who is that?"

I freeze. Dragon's teeth. I'd been so wrapped up in Regan's ar-rival that I'd forgotten all about the bed of bramble. And I suppose Regan didn't notice, either—until now. She veers in the direction of the bed. My senses come back to me in a violent whoosh. Vila or not, Regan is a stranger. With a snap of my fin-gers, the branches cinch closed. Regan has to jump back before a thorned vine whips her in the face.

"Don't touch her."

Regan backs away, one hand holding up the remainder of the scone in a placating gesture. "I mean her no harm. Is she sick?"

"She's . . ." I hesitate. Somehow I doubt that Regan will be thrilled to discover Briar's last princess sleeping under my protection. I'm not sure how she'll react if she knows. But there's no point in lying. Aurora's portrait is everywhere in this palace. It's only a matter of time before Regan figures it out. "Aurora. Princess Aurora. And she's not sick—she's cursed."

The cry of a raven carries through the room.

"Cursed?" Regan repeats, swallowing down her mouthful. Her lips twitch up. "Did you do that, too?"

"What? No. Well, sort of." Mortania's presence rumbles, and I tamp her down, uncomfortably reminded that, as much as I appreciate her power, the ancient Vila is partly responsible for Aurora's sleep. "It was my magic that caused the curse, but I didn't mean to use it against her. She's my . . . friend."

I cannot bring myself to confess more. Regan wouldn't understand. Besides, I will not repeat the mistake of the last time I trusted someone who didn't deserve it. The shadows of the room seem to dance and writhe, as they did in the black tower.

"Oh." Regan peers through the narrow slats of bramble, at Aurora. "Judging from the state of things, I didn't expect you to be a friend of the royals."

"Aurora is different," I explain. "She respects my dark magic. Before all of this, we were going to change the realm. Root out the corruption. But then the curse happened, and I . . ."

"Took matters into your own hands," Regan finishes. I nod. "I like it."

Salt-laced wind gusts in from the sea, stirring torn book pages.

And I let myself relax. Regan isn't questioning or challenging me about Aurora. She crosses back to Callow, who mutters on her perch and rearranges herself.

"You really stowed away on a ship to come here?" I ask, changing the subject.

She pets the white fluff on Callow's head. "Wouldn't you have done the same if you heard of a Vila who had set herself up in a mortal palace?"

Yes. The answer expands through every limb. I would have wanted to anyway. But would I have gone through with it? I never possessed the courage to sneak away on a ship when I was the Dark Grace. And I admit that until Regan walked in I hadn't given a thought to the other Vila across the sea. I was aware they existed, that the creatures of Malterre scattered after the War of the Fae, which was how I eventually came about. But now I feel that I've been neglecting my own kind. Worse, ignoring them.

"Will you tell me about yourself?" I ask, embarrassment nipping at me. "And about the other Vila?"

"If you like." She shoves the last crumbly bits of scone into her mouth. "But on one condition."

The walls groan in the wind. "What?"

She points to the plate. "I'm sorry, but even for a starving person, this really was quite terrible. Are you certain there's nothing better?"

A laugh bursts out of me. And I almost choke in surprise. Because today with Regan is the first time in months that I *have* laughed. An unfamiliar lightness blooms in my veins—one I haven't experienced since Aurora was cursed.

Callow settles on my shoulder as we leave the library and head toward the kitchens, where I do my best to scrounge up a decent meal for Regan. She tells me of her life roaming the realms across the sea, of living in hiding and being unable to so much as set foot in a village or town for fear of being executed. Of the loss of her mother and sister. The friendships cut short because someone was captured. And though I do not share her circumstances exactly, Regan's sorrow speaks directly to mine, resonating in the very marrow of my bones. And I tell her of Lavender House, and Kal, and the medallion. How Mortania's power joined with mine to create the greatest force of an age. Everything but my relationship with Aurora. I insist that we were friends, and Regan appears to accept my claim that Aurora isn't like the cruel humans who have sullied our pasts. But I can sense her skepticism, such as any Vila who wasn't familiar with the sleeping princess would harbor. Perhaps, in time, she might understand.

"I wish I'd been as brave as you," I say. We're back in the library, with two bottles of Tarkin's best vintage in hand. The sun is setting over the horizon, but it feels like only minutes have passed since she set foot in this chamber. "All those years, I could have used my elixirs to bargain my way out of Briar. Seek the life I wanted, no matter the consequences."

She takes a long swig, then points her bottle toward Briar. "It looks like you did, eventually."

Yes, pet. We did.

Fizzy wine dances down my throat. "I suppose you're right."

"And what now? You're not the Dark Grace anymore. And you're not alone."

Shyness creeps up my neck. "I hope that means you'll be staying awhile."

"If you'll have me." She scoots slightly closer. "But it's about more than just the two of us. How many of our kind have wanted to do *exactly* what you've accomplished here? We were pushed out of Malterre. Hunted in the realms across the sea. And you pushed back. That's why I came here. That's why the others will come."

Others? I study the gold-painted waves of the sea, imagining ships of Vila pulling into the harbor. The palace filled with my kin. "You really think they will?"

She reaches over and squeezes my wrist. A jolt gallops through me at the sight of her bone spikes against my pale green-veined skin. "I would have crossed the sea a hundred times over if it meant being here. The Nimara from our history gave us our first home. And now you can give us another."

Home. The word unfurls inside me like a flower opening. Mortania nudges against my insides, her dark presence filling me up, and even Callow warbles what could be encouragement.

But my focus travels to the bed of bramble. How would Aurora feel about a court comprised solely of the creatures of Malterre—Goblins and Imps and Demons? Or the state of this palace . . . and Briar?

"Do you think it's horrible, what I've done?" The question—one I've asked myself too often in the endless hours of night—bubbles out of me before I can stop it.

"Horrible?" Regan echoes. "You gave the humans what they deserved. Do you regret it?"

"No," I answer immediately. And I don't. Any guilt that's festered in my soul over the last year is nothing compared to the power I command. But the whine of the wind sharpens in pitch, like the screams from the citizens when I was soaring above them. The faint, ever-present smell of sulfur stings in my nostrils. "But sometimes . . . it haunts me. This was her home, too."

"Were you ever welcome in it?" Regan asks gently. "Truly welcome? From what you've described to me today, it doesn't sound like you were. She had good intentions, but . . ."

That touches a nerve. The wine is suddenly too sweet. I set the bottle down and stand, going to the other side of the gap. Smoke curls into the sky. "Aurora would have done everything she promised. You didn't know her."

Regan rises. "I can't argue with you. But if she's really your friend, wouldn't she support you? Wouldn't *she* have been angry if she'd known what happened after she was cursed?"

I'd never considered the circumstances in that light. Aurora *would* have been furious to learn of the "protections" the Fae ambassador Endlewild placed on her curse, permitting her to be woken by anyone's kiss but mine—and then painting me a villain in her memory. She'd be even angrier if she discovered that wedding preparations were already in place while she slept. I think her father was actually going to marry her off before she was fully conscious, if they let her wake at all. Tarkin might have deemed it more advantageous to lock his unconscious daughter in a tower and blame her curse on me.

"May I tell you something?" The back of Regan's hand brushes mine, and my breath catches again at the sensation of her touch. Another Vila, after a lifetime alone. "When you were the Dark Grace, they trapped you. Forced you to make elixirs every day of your life. To despise your own power." She gestures around the library. "And, forgive me, but it doesn't seem like a lot has changed since then."

A retort is ready on my lips. But then Mortania's presence sighs in its den.

Listen well, pet. And look around you.

I'm not certain what the ancient Vila means. But then I take in the books teeming on every surface, and the ingredients haphazardly piled on tables. The entire palace is open to me, and I've barely left this library. Even my current gown was pilfered from the servants' stores. Because that's all I've ever been.

I pluck at the worn laces of my bodice. "I . . . haven't really known what to do."

"How could you know?" she asks. "Your whole life they taught you that you're nothing. But you, Nimara, are *everything*."

Without thinking, I take Regan's hand and hold it tight. Energy hums between us. No one but Aurora has ever spoken to me with such raw appreciation. And a thought begins to winnow through my mind. Even if Aurora had become queen, she couldn't have pulled up *all* of Briar's rotted roots. But that's exactly what I've done—made it so that we can start entirely fresh. And we will.

Yes, pet. Mortania practically purrs. *We will.*

"Let them all come. We'll found our own court." I say to Regan, a name sprouting in my mind as if it had been planted there long ago. "The Dark Court."

She retrieves our wine bottles, passes me mine, and raises a toast. "To the Dark Court, then. And its mistress."

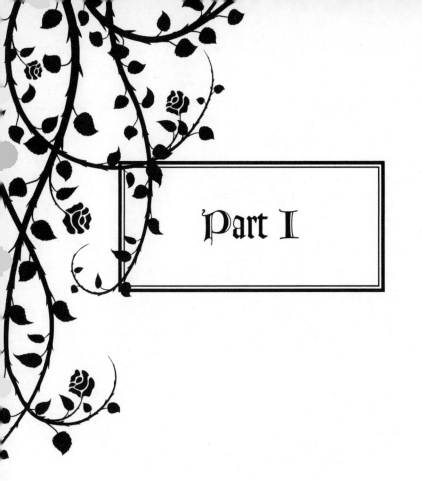

Part I

There is a prophecy.

That the High King of the Fae will lose his throne when the mountains crumble.

That a power will be released, heralding a new age. One that shall begin with a forgotten crown.

Ridiculous.

Some drivel spouted by a member of the Court of Dreams after too much ambrosia wine.

There is but one age, one crown, and both belong to me. I have ruled the Fae courts for millennia. Without me, this land would wither and die. For I am its king.

I am Etheria itself.

—From the private writings of Oryn,
High King of the Fae, date unknown

ONE HUNDRED YEARS LATER

CHAPTER ONE

AGE OF THE DARK COURT, 99

"Do you think she's dead?"

"She's breathing, you idiot."

Tinny voices permeate the twilight space between sleeping and waking. I groan and pull the thick covers over my head.

"See? I tolds you."

Something hard thunks onto flesh and the screeching wail of an Imp stabs through my skull, erasing any hope that they will find some other entertainment before I'm fully awake. I throw a pillow in the direction of their noise. "It's too early for your nonsense."

"Not nonsense, Mistress." Their squabble ceases. I open my eyes to discover two vermilion faces peering at me, only tall enough that the tips of their hooked noses hover above the edge of the bed. "We've brought you something."

With a chorus of grunts, the Imps heave a text onto the enormous mattress and slide it toward me. I push myself to sit up, curiosity overriding my irritation. "Where did you get this?"

"Valmar says to bring it right to you. Says we weren't allowed to wait, case it gots lost."

Which occurs more often than not with the Imps. I run my hands over the book's cover. It's not a material I recognize, like leather, but scaled and slightly rough. I wonder if it's dragon hide. If so, it's exceedingly rare and old.

"Has Valmar brought more Imps from Malterre?" It's been years since we welcomed anyone from those blighted lands into the Dark Court.

"Aye." One of the Imps uses his companion as a ladder and clambers up onto the bed. He points a clawed finger at the book. "Will you read it to us? Been too long since we had a story."

I trace the sigil stamped into the cover, the unique material made darker against the nearly translucent shade of my skin. A broken Fae orb of the Vila crest surrounded by a circle of raven feathers.

I knew that court, Mortania whispers from her den. *It could contain powerful magic.*

The tingling of my curiosity intensifies. I've learned so much from the relics and books the Imps carried with them from the ruins of Malterre—all manner of rituals and the history of the Vila courts. I cannot wait to see what secrets this one provides. Maybe, impossibly, even something about *breaking* curses.

"I haven't even eaten breakfast," I say to the Imps, hoping they'll scurry off and leave me to explore the book in peace.

But the first one fishes a stone out of his pocket, tosses it into the air, and claps. By the time he catches it, the rock is transformed into a glazed pastry. He presents it to me with a flourish and a jagged-toothed smile. "Your favorite."

The other Imp applauds. I accept the pastry but give him a

playful pinch anyway. It was a blessing when we discovered the Imps and their small magic. They can turn almost any bit of rock, wood, or material into a feast. And my skill in the kitchen never improved from the months I lived here alone.

"A story, then," I say around a mouthful of nutty chocolate filling, and crack open the text, releasing its smell of musty parchment.

"With plenty of guts and blood," one of the Imps instructs, the veiny ridges of his ears quivering.

"Find one with a beheading. We love those."

I thumb through the pages, scanning entries detailing various events in the fallen court. Council meetings and ceremonies and special occasions. Births and deaths. Logs and ledgers. A few diagrams illustrating how to conduct rituals I've not yet encountered, which I make a mental note of to revisit later. "This isn't a story-book," I tell them, tapping a corner of the page. "And these dates suggest that it was written before the War of the Fae, so I doubt there are any beheadings. Vila courts didn't do that to their own."

"Sounds boring." An Imp yawns.

The other nudges closer. "You sure there's not anyone having their innards ripped out?"

I eat the rest of the pastry, lick my sticky fingertips, and am tempted to ask for another. "Not that I can see."

Their ears droop in disappointment. One scrambles from his place and scurries to the foot of the bed, which, as this is the former royal suite, is fashioned to look like the head of a roaring dragon just landed from battle. Its massive mahogany tail winds down one of the bedposts, and taloned wings dip down over the sides. "I shall tell a story, then," he announces. "Of Mistress Nimara and how she turned beastie and toppled the fat old king and rescued us Imps from the Fae courts! How she swooped in with her green fire and—"

"You're telling it wrong! You left out her claws. And her teeth. Thems the best bits." The other rushes across the bed and barrels into him. Both fall in a tangle of limbs onto the floor.

I rub my temples. I definitely should have asked for another pastry while I had the chance. Or at least tea. An impatient tapping draws my attention to the window. I kick free of the bedclothes and draw the curtain back.

"Where did you get off to?" I crank the panes wide, and my kestrel wings past me with a peal of pleasure. She completes a lap of the room and then settles on the back of a chair. The Imps greet her with a cheer. Everyone at court adores Callow. "There was a storm last night. I worried about you."

She clacks her beak in a way that informs me that she has no patience for my fussing, and the Imps turn handfuls of pebbles into dried beetles and fling them at her. She catches them midair, and they are beside themselves with glee.

Of all the surprises of the last century, Callow's steadfast presence is by far the best. In truth, I'm not entirely sure how the kestrel hasn't aged. Regan's theory is that I unknowingly bound Callow sometime during my years in Lavender House. We learned of binding curses in the Vila books, and I could have unwittingly initiated one anytime the kestrel nipped me hard enough to draw blood, allowing my magic to enter her body. My power centers on intent, and I'd wanted Callow to stay with me badly enough that I ensured she always would.

There's a knock on my door, and then Regan enters. She stops short at the Imps. "What are you lot doing in here?"

But they've invented a game in which they toss the beetles to each other instead of Callow, and the kestrel is swooping back and forth between them, extremely annoyed.

I thread my arms through an ermine-lined cape to ward off the cold. "They brought me a book from Valmar."

Regan dodges out of the way before one of the Imps smacks into her. It's been a century since she first arrived in this palace, but she looks the same as when she discovered me in the old library. Both of us do, our magic slowing our years and preventing our appearances from significantly altering. Even though I can Shift, my human form is easiest to maintain.

"Anything interesting?" she asks about the book.

"I'm not sure yet." I go back to where I left it on the bed, keeping out of the line of Imp fire. "But I'm fairly certain it was written before the time of the Briar Queens, maybe even before Leythana."

Regan disappears into the wardrobe, which is a cavern unto itself. Before Briar's fall, this suite belonged to King Tarkin, and he cared about his clothes almost as much as he did about his army. "You'll have to read it later," she calls from within. "Torin is waiting in the council chamber. The Goblins sent a report of their progress in the Fae courts."

She returns with a gown draped over her arm. A rich garnet velvet cinched at the waist with a thick chain belt. Metal clasps form an inverted triangle down the front in an almost military style. I shrug off my dressing gown and step into it.

"Bad?"

"Wonderful." She helps me tighten the laces in the back, her fingers deftly familiar with the task. The bone spikes on her knuckles graze the nape of my neck. Sometimes it seems impossible that there was ever a time here without Regan. We've become closer than sisters. "They have the Court of Dreams on their toes. It's sure to fall soon, which makes six of the seven courts destroyed."

The Imps let out a feral cheer and complete a series of celebratory somersaults. I hadn't envisioned a second war with the Fae when we founded the Dark Court. But then we heard of the Imps being used as slaves in Etheria. In the course of liberating them, and as more joined our ranks, the cry for vengeance against the Etherians became all but deafening. It started with Goblins and Demons sneaking over the Etherian Mountains border just to tweak the noses of the Fae. But when the Etherians retaliated, the conflict swelled to a wildfire.

You did not argue against it, pet.

No. The Lord Ambassador Endlewild treated me like I was vermin when I was the Dark Grace, poisoning my mind against my own kind. And the Fae are responsible for the supposed protections on Aurora's curse, which ensure she will not recognize me if she wakes. I may not have set out to start a war, but I intend to finish it.

"It needs something," an Imp says, rubbing his chin and examining my gown.

"I know." The other claps.

In a puff of smoke, the skirt of the dress is transformed into a cascade of scarlet and black peacock feathers. It's excessive, but I know better than to criticize their work. "Another masterpiece."

They beam with pleasure, and tumble over themselves and out the door.

"Do you remember when you advised me to assign guards for my chambers?" I ask Regan.

"You said you didn't want a barrier between yourself and the rest of the court."

Callow settles on my shoulder. "I was mistaken."

The rest of the palace is waking as we make our way through the halls. The former Briar King Tarkin would weep to see his monstrosity of stained glass and pink stone as it is today. When Tarkin ruled, the aristocrats living in the affluent Grace District would drink their weight in wine every night and spend their coin on pearl-encrusted slippers and gowns with embroidery that was brought to life by the magic of the innovation Graces. The parties at the palace were the stuff of legend, with Briar roses that changed shade every few moments and elaborate costumes. Desserts dipped in edible gold and dragon-snouted fountains flowing with fizzing wine.

Now, a century later, green rust clings like barnacles to solid gold sconces. Crystal chandeliers are chipped and coated with silt. Cobweb curtains drape over the busts of former Briar Queens, their crowns of bramble and thorn now packed with clumps of spiders' nests. The plush carpets are muddied and moth-riddled. Fine tapestries depicting Briar's early history—scenes of the first queen, Leythana, besting the Fae challenge that earned her the throne, and those of the first Fae war—are all but unraveled.

If I listen carefully, I can imagine the laughter of the former courtiers, the slivers of gossip dealt out like hands of cards, the rustle of silks and the clip of heels. Now, Imps scurry back and forth with platters of food, lobbing handfuls at one another more often than not. Bowlegged Goblins are still blearily scratching behind their horns as they head to the practice yard, wicked weapons of their own design strapped to their backs. Demons patrol on their sentry duties, all of them trodding upon the dead king's bones. It is deliciously fitting.

Deep in the place where my magic lives, Mortania's spirit thrums with laughter.

The council chamber is the same war room Tarkin used as Briar King, complete with the massive doors fashioned to look like a dragon. The ruby-eyed beast is the only surviving motif of the old court. It reminds me of Leythana, and of the might and strength it took for me to raze Briar and establish the Dark Court—the same determination Leythana herself exhibited when besting the Fae challenge that earned her Briar's throne. I walk through its broad belly with my head held high and look out at the sprawling ruins through the wall of glass. I think Leythana would be proud of what I've done. After all, there wasn't anything left of her warrior-queen rule when I took charge. Her heirs—except Aurora—were shadows of their ancestress. Weak and inefficient. Not anymore.

"Nimara." Torin, leader of the Demons, greets us from her place as I transfer Callow to the back of my chair.

Six chairs surround the ebony table. One for me, and another for each clan leader, a representative elected by their own.

"How are the rescued Imps faring?" I ask.

"Well enough." Like all Demons, Torin's long, lithe body appears to be sculpted from living coals. Bright fissures map their way over her deep black body, glowing and fading from orange to gold to amber, as if her very blood is made of molten fire. "Valmar and his party scared them nearly to death. They'd burrowed into some of the oldest ruins and lived almost entirely underground. Valmar says they're skittish at seeing a court as large as ours."

It's a common complaint among new arrivals to the palace. When refugees aren't hiding in corners, they often gorge themselves until they're sick, as it's been so long since they've eaten any decent food. There was a Goblin some years ago who barricaded herself in a suite of rooms for a month because she was convinced it would be taken over if she ever left. I'd delivered a few of her meals myself, glimpsing only the flash of warty green hands snatching up the tray before the door slammed shut again.

You gave them a home. Mortania swirls in her cave.

"We'll have a revel," I say. "That will lift their spirits."

"You never have to convince me to throw a revel." Regan props her heels on the silver-veined table. Her staff leans behind her chair. It's a twisted yew bark that is spotted with the dried Fae blood of the Etherian she'd taken it from during a campaign. Nearly every council member carries such a trophy, including myself. "And what of Malakar's report? More boasting?"

Torin holds up a parchment. "I'm sure we'll hear plenty of that soon. He'll be home in the next days if all goes well—with Neve accompanying his party."

I frown and pick up one of the pewter markers. It's in the shape of a starling bird, which is the symbol of Neve's network of Shifter spies. Shifters—with their changeable forms—make excellent spies. But though I've had no official cause for complaint among the Starlings, I cannot help but continually compare them to Kal. He was the only other full-blooded Shifter I knew, and he turned out to be just like the duplicitous creatures I'd read about in the book Endlewild had given me. The sharp edges of the marker bite into my flesh. All those traps he'd laid—which I stupidly stepped into. What similar traps might Neve be setting?

Worry not, pet. I shall not let you be led astray.

Callow chuffs and flares her wings, as if even she can sense the ancient Vila's presence.

"Good riddance to the Court of Dreams, then." Regan slips her favorite dagger from her boot. Its handle is carved from bone, fashioned as a jade-eyed snake with its jaws screaming wide, blade protruding from its throat. "It's about time it fell, after ten years of laying siege to the place. Tonight's revel shall have dual purpose."

"Are you certain the Imps can conjure enough wine?" Torin curls a half-smile.

"That"—Regan sits up and reaches for the pitcher—"sounds like a challenge."

I hold my hand over her goblet before she can start pouring. "It isn't even midday. What of our losses. Did Malakar write of those?"

Torin's smile dims. Our power is formidable against the Fae and is sweeping through their courts the farther we push in. But Oryn's ilk are more than equally skilled in weaponry. And, though their magic is the exact opposite of our own, stemming from good intent, they can bend that intention to encompass all manner of retaliation in the name of "protection." And that is nothing compared to their skill with blades, which is not governed by their magic at all. "The Fae army wove enchanted nets that trapped my regiment in their trees and tainted their minds. I lost nearly fifty to madness."

Wind groans against the glass. Mortania surges in anger that matches mine. Such losses are inevitable, even expected, but I can't stand the thought that the Dark Court was supposed to be a haven for our kind. And too many have been killed in the Fae courts. I twist the band of my signet ring, designed like the broken-orb crest of the Vila, surrounded by ebony bramble and thorn.

Regan intuits my thoughts, as always. "There's nothing we could have done, Nimara. No one is sent against their will. They accept the risks."

"They do," I agree. "But we'll honor them before any revel. Add their names to the throne room walls."

"Plans are already in place," Torin assures me.

"And I am sorry about your regiment," I say to the Demon leader. "Was there anyone particularly close?"

The fissures mapping her limbs fade from umber to pale gold in a tempo that tells me she's melancholy. I've noticed her flit from one romantic entanglement to the next, with various court members. But she's never remained with one lover for long.

"No one I knew well," she says. "But I mourn them all."

"As does the court," I say.

A moment passes, brimming with shared grief.

"Which is why"—Regan picks up a marker and puts it in the center of the narrowing sphere that is Oryn's domain—"we need to focus on what's next. Our plan for razing the High Court and ending the war."

Torin holds up her hand. "I've no wish to deal with Malakar if he finds we've been strategizing without him."

She's right. And I can't focus on war planning anyway.

"Nor do I." Callow flaps to my shoulder as I push back from the table. "I have other matters to attend. I'll leave you two to plan out the particulars of the revel."

"What matters?" Regan asks as I head for the door.

"That book Valmar brought. I want to see if there's anything of value to be learned."

"Book?" Torin asks, straightening. The Demon leader shares my fascination with the relics of Malterre.

"An ancient court record. There might be something useful in it."

"I doubt it." Regan rearranges the markers. "Unless it can tell us how to vanquish the High King."

Regan has never possessed the patience, nor the love, for reading. Not like I do—or Aurora. A pang of grief hits me as I imagine us together in my Lair, our heads bent close as we debated the meaning of some obscure passage. The memory is so old that the edges are dimming.

But perhaps this book will be able to bring it—and her—back to life.

CHAPTER TWO

I return to my chambers to fetch the book, having decided to bring it to the old library and explore it with Aurora. I visit her daily and usually read to her in the hopes that she can hear me. But my suite isn't empty. A human servant, who should be changing the linens and tidying the mess the Imps made in my bedroom, is stealthily pawing through my drawers. She lifts a string of luminous black pearls and inspects it.

"Are you looking for something?" I ask from the shadows.

She leaps out of her skin and whirls. The pearls clack as they hit the marble floor. "I . . ." she stammers out. "I didn't see you there, Nimara."

"Clearly not." The peacock feathers on my skirt whisper behind me. "And it's *Mistress*."

She scrapes the barest of curtsies. "Mistress."

I take my time approaching her, savoring her obvious disdain— and that she can't do anything about it. "What is your name?"

A muscle in her jaw feathers, like she does not want to tell me. But she knows what will happen if she refuses. "Elspeth."

"Elspeth," I repeat, studying her dirt-smeared face and lank copper hair, which is devoid of the shine and luster she probably used to purchase from the beauty Graces. "You look familiar. Did you ever visit my Lair at Lavender House?"

The crimson flush on her cheeks is answer enough. I smirk. I love reminding the human servants of when they were haughty nobles, demanding elixirs for leaden feet or scratched voices to inflict upon one another. Of how far they have fallen and who rules now. Sometimes I brew batches of my old elixirs and force them to suffer the petty punishments they once commissioned from me. It's been a while since I've done so. Perhaps I shall send for Elspeth at our revel this evening.

"Were you stealing from me?" I point to the pearls. "I don't recall asking for my jewels to be cleaned."

"I wasn't." She keeps her eyes down.

"I don't believe you." I reach out and snatch up her forearm, turning it to reveal the circlet of bramble and thorn, the symbol of the curse that binds her to me. She hisses at the touch of my skin.

With barely a thought, my power slinks out of its cave, exerting the tiniest amount of pressure on our bond. The mark flares red. She yelps, attempting to pull back, but I hold her fast.

"You know the rules. You could have decided to wither away in the ruins of the districts. You *chose* me."

That oath was an offer I extended to all the humans as soon as I learned how. They could swear to me and serve at the palace or die of exposure or starvation in the graveyard that was Briar. A gracious proposition on my part, given the alternative. Those with enough sense accepted.

The smell of scorched flesh rises between us. But to her credit, Elspeth does not cower or beg. Fire blazes in her eyes. "I didn't choose you. I chose not to die."

I arch an eyebrow. "Would you like to reconsider?"

Mortania swells behind my sternum. Blisters pucker Elspeth's skin. But she holds out for another heartbeat. Two.

"Stop," she finally whimpers. "Please."

I release her, and she clutches her forearm to her chest.

"What were you doing in my jewelry? Thieves will be punished with far worse than a mild burn."

Indeed, depending on the severity of her betrayal, her mark might have killed her.

"I'm not stealing." She swallows. "I cannot steal something that is mine."

"Nothing here is yours."

She flexes her forearm and winces. "I'm looking for a brooch that belonged to my mother. It was a family heirloom, and I know it's here somewhere. We had rooms in the palace. I've looked everywhere else."

Of course she's searching for some trinket of her former life. I roll my eyes. "The Goblins probably have it. Go about your duties."

I reach for the book and head toward the door.

"I wish they'd never let you live."

Silence hums. Mortania sizzles across every nerve. I turn, slow and deliberate.

"Do you think to wound me with your opinion? That it's some kind of revelation? You—and the sycophants like you—reminded me every day of my life how unwanted I was. How despicable. Why do you suppose that I offered you mortals a place at *my* court?" I lean in and grin at the way she recoils. "So that you could finally know what it was like to be me."

The hollows of her collarbones deepen.

"What does your brooch look like?"

She purses her lips, her grip tightening on her forearm.

"It was a split pomegranate," she says at last. A tear splashes onto her cheek. "And the seeds were tiny stars."

"It must have been a beautiful piece. I shall ask the Goblins if they've seen it. And if they have"—I stroke the feathers on my skirt—"I shall wear it myself every day. And you'll never know when I might get the urge to take it off and grind each one of the precious stars into dust."

With that, I tuck the book under my arm and leave.

There are much faster ways to the old library, but I stick to the ancient servants' halls so that no one will follow me. As much as I trust my court, I decided long ago that Aurora should remain a secret for the time being. They did not know her as I did, and so many are suspicious of humans. I cannot blame them after what they endured in exile. Besides, Dragon knows what the Imps would do with Aurora if they were cognizant of her existence. I'd find her propped up like a living doll at their macabre tea parties. Or posed as a statue beside the busts of the old Briar Queens. Or they might make a game of hiding her. I cringe, picturing Aurora stuffed into one of the large cannons on the battlements. Better to wait for a proper introduction.

The massive limbs guarding the abandoned library shiver as I approach, sensing my magic. I slide my palm against a bough as thick as my torso, and the slick-skinned thing curves to one side.

Much of the palace has been restored in the last century, more or less, but almost nothing has changed in here. A breeze sighs through the jagged hole in the outer wall and wafts around me, laced with salt from the sea. I could have mended it, but I like the way it reminds me of the day I realized what it was to be powerful. The first day of my new life. *Our* new life.

The enclosure of wicked-thorned brambles around the bed unspools at my command, stems slithering in every direction to reveal Aurora nestled safely beneath her blanket. I sit beside her and squeeze her hands. "Hello."

And I imagine that she might answer in her mind. That she's waiting, just like I am, until we can be reunited. I pick up a comb and take my time running it through her spun-gold curls, arranging them just so on the pillow.

"More Imps arrived from Malterre," I tell her, nodding at the text beside me. "They brought another book. This one is old— maybe the oldest I've ever seen. It might help."

But I hear the wish in my voice. I've scoured every book in this library—in this realm—for answers to lifting Aurora's curse. But nothing has worked. I'm starting to worry nothing ever will. I cannot count the number of times I've almost dragged a human servant up here and commanded them to kiss Aurora, for at least then her amethyst eyes would open. But she also wouldn't remember me—*us*. I could not bear to see the hatred of former Briar reflected in her gaze. And she wouldn't want that, either.

Wind whistles through the cracks in the stone, and I shake myself out of my self-pity. I pull the book toward me. The familiar smell of aged paper greets me as its spine creaks open. At least the ink is in good condition. I'm amazed I haven't gone blind, with the amount of nearly translucent pages and illegible handwriting I've had to decipher over the years.

"It's a court record," I tell Aurora, examining the dates again. Without the distraction of the Imps, I'm able to more specifically place the time period. And I sit up straighter, interest piqued. "Oh, you'd love this. It was written during the time when the High King's staff was stolen by the Vila courts. We've never read anything about those events from a Vila's perspective." I scan a few entries. "It's describing the mortals who were trying to win Oryn's challenge and the Briar crown. I wonder if they write of Leythana."

The first Briar Queen is a subject of immense interest for both of us, and one of the reasons my friendship with Aurora had formed at all. Leythana was rumored to have sailed into Briar with a fleet of ships constructed from the carcasses of dragons, their enormous wings used as sails. Unlike the queens of Aurora's time, Leythana was fierce and decisive. Her daughters were just like her—at least for a few centuries. But then they softened, yielding their sovereign rights to their husbands until they were all but ornaments in their own courts.

I had unearthed some of their journals in the royal library, all filled with blather about balls and fashions and favorite courtiers. It was nauseating enough to make me believe that the volumes were either heavily censured, or that the queens were drinking enough wine to take the edge off their mundane lives. Leythana would never have been so complacent. She would have—grackles trade their calls above the jagged spikes of stone that make up the districts—she would have done exactly what I did, rather than let Briar slowly fester from the inside out.

Mortania stirs. *You have accomplished it for her, pet.*

Yes. And for Aurora.

"It will be a shock all the same," I say to her. The mattress rises and falls almost imperceptibly with the rhythm of Aurora's breathing. "This isn't *exactly* what we talked about when we were planning Briar's future. But you'll understand. I know you will."

Even so, an unpleasant doubt taps against the base of my skull. Will she understand? I smother the prickling question and go back to the book. I wish I could find a similar account written during Leythana's time, especially by her own hand, like the journals of the other queens. I've scoured the palace a hundred times over—even the royal crypt, where rows of stone caskets, topped with sculpted effigies, house tribute and mementos of the dead queens—but it's as if Leythana was nothing but a bronzed statue outside the palace gates. A story. Probably the doings of the old kings, who wouldn't have wanted their wives getting any ideas about governing from their ancestress.

"Ah, here," I say to Aurora. "There's something about a parley. That must be about Leythana. She's the only one who thought to negotiate with the Vila."

Everyone else who had attempted the Fae challenge went blazing into Malterre with weapons and died for their mistake. I keep reading. But this can't be right. I recite the passage aloud:

A prince from the Kingdom of Cardon arrived at the border between the unclaimed lands and Malterre. On behalf of his father, he extended his realm's hand in friendship should the Vila surrender the High King's staff. An alliance that would continue when the Cardon prince took the throne of Briar for himself. But the

mistress of the court knew better than to trust a mortal
tongue. She had no interest in such a toothless alliance,
and sent him away.

I flick the edge of the brittle page. How strange. I thought
Leythana was the only challenger to offer *her* alliance in exchange
for the staff. I've never encountered any record of an additional, if
failed, negotiation. Had the Vila courts been more tempted by
Leythana's reputation of a warrior queen than that of Cardon's?
My knowledge regarding that realm is limited to the terrible story
about a former Briarian princess whose curse was broken by a
noble's daughter. They had not been allowed to be together. Wind
whines through the cracks in the stones, and my focus drifts to the
hazy outline of the Crimson Cliffs, where the bones of those
women are buried beneath the sea. A shudder runs through me,
and I squeeze Aurora's hand.

That was a long time ago. And our story will not end like
theirs. I won't let it.

"Mistress!" The rattling cry of a Goblin reverberates from farther down the hall.

I snap the book closed, and my lingering questions with it. The
court may not know about Aurora, but they're aware of the fact
that I disappear into the old wings sometimes. Regan told me that
they think I keep a torture chamber back here, where I experiment
with the Fae prisoners. I let them have their morbid ideas if it de-
ters them from visiting.

"I'll be back later," I whisper to Aurora, hurrying from the library. The branches twist behind me just as the Goblin rounds the
corner and skids to a halt.

"Mistress," he pants, hands on his knees. "You must come at once. The storm last night, and then the Demon sentries—"

"Calm down." I place a hand on his shoulder. "What's happened?"

He wheezes a cough, his stubby snout wriggling. "There was a shipwreck. A *human* washed ashore."

CHAPTER THREE

If possible, the entirety of the Dark Court is packed into the throne room. Goblins, Demons, and Vila lean over the rotting railing of the mezzanine, with Imps shoving their way through the gaps in their legs. Some have scaled the walls, hanging upside down by their tails from chandeliers as the draft swings them back and forth.

Sometimes, I forget that I once stood in this room as the Dark Grace, cowed and trembling as King Tarkin threatened and manipulated me. The terrified girl from that time seems like a different person altogether. One I'm glad to say I no longer recognize. And there is nothing here that calls the memory of the old king, either. All of Briar's finery has been replaced with the trappings of the Dark Court. Six thrones, one for each clan leader, form a semi-circle on the dais and are decorated with the broken staffs of the Fae. Gargoyles leer from corners and eaves. Elegant sconces have been magicked into dragon snouts, roaring flame. Royal portraits have been slashed, or wickedly improved by the Imps, or are littered with knife hilts and darts.

The human is on his knees. His shirt hangs from him in ribbons, exposing the labor-hardened muscles of his chest and torso. There's a nasty cut grazing the high plane of his left cheekbone, and the brushed-copper skin of one of his biceps is sliced down to the bone. Salt crusts his shoulder-length black hair. But it's the look in his amber-brown eyes that holds my attention, an expression smoldering with fear and disgust. Mortania rumbles in her cave.

"We witnessed the shipwreck last night," one of the Demon sentries explains. "It was far enough from shore that everyone aboard was presumed dead."

"Was mine who found him." Valmar, leader of the Imps, winds his barbed tail around his staff. Smaller even than the stubby-legged Goblins, he has to stand on his chair to be properly seen. "Don't know how he didn't drown in that storm. Must be part fish."

"There were no others?"

"No," Valmar answers. "But I told a few of mine to keep looking. Might be they find something of value among the bits and bones."

Strong as he undoubtedly is to have survived the wreck, the prisoner winces with each breath. The sea was not kind to him. But he appears otherwise healthy, with broad shoulders and solid limbs. And his unlined face suggests that he probably isn't much older than Aurora was when she was cursed by the spindle—twenty, perhaps.

"A sole survivor," I muse. "And how did you accomplish that?"

"I don't know." His voice is strained. "The storm hit, and I was belowdecks. The rest is a blur."

Callow flares her speckled wings from her perch on the back of my throne.

"What were you doing near our shores? We've not encountered a human for more than half a century. Were you unaware of the fate of the previous mortals living in Briar?"

I gesture around the room. And he must have been distracted when he was dragged in by the sentries, for it's only now that his attention drifts up, then stops on a place above my head. Every muscle in his body stills.

"What in the name of . . ."

Imps chitter, and I know exactly what the boy has discovered. Rows and rows of Etherian heads are mounted high on the walls. Peeling lips are screwed into silent screams. Brittle veins hang out of empty eye sockets. One of the inciting acts of this war occurred when a Goblin was captured by the Court of Beasts. His head was sent back to us on a golden plate. Regan suggested we start a collection of our own. It was only fair, after so many of ours had been brutally murdered when we were driven from our homeland.

"Do you not approve of our display?" I lean back, rubbing my thumb over the cracked jewel of my signet ring.

"Maybe he wants to join them," Valmar suggests.

His Imps crow their approval.

"I want to hear his answer first." I signal for quiet. "Why did you come here?"

The boy inhales a steadying breath. "Our king sent us. Now that the Etherium trade has dried up, our coffers are empty. Diseases not seen in a hundred years are cropping up, sickening entire villages. We're desperate."

Etherium. I'd nearly forgotten. The ground-up mineral, mined from the Etherian Mountains, was the reason Briar was the wealthiest realm in the world. Huge crates of the stuff were traded across the sea, as close to a Grace elixir as the Briar Kings would permit to be exported. For the other mortal realms, Etherium was a medicinal powder that could cure almost any ailment. In Briar, it was mostly served at parties or in Grace parlors—to relax patrons and induce a euphoric bliss. But the Dark Court has no need of trade. The mines are abandoned. Maybe even ruined, now that the land is steeped with our dark magic.

"Etherium could not have been your only source of commerce."

He coughs. Seawater drips from the cliff of his jaw. "No. But Briar purchased much of our other goods, until the gold stopped and crippled our markets. The loss of Etherium was a double blow. The kingdom had none to sell to its people and none to tax, which stripped the coffers even further. Not to mention the healers who relied on the stuff."

I'd never spared any concern regarding what happened across the sea as the result of my siege. A strange, guiltlike feeling wends through me.

What did they ever do for you, pet?

She's right. I snip it back, close to the root.

"You will find no Etherium here," I tell the prisoner. "Nor sympathy. Your king's gold supported a realm that grew fat off the exploitation of Graces and commoners alike. If you are suffering now as a result of it, I'd say you are reaping what you sowed."

His fists clench at his sides. "And the merchants who can't feed their families? The children battling plague? Are they to pay for the sins of our ancestors?"

Unrest reverberates from the mezzanine.

"Any debt must be paid," Regan replies. The russet streaks in her tight braid light up in the dull sunlight streaming through tall windows. "A lesson *our* ancestors taught us well."

Callow flaps to the armrest of my throne, talons clacking against the metal.

"What did you predict would happen when you came here?" I continue, stroking my kestrel's back. "Assuming you *hadn't* made a spectacular mess of your arrival?" Snickers. "Did you suppose that we would let you pass with nothing more than a friendly greeting?"

He hesitates, tugging at the hem of his sodden shirt. "We did not . . ."

"Well?" A Demon sentry prods him with the toe of his boot.

"The stories we heard about this realm were too impossible to be real," he confesses. "We assumed it was abandoned."

A beat as his answer sinks in. And then the court roars. A troupe of Imps dances from a corner, swarming the prisoner and pulling grotesque faces. Their long barbed tails thrash at him. Valmar is doubled over, tears streaming down his face.

"Does it look *abandoned*?" He swipes at his long nose.

"You don't understand." The prisoner tries in vain to fend off the Imps, who are now taking turns charging him and slamming their thick skulls into his body. "The things we heard—" He grunts at a particularly vicious blow. "That there's a princess, asleep for a hundred years. That there's a dragon guarding the mountains. It's madness!"

Panic spears through me, hot and swift. I knew the wretches who escaped my wrath would spin their various tales about my siege. But I never thought the story of Aurora would make its way across the sea, especially not one so hauntingly accurate.

A pair of Goblins elbow each other in the ribs, each claiming to be the legendary princess and curtsying. Regan catches my eye and shakes her head. I need a distraction.

Callow complains and relocates to another chair as I shrug off my cloak. The Imps slide back from the prisoner like drops of oil. I bid the bones of my back expand. It's been a long time since I've Shifted, but Mortania's influence on my own magic makes the change as easy as it was on the day of my siege. Talon-tipped wings rip through my bodice, fanning out behind my shoulders. I see my outline reflected in the twin saucers of the prisoner's brown eyes—a monster from a nightmare, as I was to every other human during the time of the queens. All but one.

The boy's lips open and close, and I think his fragile human heart may explode. I can almost hear it knocking against his ribs. Mortania cackles. "You—are the dragon?" he splutters out. "We never . . ."

"Believed? That's your own misfortune." I bare every one of my daggerlike teeth and let my wings stir a breeze to ruffle his sea-matted hair. "Which pompous king sent you to your death?"

His throat bobs. "I've come from Terault. But, please. I must go home. My family needs me. I was just a ship's boy. I meant you no harm."

A laugh kicks its way free of my lungs. "Moments ago, you were all bravado. And now you plead to go home? Weak character, I think."

"Weaker limbs." Valmar smacks his lips. "Tender organs. Crisp bone."

"Please." The wound on the boy's arm weeps. A drop of his warm human blood splashes onto the floor. "I will tell my king never to return. I will give you—"

Regan sneers. "What could we possibly want from you?"

"Save his innards." Valmar pats his rounded belly. Goblins begin throwing out various ways to roast the human. The prisoner shades greener at the mention of a spit.

I pick up my staff—Endlewild's, which I'd fished out of the wreckage ages ago—and bang the end on the marble floor. "Now, now. The other humans at this court were given an opportunity to save themselves from such dire fates. This guest deserves the same courtesy." I nudge his chin to face me with the broken orb of the staff, the same one that gifted me the half-moon scar on my torso. "Swear my oath, ship's boy, and you will live."

His lips are salt-dried and cracked. "What does that mean, an oath?"

"Does it matter? If you decline, I'll let the Goblins experiment with how long you're able to survive without your entrails. And it's not as brief a period as you might expect." The snout-nosed creatures whoop.

The prisoner's attention snags on something to our right. One of the servants hovers in the fringes of the crowd, still clutching a scrubbing brush. He blinks in shock at the sight of another human.

He gestures in her direction. "Has she sworn?"

"Yes." The servant flits away into the shadows. "And you can see she's perfectly fine. Better than fine, considering that I've practically granted her immortality. She's bound to my magic, and my life is just beginning."

The boy's jaw works. The pulse at his temple is rabbit-quick. A long moment passes, and I suspect that he might actually prefer death over an existence in this macabre court. Plenty of the other humans had. But I've underestimated him. Something changes in the depths of the brown pools of his eyes, like a spark flaring. He steels himself. "Very well."

"Smarter than he looks." Regan flips her dagger from a sheath at her boot and passes it to me. The jade eyes glint. "It's too bad, though. I know the Goblins were counting on a meal."

Tooth-studded cudgels and skull maces droop in disappointment. Some mutter that they should at least be allowed to use the boy as target practice.

Regan pulls the prisoner's arm out and holds it firm. Three slashes down the inside of his forearm are all I need for the binding ritual. He curses. I cut my own palm. Green Vila blood wells on my papery skin, and then I press my wound into his.

My magic uncoils and slams into the prisoner, finding his wisp of human power almost instantly. I could extinguish his fragile mortality right now, as easily as snuffing out a candle flame. Instead, I send my intent through the connection between us. A green aura limns my hand. Heat pulses between us. He grits his teeth, his body rigid as the Demons pin his shoulders.

"Swear to serve me from this moment on," I say.

This is the crux of the ritual. The binding requires the human's magic to accept and submit to mine. If he rejects me, it will falter. And then the Goblins will get their meal after all.

Sweat beads on his forehead. He hesitates for a heartbeat, long enough that the bow-legged creatures inch closer. But then, "I-I swear."

Fire blazes beneath my hand. The prisoner howls. The scent of charred steel and rich wine fills me up and sings across every nerve. There's a flare of light, then everything stills. The wound on his forearm seals, and in its place is the wreath of bramble and thorn. The boy slumps, examining the mark with an expression of pure horror and revulsion. It's a look I've endured too many times to count.

"Don't forget what she said. Betray us, and"—Regan bends close to his ear—"your blood literally boils."

Mortania laughs. *I do hope we see it.*

The troupe of Imps from earlier bounds toward me. "Give him to us, Mistress. We'll show him around."

"Got lots for him to do." Another cartwheels.

"What shall we call him?"

The first's nose scrunches. "Squid."

"No, Cat. He has enough lives."

"Teacup." Another giggles. "Bet he breaks as easy as one."

"Derek," the prisoner interrupts them with more sterness than I would expect given the circumstances. "I would prefer Derek."

The Imps grumble, and I doubt they will ever call him that.

"Try to be gentle with *Derek,*" I tell them, picking a scrap of seaweed out of the boy's hair and flinging it away. "Welcome to the Dark Court. Do take care where you sleep. The Goblins have a penchant for midnight snacks."

CHAPTER FOUR

The Imps herd Derek off, claiming they're going to determine which of the nobles' old clothes suit him best and calculate the precise number of seconds he can stay conscious if they hang him from his ankles. I don't envy the boy. It's been a long time since the barb-tailed creatures had a new mortal to play with.

I go to my rooms and change out of the gown I just ruined by Shifting, my mind still buzzing. Another human after decades without even a whisper from the realms across the sea. What could it mean?

It matters not. Mortania rises. *Focus on the High Court.*

Perhaps she has a point. Callow hops from perch to perch in my solar until I set her free. She soars away, her happy peals resonating over the wreckage of Briar. I close the window against the brine-soaked chill and stoke up the fire. Run my fingertip along the curve of the scaled snout of a dragon molded into the mantel.

The boy imagined me to be such a beast. I could taste his fear. And I'm not sure why it bothers me.

"Brooding?" Regan ambles in unannounced and settles herself in a cushioned armchair.

"No."

"No, that's definitely not your brooding face," she agrees. I shoot her a glower. "Let's call it pensive, then. About what?"

"Everything. The war. The boy." I add a log to the fire. "I don't like that he suddenly showed up here. And he knew about Aurora."

"He also thought this land was empty"—she points at me— "and that you were a dragon. The princess is just another story to him."

"You're probably right." I pick up a dragon figurine from my desk. The jeweled scales sparkle in the firelight.

"If you're really worried, have the Starlings see what they can dig up." She examines the band of a silver ring—a snake that's wrapped around her first finger in a knot, jaws biting just below the bone spike on her knuckle. The Imps conjured it for her after she told them the twisted serpent was the crest of the Vila court to which her family belonged in Malterre. "Some of Neve's Shifters are poking around the realms across the sea. They can visit Terault."

"Neve has enough to do." And I do not trust her with the errand.

"Gathering intelligence is her job. If you—"

"Send word, then." My tone is sharper than I intend, and Regan raises an eyebrow. "I'm sorry. It's just—did you see the boy's face when he saw the Etherian heads? He hates us."

"What does that matter?" She laughs. "The human servants hate us, too, but that's never troubled you."

"They've always hated me. And they deserve their suffering." I set the dragon down.

"And you think this boy would have been any different than they were a hundred years ago? That he would have treated you any better? Don't forget that I came here on a ship just like his. And if those sailors had found me aboard"—with the fire at her back, shadows play in the valleys between Regan's bone spikes—"I would have been thrown into the sea with rocks tied around my ankles."

Indeed, pet. Mortania thrums.

I wrap my arms around myself, imagining that horrible possibility. A log collapses in the hearth. "I'm glad they didn't."

"Me, too." Regan smirks. "When the Imps aren't ransacking my wardrobe or setting their traps in my rooms."

I laugh and try to let the lingering feelings of uncertainty dissolve. Regan is right. I'm wasting energy by worrying about the boy.

"I'm headed to the practice yard, if you'd like to see any worthy sparring." She gets up and straightens her leathers. Regan loves showing off for the court. And I admit that I enjoy watching her make a spectacle of herself. All that diving and parrying. Her muscles firm and flexing beneath her leathers. A flush climbs up the back of my neck, and I busy myself with a pile of books on my desk.

"Another time," I tell her. "I've some more work to do here."

"You can't win the war by reading." She winks.

"Go on, then," I shoo her off. "Try not to maim any Goblins."

"No promises," she calls over her shoulder.

But just before she crosses through the door—

"Regan." She turns. But my tongue is suddenly clumsy, and I fumble a little, unsure of the right words. "The boy might be another ignorant human, like the sailors who would have killed you. But not all mortals are like them. When Aurora wakes, you'll see."

The clock on the mantel announces the hour. It's an Imp creation, with each chime a separate and piercing scream. I keep trying to hide the hideous thing, but it always finds its way back here. Even if I break it, the Imps fix it—and then it's usually worse.

"You believe me, don't you?"

"Of course I believe you," she answers without a second's hesitation. "I'll be glad to meet the princess when the time comes."

It's exactly what I want to hear, and what she's told me repeatedly over the years. So why doesn't the tightness in my chest loosen?

Perhaps, pet, it's better that the princess sleeps.

I shove the ancient Vila away.

Two weeks pass, and the ship's boy miraculously has not decided that a plunge off the Crimson Cliffs is more tolerable than the Imps' ministrations. Nor have we discovered him curled up in a corner, smoking and boiled from the inside out as a result of any treachery he might have attempted. Instead, Derek learns that the Goblins enjoy a bawdy joke and explicit story—the bloodier the better. And the Imps fight over turns in a rowdy game he makes of spinning them around by their ankles and abruptly releasing them, the aim being to knock down as many of their compatriots as possible. He even amuses them by gamely donning whatever costumes they devise for him and tripping about the palace imitating the accent and posture of various court members.

But I note the way he takes stock of each room when he thinks no one is watching. The dried meat and crusts of bread he slips into his pockets. His human compass is pinned to survive, and it is that instinct that will kill him if he steps a toe out of line.

"Again!" The command of an Imp shrills through the throne room.

After an early visit to Aurora, I've passed the morning on the dais. The court is busy. A Goblin proudly showed me a dagger he crafted. There's a hidden button on the hilt that causes an extra, longer blade to fire when it's pressed. Our recently arrived Imps are getting their bearings. Several have scurried to my side and recounted their nightmares, which they consider to be entertaining dreams. Another turned a broken brick into a teacake with icing piped to resemble a stormy sea. A spun-sugar ship complete with sails was half-sunk in the creamy waves, in honor of Derek's arrival. The Imp even took care to stain the icing with bits of pink.

"Them's the dead ones," he'd clarified with a grin, pointing.

The Demons converse among themselves, playing complex games with markers carved from painted Etherian finger bones. The red and orange rivers traversing their limbs pulse in a focused tempo. Derek, who is again amusing the Imps by tossing them into the air high enough that they can swing themselves onto the rusted chandelier, wipes at his brow with his sleeve. A sleeve that fits, I notice, and his breeches are only a touch loose in the waist. Yesterday, the Imps outfitted him in a uniform at least three sizes too large, cinched together with rope around his middle, with some mountainous wig bedecked with crispy flowers fastened to his head.

Two of the Imps begin quarreling over whose turn is next. Derek rolls his shoulders and kneads at the muscles of his back. For some unfathomable reason, I decide to take pity on him.

"Let him be," I instruct his keepers, rising from my throne.

The gaggle of Imps scatters. One of them pouts at my spoiling their fun and sticks out his long pointed tongue at me. Another boxes his ears in scolding. Derek bows as I approach. Sweat glistens in a fine sheen over his neck. His shirt sticks to the firm trunk of his torso.

I crook my finger, the smoky green jewel on my signet ring flashing. "Come. It's time we were better acquainted."

He wipes his palms on his breeches, glancing about the hall as though someone might come to his aid before I spirit him away. No one does, and he shuffles cautiously along behind me, out a side door and into the gardens.

It's nearing afternoon, but the sun is dull and the skies are smeared with bruise-colored clouds. I can't recall if it's summer or winter. The years are harder to track now that the Court of Seasons is gone. Derek shivers in the breeze, and I'm grateful for my fur-lined gown—one the Imps designed so that the bodice is comprised of intertwined bramble and thorn. Crimson teardrops track down the skirt, like drops of blood.

"Has this place always been so . . ."

"What?" I enjoy the moment as he scrambles for an acceptable word, and then wave him off. "Don't trouble yourself. These gardens were immaculate during the time of the queens. The palace employed an army of gardeners, and then there were the Grace-grown blooms. I once smelled a peony that made the taste of chocolate land on my tongue."

"They could do that?"

"Indeed, and much more."

But the days of the Graces are long over, and I would not resurrect them for all the enchanted peonies in the world. Gravel crunches under our feet as I navigate the untidy paths. Hedges are barren and black. The prized rosebushes have morphed into huge, rambling things with thorns the length of my hand. Fine sculptures are crumbling or missing limbs or the Imps have recast them so that maidens boast the heads of leering gargoyles or the unsettling bodies of squids or griffins. This is the same garden where I met Aurora. Somewhere, the fountain she admired sits amid stinking earth and withered flowers. Melancholy twinges in my chest, but I shake it away.

"War will do this to a land, I suppose," Derek comments.

I laugh. "The state of this garden isn't the result of the war."

In fact, there's never been a battle on our soil. Oryn and his Fae courts are quick to retaliate if we trespass on their territory, but they've never ventured here. The High King hasn't even bothered to send an envoy during these decades of conflict. Regan ascribes his silence to his pride or the fact that the Etherians cannot survive on our lands for long. Either way, it doesn't matter. We'll soon have the opportunity to ask Oryn whatever we desire—when we storm the High Court and he is kneeling at our feet.

"The barrenness of these lands is due to the Dark Court." I find the thready magic of a climbing vine and send it slithering in front of the boy's feet like a snake. He jumps back. "For the last hundred years, our magic has seeped into the land and altered the climate. The fall of the Fae courts contributes as well."

His brow scrunches. "How could the Fae courts have anything to do with Briar? I didn't think this land held any magic."

Branches rattle overhead, stirred by the salty wind.

"Not of its own, no. But we've found that it is influenced by Etheria. Each Fae court governs an area of the natural world— seasons, dreams, beasts, and so on. As each court succumbs to our army, the dominion it governs pales with it. The lack of flowers in this garden"—I touch the hollow shell of a puckered and lifeless bud—"has much to do with the demise of the Court of Earth, one of our early conquests."

He reaches for a charred vine, which crumbles in his hand. "That's . . . sad."

Mortania bridles, and I share her annoyance. I exert the tiniest amount of pressure on the bond between myself and Derek. His curse mark flames scarlet. He yelps in surprise and pain.

"That, ship's boy, is an opinion. One better kept to yourself."

A screech cuts through the heavy-bellied clouds. Callow circles into view, lands on my shoulder, and nips at my ear.

Derek stops rubbing his arm and extends a tentative hand to the kestrel. "Remarkable. I've never met a bird so tame."

Callow promptly snaps, earning herself a gullet full of mortal blood.

"She isn't tame." I stroke her breast. "She is mine. What of yours? You spoke of a family in . . . where was it?"

Neve agreed to have her Starlings investigate the boy, but they haven't sent word back. And my curiosity about this unexpected addition to the Dark Court grows by the day.

"Terault." Derek sucks his wound and maintains a healthy distance from Callow. "I have a younger brother and two sisters. And my mother and father."

"But you must be accustomed to being separated from them, what with your work on a ship."

"The voyage that brought me here was my first. Before then, I worked odd jobs. Crew hand pays better, though. And we needed the money, even if my mother begged me to stay."

So he's poor, with a mother who loves him. An irritating sense of sympathy wheedles my conscience.

"Your maiden voyage ended in a wreck? I pray you haven't carried such ill luck to our shores. And now your mother must think you dead. How tragic."

He kicks at rocks. The Imps have magicked his boots so that they appear as though they are made of the writhing tentacles from one of the sea monsters of Derek's tales.

"Do you suppose that I might send them a message? Let them know I'm alive. That there's a chance I might come home."

"You've sworn to me," I remind him, indicating his forearm. "You're not going home. And we don't communicate with the human world. Which is why they all think we're *stories*."

"Oh." A pebble goes skidding into the bushes.

"Even if we did allow such a missive, you wouldn't exactly have optimistic tidings to report. The Imps consider you amusing today. But perhaps not tomorrow."

He tucks his fingers under his arms at the next gust of wind. "There's a stipend for the families if a crew member doesn't return. That will be something for them, at least."

Somehow I thought—or even hoped—that he would put up more of a fight. And his lack of a backbone makes goading him immensely less satisfying. I change the subject.

"Were you really oblivious to the Dark Court before you attempted the crossing?" I sweep my staff in the direction of the sea and the Crimson Cliffs, barely visible in the distance. "Your king must have been informed of the fate of the fleets who sailed here over the last century. Or did you think all the ships were capsized by the giant sea serpents from the stories you weave for the Goblins?"

He doles out one of his easy, lopsided grins. "I think it interesting that you call the sea serpents 'stories.'" If he expects a laugh, he doesn't get it. He scrubs at the back of his neck. "We knew of the other fleets. Even of how the Fae used to flatten human armies who encroached on their lands before Briar was established. But the royals in Terault are desperate. Desperate people commit foolish acts."

"You sound like you resent them for it."

He runs his hands through his dark hair. It's growing out, lending him an unkempt appearance that somehow suits him. I make a note to instruct the Imps to shave it off. "I'd be whipped if any of the soldiers heard me say it, but Terault has to restructure. They cannot rely on what's worked in the past. Or what the damn astrologers say. If we're going to survive, we must forge a future that doesn't depend on Etherium, or anything else we cannot control."

"You seem to understand quite a bit about politics for someone who spent their time on a ship or working 'odd jobs.'"

He shrugs. "I kept myself informed. I was part of a group, actually—" He slides me a sideways glance, and I scent a secret hanging in the air between us.

"Go on, then. I'm not going to tell anyone. What do I care what happens in your country?"

Callow warbles something that could be a laugh. Derek scowls at us both.

"I was part of an organization. We met and planned what we might do to change the realm. Initially, it was only discussion. But then we began to map out tangible ideas."

"You're a revolutionary?" I study him with fresh eyes. He doesn't strike me as the type. "And would you have been brave enough to stage a coup? Rule yourself?"

"I would have done whatever was necessary for the good of the people."

In this moment, he actually reminds me of Aurora. That unflinching ferocity that shone through her when she refused to sign her sovereign rights over to a husband, as most Briar Queens had done, and insisted she would be the queen Leythana had been. The comparison should make me warm to the boy, but it does the opposite.

"It's too bad you'll never get the chance."

Derek looks like he wants to answer—maybe beg to be sent back home again. But then he grits his teeth and walks on in silence.

The garden wall is in shambles, granting a view of Briar's skeletal wreckage and the sea beyond. I wonder how many bodies lie at the watery base of the Crimson Cliffs. How many wrecked ships and rusted swords? Derek leans against the worn stone, taking in the hollow husks of the buildings. The murders of crows, among the only sort of animal that survived the fall of the Court of Beasts, wheeling above the caved-in domes of the Grace District rooftops. The shadows curling like wisps of smoke.

"You did all this, then?"

Callow mutters a warning. "We don't like your tone, Derek. You weren't here a hundred years ago. The people of Briar judged me monstrous. I gave them what they wanted."

"They wanted their realm to burn? Their lives destroyed?"

A hint of Mortania's silty power lands on my tongue as an achingly familiar rage begins to bubble in my chest. I take one slow step toward Derek, close enough to see his pulse flutter at his throat.

"They wanted a villain. A beast to suit their stilted narrative. One they could use and discard and punish for whatever purposes they devised." A phantom pain pierces my torso, the ancient echo of one of Endlewild's "treatments" to cleanse my wicked green blood. Even with my Shifter abilities, I've never been able to permanently remove the scar. "And so I took everything they gave me and flung it back at them."

He considers this. Watery afternoon sunlight shines in his brown eyes, brow furrowed. "Was there no one innocent?"

This boy doesn't have the sense of a goat. But a rare and elusive guilt sinks its teeth into my conscience. I think of Hilde again. I'd been so sure that the apothecary would come to me. That she would *choose* me over the greedy and vapid citizens of Briar. But she fled, like everyone else, from the monster.

Because she did not care for you, pet. None of them did.

An ache squeezes between my temples. "Not innocent enough."

Derek must have been anticipating an answer to soothe his fragile mortal nerves. That chalky pallor he wore during our first meeting returns. I let him stew in his discomfort and start heading to the palace.

"I'm sorry for you," he calls at my back. I freeze. "For what they did. And for what it made you. You didn't deserve it."

An unfamiliar mix of emotions spears through me. Besides Aurora, no human has ever apologized to me and meant it. But I do not let myself turn. Only keep walking, one step after another, as if I had not heard him at all.

CHAPTER FIVE

Thunder rumbles, low and menacing. Outside the jagged gap in the library wall, rain pours over Briar. It is the kind of endless, soaking deluge that is commonplace now that the Court of Seasons is vanquished. The sort of weather during which I would have loved to curl up with a book in my attic room of Lavender House and read for hours.

But today, a headache presses between my temples. I let the book fall closed on my lap. It's the court record the Imps brought me, and this is the second time I've read it. But it doesn't hold any clue about what might break Aurora's curse, or even about Leythana and the Fae challenge.

"Don't worry," I say to Aurora. I've folded myself into a wide chair at her bedside with a thick fur around my legs. "I'll find an answer. With the Court of Dreams gone, there's only the High Court left. If I have to force Oryn to lift your curse myself, I will."

I hope she can hear me. That she knows how hard I'm trying. Thunder growls again, and I pick up the mug of tea I'd brought with me. It's gone cold in this dank chamber, and I use my magic to reheat it, watching the steam curl in lazy tendrils.

"We'll have a huge revel when you wake," I say, forcing positivity into my voice. "The biggest yet. The Imps will conjure up a mountain of pastries and cakes, all of your favorites. And the gowns they create for you will put your old wardrobe to shame."

Lightning flashes in the distance, illuminating the silhouette of the fallen Grace District. And for some infuriating reason, Derek's words in the garden come back to me.

"I'm sorry for you. For what they did. And for what it made you."

My grip tightens around the china cup. Ignorant mortal, speaking as though I'm someone to be pitied. As though what happened to Briar was a tragedy. Perhaps the realm's fall was a loss for him and all the others who could no longer purchase their precious Etherium. But I'm not sorry about *their* misfortune. If I hadn't taken Briar and founded the Dark Court, the Vila and surviving citizens of Malterre would still be hunted in those realms. Let them rot. It's a kinder fate than they deserve.

"You would absolutely despise this *Derek*," I tell Aurora, having already informed her about his arrival. "He's as bad as your suitors were, sailing across the sea for greed and power."

But a needling worry sticks to my insides. Derek is the first mortal to glimpse Briar since its fall, and the first unconnected with who I was as the Dark Grace. I don't care that the former nobles hate me. I want them to be miserable. But the look on Derek's face when he saw the Etherian heads mounted to the throne room walls. When he saw *me*.

I push my blanket away and climb onto the bed next to Aurora. Trace the ridge of her knuckles and let my fingertip skim down every one of her slender fingers.

You were never a villain to me. Her long-ago words sigh in the rushing of the rain.

If I close my eyes, I can see her here on the night we spent together, her skin luminous in the moonlight. Her amethyst gaze drinking me in.

"You'll still feel that way, won't you?" I whisper. "You'll still . . . want me?"

And if she does not? Mortania swirls lightly.

A gust of wind bullies into the library, spraying cold rain on my skin. I go back to the book and search for something I missed.

A few days later, the palace is woken by the Demon sentries' blaring horns. Malakar and our army parade into the courtyard, and a revel to celebrate his victory begins almost immediately. I make my way through the halls, which are swarming with Demons and Vila showing off their prizes. They pass around blades that look hewn from the night sky itself, which can cut through solid marble as easily as if it were butter. Shields woven from willow branches, which don't break no matter how many daggers the Demons hurl at them.

The entire court is fascinated with this bounty, myself included. Earlier in the war, our forces returned from the Court of Earth with tree limbs of solid silver, whose branches sported flowering buds that housed glowing pixies. There was a caged songbird brought from the Court of Beasts that warbled Fae ballads before it succumbed to our dark magic. My personal favorite is the sack of oysters brought from the Court of Sea, whose pearls were filled with swirling constellations or tiny moving clouds that changed to reflect the time of day. The former Briar King was obsessed with this sort of Fae treasure, and it gives me more pleasure than I can say to display these prizes in Tarkin's palace. I hope his ghost is mad with jealousy.

I finally spot the Goblin leader near the throne room, thronged by clusters of Imps demanding that he recount his goriest war stories. But before I can reach him, I see Torin and Neve walking together through the crush of celebration. Torin spots me and waves, and then it's too late to pivot in another direction. I plaster on a perfunctory smile and join them.

As a full-blooded Shifter, Neve enjoys changing her appearance as frequently as others might their clothing. Her skin this morning is covered in iridescent scales that subtly shift color in the light. A pair of pale blue antlers climbs up from her long hair, as white and thin as spider's silk. But her most striking feature is her cloak. It's constructed of dark, multihued feathers, like those of a starling bird. And steel epaulettes of the same fashion jut out from each of her shoulders, beaks open in a war cry.

"Nimara," Torin greets me. "I was just catching Neve up on everything that's occurred at court in her absence."

Neve dips her chin, but I detect a glimmer of disdain in her ice-blue eyes. Mortania whirls in her cave. She doesn't like the Shifter, either.

"Good," I say. "And I'm eager to hear the news *you* brought. Have your Starlings learned anything regarding the boy from Terault? Or about why the mortal realms have suddenly decided to start dispatching their ships again?"

"Not as of yet," she answers in her glass-smooth voice. "We've had far more pressing matters to attend to, as I'm sure you know."

Imps gallop past. They've summoned food for the army's return and are bandying eggs back and forth among themselves. I lean out of the way before one splatters on my gown.

"And this is a celebration," Torin says pointedly. The fissures mapping her body brighten to scarlet. "We should allow Neve to catch her breath. She's been busy enough as it is."

But busy doing what? I want to ask. I'd thought Kal was my closest ally, but none of his supposed help came without a price. What will Neve and her Starlings demand later as payment for their service? What snares is she setting that I will not see until it is too late?

You are not that girl anymore, pet.

"Forgive me for being overeager," I say, letting the iron-laced taste of my power center me. "We are always grateful for your efforts."

Torchlight gleams on the epaulettes of Neve's gown. "Are you? Because my Starlings would greatly appreciate a visit from their mistress. Especially as you're a Shifter yourself. It would do much to boost their morale."

Gravelly Goblin laughter ricochets off the walls. "You want me to leave court? Put myself in danger, for a visit?"

She tilts her head at me. "Do the Starlings not put themselves in danger every day?"

The question is fanged and I try not to react.

"They do, but—"

Torin's unnaturally warm touch grazes my forearm. "The council agrees that it's better that Nimara remains here," she interjects, far calmer than I could ever be when dealing with the Shifter leader. "We cannot risk the loss of her power should she be captured or killed. But the Starlings will receive an elaborate show of our gratitude when the time comes for them to return home. As will you, Neve."

"Precisely." I smooth my skirts. "Not even Oryn follows his army."

"And you wish to behave like Oryn?" Her smile is too wide, and I want to strangle her. "But it was only a suggestion. I thought it might benefit you to practice Shifting. After all, some Shifters lose the ability if they inhabit one form for too long. You do know that, don't you?"

Of course I know it. Would that Neve could forget how to Shift and trap herself in some other body. Preferably one without a mouth. "I appreciate your concern, but I am in no danger of losing *any* of my abilities."

The feathers on her cloak flutter in the draft. "How reassuring."

I've had more than enough of this exchange, and am about to excuse myself, when a deep voice cuts through the chatter of the corridor.

"Mistress!" At the sight of Malakar's warty snout and jagged-toothed grin, my anger melts away.

"Welcome home." I bend down to embrace him. His bristly curls tickle the side of my face. "We've missed you."

The Goblin leader was one of many of his ilk who made their homes in the mountain caves of the realms across the sea. As they were so easily recognizable as being former citizens of Malterre, the Goblins rarely ventured away from their clans—or even into daylight. It took us ages to root them out and bring them to the Dark Court. Malakar was among the first to arrive, and his genial nature—if hidden beneath a cantankerous exterior—soon made him a popular leader among his own. He was unanimously elected as general for our army and is uniquely skilled in weaponry. Malakar's men take great pride in their whips strung with sharpened vertebrae and maces set with steel-spiked skulls. And the Goblin leader himself designed a special powder, dubbed blight elixir, which mixes Vila blood with gunpowder, and decimates the Fae courts when launched from flaming arrows.

"Aye, have you, then?" He pulls away and scratches beneath the corkscrew horns protruding from behind each pointed ear. "I missed the Imps, can tell you that. Had enough of dried grouse to last me five lifetimes."

I laugh. "I suggest you eat your fill before they've wasted it all in their battles."

As if to illustrate, an Imp catapults onto Malakar's shoulders and bellows, "Charge!"

"Heave off!" Malakar wrestles the creature away, who cackles and scampers to join his fellows.

Torin shakes her head. Her garnet hair—like wet mortal blood—glistens in the torchlight. "I suppose such displays of affection are the consequence of returning home in such a glorious fashion."

He waggles his thick eyebrows. "Glory, aye. Have they told you yet who's in the dungeon?"

"No. Did you bring a prisoner?"

"Did we?" His silver eyes shimmer with pride. "The High Lord himself waits for you, Mistress."

Several Demons, in their shadow forms, skirt the ceiling. Gooseflesh breaks between my shoulder blades at the draft they raise. "The High Lord? Really?"

"Aye. Found him waiting in his palace, we did. Like he was expectin' us." His ears point backward. "Strange like, really. But that's the Fae for you."

Maybe. "Did you know anything about that?" I ask Neve.

"No," she replies, adjusting the Starling brooch on her jacket. "But I'm not surprised. The Court of Dreams is unique in Oryn's domain. Surreal, as one might expect, given its breed of magic. Mysterious or eccentric behavior is commonplace."

Mortania churns, as suscpicious as I am.

"But here, Mistress." Malakar pulls something from the satchel slung across his stocky body. "I've brought you a gift."

"That wasn't necessary. I'm just relieved you're—"

He holds it out to me. It's a mirror. The frame is a wreath of willow branches with sparkling diamond leaves threaded throughout. And the glass is unlike anything I've ever beheld. It looks liquid and even ripples when I touch it.

"What is this?" I turn it over in my hands, amazed.

"Belongs to the High Lord." Malakar bends close. "Ask it what his true name is."

Beside me, Torin inhales a sharp breath. "He didn't."

Malakar's lips curl up. "Ask, Mistress."

No. There's no possible way we could be this lucky. Mortania hums with desire. I stare into the glass, which only grants a warped reflection of the lines of my face. "What is the true name of the High Lord of the Court of Dreams?"

The quicksilver surface undulates. But instead of an image, a sound drifts up—like someone speaking underwater. "Aelfdene."

Deep in her den, the ancient Vila cackles.

I am stunned. The Fae cannot lie, but they can misdirect with remarkable skill. And part of that misdirection includes disguises. We learned a long time ago that the true name of an Etherian is as precious to them as their staff. With it, you can command them to do absolutely anything—or perish in the effort to obey. As such, a true name is almost never uttered. But because the Fae love their tricks and challenges, they tend to hide them. Some Etherians have spent their entire lives searching for a name with which to control another. Years ago, we found one written on the inside of a walnut. Threaded into the ballad of a songbird. And now—in this mirror.

"I thought you would like it." Malakar's tail twitches back and forth behind him.

"This is incredible," I say to the Goblin leader. "You're a genius. Thank you."

"Thank her." He indicates Neve. "Was her Starlings who figured it out."

My good humor dissolves. Torin, however, appears delighted at this discovery. She hides a laugh behind a cough. I glare at her. "You didn't tell me," I say to Neve.

She toys with the ends of her wispy hair. "You did not provide the opportunity."

Torin fusses with her long sleeves, but I can tell she's still smirking.

"Are we going to stand here and discuss it?" Malakar's snout wriggles. "Or shall we put that mirror to good use? Let's pay a visit to our Fae guest."

CHAPTER SIX

Though it's been a hundred years, the dungeons are virtually unchanged from when I found myself imprisoned here as the Dark Grace. The darkness is a living thing, broken only by intermittent torches, which sputter and snap in the dankness, casting ghoulish shadows on the slick walls. The silty odor of mold and filth borders on suffocating. A perpetual draft cuts through my thick gown and raises gooseflesh down my back. Down one corridor, near the area where I was kept at Tarkin's command, I swear I detect the swirl of pleading whispers. I quicken my pace, having no inclination to visit them this evening.

The Goblin guards have all gone to the revel, as none of us are particularly concerned about the High Lord's escape, and our small party walks alone through the corridors.

"*Neve* found the mirror?" Regan asks at my side.

"Apparently," I mutter. We're a step behind the others, but my attention is squarely fixed on the back of the Shifter leader's head. "I'm surprised it didn't trap me when I looked in the glass."

Regan frowns. "Do you really think she'd attempt something like that?"

"I was careless with Kal," I reply. "I won't be again."

She grasps my elbow, firm but gentle. "She'd be a fool to even consider betraying you like he did. We wouldn't let her get away with it."

I grant her a grateful smile. "I don't doubt that. But in my experience, it's best to be prepared for anything."

Mortania's presence swells, obviously agreeing.

Fae prisoners do not survive long in our cells. The dark magic of our lands seeps through their bark-like skin and poisons their gilded blood. In Malterre, the effect was almost instantaneous, which is why the Fae were forced to ally with the humans at the end of the first war. Here, the sickness does not progress so quickly. Depending on their strength, Fae can last up to a week in our dungeon. And we use our time well.

Above the arched doorway of his cell, Aelfdene's staff is fastened to the wall—a trick Regan devised when we began interrogating our prisoners. None of them has ever revealed any particularly valuable information—Oryn trains them extensively— but more than a few Fae have broken their knobby-boned fingers while scrabbling to retrieve the instrument of their power. Sections of the wall are streaked with smudges of their blood, drying a rust-tinged gold with the passage of time.

Through the dimness, the Fae lord's shape begins to emerge.

Aelfdene's long and slender limbs are bent at unnatural angles to cram into the space. His face is gray and grooved, textured like the trunk of a fir. A wreath of silver willow branches, the symbol of the Court of Dreams, rests amid his matted, reedlike hair. An amber bruise blooms along one angular cheekbone. His eyes flutter open as our footsteps approach.

"Ah." He yawns dramatically. One of his dagger-tipped teeth is missing. "Is this the Mistress of the Dark Court? You have caught me sleeping."

His accent is ominous and musical at once. And I'm taken aback by his casual manner. Most of the Fae ooze with arrogance. But Aelfdene looks entirely at home in his cramped cell. Like he is happy to be wearing leathers splattered with the remnants of the cream puffs that must have been thrown at him when he arrived. And I'm reminded of what Malakar said about finding him waiting for our army in his palace. Mysterious behavior, indeed.

"I'm sorry to disturb you," I say dryly.

"No matter. But I was having the most interesting dream. Would you care to hear it?"

"Not particularly."

The corners of his lips pull down. "A shame. It is customary to exchange dreams at my court, especially at a first meeting. I would be intrigued to hear one of yours."

The last thing I'm going to do is share a dream with this Fae. Especially since mine are typically about Aurora. My cheeks heat slightly, and I swiftly change the subject. "We have far more important matters to discuss, Aelfdene."

I expect him to physically react to the use of his true name. But that maddening grin only broadens. "You found my mirror. How clever of you."

"Aye." Malakar pushes forward. "And now you will tell us what Oryn is planning. Spill every one of his secrets."

He lifts a shoulder. "I regret that I have none of those to boast. Oryn does not much care for me, you see."

"You're a High Lord," I say. "Which means you were Marked. Oryn must have approved your position."

Markings are one of the most important and sacred traditions of the Fae. When an Etherian's body dies, their power is capable of living on after them. As such, exceptionally gifted Fae, like the court rulers, are expected to Mark their successors to ensure that their power both strengthens and survives. We don't know the particulars concerning a Marking, but it largely entails an Etherian shedding a small amount of their blood directly onto their chosen heir's body, where it is absorbed into their skin. Later, when the power is released at the Fae's death, their magic seeks out that other piece of itself and melds with it—much like how Mortania was able to combine her power with mine when she escaped her medallion prison.

"Oh, High King Oryn approved." Aelfdene's sticklike fingers stroke the shimmery symbol of the Court of Dreams embroidered into his leathers. "But that does not mean he was happy about it."

Confusion flickers in my mind. Oryn doesn't strike me as the kind of ruler who can be persuaded to do anything contrary to his own desires, much less agree to the appointment of a court ruler he disliked. "How could he approve of you and not be happy?"

"A thorny subject." Aelfdene licks his lips, as if speaking of the matter is delicious. "Rulers Mark multiple candidates, you see, to ensure that there is a surviving heir at their demise. My elder brother and I were both Marked by the previous High Lord, as a sign of honor to my family. But when the court lord or lady dies, the power itself *chooses* which Marked one will carry it next. Everyone—especially Oryn—assumed my brother would be selected by the fallen lord's magic. He was the stronger Fae. The worthier vessel. But the magic came to me instead." He smiles, a slash of white in the dimness. "It made for very awkward family gatherings afterward. And Oryn despised me. He does so hate being proven wrong."

We hadn't known Fae can Mark multiple heirs. This absolutely explains why the court rulers are so arrogant. They believe they are *chosen*. I resist the urge to roll my eyes.

"Your court is closest to Oryn's," Regan insists. "You must know something of the High King's mind."

The gems in Aelfdene's crown brighten and dim. "Close in proximity, perhaps. Never in confidence." He taps his chin. "But I do know of one thing you might find interesting. A prophecy. One forbidden to be spoken aloud in the Fae courts."

I step closer, intrigued. "You will tell us, Aelfdene."

This time, he does flinch slightly. And I wonder what exactly would happen if he resisted. Would the words come pouring out of him against his will? Would he shrivel, curling in pain until he complied with my order?

He doesn't seem keen to experiment with the consequences. Aelfdene's leathers creak as he leans toward us, a conspiratorial edge to his tone. "Ages hence, a member of my court dreamed a vision. It would come to pass that the High King of the Fae would lose his throne. That a new age would begin when the Etherian Mountains crumble."

A thrill jolts through me. Regan and I exchange a glance.

"*You could bring the Etherian Mountains tumbling into the*

sea," Kal had said. The shadows of the hall seem to swell. To reach for me. I step closer to the torch, craving its light.

"Of course," Aelfdene goes on. "The prophecy did not specify *which* High King would fall. So perhaps it will not yet come to fruition. Time will tell, as the mortals say."

But Mortania stirs, and her excitement canters through my limbs. *It will, pet. We will make sure of it.*

"You don't seem especially perturbed at the fall of your king," Torin comments. "Nor at your own predicament. You must know what will happen to you here."

"That I shall perish?" He gives a dismissive wave. "To me, death appears as a very long dream. And I am the ruler of dreams." He laughs again, Fae teeth shining in the orange light. And then those gilt eyes lock with mine. "Are you certain you would not like to hear the dream I was having? You might appreciate it."

"No." But my mind begins to wander. I cannot help but think of Aurora. Is she dreaming? About what? Me? A shudder raises the hairs on the nape of my neck.

"May I inquire as to a different subject, then?" Aelfdene continues. "One court leader to another?"

His voice sounds farther away, though I haven't moved.

"What is it?" My tongue is slow, and there's an inexplicable heaviness in my body.

One spindly fingered hand wraps around the bars of his cell. "Why did you do it—burn the realm down? Oryn thinks it spite, but I am not so convinced."

"I don't have to explain myself to you." But I'm not sure I actually speak those words. I hear them, but I don't feel my lips move. My thoughts are hazy, bumbling things. The dungeon looks somehow unfamiliar. I cannot recall why I came down here to begin with.

"Oh, do not mistake me," Aelfdene goes on. "I very much admire you. The Court of Dreams, after all, is the realm of sheer possibility. And *you* are the impossible brought to life. What *made* you, Nimara?"

As if pulled from the depths of the sea, a memory surfaces. I see Aurora's hand meeting the spindle. Feel the weight of her body when I caught her as she fell. Her marble-cold skin. Her still lips, which have not moved in a century, but that were once pressed against mine on a night when the whole world came crashing down and rebuilt itself in dazzling glory.

"The princess?" Aelfdene murmurs. "But why would she have . . ."

The Fae lord is nothing more than colors smeared together on a canvas. Images of the curse-breaking come wheeling back to me. Aurora's bedroom. The library. Our limbs tangled, and the smell of her clinging to my own skin.

"True love." Musical Fae laughter skips along the curves of my skull. I try to shake my head to clear it but am too dizzy. "What a farce. I assure you, there is absolutely no such thing."

But that isn't right. I fight against his words, but my mouth will not open. I should lie down. I should . . .

Something jostles me. My own name pierces through the fog of my mind. Like breaking through water, my senses crash back to me. I gulp down a breath, then two. And *that* is when I feel it. Something in my mind that does not belong. The faint scent of honey and spring roses fills my nose. My magic races up, shoving it out.

"Enough, Aelfdene!"

The thing that is not mine slithers away. Aelfdene hisses and recoils. But then those Fae eyes twinkle. "And I was just getting to the good part."

"What"—my chest heaves—"was that?"

"His latent magic." The answer comes very close. And I'm startled to realize that Neve is gripping my arm. She must have been the one to break me out of the trance, or whatever it was. "Did you think of a dream when he asked?"

"No, I—" But then I curse myself. I'd thought of dreaming itself, and of *Aurora* dreaming. That must have been enough of an invitation. The Fae wield most of their magic with their staffs, but they possess certain innate abilities. A prisoner from the Court of Earth, for example, was able to coax the stones of her cell walls into rearranging themselves so that she could escape—temporarily. Aelfdene, ruler of the Court of Dreams, must have some control over minds. "Only for a moment."

"It was enough for—"

I wrest myself free of her. "I realize that."

But I feel like a fool. And Aelfdene is grinning at me. "It was not real, Nimara."

Unease slinks through my belly. The others appear oblivious to the exchange that passed between us, and for that I'm relieved. But a cold sweat prickles beneath my clothes nonetheless.

The "it" Aelfdene referenced wasn't what just happened. He meant Aurora and me. That *our* love wasn't real.

My power unfurls, rich and intoxicating as it was on the day I took Briar. The scent of charred steel and loam explodes in my lungs. My power slithers up the wall and coils around the beechwood bark of Aelfdene's staff. The light in the orb begins to swirl. His jaw tightens.

"I know you have more to tell us about Oryn. I command that you speak, *Aelfdene*." I draw his name out, savoring each syllable as I watch it scrape over his skin.

But that unnerving smirk does not slide from his features. "Ah. But I am afraid that I have sworn my oath to the High King. And, like all my brethren, I am bound to honor it."

And before I can do anything else, Aelfdene sticks out his tongue and bites down on it. Golden blood squirts from the wound and spatters onto my face. I leap back, too shocked to scream. Aelfdene is howling, bent over himself in the narrow space. And a moment later, something flops onto the ground. All the food I'd eaten that day comes hurtling up my throat and I vomit onto the grimy stone.

Aelfdene's tongue sits like a slug in a pool of his Fae blood. He'd bitten it off.

Malakar spews a string of curses. He slams his tooth-studded cudgel into the bars of the cell, the impact ringing around us. "There are a hundred other ways we can use your name. And when we're done, we'll drain your magic out of you drop by drop, and—"

An echo reverberates down the corridor, muffled by the stone.

"What is that?" Regan asks.

I sharpen my hearing so that I can pick it up. But it's Neve who deciphers it first.

"The sentries," she says.

Three notes, a signal I've not heard in the whole of this war.

An attack.

CHAPTER SEVEN

We sprint back down the rows of cells, into the main palace, and through to the courtyard. Outside, the Demon sentries are shouting to one another. Some of them have already transformed into shadows and are streaking into the horizon. What initially appears as a formation of birds begins to take shape. Fae steeds. At least a hundred. Winged wicked beasts with armor clamped around their necks and flanks. Even from here, I can see the glow of their riders' gilded breastplates, the pulsing light from the orbs of Etherian staffs.

Regan musters her Vila and they bolt to the battlements. I hurry after them. Malakar is close behind, barking orders at his Goblins. The sentries are readying their arrows. Never before have we encountered this many Fae warriors so near the palace, and I ache to show them who is mistress. To protect our home, which they have stolen once already.

They will not do so again, pet. Mortania snaps and sparks in her cave.

No. They will not.

"What are you doing?" A hand pulls me back. Regan. "This could be a trap to flush you out. We need you safe."

I tamp my power down, the struggle like swimming against a strong current. "I can't leave all of you up here on your own. You wouldn't."

She lets out a frustrated breath. But she knows I'm right. "Damn everything." With a short whistle, she calls two other Vila. "Protect her at all costs."

They jerk their chins in agreement, flanking me. And then Regan melts into the throng as the whinnying of the Fae steeds grows louder. A swarm of shadowy Demons masses like a cloud in front of the battlements, acting as a shield.

The Fae battalion gallops through the currents of air, their mounts' wings—the length of two human men stacked together—feathered with what look like crushed stars. Their armor, comprised of twisted and knotted golden branches, gleams in the murky sunlight. They stink of Fae magic, nectar and meadow and damp grass.

The beating of wings is like the roll of thunder as the Fae battalion soars over the palace. Demon arrows fly, striking the thighs and bellies of the steeds. Two beasts spiral to the earth, riders pinwheeling from their saddles. Imps operate the cannons, climbing atop one another's shoulders to stuff down the ball and powder. Booms rattle my teeth. Smoke creeps across the battlements. Goblins hurl their hatchets and spears, wield their specially designed crossbows that fire five bone-tipped bolts simultaneously.

I add my power to that of the Vila. Inhaling the scents of soldered metal and rich wine and pungent, rotting earth. Mortania's satisfied laughter skips behind my sternum. My power connects with a beast instantly, puncturing its heart of magic so thoroughly that the creature collapses without a sound. Another and another, until the palace grounds are a graveyard.

And it's then that I realize the Fae aren't fighting back.

The sky should be lashed with gilded arcs of Etherian magic. The riders should be swooping low, aiming for the Demon sentries and Goblins crowding the edge of the turrets. Yet they remain aloft. The translucent, golden spheres of their shields expand from their bodies when a Demon gets too near. Most of the Goblins' shots bounce off those glittering surfaces, though some are quick enough to sink into a hindquarter or neck or flank. But there is absolutely no retaliation from the Etherians.

"What are they doing?" I shout over the tumult.

The Vila beside me are too absorbed in their attacks to reply. The horde of Fae arranges itself into formation and circles around the palace. A blur of black and blue plummets from a saddle. There is a final war cry, and then they're flying back toward the rose-capped peaks of the Etherian Mountains.

I grip the edge of the battlement, the moaning of the fallen Fae swelling from below. None of ours appears to be wounded. I race down the stairs and into the courtyard, where a crowd has already convened around whatever the Fae left behind. It's a bag. Some sort of silky midnight blue fabric, cinched at the top with a gilded rope of laurel leaves.

Malakar followed me from the palace, filthy with cannon powder but otherwise unharmed. He kicks the bulging sack with the toe of his boot. "Don't feel alive. But there's only one way to find out."

He yanks the bindings loose. The fabric of the sack slackens and several objects spill out—stumps smudged with a tarlike substance, black and oozing. Malakar picks one up and abruptly drops it. If my stomach wasn't already empty, it would void again. That isn't tar pooling on our land. It's blood. And there's only one sort of creature who bleeds like that.

"What is it?" Neve maneuvers her way to the front of the crowd, her starling-feather cloak billowing behind her. She's stunned into stillness for a moment, and then she rushes to the bag, knocking a few disgruntled Imps out of her way before dropping to her knees.

The wind whips in from the sea, salt stinging our cheeks. Neve does not sob—doesn't make a sound. She stares, vibrating slightly around her edges as she gently touches the pieces of the Starlings. I can't tell yet how many there are, but they've been hacked to bits. The scent of decaying flesh is thick enough to chew.

Torin hurries to Neve's side and throws her arms around the Shifter leader.

Do something, she mouths to me.

"Neve, I . . ." But the words stick in my throat. She picks up a hunk of flesh. Black Shifter blood rolls down her wrist and splatters onto the ground. "We all grieve the loss of your—"

"Our," she corrects, her fist clenching. "These are *our* kin, Nimara. Yours as well as mine."

My face heats. "I was going to say your *Starlings*. We'll have a ceremony to honor them. You can preside over it. We'll do whatever you want."

A cold wind lashes between us. "Whatever I want," she repeats flatly. "Do you not even know the burial rituals for *our* kind?"

Silence hums. I do not know. I've read hundreds of books about the Vila. Listened to countless stories from the Goblins and Imps and Demons describing their own traditions. But the Shifters . . . they don't remain long enough at the palace for me to learn anything about them, I tell myself. But the excuse is feeble. I've no desire to learn because I already understand enough about Shifters to last my whole life. In my mind's eye, I can see Kal Shifting into my body to lure Aurora to the spindle. Laughing as she fell. Using me because it was *easy* to do so.

"We will do whatever is required," I say.

But it isn't enough. Neve swallows, and the expression on her face could melt stone.

"Over here!" From behind us, an Imp shouts. "One's still alive!"

I turn, grateful for the distraction. The Imp is waving wildly, indicating a Fae steed. There's an arrow in its hindquarters, and its lips are frothing, star-bright eyes rolling with fear.

"Shall I kill it for you, Mistress?" the Imp asks excitedly.

"Wait!" Demons part as Derek elbows his way forward. "Don't harm the horse."

"It's not a horse." Regan removes her knife from her boot. "It's Fae. And it has no place here. Rather like you, actually."

Imps chitter their laughter. And a few of the Goblins chuckle, tossing out jokes about how best to roast a tender mortal heart.

"Please." Derek positions himself between the Imp and the steed. "It's done nothing wrong. The wound might heal."

The beast nickers, breath steaming from its nostrils.

"And what would you know of it?" I ask. "Have you cared for many of its fellows on your ships?"

"I . . . no." More laughter. "But I did mind horses."

"I thought you were a crew hand."

"I was." He scratches at the line of his wig. "But I once held a position at an estate in the country. I groomed the horses and exercised them, and helped treat their injuries. And I'd like to tend this creature."

I cross my arms. "Why?"

Derek blinks, as if the answer was the most obvious in the world. "Because it doesn't deserve to die."

If he intended his comment to wound—with the slaughtered Shifters mere feet away—it hits its mark. I stand taller and adjust the belt of my gown, which the Imps have designed as a pair of skeletal hands wrapped around my waist.

"What if you bound the horse to you?" Derek rushes on. "Such a thing must be possible."

Curiosity undulates among the onlookers.

"You might be able to do it," Regan says at my elbow. "You did with Callow. And then we could use the beast to fly over the High Court during our campaigns."

It's an intriguing theory. With the exception of the Shifters and Demons, our army progresses through the Fae courts on foot. Briar's horses did not fare well after the Court of Beasts met its end. The lack of transport adds weeks to our journeys now that we're laying siege to Etheria's inner courts. But if we possessed our own flying battalion . . .

Dimples appear on either side of Derek's lips. I itch to slap them into the mud.

"Don't be too excited." I elbow him aside. "It's not done yet. And if it works, you're responsible for them. Do you understand? Feeding, grooming, shit-mucking, the lot. Don't come to me whining for the Imps or anyone else to help you."

He agrees, and Regan passes me her dagger. Several Demons secure the Fae steed. It screams and tries to buck as I slash the flesh of its hindquarters. I do the same to my own palm and then press the wounds together. The Fae steed rears. Its massive hooves strike the ground, kicking up clumps of dirt. The moonlit surface of its hide warms beneath my touch as I send my power through my hand and into its body.

Serve me. My intent pumps through the cord of my power, finding the heart of the steed's magic and twisting tight. One heartbeat. Two. An aura of green limns my hand. The beast whinnies and tosses its head, and I expect its magic to push back against mine in refusal. Or that the creature will burst into a thousand pieces. But to my immense astonishment, I sense acceptance pulsing from the other magic.

The halo of green light fades, and I can only stare at the brand left behind—the wreath of bramble and thorn. It worked. The creature is calm. Tame, even. It paws at the ground and blinks at me as if awaiting an order. In the cave where she dwells, Mortania cackles.

When I'd bound the human servants, I'd been filled with a glorious vindication. Heady triumph, after administering the punishment they so richly deserved. But this is different. My connection with this steed is closer akin to the bond I share with Callow. I place a hand on the creature's nose. Its ears twitch back and forth, as though it already recognizes my touch.

"And what do you say?" I ask quietly. "Shall we pay a visit to your master?"

The beast thumps his front hoof in what I interpret as agreement.

It brings a smile to my lips.

CHAPTER EIGHT

The next night, on the Crimson Cliffs, we burn the fallen Starlings. As the only other Shifter in attendance, I stand with Neve. But the space between us is prickly and loaded and I would rather be anywhere else.

Disdain seeps from the Shifter leader's very pores, and she barely even looks at me. She acts as though it's a crime that I don't know we're supposed to use cedar wood, with its spiced-smoke scent, to build the pyre, or feed the flames with jasmine and yarrow to speed the souls of the lost into their next lives. That the ashes are to be smudged in stripes along our cheeks and foreheads, or that there is a song to be sung when we scatter the rest to the sea winds.

When was I supposed to learn these details? In the black tower, when Kal was filling my head with lies? Or in the vile book Endlewild forced me to read? Neve behaves as though it is my own fault that I was taught to fear Shifters, and that the only other one I knew turned out to be just as horrible as those stories claimed.

It's a relief when she decides to return to her Starlings rather than stay the night. Maybe she'll stay away the rest of the war.

The court continues its mourning with copious amounts of drinking, the funeral quickly evolving into an extended celebration of Malakar's victory. And I'm more than happy to leave the disastrous ceremony behind me. I clean the ashes from my face at the earliest opportunity. Derek joins us in the throne room, wearing bright fuchsia breeches that clash terribly with a dingy yellow jacket. His wig is a mountain of frizzy ringlets strung with faded ribbons and chipped pearls. The Imps stuck in dead beetles for good measure, snacking on them as they take turns demanding to be whirled in dances.

When given a reprieve from the Imps, Derek—who has never experienced a revel before—feasts on as much of the food as he can. But apparently no one explained to him that, while the Imp food does not adversely affect those with dark magic, Derek's human magic is far too minuscule to be of any protection. Since his arrival, he has ingested only small portions of bread and dried meat—not enough for him to experience the full effects of the enchantment. Now, he shovels chocolate pastries into his mouth like this might be his last meal—and then promptly vomits black sludge in a corner while the Imps point and giggle.

"I feel like a complete idiot," I say to Regan, as our conversation returns to what transpired in the dungeons with Aelfdene. "I had the true name of a High Lord at my command and completely squandered the opportunity."

And I'll never get another. Even if we could compel him to write or mime his secrets, the Fae lord perished from his wounds, which had been exacerbated due to his exposure to our magic. Soon, his head will be mounted with the others, and the Goblins are talking about bronzing his tongue.

"Stop blaming yourself." She waves away a pitcher of wine, claiming she needs to stay sharp in case there is another visit from Oryn's forces. "He tricked all of us. What was he saying to you anyway? You looked half dead until Neve roused you."

Guilt prickles up the back of my neck. I can't exactly admit the whole truth about what Aelfdene glimpsed in my mind. I sip my wine. "He wanted to know why I seized Briar."

Her brow rumples. "Why would he have cared?"

I shrug. "He said he was interested in me. That I was the impossible come to life, or some other nonsense."

A trio of Imps chitters past, yanking one another's tails.

"Neve wasn't exaggerating about the strangeness of that court." Regan runs the blade of her snake-handled dagger through her fingertips.

I swallow more wine. The spices burn down my throat.

"It was not real."

The dead lord's words dig their talons into my soul. He was just being cruel, I tell myself. Twisting a knife while he still could. But doubt clings to me, like the smell of the cedar smoke from the pyre. Even Aurora questioned the "true love" her parents supposedly shared while they lived. Their kiss might have broken the late queen's curse, but the former royal couple had been miserable together—as were many before them. Aurora assumed that power and money had tainted their relationships, a more than plausible explanation. But what if Aelfdene *wasn't* being cruel? After all, the Fae cannot lie. What if Oryn had claimed true love could break

Mortania's curse on the princesses, but it was actually lifted by some random kiss? One that *might* have inspired love in the right circumstances?

"Do you believe in true love?" I ask Regan before I can think better of it.

A group of Goblins roars when their game of wager sours. Jewels and coins go flying, and Malakar descends upon them to break up the fight.

Regan angles herself to look at me properly. "*True* love?"

"You know." I rub my thumb over the embossed Briar rose on my goblet. "That there's only one person for you. And that, no matter what, you'll always be drawn back to them. That your relationship is . . . fated."

She steals my wineglass from my hand. "How much have you had?"

"I'm not drunk," I huff. Though I almost wish I were, after the day I've endured. "Do you think that sort of connection is only for tales and ballads?"

Regan sighs and crosses one leg over the other. "I don't know about true love," she admits. "But look around you. Everyone here adores you. The Vila used to bow to you when they started arriving from the realms across the sea. And the Imps tried to make a shrine."

With various old bones they plucked from the human skeletons in the corridors. I still shiver when I think of the macabre display. But that wasn't why I made them take it down or refused to let anyone kneel or bow in my presence. I don't want to be that kind of leader. We're all equals here. This is our home.

"That wasn't exactly what I meant."

"But it's enough, isn't it?" she asks. "And it's more than most of us have ever experienced. What does it matter if it falls under some magical category of *true love* or not?"

She's right. It should be enough. More than enough. A group of Imps blurs past, and I watch the dancing. The joy on the faces of so many who were exiled. A joy I helped to cultivate. And I try to let Aelfdene slide away. He was goading me. Reshaping my thoughts into something ugly, just as Endlewild used to do. But I don't have to let him.

"Come," I say to Regan, offering my hand. "We're going to dance."

"You're a horrible dancer." But she grins and sets down my glass.

Her hand is so familiar in mine, bone spikes against my green-veined skin. And I let myself be spun in dizzy circles, let the court blend into a wash of distorted shapes, and think of nothing else until morning. Not even Aurora.

Derek is indeed suprisingly skilled with the Fae steeds. A half-dozen more were found pawing around the palace grounds, and though they're nothing like the horses he tended in Terault, the apparently multitalented crew hand soon has arrow wounds packed with poultices and gashes stitched, and sets to exercising the string around the courtyard. He even mucks out the stalls without complaint, which is a huge disappointment.

The Imps regard the Fae steeds as their newest pets. There are always a dozen or more of the barb-tailed creatures crowding around Derek as he tends the animals, begging for rides. They seem to delight in being bucked off, which happens more often than not. Before long, the beasts are flying again, and the trilling peals of the Imps as they swoop and soar on the steeds' backs can be heard throughout the palace.

At the next council meeting, Malakar's stubby snout wriggles with anticipation. "We cannot let what happened with the Shifters go unpunished. Neve's lot shoulders the greatest risk of any of us. They deserve our support."

"True," Torin agrees. "But we cannot go barreling into the High Court in the name of justice. Oryn is likely expecting that. And his protections might have been what killed the Starlings."

An image of the hacked-up Shifters rears, and along with it my uncomfortable guilt from the funeral. I try to drown it in a swallow of tea, feeling as though the Shifter leader's eyes are boring through my skin and into my bones.

"Bah." Malakar waves Torin off. His ears twitch between his horns. "Enough blight elixir will blow those shields to bits. Or mine will invent something else to get the job done."

"Perhaps." Torin picks up a marker. "Or should we formulate another strategy? Our focus so far has been on the outer courts. But now . . ."

The great dragon doors burst open and an Imp barrels through, fuming. "He pushed me!"

Malakar hops from the seat of his chair. "Take your games somewhere else."

"Not a game." The Imp rubs at a spot on his hip. "The boy pushed me. Hateful, wicked thing. You'll punish him, Mistress?"

"The boy?" I ask. "Do you mean Derek? I can hardly blame him for retaliating with the torture you lot devise."

Regan flips her knife from one hand to the other. "That's what he gets for sailing across the sea to the land of *stories*."

"Aye, and he should get worse." The Imp lifts his chin, indignant. "We was going for a ride on a beastie, and as soon as we gets off the ground, he shoves me away and goes off hisself."

Regan laughs. "He did what?"

"Just what I says!" His crimson tail thrashes. "I tolds him I wants to fly past these windows. Do a trick for you, Mistress. I knew you was at council. But as soon as the beastie makes for the sky, he flicks me off like I's a bothersome flea."

There is something I do not like about this story. An itching in my mind. Derek knew we were occupied. That the sentries on the battlements wouldn't think twice about seeing him flying, and that none of us would be close enough to interfere. Could he be making his escape? Is that why he begged for the life of the steed?

"Where is he now?" Regan asks.

"How should I know?" The Imp pouts. "He takes off, like I tolds you. You'll bring him back, won't you, Mistress? See he gets a proper whallop?"

"He can't have gone far." Malakar watches the windows, snout scrunching. "Unless . . . would he be daft enough to take the beast to sea?"

"The bond would kill him if he tries to leave us," Regan says. "It would kill the beast, too."

"Look!" The Imp points. "There he is!"

Across the seamless glass of the windows, the steed streaks through the sky, its gold-dusted wings shimmering in the sunlight. But it's not headed toward the sea. It looks like he's steering toward the old wing of the palace.

Stories of a princess . . . asleep for a hundred years.

My blood flashes hot, then cold. No—it isn't possible. He

doesn't know where she is. Doesn't know *who* she is, or that she's even alive. And no one can get to Aurora through my barrier.

But, I realize with a sickening jolt, there is no such barrier blocking the gap in the wall—a gap wide enough for a Fae steed and a worthless ship's boy.

"Nimara." Regan nudges me, and I'm dropped back into the present like a stone.

"Find him." I push away from the table. "Have the sentries shoot him down if they must. And then bring him straight here."

Amid a volley of questions, I leave the chamber and Shift into invisibility so that they cannot follow. If Derek is going to the library, I must get to her before he does.

CHAPTER NINE

My feet pound the dusty stones of the back corridors. Not fast enough, even with my Shifter magic pouring into them.

I'm overreacting, I tell myself for the thousandth time. Derek has no reason to fly through the gap in the wall. No one else has disturbed Aurora in a hundred years, and—

The Fae beast's snorting and chuffing reach me as I near the wall of bramble, shattering my impossible hopes. My hand slaps down on a thick vine. A thorn pierces my palm, but all I feel is a blind, frantic panic as I tear through the entrance and find Derek leaning over Aurora.

Horror consumes me. The bramble enclosure on Aurora's bed is open. I must have neglected to close it the last time I visited. And the boy's lips are inches from Aurora's, the space between them narrowing by the second.

"Get away from her!" I scream.

Derek jerks back like a marionette tossed aside by its strings. But it's too late.

There's a rumbling, like one I never thought to feel again. Small stones ping down from the ceiling. Books spill from their shelves and clatter to the floor. The Fae steed whinnies in terror and vaults through the gap in the wall, abandoning his rider.

"What have you done?" I yell at him as the room finally settles.

Derek gapes at me from where he landed. He starts to stammer out an answer, but then—

"Alyce?"

I've not heard that name—that voice—in a century. An exquisite ache blooms in my chest. I can hardly breathe around it.

Aurora is sitting up. Her golden hair falls around her shoulders. Her eyes—those glimmering amethysts—are open and alert. So beautiful that I will split right down the middle, the pieces of me floating away on the wind.

"Aurora."

Tears clog my throat, of happiness and relief and a hundred other emotions. But then everything is smothered by confusion. Derek kissed Aurora awake. Which means the Fae protections on her curse should be in effect. Her expression should be fearful, or at least clouded with uncertainty, for she should know me only as a monster—if she remembers me at all. And yet she's looking right at me. She said my name.

"Are . . . are you the princess?"

Derek. The boy is irritatingly unscathed. "You will not—"

Aurora cuts me off. "Who are you?"

He bows, but it's an unpracticed gesture that makes him look foolish. And I notice there is manure smeared over his breeches.

Good. "Derek, Your Majesty. Highness. I mean . . . I'm actually not sure what to—"

"And you kissed me."

He swipes his unkempt crow-feather hair off his forehead. "I—well, yes."

Aurora's knees wobble as she stands. Derek rushes to help her, but she leans out of his reach. "I require no further assistance."

"Don't pay him any attention. He's not important," I say before he can cause any more distraction, and Derek wisely takes the hint to be silent. I inch toward the bed, hardly able to speak the words that are burning through my mind. "Aurora. Do you . . . remember me?"

But she doesn't answer. Slowly, she assesses the room. Apprehension skates across my nerves. Even a hundred years ago, this chamber was a decrepit ruin. But now it is far worse. Cobwebs drape the shelves like shredded curtains. The windows are grayed with grime. The furniture is warped and stained with rainwater from a century's worth of storms. The wreckage of Briar looms in the distance. What does she think of it?

"How long has it been?" There's a tremor in her voice.

I twist my fingers together, the bramble band of my signet ring digging into my flesh. I'd imagined this conversation a thousand times. Practiced it, even. But now the words slip about like eels, completely out of my grasp. "Not terribly long. Well . . . a hundred years."

Wind stirs her spun-gold hair. "One hundred years."

At last, she turns. Takes one foal-like step after another in my direction. I bite the inside of my cheek and hope that my thudding heart doesn't explode out of its cage, then hope that it does. Her scent washes over me, far more potent now that she is awake—

apple blossom and summer nights. I drink it in, a single wild thought whirling through my brain: Does she taste the same?

A sharp sting cracks along the side of my face. The room blurs past me and I stumble.

She slapped me.

"How could you?"

The question is low and lethal, unlike any I've heard from Aurora before. Because it isn't really her, I register. It's the curse taking root. I clutch the throbbing in my cheek. And for the first time since my siege, I wish Endlewild were alive so that I could kill him all over again. "You don't understand. Laurel and Endlewild altered your memories while you slept. They deliberately confused you so that you would think I was . . ."

But I can't even finish. Laurel. My blood roils. While I was living in Lavender House, I thought the wisdom Grace was my friend, or as close to a friend as I ever had. But she'd been spying for Endlewild, reporting all of my activities to the Fae ambassador.

"They altered nothing." Brittle pages flap around us. "I remember it all. The fountain. Your bird. The summoning ritual. The night we spent here."

An image of those hours sear through my mind, the two of us tangled together. And I am suddenly acutely aware of Derek's presence. No one in the Dark Court knows of my history with Aurora, and I certainly can't start with *him* piecing it together.

"Get out." I jerk my chin toward the entrance.

The boy has the gall to stand straighter. But his feet begin to shuffle as the bond between us compels him to obey my command. He grabs at his arm and grits his teeth.

"What are you doing to him?" Aurora wrests Derek's arm

away from his chest and pulls up his sleeve. The wreath of bramble and thorn is glowing like a burning coal. "What is this?"

"Nothing to be concerned about. He swore his service to me. Willingly," I add, at the judgment on her face. "This is the consequence when he doesn't honor his vow."

Aurora touches the mark and Derek hisses in pain. "Yes, it looks like 'nothing.' Let him go. Immediately."

Mortania rouses in the place where my magic lives. *Is SHE the one giving orders?*

I tamp the ancient Vila down. Aurora simply doesn't understand yet. Tiny curls of smoke are rising from Derek's brand. The scent of scorched flesh stings in my nostrils. "You may stay," I grind out.

The ancient Vila rumbles her displeasure, and Derek exhales in relief. The mark fades to black, but I sorely hope the pain lingers.

"Thank you, Princess," he says. "If I can ever be of service to you—"

"I do not know you, Sir Darren." Aurora steps away from him. "And I would thank you not to presume an acquaintance you do not enjoy. Do you make it a habit to kiss women while they sleep and are unable to fend you off? And why did *your* kiss wake me anyway?"

Sparks of surprise and relief flare in my veins. She doesn't know that anyone could have woken her—anyone but me. And she *cannot* find out, not after this.

Derek's face shades the color of a ripe plum. "No. I don't know. I just—"

"We'll deal with him later," I interrupt, putting myself in front of Aurora. "You're angry, I understand. But please listen to what I have to say. When you were cursed again, Laurel and Endlewild tainted your memories of me with an elixir or something. They wanted to change your perception of me. Whatever they did is the reason you can't see clearly right now."

"See clearly?" she repeats. "My home doesn't exist anymore. What else is there to see? There's nothing *tainting* my memories."

"There is," I insist.

"Really?" She ticks items off on her fingers. "Your bird's name is Callow. You muddied up a fountain in the gardens on the night of my birthday. I rescued you from a prison cell after my father was going to use you as his weapon against the Etherians."

My mind is spinning. She does remember. And a cold understanding pools in my belly. Could I really have spent the last hundred years seeking a way to lift protections that were never in place?

"But Laurel *told* me," I repeat.

"Then her elixir either didn't work, or she lied."

"She had no reason to—" I stop short, that terrible day coming back to me in waves. Laurel in Aurora's bedchamber, urging me to run before Tarkin's guards broke down the door. Before the light Fae arrived, deposed the king, and executed me. "She knew I wouldn't leave Briar without you," I whisper. "She lied so that I would go . . . and live."

Dragon's teeth. What a fool I've been. Despair settles over me like a wet woolen blanket. But this revelation, if it's true, does nothing to quell my anger toward the Grace. Laurel might have been trying to help me, but she achieved the opposite. I think of all the days I've lost, when Aurora and I could have been—

"And I assume Laurel is dead now, for all her gallant attempts to rescue you." Aurora folds her arms, and guilt jabs at me. Laurel had helped her rescue me from Tarkin's dungeon. She was part of our plan to stage a coup.

Until she changed her mind and allied with the Fae, Mortania whispers.

She's right.

"What Laurel did doesn't excuse—"

"And everyone else?" Aurora asks. "Are they all sleeping in their own cages, waiting for Eric to come and free them?"

"Derek," he corrects, rubbing the back of his neck.

"Quiet!" I snarl at him. This is worse than any curse. "You were never in a cage," I say to Aurora. "I was protecting you from your father. You'd be married to that infernal prince right now if it weren't for me. You remember *him,* don't you?"

"Protecting me?" She laughs again, but it does not sound like the same laugh we shared together in my Lair, mocking the vapid courtiers. "I thought I had died and been delivered to some sort of personal hell. I saw visions of the Grace District burning. Courtiers and merchants and *children* reduced to charred corpses—by *your hand.*"

"You weren't here," I say, anger spiking. Why won't she listen to what I'm trying to tell her? "You're confused right now, but—"

"Confused?" The cry of a raven carries through the room. "You know, Alyce, I think Laurel's elixir was more effective than she guessed. I don't recognize you at all. But not because of any Grace magic. Because of you. *You* are the curse."

Thunder growls as yet another line of storms trudges inland. Salt stings on my lips, tears track down my face. But whether they are from shock, or sadness, or rage, I cannot tell. I swipe them roughly away.

There's a stampede of feet in the distance. Dragon's teeth. The others. And it is far too late to do anything to salvage the situation.

Malakar is the first to skid to a halt inside the entrance, followed by Torin and a few Demon sentries. An Imp points, open-mouthed. "Wha's that pretty one doin' here?"

"Never seen her before," another agrees.

Regan elbows her way to the front of the crowd, then freezes as she comprehends what's occurred. She mouths something to me, but I shake my head. I'll explain later—if I survive whatever disaster is about to fall upon my shoulders.

"Nimara?" Torin asks, expectant.

The taste of loam fills my mouth from where I've been biting my tongue.

"This is Aurora," I force myself to say. "The last princess of Briar."

And apparently, from the way she is glowering at me, my enemy.

Part II

Another child. She will be my last, I know. Tarkin shows barely any interest in me on the best of days, though there was a time, long ago, when a dashing prince of Paladay lifted my curse with his kiss—true love's kiss—and guaranteed me every happiness.

I envy my younger sisters. Due to the curse, they are not allowed to bear their own daughters. They do not have to stroke their baby's down-feather hair and hold their plump starfish hands and know the heartbreak that is to come.

But this daughter.

Aurora.

Tarkin judged it a ridiculous name, pretentious and indulgent. I don't care. This violet-eyed girl may be the last—the only—gift I bestow on my realm. For if the thorn-and-bramble crown ever rests on her head, she will very much need to live up to such a name.

She will need to bring the dawn to this interminable night.

—Excerpt from the lost diary of Mariel,
Briar Queen. Age of the Rose, 956

CHAPTER TEN

The unsettled energy of the court eddies in a rush of whispers and rustle of bodies. A familiar feeling of pins and needles prickles through my limbs—so like what I endured as the Dark Grace that I have to resist the urge to huddle under an invisible cloak. It is a sensation I have not experienced in a hundred years, and I despise it. Despise the fact that, after everything, I can still be reduced to that girl again. Mortania undulates in her cave.

You are not that girl, pet.

It had taken a long time and much shouting to convince the others to leave the old library and convene in the throne room, then far longer for Aurora to complete the journey. After a century of sleep, she is as weak as a fledgling, but she refused to let anyone carry her—even though it meant frequent stops during which she had to brace herself against a wall to recover. And then she had halted for other reasons, like when she found the statues of ancient queens defaced, and her mother's portrait shredded and—

most disastrously—when she glimpsed the great doors of the throne room, relieved of their array of jewels.

"Are those," she'd whispered, "eyes?"

The Imps proudly confirmed that they were, and that they had embedded the Etherian eyes into the doors themselves. Then the creatures happily pointed out the tattered banners hanging from the ceiling, the crest of Briar's royal family obliterated. The thrones with their assortments of broken Fae staffs. The Etherian heads mounted to the walls. Aurora accepted each display with steadfast silence, but I know there is a storm brewing between her bones. I just need to get her alone. Her waking was too much of a shock. But I can explain.

Torin's staff, carved from the diamond-grooved trunk of an ash tree, taps against the marble floor as she approaches Aurora. "This is the crown princess? The very same whom we assumed to have perished with the royal family?"

"The *sleeping* princess from the boy's story?" Malakar's snout wrinkles. I overheard several of his Goblins muttering to one another about the supple, peach-pink hue of Aurora's skin, and the luster of her hair—fine spun gold they yearn to add to their collection. This is not the way Aurora's introduction to court was supposed to happen.

A few heads turn to Derek, who is hovering near the east bank of windows. He's kept as close as possible to Aurora since we left the abandoned library. His muscles are coiled, as if he's waiting for the right moment to swoop in and rescue her. But he's done quite enough of that today. Perhaps it will soon be time for the ship's boy to take his leave of us. Permanently.

"You knew she was alive, Nimara?" Torin's coal-bright attention only intensifies my discomfort.

"She was under a sleeping curse," I reply with as much dignity as possible. "I did not know how to lift it. I've been housing her in the old wings since my siege."

"A hundred years you kept this from us?" Wisps of shadow curl from Torin's skin, signaling her anger. Anger that is, admittedly, deserved. "Regan—did you know?"

The Vila leader lifts her chin. "I did."

Demons whisper to one another. I twist the signet ring on my finger.

"She kept the secret because I asked her to," I explain, clearing the hitch in my voice. "I wasn't sure how you would react if you knew."

"And how should we react?" Malakar's ears lay flat beside his horns. He points at Aurora. "Her family destroyed Malterre and banished our kind. Allied with the light Fae. They would have seen us all dead."

"Aye, kill the princess!" A few Imps shout. Cheers.

Vila propose that Aurora's body should be chopped up and dumped over Etheria, as Neve's Starlings were in our courtyard. Though I can tell she's trying to fight it, Aurora's shoulders bow slightly inward. No—I will not let them treat her this way.

"Enough!" The word echoes in the chamber like the lash of a whip. Several Imps, who had been creeping closer to the dais, shrink back. "I've spent the last century welcoming each and every one of you into this court. Creating a home for you when you had none. If Aurora is the sole surviving royal, don't you think I had good reason to protect her?"

"Aye, and what reason was that?" Malakar asks. "Was she to be some kind of hostage?"

"No," I say, exasperated. "I'm aware of your opinions concerning the former rulers." I gesture around at the ruined portraits hanging at crooked angles. "And I cannot fault you for assuming the worst of one of their princesses. But Aurora is different. She's my . . ."

Aurora arches an eyebrow, and my throat tightens. She's *every-thing*. But I cannot admit that when, only a moment ago, the court was talking of scattering her broken body over Etheria. Later, when they get to know her, their hearts will soften.

"She befriended me," I say. Aurora tenses. "Accepted me, when no one else in this realm would. She deserves a place here as much as the rest of you do."

Uncertain murmurs swell. But I sense that a fraction of the court's bloodlust has cooled to curiosity, and I count that as a victory.

"Aye, and what does the princess have to say about it?" Malakar drums his stubby fingers on the arm of his chair. "Does Nimara have it right? Are you *different*?"

The seconds drag on. I hold my breath, silently willing Aurora to say *something* that will support my claims. They will love her as I do if only she would—

"Your . . . Your *Highness*."

There's a stir in the court as a human servant slips her way through the sea of onlookers. The Goblins and Imps block her path and pinch her limbs. One of them sticks out a foot and trips her. She goes skidding across the floor, then crawls on hands and knees toward the dais.

"Do I know you?" Aurora asks.

The human rakes her matted auburn hair out of her thin face. "Elspeth, Highness."

The same servant who was digging around in my drawers. The skin around her curse mark still bears faint scars from our encounter. I let out a sigh. This day keeps getting worse.

"My mother was a member of your household when . . ." Her focus flicks to me, and I dare her to continue. That bright spot of lapis fury from my bedchamber leaps and dives within her gaze.

I never did ask the Goblins about Elspeth's brooch. Perhaps I will.

Aurora kneels to the servant's level, still wobbly. "Who was your mother?"

"L-Lady Elipsa." A tear tracks through the layer of grit on her cheek and drips onto her uniform, which is blotched with colorful stains and ripped at the sleeves. "But she is long passed now."

The first real happiness in a hundred years illuminates Aurora's face. And it's directed at someone else. My fists clench.

"Yes, I think I do remember her," she says. "Lady Elipsa was a skilled dancer."

A vague recollection of this courtier surfaces. Her laugh sounded like crows cackling, and she frequented my Lair regularly for hair-thinning and waist-thickening elixirs she used to sabotage the other ladies of court. And Elspeth is a greedy vulture, who is likely already plotting how she might use this situation to her advantage. But Aurora is reaching for her hand. Regarding her like she's a saint.

Ignore them, pet.

I cannot.

"Yes, Highness," Elspeth goes on in that breathless, simpering tone. "My mother adored you. The others will be relieved to know that you're alive. I'll be sure to—"

Regan slams her staff on the stone close enough that Elspeth half-tumbles down the steps. "You're disrupting the business of court." She jabs the staff at the door. "Get back to your duties."

Aurora rises stiffly. "You will not speak to her that way. She deserves respect."

"Respect?" A Goblin spits. "What gives you the right to instruct this court on its manners?"

Giggles from the Imps. But Aurora doesn't even flinch at their derision. She adopts that regal posture I've seen too many times to count, and my stomach drops. "Because this is *my* home. *My* court. Because I am the Briar *Queen!*"

Silence thrums, ringing in my ears. The court stares at her, open-mouthed.

And then they explode into laughter.

Goblins stomp their feet. Imps fall over one another, kicking at the air as they roll back and forth. My head pounds, and I curse this wretched day. Of all things Aurora could have said, that has to be the worst. I wrack my aching brain for something to say to defend her, but how can I? This isn't Briar anymore.

"There are no queens here, *m'lady*." Malakar snorts.

Splotches like long-ago Briar roses climb up Aurora's neck. If only I'd had time to warn her how they'd be. But she's always so ridiculously stubborn.

The Imps begin to dance and climb one atop the other, ordering charges in the name of their pretend queen. Goblins raise their cudgels and take up the cry. Demons and Vila grin in a manner that could only be described as carnivorous.

"And you claimed she's different than the other royals?" The fissures on Torin's body pulse scarlet.

"She's been asleep for a hundred years," I reason, "and has

woken to find her home in ruins. You can understand what she's feeling."

But the Dark Court entertains no interest in empathy. And I feel as though Aurora and I are farther apart than ever before. Standing on opposite sides of a widening chasm.

And which side will you choose, pet?

I squeeze my eyes shut against the ancient Vila.

"I agree with Nimara." The back of Regan's hand brushes against mine, her light yet steady touch filling me with gratitude and relief. "We welcome the former Fae into our midst, why not a human?"

"Those Fae are turned Vila," Torin points out.

Several of such courtiers are sprinkled through the crowd. Turning was a fairly common practice before the War of the Fae, beginning with the mate of the first Vila, who changed his golden blood to the green of the Vila rather than forsake his love. After him, Etherians who were tired of the rigid rules of Oryn's domain frequently abandoned the Fae courts to join those of Malterre. Dozens of former Fae are now members of the Dark Court, their outward appearance unchanged, though their blood runs emerald.

"The princess cannot turn," Torin continues. "Nor does it sound like she would."

Aurora crosses her arms. No, she would not. And I wouldn't ask that of her.

"She could be bound," Malakar suggests. "As the other humans have done."

"I will not wear another curse mark," she grinds out, glaring at me.

Tension masses between us and undulates through the onlookers. This is a catastrophe. I berate myself for not having planned Aurora's introduction with more care. I should have detailed every step. Devised plans and counterplans. I was an absolute idiot to think it was going to be simple when she woke—that she could just slide into place like she'd been here all along. Then again, it *might* have been easier if not for the boy's sneaking around where he didn't belong. I pin him with my most vicious glower, and he shrinks farther into the crowd. We will have much to discuss later.

"You claim there was a friendship." Torin angles her staff between me and Aurora. "But I do not see it. Whatever you two shared has clearly withered beneath the curse."

"It was not real."

Aelfdene's words come crashing back. A lump congeals in my throat. And for the first time in a century, Aurora smiles at me. But it is a rueful thing, intended to wound.

"*Clearly,* you're all forgetting who stands before you." Regan speaks above the rising clamor. "Without Nimara, we would still be wandering the realms across the sea, in exile. Or," she gestures at an Imp, "be enslaved in the Fae courts."

A tremor of unease ripples among the court, each of us battling our memories.

Regan puts her hand on my shoulder. "We owe her everything. And all she asks is that we trust her word when it comes to this mortal princess. Obviously, she saw something worth saving in the girl. And that's enough for me."

A weight lifts from my chest. And Regan's confidence finally seems to penetrate the icy veneer of the court. Weapons droop and sneers soften. I slide a sideways glance at Aurora. But she remains as contemptuous as ever.

"Perhaps"—Torin tugs at the pendant around her neck—"we could grant the princess time to adjust."

It's as close to kindness as I could hope for.

"Time, aye. For her to traipse about, shouting that she's queen?" Malakar scratches behind his horns.

"Let her say what she likes. I find her assertions rather humorous, actually." Regan grins. "But we can assign her some keepers to make sure she doesn't get herself into trouble."

My gratitude sours into irritation, but the idea is met with appreciation from the others. And I cannot argue against such a compromise if it keeps Aurora alive.

"Yes, give her to us." An Imp creeps forward, rubbing his hands. "Never had a princess to play with before."

"She's not a toy," I say sternly. He slinks back.

"Then what am I?" Aurora hurls the question at me like a blade. "A hostage in my own home? Held by someone I thought . . ."

Her jaw sets, lips pursed together until they're bloodless. And a fresh crack forms in my heart, imagining what she might have been about to say.

"You cannot be a hostage." Malakar displays his jagged teeth. "There's no one left to offer ransom."

Aurora's amethyst eyes shine. But she does not allow the tears to fall. Not even as the court laughs and swarms around her.

A terrible thought takes root in my mind. That Torin was right. That the fragile, beautiful thing between us has withered. And there's no going back to the way we were before.

CHAPTER ELEVEN

"And how did *that* happen?"

Regan pulls me aside as the court launches back into its routine. Valmar assigns his best Imps to be Aurora's keepers, and they lead her away amid a flurry of excited chittering. She'll be housed in her old rooms, at least, which I hope is a comfort to her. They're technically Neve's chambers now—but the Shifter leader is so infrequently in residence that I determined it wouldn't matter if Aurora occupied them.

"The horrible boy," I answer, jerking my chin to where Derek lurks near the windows.

"Him?" She laughs. "But he's mortal. How did he manage to lift a curse?"

I press my thumb into the cracked jewel of my signet ring. "He kissed her."

"Oh." Regan crosses her arms and considers him. "Do you think it was one of those 'true love' instances, like what you were saying? Fate, or something?"

The image of Aelfdene's grin rears in my mind.

"No," I say, with far too much force. Regan deals me a quizzical expression. She's aware of Aurora's first curse, but not that I'm the one who broke it—or *how* I broke it. "He's not interesting enough to be anyone's true love. And I thought you didn't believe in that anyway."

"I never said I didn't." She runs a fingertip over the bone spikes on her knuckles. The Imps tow Derek away, and I hope they run him ragged. "It is strange, though, that all this should suddenly happen. Why him? And why now?"

My head begins to ache, and I do not like any of the possible answers buzzing inside my mind. "Could we continue this later? I have something to do."

She frowns at me. "Are you all right?"

"Fine," I lie. "I just need to think."

Regan squeezes my shoulder. "Let me know if I can do anything. I promised Malakar a round of sparring anyway. And try to sleep. You look awful."

She tosses me a teasing grin as she turns to walk down the dais steps, but I catch her wrist. "Thank you for standing by me today."

Regan shrugs in that gruff way she does when receiving praise. "It's easy to do. But . . ." Her green eyes darken. "I know you said she was your friend."

"Is," I correct, bristling.

"I believe you. Just . . . be careful. I won't always be able to help you. And"—she indicates the rest of the court—"if every day is like today, they won't warm to her. And I can't say that I would blame them."

Though it pains me to admit it, I can't say I would, either. But

I let that go. "Aurora will come around," I say. "She'll understand."

She has to.

It's been a long time since I've stood outside Aurora's chambers. The dragon engraved on the pale wood of the doors is barely visible through the scars of soot and decay. The first time I saw its jeweled eyes, I'd been disguised as a pleasure Grace after Aurora was cursed by the spindle. Amid the other sounds in the corridor, I can even imagine the phantom strain of the palace bells announcing her upcoming wedding to the star-chosen prince. But I squash that memory as quickly as it surfaces. Things are different now. Better, even if Aurora doesn't see it that way. Still, part of me thinks I should do as Regan suggested and rest. Get my bearings before I undertake this mad endeavor. But sleep would never come, not with the way my nerves jangle. And I must speak to her. My hands are restless as I debate whether I should knock. Probably, but I'm too afraid that Aurora won't answer. I test the lock. The handle gives, and I slip inside.

The sitting room appears much the same now as it did a century ago. Just after the siege, I'd righted all the toppled pieces of furniture and cleaned up the shards of glass and plaster. Patched up the holes in the windows and made sure Aurora's books remained in decent condition. Neve hasn't added a single trinket of her own to decorate the suite, and I'm glad of that. I'd always secretly hoped Aurora would occupy it again. If, I blush, she wasn't with me in the royal suite.

But there's no evidence to suggest Aurora appreciates my efforts to keep up her rooms. She hasn't removed the sheets from the silk-upholstered chairs. She isn't reading any of the books I took such care to salvage. Muffled conversation filters from behind the closed doors to my right, those that lead to her bedchamber. I tiptoe toward them, then Shift my hearing and listen at the keyhole.

"So you're Imps?" I hear Aurora ask, using the tone she once reserved for irritating nobles. "I thought all the creatures of Malterre died during the War of the Fae."

"Aye," one replies, "and we thought all the princesses died when Nimara turned beastie and burned this realm."

A chorus of cackles.

"I'm sorry to disappoint you with my existence."

"Not disappointed. Not when there's such fun to be had. This hair—" A sound like a warbly cooing. "So lovely. Will you give me some of it?"

"Or all of it? You won't miss it."

"It grows back."

"And your teeth are so white. Like rows of pearls."

"I do love pearls. Open your mouth."

This has gone far enough. I push the door wide. Aurora is seated at the window, and the trio of Valmar's creatures are far closer than they ought to be. One has his spindly claw-tipped fingers hovering near her face.

"Mistress!" He freezes and backs away with a hasty bow.

"What were you three doing?"

They nudge one another.

"Welcoming the princess," one attempts. "As you wished."

"I see. I've already told you that she's not your plaything. You'll take none of her hair, nor anything else that belongs to her."

Groans of disapproval.

"Shall I *turn beastie* and demand your obedience? Or better yet, deny you access to my wardrobe?"

Their ears droop. "No, Mistress."

"Good. Now go and find something else to do for a while—but leave tea."

The one who had been angling for Aurora's teeth fishes a few stones from his pocket and places them on a table. He claps his hands over them, and a tea set appears, steaming and complete with a jug of cream and a plate of tarts and sandwiches. The trio scuffles out, shooting Aurora sidelong glances and murmuring about the length of her eyelashes.

"Don't worry about them," I say to her, pouring two cups of tea and adding cream. "They're harmless, really. Just easily over-excited."

"I'm not worried," she replies. "The worst thing that ever could have happened to me already has happened. Why should I fear anything else?"

An auspicious beginning. I roll my shoulders against the knotted tension there, stacking sandwiches on a plate and offering it to her. "You must be hungry. The magic in the Imp food shouldn't harm you seeing as you've lived under Mortania's curse for so many years. But try not to eat too much. It might cause discomfort at first, until you become accustomed."

She doesn't move. "Accustomed? To the food, or to the fact that you'll obviously be listening to every conversation that I have from now on?"

My cheeks heat. "I couldn't help but overhear."

"I imagine not, when you were standing right outside my bedroom door with your ear pressed against it."

I set down the plate and pull a chair across from her, doing my best to smooth out my own irritation. "You're right. I'm sorry. About that, and about how things went earlier in the throne room. I never thought . . ."

"That I would wake up?"

"No! I mean, yes," I say, flustered. "I wanted you to wake up more than anything. I must have crafted a thousand elixirs over the years. Nothing worked."

She crosses her arms. "Except Derek's kiss. Do *you* know why?"

I fidget with the embroidery on my skirt and hope she cannot scent the lie beneath my silence. Part of me thinks I should tell her. But she's already so angry about Briar. She wouldn't take the news that I'd let her sleep for a century very well, regardless of my intentions. Better to wait until I can clean up the other damage.

"All I know is that mine wouldn't," I say. And it's not totally untrue. "Laurel and Endlewild did something to the curse to make sure I could never be the one to wake you that way. And then they took you back to the palace, where the servants were already decorating for your wedding to Elias. I had to do something to stop it."

She huffs. "Fire and murder were your first lines of defense?"

I can no longer stopper my annoyance. "Do you want to know what happened? Or are you content to keep inventing a story of your own?"

A muscle feathers in her jaw, but she nods—all the invitation I'll receive.

I take a fortifying sip of tea. This is what I came here to do. But it still feels as though I'm stepping onto a thinly frozen lake. And I proceed in kind, explaining slowly and deliberately about the black tower. Kal and his secret lessons and the broken medallion.

How he Shifted to mirror my appearance on the night we were supposed to stage our coup, then lured Aurora to the spindle and the second curse. Endlewild ferrying her back to Lavender House, and then the palace. Laurel's treachery. King Tarkin and his men trying to beat down my barrier in the library. And then, finally, how I'd Shifted and made sure no one could ever keep us apart again.

"They would have killed me," I tell her. I've been talking for so long that the teacup is cold in my hands. "And they probably would have locked you in some tower after you were wed, still asleep, so that Elias could rule on his own."

This is when I expect Aurora to soften. For understanding to spark in her eyes, realizing the impossible situation I was in. The dire fate that had nearly swallowed us both. Maybe she won't be *happy* about what happened, but she should at least see that I did what was best . . . for both of us. But she only sits and watches me with that stoic stare. She's silent for so long that I'm half worried that she's in some kind of trance and hasn't heard a word.

"Had you always known you were capable of Shifting like that?" she asks at last, and I'm slightly disgruntled that this is her first question.

"No," I answer. "Shifting always proved difficult for me, actually. Until Mortania's power melded with mine. Her magic must have bolstered my Shifter abilities as well as Vila."

Yes, pet. I made you what you are. The ancient Vila whirls, and the scent of charred steel and loam tickles my nose.

"And this Mortania. She was in Kal's medallion the whole time? The same Vila who cast the curse on Leythana's line?"

The one we broke, though it doesn't appear she cares to remember that particular detail. A clock chimes the hour.

"Yes."

"The same Vila whom we were trying to banish?" her voice rises. "The one who killed my sisters and would have killed me, *lives* inside you now?"

I set my cup down. China rattles. "It's not that simple. Yes, she was responsible for your first curse. But her magic is also the reason you're here today instead of lying unconscious in some tower, a pawn of the Briar Kings. I couldn't just let them have you."

"Have me?" Her eyes blaze. "What am I, a barrel of Etherium to be traded?"

"That's not what I mean and you know it."

"What I *know* is that I've woken to find my entire life upended. There are severed heads on the throne room walls, and my palace is filled with cre—"

A raw and brutal anger kindles, sharp and swift. Such as I've never felt with Aurora. "Creatures?" I repeat. "Is that what we are? What *I* am?"

She doesn't answer, but her breathing quickens. "I don't know what to call you. Alyce. Nimara." She wields the names like weapons. "All I know is that I trusted you. And you took everything I loved and ripped it to pieces. And now you expect my thanks?"

Everything? I saved us. Was that not enough?

"You want to speak of trust? I trusted *you.* That you didn't care that I was Vila. That you would change Briar for the better. But now I see how you really feel about me and mine. I was nothing more than your pet Grace."

Her nostrils flare. "If you were my pet, at least I didn't keep you in a cage for a hundred years. And now I'm in another. How long until your court decides to add my head to the walls?"

Mortania's presence swells and crests, sizzling across every nerve, and I do not fight her. "Do you want to know why there are heads on the walls? Because of Endlewild. And the Fae courts, who tried to drive all of *my* ancestors to extinction. Ask the Goblins and Demons and Imps what their lives were like after the War of the Fae, hunted and exiled. The murdered families and degradation. You were pampered and spoiled. A *princess*. You have no idea what it's like to be one of us."

For the briefest instant, the fire in her eyes dims. "I may not know exactly what hardship they suffered, but I never treated you with anything but respect. I loved you."

Loved. The fissures in my wasted heart expand. Unwelcome tears sting in my eyes. I blink them away.

"But you could not even claim me in front of your court," she goes on. "What did you think was going to happen when I woke? I've seen the human servants. It might be kinder to keep them in the dungeons. Leythana's crest has been chipped out of the stone, the tapestries of the early queens are destroyed. All evidence of Briar has become a mockery. *I'm* a mockery."

I grip the arms of my chair. "Is that what you care about? The trinkets, and the jewels, and the gowns? The statues and the sigils? What will you do—cry and whine for what you deem is your right? Throw tantrums until someone hands it to you?"

Wind bullies against the glass. The walls creak.

"I hate you," Aurora whispers. It steals my breath. "I hate what you've become. You're not Alyce anymore. And I . . ." She swallows. "I wish I was still asleep."

My pulse thuds in my palms against the carved wood of the armrest. I cannot keep the tears back now, but I will not let her see them. I gather myself and go to the door. "Whether you choose to believe it or not, I did this for us. I won't apologize for making a home for my kind after the hell we endured. Briar may not be glittering or gilded anymore, but it is still the world we imagined. I still want you to be part of it."

I risk a glance back. But Aurora isn't looking at me. She's picked up a tarnished hand mirror from her dressing table and is examining her warped reflection. A fresh wave of anger crashes into me. Is she worried about the Grace magic in her blood Fading, and her famed beauty draining away?

"*It was not real,*" Aelfdene's vile words lodge themselves into my very soul.

CHAPTER TWELVE

I hate you.

It chases me through the next days and nights. Invades my dreams and smothers my appetite. Aurora refuses to come out of her rooms, and I will not go and see her again after what happened. The Imps tell me that she's barricaded herself in her bedchamber. That sometimes they can hear her crying.

I have her favorite foods sent to her rooms, and books I think she might enjoy. She ignores my notes and invitations to join the court. I should spend my time in the council chamber, or my solar, and lose myself in strategizing. I wander the corridors instead, my argument with Aurora replaying mercilessly in my mind. She was so cruel. Utterly unwilling to see my side of things. When Briar was at its height, Aurora abhorred the nobles like Elspeth, a bunch of sycophants obsessed with climbing the social ranks. But the way she looked at the servant—far kinder than she's looked at me since she woke. Or perhaps ever will again.

Let her go, pet, Mortania urges.

At times, I wish I could.

Some days later, I find myself on the battlements after sunset. The Demon sentries are accustomed to seeing me here and dip their chins in greeting. We've had no further visits from Oryn's forces, and I know the sentries are hungry for Etherian captives— and for more steeds to add to the number Derek is training. Malakar and his Goblins enthusiastically await the chance to utilize them during our next campaign. Which reminds me—I owe the ship's boy a visit. There are many more questions I want answered.

There's a high shriek above me, and then Callow lands on my shoulder. She ruffles her tawny wings and knocks her head against my cheek. I stroke her back and look out at the Grace District. Callow fought beside me when I razed it. Slashed the faces of our enemies with her talons as fiercely as if she were a dragon instead of a kestrel.

"What do you think?" I ask her quietly. "Am I a monster?"

"You're keeping strange counsel these days."

Torin seems to peel herself from the shadows. Given the molten fire that is their blood, the Demons can tolerate the cold far better than the rest of us. I'm wrapped in furs against the bitter wind, but she's in a thin silk gown, its ruby color striking against the black and amber of her skin. "Does the bird have any wisdom to impart?"

As if in answer, Callow chuffs and rearranges herself. I laugh. A sentry passes us and raises his fist to Torin in salute. "I wish she did."

"Is the advice of your council not sufficient?"

There's an edge to her tone that grates against my conscience. "I didn't mean—"

"I know you didn't." She picks at the loose stonework. "But

many of us are still reeling from the discovery of a princess in the palace. I, for one, did not realize there was information you did not trust me to handle."

I study the bottomless black of the horizon, chastened. "I'm sorry. You're more than my council. You're my friends. My family."

"Family doesn't keep secrets like that."

The wind whistles around us. I sigh. "It was just . . . easier. I worried that you would all think less of me because of her. Humans haven't been kind to us in the past."

"Nor at present," she comments, "if the princess's attitude in the throne room is any indication of her future behavior."

"She's only—"

"How long did you know her before?" Torin asks. "Her whole life? Twenty years, perhaps?"

Metal clinks together as another pair of sentries passes. Heat climbs up my neck.

"One year."

Less than that, actually, as Aurora and I met on the night of her twentieth birthday, and she was cursed again just before her next.

The fissures in Torin's skin change abruptly from deep gold to canary yellow. "A single year?"

The flush on my face deepens, and I busy myself with petting Callow. "Does that matter? Don't you think two people can get to know each other in that time?"

"I do," she hedges. "But we have been friends for decades, and yet there are still things I am discovering about you."

The distant crash of waves drifts in from the sea.

"I said I was sorry."

Torin, cool and collected as ever, examines what scant stars are visible in the murk. "Do you recall the story of how the first Vila was created?"

I'm not sure why she's bringing this up now. Besides, she knows I've read Nimara's tale hundreds of times. "Which version?"

In Briar's, Nimara was angry and vengeful after being turned by the Demon, and laid waste to the Fae courts in her wrath. But the Vila paint her as the founder of a mighty race, establishing Malterre for all who would join her.

"Precisely." Torin slides me one of her enigmatic smirks. "It has always interested me the ways in which a tale will change based on who is telling it. In most renditions, so much of that particular story centers on Nimara as a victim. She's attacked by the Demon, and then either rejects or embraces her fate. But what of the Demon himself?"

I shrug. "He vanished, I suppose. Is it important?"

Torin fiddles with the pendant around her neck. Her rich garnet hair drinks the torchlight. "It might be. If the Demon did not *lure* a Fae female out of her court. If he was *invited* to cross the border into Etheria."

Invited? Callow chuffs and rearranges herself.

"After all, if it was so simple to outwit and then overpower an Etherian, why hadn't it been done before?"

"I always thought the Demon was exceptionally clever."

"Maybe. Or perhaps the Etherian female was curious about the dark creature and his power. Maybe she befriended him. *Desired* to become Vila."

My mind spins with these suggestions. This is not the story I know, but does that make it false? Briar had no trouble casting the Vila as the villains in their version of the birth of Malterre. Who's to say that the Vila didn't do the same to the Demons?

"But . . . Demons were members of the Vila courts—and kin, because their magic is what turned Nimara's blood," I reason. "It would have been disrespectful to portray them as being so vicious and wicked."

"And that"—she points at me—"is why many Demons refused to set foot in Malterre before the first war."

The next howl of wind grabs at my furs. The torches gutter. "I wasn't aware."

"You couldn't have been. And there's no way to know for certain what happened between the demon and the Fae he turned. Perhaps he was as cruel as the Vila's depiction of the legend claims. But those of us who did have cause to dispute that portrayal of one of our own could not share the home of the creatures who judged us ravenous, blood-lusting beasts."

I don't blame them. It had been intolerable to live in Briar as the Dark Grace, a resident monster. I wouldn't wish the same fate on anyone. Well, mostly anyone. "And was your family among those who would not live in Malterre?"

She nods. "Most of us took refuge in the forests of the southern kingdoms across the sea. It was a nomadic life and an arduous one. Not least of all because, in a way, we were turning our backs on our own. As you point out, some of our magic flowed in Vila blood, and yet we could not bear to count them among our kin."

Something scratches at the corners of my mind. A deeper purpose I cannot quite grasp. "Why are you telling me all this?"

It's a few moments before she answers, as if she's weighing her words. Callow mutters at something and picks at her feathers.

"Because you are asking us to put aside all of our prejudices and differences when it comes to the mortal princess," Torin says at last. "Based solely off your word."

I heave a sigh. It clouds in front of my face. "I understand it will be difficult, but—"

"And yet you are not willing to do the same when it comes to your own."

"My own?"

She arches an eyebrow. "Neve."

Neve? My irritation spikes. I start to protest, but Torin holds up a finger.

"Have you ever wondered why Neve prefers to sleep elsewhere? And why her visits to the Dark Court are so brief?"

"She's head of the Starlings. She has to go and do . . . Starling things."

"Or she doesn't feel welcome at court."

A raven shrieks, far away.

"That's not it," I insist. "The Imps love dressing her up, and the Demons adore her. I've witnessed the two of you together on countless occasions, and—"

"And I have never seen *you* two together, not when it wasn't required. You're the head of this court, and yet you looked like it physically pained you to attend the Starling funeral—and not because of grief. The Imps exhibited better decorum than you did."

Now I'm sorry I came to the battlements. There seems a trap waiting for me at every turn. "That isn't fair. I didn't know what to do, and she made me feel completely inadequate."

"One day, this war will end," Torin goes on as if I hadn't spoken. "And then Neve and her Starlings will come home for good. What then?"

I frown. The war has stretched on for so long that I haven't given the prospect much thought. It settles like a stone in my belly.

Torin holds out the pendant she wears around her neck. I must have seen her tugging at it a thousand times, but I've never paid close attention to the detail. Torchlight ripples over the onyx stone, lighting up fissures of amber and gold. It looks almost like a piece of Torin herself. "This is the token of the Demons; those who allied with Malterre were required to surrender it to demonstrate their loyalty to the Vila courts. It was passed down in my family for generations. I count myself a member of the Dark Court, but I still wear it. Do you know why?"

"To honor your past?"

"Partly." She lets the obsidian pendant fall against the glow of her chest. "And partly because you would never ask me to surrender it. It reminds me of the progress we've made since the days of Malterre. You *have* created a home here for us. That is why I came, and why I stay. Had I refused to join you because of how the Vila used to treat the Demons, I would have allowed my past to poison my present."

"And you think that's what I'm doing with Neve?"

"Your distrust of the Shifter leader is understandable given what happened before your siege of this realm." I squirm at the mention of Kal. "But Neve has nothing to do with the shadows of your past. Stop punishing her for them."

Flags snap in the wind. And I cannot deny that Torin has a point, much as I wish otherwise.

"I'll try harder with Neve," I grumble. "But that means you have to try with Aurora. She doesn't deserve your distrust, either."

Torin frowns and smooths her sleeve. And I grin. It's a rare feat to trap the Demon leader in her own logic.

"A fair bargain," she relents. "But any effort on my part would require the princess to emerge from her rooms. It's been nearly a week with no sign of her."

Callow mutters again, and I share her frustration.

"She'll come out." But I actually have no idea if that's true.

A Demon in shadow form whispers past us, raising gooseflesh over my entire body. I huddle in my furs, but Torin leans into the swirling darkness.

"Are you certain she's well?"

"What do you mean?"

"I possess little experience with curses, but do you have any clue as to what will happen now that the princess's is lifted? If you or I were to sleep for a hundred years, our magic would preserve our physical bodies. But she is mortal. Will she continue aging as a typical human from this point forward? Or not at all?"

Or all at once? I grip the edge of the battlement, imagining Aurora's years draining away like sand through an hourglass. Opening her bedchamber to find that she is nothing but bones and dust, as every other mortal who didn't take my oath. "I'm not sure."

There must be some way to prevent such a nightmare. But without binding her to me, how can I—

Dragon's teeth. An idea plops into my mind, and my temples immediately begin to throb. It might work. But it means visiting the one person I hoped never to encounter again.

CHAPTER THIRTEEN

The Garden is what I now call the block of the prison cells where Tarkin incarcerated me all those years ago. I used to visit in order to attempt to glean information from its inmates, or to taunt them with my very existence. But the excursion soon lost its luster. Now I let the Goblin guards run the place as they see fit.

Iron squeals as I unlock the various gates. The guards are confused to see me when we have no Fae prisoners, but they let me pass without much more than a greeting. Torchlight licks the rusted row of cells. The prisoners are awake. I detect muffled mewling and the scuffle of feet. My train swishes on the slimy stone until I reach the fifth cell on the right. A hand curls tentatively around an iron bar, then another.

Even in the dimness, I can make out the singular shade of pink in a tangled nest of curls.

Rose.

• • •

I'd lain waste to every Grace house in the realm during my siege, but there were many Graces who hid in cellars, or private homes, or whatever holes they could unearth to escape my vengeance.

As they're part Fae—gifted with just enough Etherian magic to bestow temporary blessings and charms in the form of elixirs—some Graces fled to Etheria. They supposed, I assume, that their distant kin would take pity on them and usher them into the refuge of the Fae courts. But the Etherians know nothing of pity. The Graces who attempted to cross the mountain border either died during the journey or were killed by the protections surrounding Oryn's domain.

Other Graces cobbled together flimsy rafts and set sail from the wrecked harbor. I usually let them get just beyond the sight of the shore before I went after them, rounded them up, and deposited them in the palace dungeons. At the time, I suspected that I could use the magic in another Grace's blood to undo Laurel's alterations to Aurora's curse. But it was a fruitless effort.

Though their magic was useless for my purpose, I couldn't simply release the Graces. Not after the decades they spent lording their status over me. Instead, I offered to allow them to swear to me, as the humans had done. But they refused, preferring to wallow in the prison cells for the rest of their lives, which appear to be the same interminable period as that of the Fae, now that they're not draining their power at the demand of the nobility.

"And to what do I owe the pleasure of this visit, *Malyce*?"

Rose's voice is raspy with disuse but laced with her usual venom. That nickname—the one she invented for me in Lavender

House—used to raise my hackles. But I let it slide from my body like a discarded cloak and smile. "I see your tenure in this cell has done nothing to improve your manners. Perhaps I shall have to instruct the Goblins to educate you on appropriate conversational skills."

Rose's cheeks smudge amber, but I have to say I admire her spirit. No matter the circumstances, she never loses her fire.

"I beg your pardon." She bobs a mocking curtsy. "What is it they call you these days? Mistress? If only our own Mistress Lavender could see you now. I'm sure she'd be pleased to learn what her generosity in not drowning a green-blooded infant has wrought."

Mistress Lavender was the only house mistress brave enough to take me in after I was discovered in Briar. But it wasn't out of the kindness of her heart. She received a healthy stipend for the expense of housing a half-Vila, and made sure my patron schedule was booked to the gills so that I would earn as much coin for her as possible. It should come as no surprise that my former mistress had not been one of the Graces I'd plucked from the ruins of the districts. Her escape seemed unlikely after I plugged the windows and doors of Lavender House with fire.

"Would you like to reminisce?" I grip my staff tighter. "Or would you like to hear what I've come to propose?"

One pink eyebrow rises. The other Graces murmur in their cells. I inhale the smell of unwashed bodies and damp mold. "What is it?"

I let my hand dip into my pocket, fingertips skimming over the chains of stranded white gold twined together like brambles. An expensive piece, set with diamond thorns and ruby Briar roses, which I'd selected from my own jewels.

"Princess Aurora is awake."

Noises of disbelief from the others. I throw them a scathing glare and they retreat back into darkness. "Awake. You mean—she's *alive?*"

"She'd have to be alive to be awake, wouldn't she?"

Rose sucks her teeth, and I take a moment to enjoy how the power dynamic between us has reversed. Perhaps I was too hasty in stopping my visits to the Garden. It is immensely satisfying to play the part of tormentor.

"It was her curse, wasn't it?" Rose says, brow furrowed. "The enchanted sleep allowed her to survive all this time. And if she's awake, then the curse must be lifted . . ." Her signature snide smirk takes residence on her dry lips. "Which means someone *kissed* her. Someone who wasn't you. How absolutely thrilling. Does she see you for what you always were now—a mongrel?"

Rage builds and snaps behind my sternum. I'd forgotten how much I despise this Grace. Mortania's presence rumbles. And before I know it, my power leaps out and pummels into Rose. She chokes and sinks to her knees. I wait long enough that she will wonder whether I will actually kill her, and then I release her magic.

"It was a mistake for me to come here."

Graces whimper, scampering away from my shadow as I make to leave the Garden.

"Wait!" It's more croak than word. "Please. You said you had an offer."

I'm not sure I've ever heard Rose beg before. "Apologize, and I might reconsider."

"I . . ." This might pain her more than when I held her magic in my fist. "I'm sorry. Please. If the princess is awake, I want to help her."

"Would you?" My staff taps against the slippery stone as I walk back to her cell. "Even if it means shedding your blood again?"

The wheels behind her gilded eyes spin. "You want me to . . . craft elixirs? But I haven't done that in years."

"I'm concerned about Aurora's health. Her body wasn't meant to live as long as it has, and I'm worried . . ." I swallow, loath to dwell on the idea. "Could you do anything to help her? You're not a healing Grace, but . . ."

"No. *They're* all dead."

I rub my thumb over the bramble band of my signet ring. "It will not trouble me at all to let you languish down here until you die with them. Can you craft the elixirs, or do you lack the skill? Perhaps you're close to Fading?"

It's a simple spot to irritate her with, which strikes me as funny. Rose shouldn't care whether her blood is turning silver, signifying the end of her gift. There aren't any Grace competitions anymore. And certainly no coin to be earned. But she crosses her arms and scowls. "You know that I'm not. And I might be able to bend my magic for the princess's benefit. With the right elixir recipe, of course."

"You'll have access to all the relevant books in my library."

"Fine. But I'm no fool," Rose says. "There's always a catch with you. What is it?"

I tug out the necklace. Ruby Briar roses dazzle, and rainbows dance along the dungeon walls as torchlight strikes diamond thorns. Rose stares at it hungrily. She was always like a magpie with her wardrobe, collecting the best and brightest fashions, and she hasn't worn anything decent in a hundred years.

"If you leave this cell, you'll be wearing this. It's cursed. If you betray me, such as tell Aurora anything about the sleeping curse or attempt to poison her mind against me, it will strangle you."

A simple feat, the work of moments. My blood shed and guzzled up by the diamonds, the same as when I cursed items for Tarkin.

Rose considers it. "Why not simply demand that I swear to you? Or bleed me like you used to do and craft your own elixirs?"

I'd entertained that course. But I lack the time to experiment with the recipe. And if Rose swore like the mortals did, Aurora would see her mark and guess what I'd done.

"Because Aurora needs to trust you. In addition to the elixirs, you'll be her companion. But you'll be reporting to me."

She huffs a laugh. "So you want me to spy on the princess? I suppose I shouldn't be surprised. And what am I supposed to tell her when I show up from thin air? I assume you don't want her knowing about this particular 'wing' of the palace."

No, I do not. "You'll think of something, or you'll wish you had. But if you're not up to the task . . ." My fist closes around the braided metal.

Rose steps forward quickly. "I'll do it."

"You're sure? You've witnessed my magic at work. I'm not bluffing about this necklace. And I'll not shed a tear if I find you with your throat sliced open by these thorns." A diamond winks in the torchlight.

She smiles at me, as if we were both back in the parlor of Lavender House and she was ordering me to fetch ingredients from the apothecary. "I would expect nothing less, Nimara."

• • •

I wait a day—long enough for me to deposit Rose in the Imps' care and have her scrubbed and made presentable—before taking her to meet Aurora. The Imps are morbidly delighted at the thought of a Grace among the court, especially after I let them know that Rose is not much different from the human servants. The look of pure terror on Rose's face when they started devising various "games" they wanted to play with her was worth more than a pile of Goblin treasure.

"Remember what I said," I warn the Grace as we walk to the princess's chambers. "Nothing about the Garden, nothing about when you helped to 'soften' the curse, or how it could be lifted."

"Yes, Malyce." She fingers the necklace, which cannot be removed by anyone but me and would not react to so small a slight as my old nickname. I can't curb Rose's temperament too much without raising Aurora's suspicions.

The Imps have replaced Rose's grime-stained rags with a pastel pink taffeta gown, accented with floral embroidery. I marvel at the way she's transformed. There's a golden blush on her cheeks and her hair is styled into flawless ringlets. She could be on her way to one of Briar's famous royal parties.

I stop us outside the doors to Aurora's chamber. "I'll expect your first report tomorrow. Find a discreet way to send them to me. She's never to know of our agreement."

"Why not?" Rose stops fluffing the ivory lace at her neckline. "You don't think she would approve?"

I exert a small amount of pressure on the magic in the necklace. The thorns lengthen enough to graze Rose's neck. "Keep testing me. We're not in Lavender House anymore."

"Maybe not, but I see that you're exactly the same. The Dark

Grace, eager to win the love of a princess. One who could *never* love you back."

A shiver runs through me. And a terrifying part of my soul whispers that she's right. That underneath everything, I am *still* that ugly half-Vila. Despised by a realm. My fists clench, nails digging into the flesh of my palms.

You are not, pet. Mortania's voice skates along the curve of my skull. And I lean into the scent of her magic—steel and loamy earth—twined with mine. An anchor.

"Would you like to return to the—"

The doors to Aurora's rooms swing wide, and she's standing between them. She's dressed in a silk robe embroidered with trailing Briar roses. Her hair is mussed and her eyes swollen and red-rimmed. My heart clenches. She looks terrible. But I can't tell if it's the result of the curse lifting or simply unhappiness. And the uncertainty makes it worse.

"What do you—" But then her focus drifts. "Is that . . . Rose?"

The Grace dips into an elegant curtsy, though I can tell that she's also unsettled by Aurora's appearance. "Your Highness. After all this time, I am relieved to see you well."

"And you." Aurora rushes to her and clasps her hands. "Where have you been? How did you survive . . ."

Aurora seems to remember that I'm present and trails off. There are dark smudges beneath her violet eyes, and tight lines bracket her lips. Her Imp companions are busying themselves by hopping over one another's shoulders and headbutting in the room behind her.

"I've brought her for you," I explain. "Rose has offered to serve as a more . . . familiar companion to you. And as your maid."

Rose bristles at that impromptu addition, but her beatific expression doesn't falter. "I'm happy to assist Briar's princess in whatever capacity she might need."

Aurora nods, grateful. And there are clearly a thousand other questions she wants to ask, but she holds them back. She doesn't even thank me for my efforts.

In another instant, Rose is ushered inside, and the doors to Aurora's rooms close. I hear the bolt slide into place, shutting me out. Pride stinging, I smooth my skirts and turn away.

CHAPTER FOURTEEN

In the throne room, the Vila are practicing their knife skills—using apples balanced on the Imps' heads as target practice. Black sludge splatters in every direction whenever a hit lands. Regan and a few others are laughing and showing off their tricks. A few Imps get bored and start pelting the fruit at unsuspecting Vila. Part of me wants to join them. Release some of my frustration about Aurora with the physical exertion and surround myself with those who accept and love me. I keep imagining what might be happening now that Aurora and Rose are alone—the Grace comforting her. I might have been jealous of Rose's status while we both lived in Lavender House, but it's nothing compared to this.

Worry not, pet, Mortania soothes. *You are in control now.*

It doesn't feel that way.

Movement snags my attention, and I see a Fae steed streak across the window. I never did have that discussion with Derek, regarding how he found himself in the library, kissing Aurora.

Perhaps now is a good time to do so. I rise from my seat and head to the stables.

Paladay, the late King Tarkin's home, was renowned for its horse trade. And though Briar never experienced another military threat following the War of the Fae, Tarkin was only too happy to spend the realm's inexhaustible coin on building up a cavalry to vanquish imaginary enemies.

But the horses are long dead, and the stables were badly damaged during my siege. Even if they hadn't been, a century of foul weather and disuse crumbled the pink stone, bent sturdy columns, and caved in the roof. The remaining marble dragon heads snarling down from the eaves sport snubbed and blackened snouts, and the Briar rose badges stamped into the brick are unrecognizable. But now that we have a string of Fae steeds in residence, the Imps and Vila have worked to restore the place. It's nothing like what it was—larger than a row of ornate Grace District manor houses and strictly managed by dozens of ostlers—but it suffices.

Derek hasn't yet returned from his flight. I take a look around anyway. Hooves thump fiercely behind locked stall doors. Steam plumes from the Fae steeds' nostrils. Gently, I extend my palm to a mount the color of quicksilver. Currents of bronze and ruby traverse its hide at every movement, and its mane sparkles like the tail of a shooting star. The massive beast sniffs me and doesn't recoil. And that same feeling from when I bound the first steed resurfaces. That the creature *belongs* to me. But something about this beast is different. Stronger. I dare to place my palm on its forehead, which feels silken and somehow charged, like there might be lightning in its veins. It angles closer, nosing my body.

"Your former Fae master would not approve of us being so friendly," I tease. After the tension of the last week, it feels good to enjoy such a simple interaction.

The steed snorts and twitches its ears, as if dismissing the need for anyone's approval, then starts lipping the skirts of my gown. I can't help but laugh.

"I'm afraid all I have for you is dried beetles." I fish one out and offer it. The creature sniffs it and thumps its hoof in distaste. "They're good enough for Callow, I'll have you know."

"Here—try this."

I'd been so absorbed with the steed that I didn't hear Derek approach. He stands a few feet away, half an apple cupped in his outstretched palm. I accept it without comment, trying to disguise my embarrassment at being caught in such a candid moment. The beast's huge teeth crunch noisily through the apple's flesh, head nodding as it chews.

"He likes you," Derek says. "And that's a compliment. He's never so docile with me. Nearly chomped half my finger off the first time I took him out of the pen."

"A clever beast, then." I smile, offering the other bit of apple.

Derek, to my annoyance, laughs. "His name is Oof."

"Oof?"

"The Imps named them all," he explains. "They call him Oof because that's the sound they make when he throws them—which happens quite often."

The steed tosses his head, apparently proud of earning such a name, and a real laugh climbs up my throat. "Well, we can't call him Oof. How about . . ." I let my fingers play in the creature's mane, which is as silky and as sparkling as his tail—threads of stardust. He blinks at me, and I see myself reflected in the dark, liquid pools of his gaze. "Chaos. For that is what he shall deliver to the High Court."

Chaos's nostrils flare, and he emits a low whicker. One that is unmistakably approval.

Derek grunts. "He's certainly *delivered* enough of that already. The stubbornest creature I've ever met."

I like that. But Chaos is not the reason I've come to the stables. "I believe we're overdue for a chat," I say to Derek. "About what you were doing in the abandoned library."

His easy manner crumbles. "I don't have a good answer for you. I saw the opening in the side of the palace during my flight and felt . . . drawn to it."

"Drawn to it," I echo. "Then why did you push the Imp from the saddle before you left the yard? One would think you wanted to be alone. Undisturbed."

"Undisturbed is right." He snorts a laugh. "Those Imps have developed a nasty habit of trying to make me fall when we're above the palace. That day, one snuck on just as I was taking off. I knew better than to let him stay."

Plausible—no, likely—that the Imps would invent such a game.

"And the kiss in the library? Was your mouth *drawn* to the princess's mouth?"

He scuffs his feet, brushed-copper skin brightening to the color of a ripe strawberry. "I don't know. It was almost as if . . . as if I were watching it happen outside myself. That's the best I can explain it."

I throw a glance at his forearm. The mark doesn't react. He's telling the truth, which is infuriating.

"I believe you," I mutter to Derek, though I still don't understand it. "But no more wandering the palace, poking your nose where it doesn't belong. And the princess has made her opinion of you quite clear. Leave her be."

He sets to work untangling ropes. "That won't be a problem. I've plenty to keep me busy around here. Shouldn't be too much longer until some of the steeds are trained enough to be ready for service. The Fae did most of the work, really. I'm learning more from the steeds themselves than anything else—which commands are best and all that."

This is boring. But I'm not yet ready to leave Chaos and hope that Derek will go off with another mount and leave us alone. He dumps a bucket of oats into a trough, and I sigh.

"Malakar and his Goblins are impatient for them to be ready for the campaigns," he says. And then, "You don't really think he'll fry me up in a vat of oil and eat me, do you?"

I laugh, and even Chaos flicks his tail in what could pass for amusement. "I've no idea. But better to hurry up with the steeds if you don't want to find out."

Derek makes something between a groan and a grimace. "How long until you're ready to attack the High Court?"

I'm not sure. The siege of the Court of Dreams stretched on for an entire decade, as Oryn kept sending reinforcements to bolster Aelfdene's army. The High Court itself is a much larger and stronger target. We'll need to determine how best to breach Oryn's protections, defensive enchantments that very well could have been what dismembered the Shifters.

Worry not, pet. Mortania swirls through me.

"That depends."

Derek frowns at the vague answer. "And has the war really been waging for the last century?"

"No. We made that up to impress you." I cross my arms. "Why

do you care so much about the war? If you're interested in military endeavors, wasn't there an army you could have joined instead of sailing here?"

He heaves a saddle onto its peg. "Not much of one. My country hasn't experienced any wars in my lifetime. Without the trade, no one can afford to wage them. But I read about some. They seem wasteful to me. Oh—" He realizes his blunder. I arch an eyebrow. "Not that *this* one is. I only meant . . ."

"And I suppose you would have reacted differently? If some other land had poisoned your people and cast you into exile, and then you found yourself with the means to exact your revenge? I thought you were some sort of revolutionary. That you would have done 'whatever was necessary' for your people. Isn't that what you claimed?"

"I did say that." He scrubs at the back of his neck. "Truthfully, I don't know how I would have acted, or what I would have condoned for my family's sake. Even so, I believe it's easy to answer violence with violence. To demand blood for blood. But who's left standing in the end?"

The question presses on a tender spot I didn't realize that I had. It dredges up a memory. Aurora in my Lair, reading a logbook from the first war, one that included a record of all lives lost.

"*So much death,*" she'd said.

The names of our own dead, those lost in our campaigns, are engraved into the throne room walls below the Etherian heads. It's a gesture intended to honor them, but how many more will we add before the war is over? How many lives snuffed out?

It will be worth it in the end, pet. The scent of Mortania's power winds through my veins, silty and loam-laced.

"I didn't come out here to be entertained by the prattle of a stable boy," I say.

He fiddles with a leather rein. "I apologize if I spoke out of turn."

Chaos chuffs. I pat his flank. Derek reaches for a pitchfork but then winces.

"What's the matter with you?"

"Nothing." He flexes his fingers.

It's not nothing. I step closer and gesture for him to show me. There are angry blisters spread across his palms. One of them has opened and is oozing.

"Dragon's teeth. What did they have you *doing* on that ship? Serving tea? Don't you know enough to wear gloves?"

"I know," he answers, defensive. "But the Imps turned my only pair into . . ." He picks one up from a bench. What should be strong leather has been magicked into chain mail. And claws protrude from each of the fingers. "These. I can't grip anything with them."

"I imagine not." I sigh and find a clean-looking rag. "I'll send you another pair. Hold out your hands."

Derek obeys, and I do my best to wrap them. "I might have the makings of a salve, too. And I'll talk to the Imps about their behavior of late."

"Thank you," he says. Twin dimples peek out on either side of his lips.

I tie the wrapping too tight and he hisses. "We can't have you injured and holding up our progress, can we?"

For a minute, it's quiet. Chaos munches on the hay in his pen.

"If you don't mind my saying so," Derek says as I finish.

"I assure you, I do."

He grins anyway. "Your court loves you. And I admit that I had my misgivings when I arrived here, but I think I understand a bit more about what you did to Briar. And why."

"I'm not interested in your approval."

"I know." He flexes his hand, testing the wrapping. "I only mean to say that they will follow you. Whatever you decide to do."

Maybe I won't send him new gloves, and his hands can simply fall off. But that uncomfortable nerve thrums. Aelfdene said that the Fae prophecy claimed a new age would begin with the fall of the Etherian Mountains. At the time, I believed that meant Oryn would perish, and everything on this side of the sea would belong to the Dark Court. But those mountains also represent the barrier between the Fae world and ours. What if the prophecy was figurative, and it meant that the worlds would unite by choice?

And do you think Oryn will ever agree to such a union? Mortania asks.

No. He will fight until his last, rattling breath. But the question lingers: What if?

"Hurry up with the steeds," I say to Derek. "They're the only reason you're still alive."

CHAPTER FIFTEEN

bout a week later, Aurora shows herself in court. My heart thuds at the sight of her. Her eyes are still dim with fatigue, but she looks far healthier than she did when I brought her Rose, and so I suppose I have to thank the Grace for whatever elixirs she's been whipping up. Aurora wears a pale blue gown that the Imps have seen fit to enhance with their magic. A collar of alabaster branches clasps around her throat and encases her shoulders like armor. Gems the color of sea glass sparkle in nooks and grooves. It's beautiful. *She* is beautiful.

Rose is obviously trying to keep Aurora away from the others, tugging at her arm and whispering emphatically from her post on a window seat. But she could never manipulate Aurora into becoming another minion like Marigold was. At least she's doing her job. I've learned through the Grace's reports that Aurora is sleeping and eating. That she's reading and taking an interest in some of her old hobbies. And I hope her presence here today means that she's beginning to warm to the Dark Court as well.

My first instinct is to go to Aurora and welcome her properly, but I'm too afraid I'll scare her away. And so I watch from the dais. After a while, Aurora extracts herself from the Grace's clutches and begins hesitantly mingling with the Goblins and Imps, who are fascinated with her delicate mortality. Unlike their bawdy behavior with Derek, they are shy around the princess, sometimes peering at her from behind columns and broken statues.

Not long after, Aurora smiles when the Imps stack themselves into towers and flip from the chandeliers. Laughs when they filch the cudgels from the Goblins' belts or magic their whip tails into worms. When she praises the Vila for turning the torchlight green and teasing it into various shapes with their power, it is so similar to the instances during which she delighted in the tricks my dark magic could accomplish that my chest aches. But then she notices me and her excitement shrivels.

"Well, she's out of her rooms," Regan remarks from the chair beside me. "That's a good sign. No one is trying to kill her."

"No." In fact, a few of the Demons have invited her to play their game, gesturing approvingly as she executes her moves.

"I thought you'd be happy." Regan nudges me. "I invited her myself, you know."

I turn to her, incredulous. "You did?"

She pops a handful of grapes into her mouth. "Don't look so surprised. I told you I believe you about her. And I thought she might simply need some friendly encouragement. So I went to her rooms and introduced myself. Told her we'd love to see her at court and not to worry, for we've been forbidden to eat her."

I smack her. "You didn't say that."

"Not in as many words." She waves toward Aurora. "But it worked."

"Yes." I squeeze Regan's arm. "Thank you. I just wish . . ."

That she would look at me without revulsion.

Regan unsheathes her dagger from her boot and slices an apple in half. "Give her time. Today's going well. Tomorrow might be better."

I hope so.

"And in the meantime, Malakar is eager to discuss plans for the next campaign."

"I can guess his strategy." The Goblin leader is demonstrating his favorite crossbow. It's a masterful piece, with a special chamber that lights the shafts as they fire. "But we cannot go charging into the High Court. We saw what happened to the Shifters. We need to take our time, like we did with the Court of Dreams."

"Yes, I was thinking about that. And I don't disagree." She wipes apple juice from her lips. "But what if you accompanied the army?"

I wasn't expecting that. "I haven't gone since the early sieges."

"Because we needed to protect you. But now there is only the High Court. And yours is the most powerful magic of all of us. It might be time to use it."

Mortania whirls, the scent of her magic filling me up. I should want to go. Should *burn* to go, as I did when this conflict began. But something holds me back.

"You remember how it was . . ." Regan bends close. "Giving the Fae what they gave to us. Rescuing the Imps. It will be a fitting end to the war. Our Nimara against the High King himself."

Yes, pet.

But as much as Mortania's desire resonates against my bones, all I can think about is that idiot stable boy and his ideas of peace. *"They would follow you anywhere."*

Would they? Or does the court prefer me as its warrior mistress?

A shrill screech cuts through the chatter of the hall. I'm yanked from my reverie and back into the present. Malakar allowed the Imps to play with his weapon, and one of them has misfired it. The bolt goes whizzing through the throne room. Goblins and Demons duck, but an unfortunate Imp isn't fast enough. He spins like a top as it grazes him, then punctures a stained-glass window. Shards of brilliant glass explode outward.

Dragon's teeth.

I'm on my feet in an instant. Malakar is hurrying to tend to the injured Imp. But it's Aurora who reaches him first. She kneels to his level, gently stilling him as he howls and clutches his head. Malakar tries to push past me, but I motion for him to wait, curious as to what she will do.

"Let me see," Aurora says, prying his clawed hand away. Blue Imp blood pours from the wound, staining her gown. But it doesn't seem to bother her. "I think it only nicked you. It might have been worse."

And to my utter astonishment, Aurora rips a swath of fabric from the skirt of her gown and presses it to the wound.

"Whining about a scratch?" another Imp taunts with a cackle.

"Aye, and would you like one of your own to match it?" Malakar threatens him.

The creature pouts and skulks away.

"What's your name?" Aurora asks the injured Imp.

He snuffles. "Grigor, Princess."

"Call me Aurora." She dabs at his head. "And I believe you will live, Grigor. Does it still hurt?"

He pulls himself up, and I think he's trying to look brave for her. A smile twitches at my lips. "Not so much now, Aurora." He lingers on the syllables of her name. "Got worse at the Fae courts, I did."

"What do you mean?"

"See here?" He holds up a hand, which is missing two fingers. "The Fae would take bits of us, they would, when we was bad."

Aurora sits back on her heels. "You came from the Fae courts? Not Malterre?"

"Fae takes us to Etheria when they catches us," Grigor explains. "Made us work in their courts. Dance for them, magic like. Sometimes, they would forget to make us stop."

"Aye," another mutters, long ears lying flat. "Saw some die like that."

A tremble of fury and sadness ripples among the court. Aurora looks around at them, sympathy etched in the lines of her expression. "I didn't know that."

"Not to worry." Apparently healed, Grigor hops up and tugs at Aurora's hand, leading her toward the front of the throne room. "Mistress gave 'em theirs, she did."

My stomach sinks. He lifts his arms to indicate the display of Etherian heads. Aurora's shoulders stiffen.

"Ah, there." The Imp points to a head. "That's the court leader. Mistress swooped in with her claws and wings and—"

"That one's a lady, you idiot." Another bounds up and thrusts his bone-tipped spear at another head. "That's the one."

"No, it isn't!"

"It is!"

"Mistress," Grigor calls to me. "Tell him."

Aurora turns. The softness in her eyes has glazed over with ice. "Well?" she asks crisply. "Which one is it?"

My head pounds. From her spot across the chamber, Rose smirks. The diamond thorns on her necklace sparkle, and I am very tempted to demonstrate its abilities.

"That's not important," I answer, trying my best to keep my tone level. "What matters is that I rescued the Imps."

"Tell us a story about it, though," Grigor begs. "I remember. Your wings were this long." He sticks out his arms as far as they will go. "And you turned the fires green and bound the High Lord and—"

"I have a story."

The room quiets at Aurora's interruption. Grigor claps his hands, and several other Imps scurry forward, tails twitching with excitement. "Oh, do share it, Princess."

This cannot be good.

"Once upon a time"—Aurora pitches her voice loud enough to carry through the chamber—"there was a princess who befriended a monster."

The Imps chitter. "A monster," one warbles. "Lovely."

Regan shoots me a confused look from the dais. My palms prickle. Is this a story about us? I should find some distraction to stop her, but I'm rooted to the spot.

"Everyone warned the princess that the monster was wicked, and that it would bring only harm to the realm," she says. "But she wasn't particularly interested in what anyone else had to say. The princess ignored the advice of her closest friends and kept the monster near her anyway."

"And what happened then?" Grigor asks. "Did they kill her because she disobeyed?"

Aurora shakes her head. "No. For a time, the princess was happy. She gave the monster rooms in the palace. Dined and danced with it. Shared her many secrets and believed all the vile stories about the creature were wrong. Misunderstandings, based on prejudice."

I hold my breath. This is definitely about us. But where is she going with it?

"But then," Aurora continues, "just when the princess was sure that the monster was not a monster at all—the creature revealed its true self."

The Imps gasp. "What did it do?"

Sunlight glimmers in the threads of red in Aurora's golden hair. "It waited until the princess wholly trusted it. When her feelings rendered her incapable of defending herself." She pauses. "And then it tore her apart, piece by piece, until there was nothing left of her."

Her words slam into me. Tears well in my eyes, and I have to blink them away before anyone sees.

"Wonderful ending!" The Imps applaud. "Perfect!"

"Would you tell another?" one begs. "With more dead people in it this time. And don't leave out any details. We want all the gory bits."

But Aurora gathers her bloodstained skirts and makes for the doors. Rose sweeps a flawless curtsy, winks, and sails after her.

And I am left standing alone.

CHAPTER SIXTEEN

Shortly after Aurora leaves, I excuse myself, as I cannot remain and pretend that what she said hasn't hurt me. Furious and heartsick, I want nothing more than to go to her chamber and demand an explanation. But it would only instigate another nasty argument. I wander back to the abandoned library instead. The bed, with its brambles and tangled bedclothes, waits like the prickly beast from Aurora's story. A cage, she called it. I cannot stand her habit of looking at everything I've built and deeming it unfit. Ugly. Monstrous.

Rage crackles against my bones. How much can a person hold before they burst into a million pieces? It seems I am a bottomless vessel for it. My limbs ache with the molten heat. A feral scream builds in my lungs and claws free of my mouth. My magic pummels into the first targets it can find. The mattress and pillows explode, feathers and dust swirling like snow. The branches encasing the bed snap and fly in all directions, cartwheeling out the gap in the wall. A stray thorn grazes my cheek, but I don't even flinch.

My power hurtles into the shelves. Wood groans and splinters as they smash into one another, down and down the rows, like felled trees. Books clatter to the floor like shot birds, covers splayed out like wings.

It is not enough. I descend on one of the many piles of books I thought held the answer to lifting Aurora's curse, ripping pages from spines until my arms are shaking and my palms raw. The broken jewel on my signet ring glares at me. I want to smash it to shards and dust. To—

"I thought you'd be done with this place."

Regan. I swipe my sleeve over my nose. "You followed me."

"I could sense something was amiss." Glass crunches under her boots as she makes her way to my side and takes a seat. "Would the state of this room have anything to do with the story the princess told?"

Of course Regan would have caught on. I hope no one else in the court did. Most of them know about the curse on the royal princesses—it would be impossible for them not to know, with all the books that used to be in the royal library, and the paintings honoring "true love's kiss" strewn about the palace. But I've never admitted to anyone that I was the one to break Aurora's first curse. And I'm not going to start now.

"I don't know what to do with her," I confess. "I understand that she's angry, but she won't even try to see my side of things. It's like she's a completely different person."

Thunder rumbles in the distance. I look out at the wreckage of the Grace District, wrapped in a misty haze.

Regan plucks something from my hair—a feather—and lets the breeze take it away. "I haven't been entirely honest with you about my past."

I turn back to her. "What do you mean?"

She rubs her thumb absently along the silver curves of her serpent ring, as she does when something is troubling her. I scoot closer. "I've told you that I lost my family—but never how it happened. My sister . . ." She trails off.

"Please." I put a reassuring hand on her arm. "I want to know."

Her green gaze flits to mine, vulnerable in a way I've rarely seen it. She presses her lips together, but nods. "Like everyone else exiled from Malterre, my mother and I were always in hiding. One night, while we were hunting in the woods outside a village, we heard a cry. It was a child—a baby left to the wild."

I can picture it, a swaddled infant half-buried among leaves and bramble. Cries smothered under the whine of the wind. "Who would do that?"

She lifts a shoulder. "There was a bright red blossom on one side of her face. Mother said that the humans likely supposed that the infant was a changeling or touched by a Demon. They were giving it back so that the real child would be returned to them."

"All because of a scar? That's awful."

"We thought so," she agrees. "Mother raised the child as her own—as my sister. We named her Pansy, for the shape of the mark on her face, and taught her that she was beautiful and loved."

"So your sister wasn't Vila?" I say, surprised.

"No. Pansy was fully mortal, but that didn't matter to us. We lived together as happily as we could, ears always pricked for danger, and faces always hidden. Pansy grew to be quite pretty. Not a changeling. Not magical at all, except for the spell she cast over our hearts."

Wind sighs through the gap in the wall, stirring the mess I made.

"And then Mother went hunting one day and did not come back." Her fists clench, the skin covering her bone spikes stretching pale. "I searched for her, leaving Pansy to guard our camp. There was a town a few miles away. I could hear the celebration before I reached the gates. Apparently, there'd been an illness or a plague of some kind, with villagers dying right and left." Dread festers in my stomach, guessing how this will end. "But it would soon be over for they'd found the cause."

"They didn't—"

Her grief is palpable. "I climbed a tree high enough to see over their walls. They strung my mother up by her neck and cut her open, letting her green Vila blood spill over their square. She was still alive. It took her a long, long time to die."

The Imp food I'd eaten earlier threatens to resurface. "Regan, I—"

"Just . . . wait." Her throat works. "I went back to Pansy and told her what had happened. She was so young—only thirteen— and I didn't want to frighten her. So I kept most of the details to myself. But we departed immediately. Roamed to place after place, with only each other for family. I thought it would be enough."

I can tell by the hollow ring in her tone that she was wrong.

"Some years later, Pansy went gathering. The next day, it was time for us to move on, but she insisted on staying. She was tired of roaming, and I didn't have the heart to refuse her. One week stretched into two. And then a month. And then I followed Pansy into the woods and saw what had captured her interest. She had taken a lover. A man from a nearby village, whom she'd met in the woods."

"Oh, Regan."

A gentle rain begins to fall.

"I wasn't angry," she says. "I wanted my sister to be happy. And she swore she was with him. I carved out my secret home in the forest while she married. She couldn't tell her husband about her Vila sister, but she made me promise not to venture too far. She would come and visit me and bring me warm bread and fresh milk. Pansy baked the best bread, flecked with herbs and so light it melted on my tongue."

Regan inhales, as though she can still smell it.

"And then she began to thicken." She laughs, but it's tinged with emotion. "I teased her. Called her a spoiled housecat. But it wasn't that. Pansy was with child, and I was going to be an aunt. It seems silly, but I was overjoyed. I wanted to help raise the baby more than I've ever wanted anything."

"It's not silly," I whisper.

"It was." A tear rolls down her cheek, and she swipes it roughly away. "I should have left when she married. Let her have her life."

"What happened?"

Thunder growls, closer this time, and the rain picks up.

"Pansy didn't visit me for so long that I grew concerned. I debated going to the village and checking on her myself, though I knew such an errand was insanity. In the end, I didn't have to. Pansy finally returned—with the baby." She pauses as if the memory might disintegrate if she speaks it aloud. "A girl. Beautiful and chubby and perfect. She lay nestled in my arms for hours, my heart fuller than I ever conceived possible."

Regan pauses, savoring the images that must be painfully vivid. Book pages rustle over the floor.

"Shortly after seeing me, the child took ill. Pansy came to me, frantic and desperate, but there was nothing my power could do. And then—" She pauses. "The little thing died. Babies do sometimes. They just go. It could have been a chill in the woods, or anything else."

"Yes," I agree. "It happens."

"But my sister blamed me. Like the villagers blamed my mother for their sickness. She told the men in the village that she'd seen a Vila skulking about in the forest. That my dark magic had seeped into the town and infected her baby."

The roots of my hair tingle. "No."

"And they believed her. Why wouldn't they?" She laughs again, a haunting, mirthless sound. "I woke to the crunch of their boots and the blaze of their torches. I made it out alive." Regan unlaces her jacket and peels it off. There's only a thin chemise beneath. She angles her body so that her back is to me.

I gasp at the garish, puckered scar, visible even through the fabric.

"But not before they gave me this."

"Regan." My fingertips brush against the groove of a scar that almost grazes her spine. She shudders at my touch. "Your own sister. How could she?"

Leather snaps back over Regan's shoulders. "I was convinced that there'd been a misunderstanding. They'd tricked Pansy or coerced her. And so I went back. Waited until I found her gathering outside the village."

"And did she—"

"She spit in my face. Threatened to call for her husband, flush me out of the woods, and finish what they started. There was no *misunderstanding* that day. In her mind, my touch contaminated her baby's blood. I was not her sister anymore. I was a monster."

The purpose of her story hammers home. Thunder claps. "You mean like what Aurora said. Her story. But she wouldn't—"

Regan grasps my arm. I can feel her pulse against my skin. "I understand that you care for her. That she was kind to you before. But sometimes, Nimara, people are not who we believe they are."

The room blurs, my own tears sticking in my throat. "Why didn't you ever tell me about this?"

"Because I wanted to forget it myself," she says softly. "Pansy was my *sister,* or so I thought. But she betrayed me. Sacrificed me, after I'd given her a lifetime of love and loyalty."

My heart pounds out an iron-clad cadence. Mortania slithers between the beats.

Listen well, pet.

"Aurora isn't . . ." But I cannot finish.

"*I hate you,*" she'd said.

"Tragedy teaches us things about ourselves and about others," Regan goes on gently. "Sometimes we do not like what we see. But we have to look anyway. We have to know."

A chill shivers through me, laced with the whisper of Mortania's presence. "Are you saying you want me to turn my back on Aurora?"

"I cannot tell you what to do when it comes to the princess," Regan replies. "And I genuinely hope that I'm wrong about her. That she is still adjusting to the Dark Court and will warm to us in time. But, Nimara, you must at least begin to consider the possibility that too much has changed between you. That she *is* different, like you feared."

"*It was not real.*" Aelfdene's musical voice twines with the wind.

But I don't want to believe it. Not even after today.

"Please." Regan tucks a lock of my hair behind my ear, a bone

spike on her knuckle grazing my temple. "For your own sake—
and ours—be careful."

Lightning forks outside, glazing the room in white.

"All right." I nod, though the promise tastes bitter. "I will be."

"And, Nimara." She nudges my chin so that our eyes meet.
Hers carry a silver sheen in the night. "You are *not* a monster."

CHAPTER SEVENTEEN

Pansy's story haunts me for the next few days. What happened between Regan and her sister is not the same as that between me and Aurora, I tell myself repeatedly. But even I am not convinced. If Pansy was willing to reject her own sister because of the accidental death of her child, isn't Aurora capable of abandoning me? When we fell in love, she was a princess—a future queen—and I was a Vila, the only known member of a race *her* realm worked to stamp into extinction. Maybe Aurora only cared for me because it was easy to do so. Because *she* held all the power. And now that the situation is reversed, she is no longer interested.

My fear is a visceral thing. It congeals in my blood and hinders even the simplest of tasks. And I do not know how to banish it.

When not with the council or the court, I've taken to visiting Chaos. The magnificent steed has come to expect me, and the warmth of his strong body beneath my palms soothes the tempest in my mind. I choose times when I know that Derek is occupied elsewhere, as I have no wish to endure the boy's presence any more than absolutely necessary, and bring the steed sugar cubes and apples and comb his sparkling mane with my fingers. I've not ridden him. It feels silly to do so when I can conjure wings of my own. But perhaps I'll let him fly beside me. Give him a tour of former Briar, with Callow for company. My kestrel is also fond of the Fae steed. Half the time, she's already perched on the door of his stall when I arrive, conversing with him in her chirrups and warbles.

But such is not the case when I slip away from the throne room one afternoon, having escaped the particularly restless court. Aurora is back to barricading herself in her rooms, and I can only tolerate so much of the Imps' mock charges and battles, in which they use tarnished serving plates as shields and broken spears for lances. The sound of wood thumping into rusted helmets echoes through the corridors.

Chaos's large head lifts over his pen when I enter, and I smile.

"You might be the only good thing that bothersome boy brought to these lands," I tell him, fishing a sugar cube from my pocket. Chaos lips it from my palm, whiskers tickling and tail swishing in pleasure. The enormous muscles beneath his quicksilver hide tremble, sending rivers of sapphire and indigo racing from his shoulders to his belly.

A whicker carries from outside. Then voices, one of which I'd know anywhere. Dragon's teeth, what is she doing here? I'd told the boy to stay away from her. But then, I suppose if Aurora sought *Derek* out, he wouldn't be violating my command. The idea that she might prefer his company raises my hackles. I let myself inside Chaos's stall, who chuffs in what is probably annoyance.

"Don't give me away," I whisper to him, Shifting to invisibility for good measure. Hopefully the steed doesn't decide to squash me with his hooves, which are almost as wide as my face. His tail flicks in what I sorely hope is assurance.

"Have you always been fond of horses?" Aurora asks. The chattering of the Imps floats down the row of stalls. Hooves clop—the mount Derek must have been training.

The Imps begin challenging one another to races. Cries and curses bounce off the walls, coupled with the sounds of sharp thwacks and falling bodies.

"I wouldn't call these horses." A gate squeals open on the other side of the stable. "But yes. I loved training them back home."

"You're very good," she remarks. "You must miss your country. I'm sorry you can't go back."

The gate closes and the bolt whines back into place. "I'm sorry you can't. At least I made the decision to come here, reckless though it was. You woke to find everything . . . changed."

He must worry about what his mark will do if he says anything negative about the state of Briar. Good. Straw rustles. Aurora doesn't reply.

Derek clears his throat. "I'm glad you visited me, though. I've been meaning to speak to you—to apologize for the way we met. You were right to be upset with me. After all, you woke to find some oaf leaning over you. I count myself lucky to have escaped the encounter unscathed."

An Imp howls about some slight, and I wish they would be quiet.

"As my limbs felt like boiled nettles at the time, I doubt I could have attacked."

"You seemed strong enough to me. And, so you know, I don't make a habit of kissing sleeping women. At least, not those who don't already know they're in bed with me."

There's a *wink* in his tone. She should slap him for that. Banish him. Instead, her surprised laughter punches through the stall and into my own heart.

"I've been cold to you," Aurora says. "And now it's my turn to apologize."

"Please." Chain jangles and something thumps to the ground. "There's no need."

"I suppose I should thank you for making the exception about kissing." I peer through the slats in the door, but glimpse only shadows and outlines. "But I am curious, do you have any idea why your kiss broke my curse?"

Every muscle in my body stills. She's still investigating this?

"Don't kisses break curses?" Derek asks.

"Certain kinds," she replies. "True love broke my first curse. I don't think it broke my second."

I hope that crushes his stupid heart.

But he doesn't sound even mildly offended. "Your first curse—Oh, yes. All Briarian princesses carried it, right?"

"So you do know something about my history."

Straw crunches and metal clangs as he moves from one pen to the other. "A little. I thought most of it was made up, to be honest. Princesses dying unless they found their 'true loves.' It was too extreme to be real."

"It was very real," she says. "I lost my two older sisters because their curses were never lifted. Not that my parents didn't try. Cordelia and Seraphina—and all Briar princesses along with them—were kissed by as many men as possible in the hopes that one of them would prove to be that love."

"But that must have been . . ."

"Quite a lot of men, yes," she finishes wryly. "You understand now why I was so angry to find yet another with his lips on mine."

As she should have been.

"I'm sorry," he says again. There's a scuffing sound, like boots kicking at the dirt-packed floor. "I wish I knew what to tell you about that kiss. I honestly don't know what compelled me. I just . . . acted. And I'm sorry to hear about your sisters. I wasn't aware."

"You couldn't have been," she says. "And I am grateful to you—for whatever reason, your kiss *did* wake me."

A reason she will never discover if I have anything to do with it.

Another steed chuffs.

"That one likes you," Derek says, mercifully changing the subject. "Here, feed him a carrot."

"His nose is like velvet." The beast chomps. Aurora laughs, then goes quiet. "Is what . . . Did Alyce hurt them at all when she bound them?"

"I don't think so," Derek answers. Bristles brush in a rhythmic tempo. "They seem well enough—hardy and strong. She's taken a shine to one, too."

"Alyce has? Which one?"

He dumps out a bucket of something and I curse under my breath as their footsteps approach. "Calls him Chaos," he says, directly outside the stall. "And she visits him often, though she doesn't think I know. I don't get the impression that she likes me very much."

My fists clench, wracking my brain for the evidence I must have left behind. Bits of apple? A tousled mane? Chaos thumps his back foot and huffs. His shimmery tail swishes against the side of my face.

"Don't take it personally. Alyce has always been . . . thorny."

"I noticed you call her Alyce. But I thought she's Nimara."

"Yes." The word is brittle. "Much has changed in the last century. She thinks she can simply slip on a new name like a fresh gown, as if it could shield her from the responsibility of what she's done. But she'll always be Alyce to me."

I glare at the back of Chaos's forelegs. I didn't just *slip on* another name for the fun of it. And I'm not trying to escape responsibility for anything. I huddle deeper into my cloak. The door to a neighboring stall rattles as an Imp barrels into it. Through the cracks in the wood, I watch him rub at the back of his head, brandish his fist, and charge his fellows. And I make a mental note to have a stern discussion with them later. They're supposed to be guarding Aurora. Keeping her away from the likes of the filthy steed trainer—whom I do *not* like at all.

Derek chuckles at the Imps' antics. "Quite the bunch of keepers you have."

"Never a dull moment," Aurora replies. "Rose detests them, though. Which is too bad. They seem quite taken with her, for some reason."

"And with you. I've seen the treats they conjure for you. Far better than the stringy scraps of meat they toss to me. And the additions to your wardrobe."

Where the Imps are endlessly amused by making Derek look as ridiculous as possible, they take nearly as much pride in Aurora's gowns as they do my own. The other day I saw her in what was clearly an Imp creation. Layers of garnet so dark it was almost black. The puffed sleeves had been altered to fall so that they exposed the sculpted angles of her shoulders. Cobweb lace accented the skirt and bodice, as well as onyx beads stitched in scrolling patterns. But the boy has no right to be noticing things like that.

"It must be unnerving," he says. "Being followed in your own home."

"I was raised as a princess, Derek," she answers. And the two finally begin to move away. "I was almost always followed or surveyed in my own home."

Except when she was sneaking out to meet me, which apparently isn't worth mentioning.

"And that's actually what I've come to talk to you about."

Chaos shakes out his wide silver-dusted wings, knocking the walls of his stall. A feather floats down and sticks to my skirt.

"Do you think you could help me with something?"

Water sloshes. "That depends on what it is. You know I swore to Nimara."

"Yes." And I think she might put a hand on his arm. My blood boils. "I'm sorry she forced you to do that."

"She didn't," he says.

"Well, you couldn't have felt like you had much of a choice."

My jaw aches from clenching my teeth.

"What did you have in mind?"

"It will take a bit of maneuvering, but I think we can manage it. And it would mean so much to me . . ."

I try to sharpen my hearing to pick up what she says next, but the Imps begin a boisterous song about severed heads. Movement flits between the slats of wood—Aurora and Derek leaving with another mount. The Imps stream out in a noisy cluster behind them, smothering all chance of overhearing any more of their conversation.

What is she planning? Rose's reports have been filled with Aurora's day-to-day activities, along with searing little jabs about how she cries out at night, or how sad it is that she's homesick in her own home. But nothing that sounds even close to a secret plan. Has the Grace found a loophole in the necklace's limitations?

All I can think about is Regan's story about Pansy. Aurora could have come to me with whatever she needed. But she went to Derek instead. Plotting behind my back. I feel like an idiot.

After I'm sure they've gone, I emerge from Chaos's pen. And then I spend a solid half hour shoveling manure over the stable floor and caking it over every clean surface. I upend buckets of Imp-conjured oats. Pour water over fresh hay. Dismantle bridles and tie ropes into impossible knots. The Fae steeds are furious, especially Chaos. But I ignore him.

Regan was right. Sometimes people aren't who we believed them to be.

CHAPTER EIGHTEEN

I go to my rooms to change my dress, and then make my way in search of Rose—who obviously needs to be reminded of her duties. The restrictions of the necklace's curse may need to be tightened as well. But I'm not halfway to Aurora's suite when I round a corner and nearly smack into another body.

"Forgive me—" But the rest dies when I find that the body belongs to Neve.

She's Shifted to resemble some kind of sea nymph, with coral-textured limbs and eyes a striking shade of blue. Shell combs hold up her green locks, and she straightens her gown where I've rumpled it, the silky material flowing as if waves were stitched together.

"The fault is mine," she replies in that oil-slick voice of hers. "My mind was otherwise occupied. I fear you've caught me wandering the palace in search of new rooms, as it appears that mine were gifted to a recently woken princess."

Embarrassment burns the ridges of my ears. I may have accidentally forgotten to alert Neve to the change in her apartments, and to assign her new ones.

"The matter was decided quickly," I say. "As you're so frequently absent, we determined your rooms would be best to house the princess."

"We?"

"The council." Though I *was* the one to suggest it.

"The same council that was unaware of the princess's existence in the first place?"

There's challenge in her cerulean eyes, and I do not like it. Nor do I like her habit of speaking only in cryptic riddles or needling questions. I've apologized enough for keeping Aurora hidden, and I certainly don't owe Neve anything.

"If you're at court," I say, "then I assume you have information. What is it?"

I half-expect her to refuse to tell me out of sheer spite. But Neve adjusts one of the shell combs in her hair. "I received word from my spies across the sea, those in the mortal realms."

"About the boy?"

"About the Fae. They've taken residence in several courts."

"Fae?" I step closer. Curiosity overrides my thinning patience. "How long have they been there?"

"That is yet to be determined. Years, possibly, especially if they were in disguise or caused the humans to forget them when they departed."

Dragon's teeth. "But the Fae despise the mortals."

"True. But they clearly want something."

"And I trust you'll tell us what that *something* is as soon as you know?"

"Of course."

From anyone else, that would be all the assurance I needed. But this is Neve. I may have promised Torin that I would try harder with the Shifter leader, but her condescension does not make that an easy, or even appealing, prospect. Maybe her rooms should be somewhere where I can keep a better eye on her. Mortania's dark laughter wends through my mind.

"See that you do," I say, pushing past her.

"Nimara," she calls at my back. I halt. "My Starlings send their condolences on the loss of our kin. They regret their inability to attend the ceremony."

An unwelcome guilt twists around my bones. I clench my fists against it. The shadows of the hall seem to reach for me, raising gooseflesh on my body. When I look back at Neve, she's smiling, the tips of her pointed teeth gleaming in the torchlight, like rows of waiting knives.

The door to Aurora's suite is unlocked, and I let myself in. As Rose's reports claimed, she's obviously made herself more at home. The sheets are off the furniture, and there are books scattered about. One is still open next to a plate of half-eaten pastries. I pick it up. *The War of the Fae,* the title reads. It appears Aurora had been exploring a passage on Oryn's inner court, or what was known of it at the time of this writing. The volume is among those brought from Malterre, and there's an abundance of salty commentary on the Etherians.

"Am I beautiful now?" A shrill voice carries through the stillness.

My brow rumples and I set the book down, drawn to a door half hidden by a tapestry on the other side of the room. It leads to the maid's chamber. Rose's room.

I angle close to the sliver of pallid afternoon light spilling out through the crack. An Imp struts about in a gown far too large for her, the skirt hiked up in one hand. In the other, she carries a mirror. Her lips—usually thin and black, like that of the rest of her kin—are voluptuous, and a rich burgundy color. She twirls, puckers her mouth, and kisses her reflection.

There are two other Imps present, perched on the narrow bed among fluffy petticoats and fringed pillows. The bedframe squeaks as they bounce up and down on the mattress, their faces smeared with various shades of powder and rouge. Aurora's Imps are outside with her, so why are *they* here?

"I'm next," one crows, rubbing his small hands together. "I want hair like yours. But blue. No, green. No, yellow, like the princess's."

"*Her* hair is *gold,* you nitwit. And it's my turn." The other socks her companion in the stomach with a pillow. A feather escapes through a ripped seam and drifts to the floor. "I want eyes like the princess's. That lovely, beauteous lavender."

"Be patient," Rose scolds. I can't see her, but I hear metal clink against glass. "You know, there is another Grace in the Garden who could sweeten your laugh. You could sound as if a chorus of bells lived in your lungs."

"Bells?" The Imp sticks out her tongue in disgust. "Ravens would be better. Vultures, maybe."

Is Rose making elixirs . . . for the Imps?

I push into the room. "What are you doing?"

The Imps' grins vanish. Wispy-haired heads duck into petticoats, only the tips of quivery ears poking up through the lace. Rose's "patron" sucks in her newly minted lips. "Nuffing."

"It doesn't look like nothing to me." I pick up the stem of a lavender flower on the table. "These are supposed to be for Aurora. Why are you wasting them?"

Rose's usual snobbery locks on like armor. "I need the creatures nearby to conjure my enhancements. The gardens here are atrocious. Not that I'm surprised, given everything else you've sullied. Quite useful creatures, these Imps. We would have welcomed the darlings in our parlors. Then we wouldn't have needed those dreadful apothecaries, with their filthy fingers and stinking shops."

As if Rose ever deigned to visit those shops. One of the Imps makes a sound like a satisfied purr. I shoot him a look, and he burrows back into the mountains of pastel skirts.

"Do you mean to say you haven't given Aurora any elixirs yet? That's the entire reason I let you leave the dungeon."

"I haven't perfected the recipe." She busies herself with the ingredients. "You don't expect me to give the princess just anything, do you?"

"But what of the curse? She could . . ."

"Perhaps you should have thought of that when you bled all the healing Graces dry," Rose snipes. "My gift is *beauty*. I'm doing my best. And I've been monitoring her. The princess is fine for now, which is no mystery. She's ingested so much of the Royal Graces' elixirs in her life, the effects would probably last two hundred years."

That's true, I suppose. Aurora told me that the palace maids used to slip elixir into her tea when she refused to drink it. But I still do not appreciate the Grace's defiance.

"Even so, if you cannot complete the tasks I require of you, there's no purpose for you being here."

She crosses her arms. "Are you the Grace Council now? Threatening consequences for poor performance?"

The jab lands as intended. I suck my teeth.

"Don't send her away, Mistress," one of the Imps pipes up. "We like her potions."

"Do you?" I tilt my head at Rose. "And why have you selected the Imps for your experiments? Wouldn't the human servants be better?"

Rose fusses with her instruments. "Because—"

"She gives them to us so we don't dress her up like the other one," the other Imp supplies. "Fair trade, it is."

The other one? They must mean Derek. And I've wondered why Rose's appearance remained unfailingly flawless when the Imps could have outfitted her however they deemed fit. I'd assumed Aurora had a hand in the Grace's wardrobe, but this explanation makes far more sense. "A century later, and you're still obsessed with your gowns and trinkets. I should have guessed."

She snatches the lavender out of my hand. "And what are you obsessed with, *Nimara*? Severed heads and broken staffs? Oh, and the princess. I'm happy to present her with inadequate elixirs if you wish. What do I care if her hair turns blue?"

"Oh, blue, yes!" An Imp bounces on the mattress. "Do mine that way."

The silty taste of my power lands on my tongue, magic poised to call on the necklace. No, to reach into her body and crush her cord of magic, as I should have done before I left Lavender House that last day. Would that I could go back.

"I warned you not to test me."

Rose toys with the charms on her bracelet. A minuscule golden seahorse. An oyster with a pearl. "You think I give a dragon's tooth about your *warnings*? If you send me back to the Garden, who will report on Aurora?"

Her arrogance knows no bounds. "Because *you're* doing such a good job of it? I know you've been keeping something back."

Confusion flashes within her gilded gaze. Did she really think I wouldn't find out?

"I've done exactly as you instructed. See for yourself." She lifts her chin, displaying the rose-and-thorn necklace, which rests harm- lessly against her throat.

My brow furrows. Aurora must not have told Rose about the secret plan. Why not?

The Imps have begun playing a gambling game with dice and finger bones. One argues about a bad throw, and the other tears off her shoe and clobbers her accuser over the head with it. He curses and scrambles backward, knocking over a table and upset- ting several books. Then they're fighting in a tangle of knobby limbs and feathers and skirts.

"Can't you imbeciles see that I'm working?" Rose shouts at them. "Calm down or get out."

"We don't leave without you, Rosey Posey," the Imp with the burgundy lips announces with a stump-toothed grin.

Rose picks up a book and chucks it at them. It thuds into flesh, and an Imp howls.

"Rosey Posey?" I repeat.

"Don't you even dare, *Malyce*. She won't be getting any elixirs for at least a week for that." The Imp splutters in outrage. The others laugh until she starts pelting them with finger bones. "If you're done accusing me of imaginary transgressions, I need to concentrate." Rose swivels back to her work. "The princess was provided her elixirs by the Royal Graces, and they didn't publish their recipes. I'll never get these done in time for—"

She stops herself and flushes, bright dandelions blooming on her cheeks. But she's caught. Rose might not know of Aurora's plans, but she knows *something*. I select a sprig of mint and begin rolling the leaves between my fingertips. "In time for what?"

The Grace dumps a spoonful of powder into the mortar. "It's not important."

But the necklace tightens at her lie, diamond thorns pricking her throat.

"That's not true and we both know it."

Stone thumps on stone as Rose drops her pestle and faces me. "Go on, then. Let this wretched collar leave a wound she will see. Or better yet, kill me."

Her tone needles me the same as it did when I was the Dark Grace.

You are not that person anymore. Mortania's presence whips inside me like a maelstrom, sucking every other thought inside it. I'm hit with the scent of rich wine and molten steel.

The Imps have given up their game and are gaping at us, saucer-eyed.

"Careful, Rose." I run my knuckle along her jawline so that the onyx thorns on my signet ring graze her gold-tinted skin. "I might feel compelled to rise to such challenges."

A bright flash of fear finally shows in her eyes. The necklace continues to cinch around her throat. But I am patient.

"Her birthday," Rose says at last, the words slightly breathless. "It's nearly Princess Aurora's birthday."

Birthday?

Aurora was born in late summer. I look out a high window. The sky is a sheet of steel, low-hanging clouds the color of smoke. Since the fall of the Court of Seasons, it's nearly impossible to tell what time of year it is. But I used to count the days religiously. Bring Aurora trays of delicacies I'd inevitably get sick eating myself, and read to her all day on her birthday, the anniversary of our first meeting.

The last time was only a year ago. Wasn't it? Or has it been two years? I rub my thumb over the cracked jewel on my signet ring. When had I stopped counting? Stopped noticing? And, far more important—why?

The necklace loosens and Rose sags in relief. Anyone else would be panting and horrified. But the beauty Grace was never one to be cornered. She smiles that saccharine simper she always reserved for me at Lavender House.

"If you came here hunting secrets, that means the princess is smart enough to keep them from me. I hope she has a thousand plots. That she finds just the right place to dig her knife in, and that she chops off your head and displays it in the throne room. But most of all . . ." Rose leans close. A pink curl flutters against her collarbone. "I hope I'm here to see it."

A mix of horror and indignation surges up from my toes, even though I know that's exactly the reaction Rose is hoping to achieve. Aurora wouldn't hurt me. But then Mortania's voice skates along the curve of my skull, repeating what Regan said in the abandoned library.

Sometimes people are not who we think they are.

My head throbs with the force of my unspent adrenaline. But I will not let Rose see the effect of her blow. I force my shoulders to relax. "Do be careful making those." I gesture at the mixture.

"Perhaps you'll be like Marigold when I brought her to the Garden—Faded and dead in the same instant."

The pulse at her throat quickens.

Satisfied, I head for the door. But I'm not two steps into Aurora's sitting room when I hear the pop of an Imp's conjuring. I melt into the shadows and watch as the creature sets a tea cake on Rose's table, delicately frosted with a strawberry on top.

"Sorry for being noisy," he says sweetly. "Since Mistress didn't kill you, could you change my hair again? Green this time."

"Wicked thing," Rose admonishes. But she scoops a bit of icing up with her fingertip and licks it off. "Later perhaps, if you behave. Fetch me a mirror so I can see what damage this horrid necklace did."

The Imp giggles and scampers off to obey. And something about the interaction makes me even angrier. Even the Imps possess a crumb of affection for Rose. Aurora does, too. It's as though the years when the Grace was so cruel to me never happened. As if *we* never happened.

Perhaps, Mortania suggests, *you did not.*

CHAPTER NINETEEN

"Neve is back."

Regan and I are sitting together with the court in the throne room after dinner that night. The Demon's game of strategy is between us, various pieces strewn about the board. She taps her chin, contemplating her next move.

"I know," I say. "I ran into her earlier. She told me that the Fae are visiting the human realms, but she doesn't know why yet."

The mournful music a few Demons are playing on their lute-like instruments floats around us. Across the chamber, the Imps are cobbling together sculptures out of leftover food. Malakar is the center of his own court, recounting a war story for the thousandth time. The Goblins roar when he tells a joke.

"Really?" Regan looks up. "I wonder if Oryn's strategy is to involve the humans, now that all but one of his courts have fallen."

She captures a gargoyle-shaped piece, and I mutter a curse. Regan tosses it up and catches it, laughing.

"Though I'm not sure what Oryn thinks the humans can accomplish now." She shrugs. "Neve's Starlings will figure it out."

Torin and Neve are on the dais, their heads bent in conversation. I'm about to change the subject, having no desire to discuss the Shifter leader, when there's a stir in the crowd, near the throne room doors. I angle myself to see better. And then—Aurora strides into our midst. The Imps have her in a black gown with silver branches accenting the low neckline and fitted sleeves. Her lips are painted dark red, and kohl lines her eyes. She looks like some kind of night goddess, and my heart beats harder.

"This is a surprise," Regan comments. "I haven't seen her in a few days."

I don't tell Regan that Aurora was in the stables with Derek earlier, possibly hatching some plan, as I'd prefer to find out whatever she's doing for myself.

"Invite her over," Regan says.

My eyebrows jerk up. "Really?"

"Why not? I haven't had the chance to spend any time with her." She gestures at the board. "The game can accommodate three players."

For some reason, the thought of Regan and Aurora playing together—even sitting together—sends a shiver of apprehension down my spine. But I can't summon any viable objection. And Regan doesn't give me the chance to voice it even if I could.

"Princess," she calls, waving. "Join us."

"We don't have to—"

But to my absolute surprise, Aurora glides across the room and settles herself at a chair to my left. The scent of her washes over me—apple blossom and cool water—and everything inside me softens.

"It's good to see you up and about," Regan says, resetting the pieces. "I'm happy to explain how everything works if you—"

"I understand already," Aurora replies, not unkindly. But not exactly kind, either.

"Excellent." Regan lifts a piece in salute. "Then it shall be a worthy match."

The game begins in awkward silence, the only sound that of the pieces clacking softly against the board as we pick them up and set them down. And with each passing moment, it becomes increasingly painful that Aurora and I are not talking to each other. Not even looking at each other. My tongue feels glued to the roof of my mouth. I cannot think of a single thing to say, though thousands of possibilities swarm through my mind. Each is more ridiculous and stupid than the last.

"And how are you finding the Dark Court?" Regan asks her at last. Goblin laughter travels from across the hall.

"As well as can be expected." Aurora moves a piece over mine, capturing it. I slide her a sidelong look, but don't comment. "How long have you been in residence?"

"I was the first," Regan informs her. She smiles at me, proud, and I smile back. "I stowed away on a ship bound for Briar and nearly drowned upon my arrival, actually."

Aurora pauses at her next move. "Drowned? Is that because of Alyce?"

"Yes." Regan laughs. "But I don't blame her for it."

Imps scamper past. A few of them shout a greeting to Aurora.

"Why not?" She captures two of Regan's pieces in one fluid move. "Don't you care that you almost died?"

The Vila leader's smile is tight, gaze fixed to Aurora's growing collection of markers—both of ours are paltry in comparison. "No. I don't. Sometimes, Princess, I believe the ends justify the means. Do you not agree?"

I sip my wine, pressure building between my temples.

Aurora trails her fingertips down the spiny collar of her gown. "I think justice can be rather subjective. To you, it clearly entails razing realms and collecting trophies." She gestures to the Etherian heads. "But I wonder how Oryn would define the term. Or even the realms across the sea."

Regan grins in triumph as she seizes a piece of Aurora's. "And why should their opinion trouble us?"

She studies the board. "Because by your own logic, if *they* came seeking their justice, wouldn't that mean you would deserve whatever means they employed?"

In a move I would never have seen coming, Aurora picks off the last of Regan's pieces and sets them neatly in her corner. She folds her hands on the table and gazes serenely back at the Vila leader. And I do not know whether to be proud or horrified.

Regan goes perfectly still. "I see I am outmatched."

"Don't take it too hard," Aurora says. "I am often underestimated."

The Vila leader bristles.

"It's no matter," I attempt, sensing the storm brewing. "We can—"

But Regan raises a hand to stop me and rises from the table. "I have endured enough games for one evening."

Her boots clip as she strides across the chamber, and I fist one of the abandoned pieces in my hand, the edges biting into my palm.

"Did you really need to be like that?" I ask Aurora when we're alone, not bothering to curb my tone. "It was her idea to include you, and she was being perfectly welcoming, and then you—"

"Oh, *now* you have something to say to me?" Aurora crosses her arms. "You think her invitation was a coincidence? I've dealt with countless courtiers just like her, who—"

"No, you haven't," I snap. "Because this is not Briar's court. It's not filled with vipers who don't care who they step on to get ahead."

She pushes back from the table. "Believe what you like."

"Where are you going?" I call after her, exasperated.

"Why should I tell you?" The branches on her dress shine. "Every movement I make in this court is tracked. Every word repeated, probably. I'll let the mystery linger until someone else informs you."

And then she's gone, melting into the throng of my court. And I'm so angry I could burst into a million pieces. I hate that she's being this way. Throwing every kind gesture back in my face. Through the press of bodies, I see a Demon ask Aurora to dance, and she accepts, allowing herself to be glided about the floor. Jealousy piles in my belly like hot coals, spitting and seething.

But then my attention catches on something else. Derek stands at the fringes of the crowd. He's wearing breeches that are far too short and tight-fitting, coupled with a footman's tattered jacket and a moldy cerulean wig that now sports peacock feathers jutting out at haphazard angles among the ratty braids.

Like Regan, I'm tired of Aurora's games. I *will* know what she's planning. If Rose doesn't know, the ship's boy certainly will.

• • •

"This isn't the way to the stables," Derek says as we traipse up a set of back stairs. "And I promise you, Chaos is doing quite well."

"Is it not?" I ask, feigning ignorance. "I must be lost."

He scratches under his wig. "If we're not going there, then . . ."

"Are you nervous to be alone with me?"

"No."

"Then you're not as smart as I thought, and I didn't have high expectations to begin with."

I lead Derek through countless twisting corridors, a path intended to incite confusion and anxiety. I assume he guesses we're headed to some remote torture chamber or to a rat-infested tower cell. But we emerge from the top levels and onto the battlements.

The night wind is brutal. All of ruined Briar rolls out to the south and west, ending at the cusp of the obsidian sea that engulfs the horizon. Mist curls in tentacles around our legs. The wrecked structures of the Grace District wallow in the murk like skeletal creatures from a story.

"Why have you brought me up here?"

"You enjoyed exploring the palace, abandoned libraries and whatnot. I thought you might appreciate the opportunity for a similar excursion. How does this view compare with that from the back of a Fae steed?"

He tugs on the sleeve of his jacket. "It's . . . different."

"Not as good. I understand. Flying has always been a favorite pastime of mine. Nothing can match it." I lean out over the stone wall. The Demon sentries rarely patrol this area, as the vantage point is much better higher up. Which means no one will be disturbing us.

There's a screech and a flap of wings and Callow lands neatly on my shoulder. She nudges her head against mine, then clacks her beak at Derek.

"That bird hates me."

"She has excellent intuition." Callow also despised Endlewild.

I didn't bring a torch with us and his brown eyes look liquid black in the night. "Have I offended you in some way?"

"You've been keeping interesting company recently. Someone a *ship's boy* should have no opportunity to meet."

A peacock feather brushes Derek's nose. He tugs it out and lets the wind take it. "Do you mean the princess?"

"Is there someone else I should know about?" He fumbles out an incoherent reply. "Giving her riding lessons, were you?"

"How did you—" His brow scrunches. "You saw us together at the stables. I thought the Imps made that mess as some kind of prank. But did you—"

"Did I *what*?"

Defiance flashes in the way his jaw works from side to side. "Nothing."

"Indeed." The growl of faraway thunder creeps toward the shore. Lightning forks over the horizon. "If Aurora decides to ride, I will arrange for someone to teach her. You do not need to trouble yourself."

"It's no trouble."

"I did not request your opinion on the matter."

He ducks his head.

"If . . ." The boy ventures too near and Callow warns him back. "If what *happened* in the stables was because of the princess visiting me there, she's never done so before. I've kept away from her like you told me to, and I'm sorry if you thought—I mean . . ."

"What 'happened' in the stables was your own fault. Because

you seem to have forgotten your place—as a servant. Entirely insignificant." I advance one step. Two. Large chunks of stone are missing from the walls. Callow flaps to the piecemeal ledge and chuffs. "So much so that if you were to disappear, absolutely no one would notice. Least of all a princess."

Derek glances behind him, where the husks of buildings sprawl like waiting jagged teeth. His boot skids on loose stone and pebbles fly, pinging down the side of the palace.

"I know she asked for your help with something. What was it?"

"I . . . It's nothing bad."

"I'll decide what it is," I all but growl. Another inch and he'll be nothing but mangled bones. Callow screeches, and possibilities tumble over themselves in my mind. Is Aurora plotting escape? A coup? How far have matters progressed?

His throat bobs. "She wants a funeral."

Wind whistles between us. "A what?"

"A funeral," he repeats, his knuckles white as he grips the crumbling stone. "For everyone she lost when Briar fell."

The answer pulls me up short. I step back and Derek drops forward, scrambling away from the perilous edge. A funeral. Callow warbles. "But why wouldn't she have told me that?"

"I think," he says from his knees, "she assumed you wouldn't be keen on the idea."

Waves crash in the distance. "I don't understand. Briar was broken and corrupt, and . . . they never cared about her. Not even her family." Not like I did. "They were horrible, all of them. She *mourns* them?"

Derek rises, legs wobbling. "It's still possible to mourn horrible people. Was there no one you missed . . . after?"

Hilde. My attention travels over the battlements, picturing the last time I saw her. I pretended it didn't matter when she didn't come to me. Choose me. But her rejection stung. Is that the same as mourning?

"No one I missed enough to mourn."

No, pet. Mortania stirs. *No one who mattered.*

"Well." He prods a loose stone with the toe of his boot. "I understand what it's like to have complicated relationships with family. I'd still mourn them if they died."

Callow chuffs, and I recall Aurora's fury when she woke. Her haggard appearance when I brought Rose to her. I knew she was furious with me, but for the first time I realize she was grieving. That *I* caused her to grieve.

My throat tightens. "And why did she come to you about such a request?"

"She asked to hold the ceremony in the stables," he explains. "I think she knew better than to try to organize anything in the palace."

In her own home. The blade of my conscience digs deeper. A raven's cry carries on the wind.

"She's right. That wouldn't go well." But as much as I despised former Briar, I hate to think of Aurora honoring her dead in the stables. I suppose she could go to the crypt. But that is a place for effigies and relics of the former queens. Briar always sent its dead out to sea on floating pyres, a tradition started by Leythana herself. "She'll want to be near the water. There are tunnels leading from the palace and under the main gates. Take those so that the sentries don't see you. I'll send you a map."

He must have expected me to forbid the memorial. "Thank

you," he says. "And I know she wanted the servants to be able to come, too."

I care far less about *their* grief. But if it's what Aurora wants . . .

"Fine. I'll hold a revel. Hardly anyone notices what the servants are doing once they get drunk enough. And I'll find a way to distract her Imps."

Callow mutters in what might be approval. And the boy is tripping over himself in gratitude. I'm suddenly weary of his company. "Don't get caught," I say, turning back the way we came.

"Nimara," Derek calls after me. "Are you the one who broke her first curse?"

I whirl. "How dare you ask me such a question?"

He puts up his hands, placating. "I mean no offense. But there was clearly something between you. And if I'm correct . . . you should know that she cares for you."

An intoxicating warmth blooms in my chest. Does she really care? It's hard to believe, after everything that's happened, especially tonight. But I don't let the ship's boy see the effect of his words. I leave him without a reply and bolt the door behind me. Maybe he'll topple off the battlements without my assistance.

CHAPTER TWENTY

The revel is easy enough to suggest during the next council meeting, in which Malakar is again advocating for our immediate charge of the High Court. The others toss out ideas regarding strategy, and speculate about what the Fae might be doing in the mortal realms. But I don't contribute much. My thoughts are fixed on what I'd learned from Derek—the funeral that will be taking place. Regan had said that tragedy changes people. The death of Pansy's child was what had driven her to lash out against her own sister. Grief could explain a great deal about Aurora in these last weeks, her obstinance and smoldering hatred. Perhaps this ceremony will allow her to put the past behind her. Accept the Dark Court—and me.

If so, I want to do whatever I can to help her along. As soon as the meeting is over, I disappear to the royal library. The shelves are painfully bare, as these books were some of the first relics of the old regime to be destroyed. I'd happily fed dozens of volumes to the flames myself, eager to cleanse the palace of the sort of stilted history that had all but smothered me during my years as the Dark Grace.

But a small number of books survived the purge. I sift through them, searching for something about Briarian royal funerals. I barely remember when Aurora's elder sisters perished for lack of kissing their right suitors. There had been a gathering at the shore. Princess Seraphina's pyre had been massive—the size of several carriages put together—and teeming with her favorite foods, and gowns, and paintings. Aurora will not be able to manage such an elaborate display. But there might be some other tradition—songs or words that need to be spoken. Anything I can dig up to show Aurora that I respect her grief, even if I don't share it.

Something rustles at the far end of the library. It sounds heavier than a rat. Maybe the Imps have decided to get up to mischief. I sink into the shadows and creep toward the sound. It's not a rustling after all, but sniffles. And then a quiet sob. Who would come here to cry?

Holding my breath, I peer around a shelf. Someone is hunched over an open book. A shaft of dull sunlight fights through the grimy windows and illuminates a shock of red hair.

"Elspeth."

She spins around, hugging the book to her chest. Tears streak down her face. "W-what are you doing here?"

"I am mistress. I go where I please."

Mortania laughs. But the flex of my authority doesn't feel as satisfying as it typically does. Instead, shame prickles up my neck, and a rotten taste cuts between my teeth.

Elspeth swipes a dirty sleeve over her face and scoots away. "I didn't realize. I'll go."

"Wait." Her shoulders hunch, and the defensive gesture bothers me. The fact that I'm bothered at all is worse. "What were you looking at?"

She hesitates, and the look on her face tells me that she's worried I'll burn the book simply for the pleasure of watching her beg me not to. But she eventually holds it out to me, another bout of silent tears dripping from her chin.

The volume is heavy. It must have been designed by the innovation Graces, for the pages are in stark and living color. It's filled with paintings whose subjects move slightly as they pose. Elspeth was studying a woman wearing a gown that would have made Rose green with envy. It's constructed entirely out of wildflowers that bloom, burst, and sprout again in various shades and species.

"What is this?"

"A record of the best gowns for each season," she says. "The royal designers put them together every year, in time for the Grace ceremony."

The annual event when the Grace houses would be honored for their achievements. Not that I would know much about it, seeing as I was never invited. I'm not sure how the book has survived this long, and I'm surprised that, despite what it represents, I feel no urge to rip it to pieces. In fact, I almost *enjoy* seeing this glimpse into former Briar. The innovation Graces, whether they were designing fashions or jewels or ingenious contraptions, were immensely talented. The woman in the portrait fans herself with an array of plumy feathers, eyes twinkling. They're a striking enough shade—and her attractiveness is so perfect—that I know she commissioned a beauty Grace's elixir to manifest them. But there's something else about her. My gaze flits up to Elspeth and back.

"This was your mother."

She swallows and nods. Sure enough, I notice a pomegranate

brooch on the painted woman's bodice—the tiny star-shaped seeds dazzle on the page.

"Please." Elspeth steps forward. "It's all I have of her."

She does think I'm going to destroy the book. And why shouldn't she? The portraits in the throne room are riddled with knife wounds. An uncomfortable feeling slithers in my belly.

Ignore her, Mortania insists.

But I cannot. "Keep it." I thrust the volume toward her.

Elspeth blinks, her mouth going slack.

"Go on. Take it with you."

"I cannot." She shakes her head. "It's safer here. If the Imps ever found it . . ."

Oh, yes. This book would not last an hour in their clawed hands. I frown. But then— "I think the princess would appreciate seeing this. Take it to her. I'm sure she'll keep it safe and allow you to look at it when you please."

Elspeth gapes at me like I've Shifted into some kind of gelatinous slug, and it only makes me feel smaller. I shouldn't care what she thinks of me. *She* never would have given my happiness or well-being a second thought when I was the Dark Grace. How many elixirs had she and her mother purchased from me to dole out petty punishments to fellow courtiers?

"*It is easy to answer violence with violence,*" Derek had said.

Damn that ship's boy.

"Take it before I change my mind."

That is all the encouragement Elspeth requires. She snatches up the book and scampers away. The slapping of her footsteps echoes in the cavernous space. But just before she reaches the door, she turns back. I might hear a whisper beneath the creak of the walls.

"Thank you."

And then she's gone.

The encounter with Elspeth stays with me, even to the revel that night. I watch Imps swing from the chandeliers by their tails, launching one another from one pair of arms to the next. Goblins are clustered together near the windows, playing a game of wager. Pearl necklaces and jeweled brooches collect in the center of their circles as they toss down cards. The Demons are dancing. Some of them are in their shadow forms and skim across the ceiling, at times assuming horrifying shapes to rattle unsuspecting court members.

Little by little, the human servants begin to slip away. I know better than to presume I'm invited to the funeral. But my restlessness will not permit me to remain at the revel for long. I take my leave as soon as I'm sure I won't be missed. And I wonder where Aurora has decided to hold her ceremony—if I might be able to see their lights from the council chamber windows. I make my way up the endless flights of stairs. But when I reach the dragon doors, I find I was not the only one who sought this chamber tonight.

"She wants nothing to do with me." Neve's voice floats into the hall, carrying an edge I'd never associated with the Shifter leader. Usually, she's all innuendo and sarcasm.

"I understand that," Torin answers, calm and steady. "Give her time."

"I've been here nearly as long as you have. How much more *time* does she need?"

"I'm working on her, as I promised you I would."

My brow furrows. Are they talking about me? They must be. And I sense that there is more than irritation in Neve's words— there's hurt. No matter what I'd promised Torin, I hadn't tried in the least to repair my relationship with Neve. I assumed the Shifter leader didn't care about the tension between us, but this exchange suggests otherwise. My conscience is already raw after Elspeth and the library, and this does not help to assuage it.

"You can promise the moon and stars. But I will not stay here while she disrespects me at every turn. The others notice. My Starlings notice. Why should they serve a court that doesn't value them?"

"We value them," Torin insists.

Neve huffs. "You do. But—"

On some insane impulse, I push through the door and into the light. For a heartbeat, Neve's eyes widen. And then her calculated stoicism slides on like a mask.

"Nimara," Torin greets me. The candles are burning low on the table, where the map is spread out. "I thought you'd be at the revel."

"I preferred the quiet tonight," I say. Awkwardness hangs heavy in the air. I gesture at the map. "Still strategizing?"

"You know our Demon leader doesn't know how to have fun," Neve comments with a slight quirk of her mouth.

The grooves mapping Torin's body flare an exasperated shade of citrine. "Neve shared a few of her ideas with me."

"Really?" I try to offer a smile that does not appear forced and disastrously fail. "I'd like to hear them, too."

I position myself to better inspect the map. Some of the markers have been arranged around the border of the High Court. Others are scattered in the mortal realms.

"I'm not ready to divulge them just yet. There's a missing piece I need to unearth."

"But I thought you just told Torin—"

"That I have hunches," she says. "But I would prefer to present you with facts, Mistress."

An argument presses behind my teeth. She's keeping things from me. But then Torin's amber gaze catches mine. She shakes her head, a warning, and I dig my nails into the flesh of my palms to maintain my civility.

"I think I'll retire for now," Neve announces.

"I'll be up later," Torin says.

I gesture between them. "You two are staying together?"

"Yes, Mistress." Neve pauses at the door. "Torin was gracious enough to extend an offer, as her suite is so large—and mine now belongs to a princess of the deposed realm."

Irritation hums, but I tamp it down. "I wasn't aware that you weren't able to secure suitable chambers." I also hadn't checked.

She waves me off. "The companionship is a welcome change. I spend much of my time in solitude."

Neve gets lonely? I frown.

When she's gone, I stand at the windows and look out into the night. There's no light to be seen, which is probably better. If the sentries discovered the funeral, they would not be forgiving. And I'm loath to be put in the position of needing to stop them from interfering.

"How much did you overhear before you came in?" Torin asks.

The Demon leader is more intuitive than she has a right to be. "Enough."

"She is not your enemy."

I go back to the table and pick up a pewter marker. It's the Starling one, set in the center of Ryna—the kingdom of the long-ago, star-chosen prince. "Then what is she?"

"I think"—Torin's long sleeves whisper over the map—"that depends on you."

An annoying answer. I set the marker back down with a sharp clack. And as I examine the outlines of the Fae courts, I'm reminded of when I first saw this map—in this very room—as the Dark Grace. It was the day Tarkin recruited me to craft his cursed objects. "The old king was planning to invade Etheria."

"I think you told me that," Torin half-mumbles as she studies the arrangements. "He wouldn't have gotten far with nothing but a human army."

"No," I agree, trailing my fingers over the faded colors of the ruined courts. "What do you think will happen when our own campaigns are over?"

"Assuming we win, you mean?"

"Do you doubt that?"

Torin consults an open book. "Part of being a strategist means I doubt everything."

I laugh. "Don't let Regan catch you talking like that—or Malakar."

"They wouldn't hear me if I did."

She's not wrong. Regan insists she's always known we'll be victorious, and Mortania is nothing but confidence. She trembles in her cave, and I pace the perimeter of the room, unsure what to believe. There's a table set with a decanter of wine and some Imp food—and a book. The cover is stamped with the emblem of a Vila court.

"Is this yours?" I ask Torin.

She glances over her shoulder. "Ah, yes. An interesting read."

I thumb through the pages. "Is it a court record?"

"No, philosophy, actually. And quite fascinating. The Vila who wrote it posited that the hatred between the courts of Malterre and the Fae was habitual. There was no real root to it, save that the two sides had always despised each other. And then the hatred was passed down from generation to generation, a never-ending cycle that became more entrenched in our cultures the longer it was repeated."

That touches something deep inside me. "Do you think it's true?"

"I'm not sure. And I'd never given the theory much consideration until now. I read that book years ago. But I picked it back up after our interview with Aelfdene." She taps the jagged line that represents the Etherian mountain range. "The Fae lord's prophecy—about the mountains crumbling and signaling a new age—made me think of it."

"What would the prophecy have to do with that theory?"

She moves another marker. "Because, if the writer is correct about the relationship between Fae and Vila, something as drastic as a new age is the only way such bone-deep hatred would ever be eradicated. And I thought it interesting that we should learn of that prophecy now, when the war is coming to a head."

The candles flicker in the draft. "Do you think it's our age—the one Aelfdene predicted?"

Her amber eyes shine. "It could be ours. Or the High King could surprise us all, and it means the end of our kind."

Mortania undulates in the place where my magic lives, despising the idea that Oryn could ever defeat the Dark Court.

"Or," Torin continues. Wind groans against the glass. "Perhaps it is a force unto itself. And neither side survives."

A chill races down my spine.

"You need more sleep," I tell the Demon leader.

She quirks a wry smile. "As do you."

But neither one of us leaves. And for a long time, I stare into the bottomless black of the horizon, toward where the Etherian Mountains wait like stone guardians. Thinking of Aurora, and what this new age might mean for the two of us. If *we* could survive it.

CHAPTER TWENTY-ONE

Aurora and the others must have eventually returned to the palace, for a servant has left a breakfast tray in my solar the next morning. I take my time pouring out my tea and eating the pastries, mulling over the events of the last few days.

Restless, I pull books from my shelves—court records and journals—and comb through the endless diatribe against the Fae. There are probably innumerable books like these in Oryn's libraries, except stuffed with tales of the Vila's treachery. Hatred passed down from generation to generation, just as Torin's philosopher suggested. It is enough to cause me to question the entire purpose of this war. Are we delivering justice to the Etherians as I've always believed? Or simply inflicting wounds on one another because that's all we know how to do? Wounds that never heal because we leave them open on purpose. We like to bleed.

And what is the alternative, pet? Peace with the Fae?

No. I sigh, rubbing my temples. I do not know. But I think

Torin may be right—if there is any force capable of bringing the mountains down, I'm skeptical that any of us will survive it.

A soft knock brings me back to the present. And then my breath catches.

"Aurora."

She stands in the doorway. Her gown is fresh, but there are tired lines bracketing her eyes. She's been crying. "Hello. May I come in?"

"Please do." I go to the hearth and stoke up the fire.

She glances around. "I was never allowed in this room. Father said it was where he did his important work, and I needn't trouble myself about it."

The bitterness in her voice is unmistakable. "You're welcome here anytime."

A few moments pass. An ember pops in the fire. "Derek told me you helped him . . . with the funeral."

Oh. "He wasn't supposed to. I didn't intend—"

"And Elspeth brought me the book you let her keep." There's a light in her violet eyes I've not glimpsed in a hundred years. "It was wonderful to see those portraits. It meant so much to her. And to me."

Emotion makes me fidgety. I set the poker down. "I'm glad to hear it."

Aurora drifts to the bookcases. "These look a bit like the ones you've been sending me. But I don't recognize them from Briar's collection."

"They're from Malterre," I explain, somewhat grateful for the change in subject. "The Imps brought all sorts of relics here with them from the ruins of those courts."

She trails her fingers along the spines. "I thought the blight killed everyone in those lands."

"Mostly. But the Imps' magic wasn't strong enough to be touched by that poison, which is why their food won't harm you."

Aurora selects a volume and sifts through the pages. "And they were really used as slaves in the Fae courts?"

I lean against my desk. "Slaves and playthings. I know we associate the Etherians with light magic, but they can be brutal when they have a mind."

"I'm not surprised. I remember how cruel Endlewild was with you."

Aurora hasn't uttered a word in my defense since she woke, and hope flutters in my chest.

"And the rest?" she asks. "The Goblins and Vila and Demons? Where had they been, if not in Malterre?"

"Exile," I explain. "Those who escaped the blight remained in hiding in the realms across the sea. Families were often separated. Regan lost her mother when a village caught her and blamed her for a plague. They murdered her."

I don't tell Aurora about Pansy. It doesn't feel right to share that story without Regan's permission.

"I'm sorry for her, then," Aurora says.

It is a much gentler tone than the last time she spoke of the Vila leader. The funeral clearly did something to soften her heart. And I decide to further test the waters. "I know you're not particularly fond of Regan, but I think you two might like each other. She's as fierce as you are, in her own way."

Aurora doesn't reply to that, and I immediately let the matter drop. This is as close to a normal conversation as we've shared thus far, and I don't want to spoil it.

"What's this one?"

She's found the latest book the Imps brought, letting her finger-tips trace the wreath of raven feathers stamped into the cover.

"A court record," I tell her. "The oldest I've ever encountered. From the time before the Briar Queens, in fact."

She picks it up with a speed that betrays her interest. "Really?"

"Yes, here." I help her navigate through the book, and our hands brush, sending sparks firing over my skin. I think I see a blush paint her cheeks. "Did you know there was another realm that attempted to negotiate with the Vila during the Fae challenge? I always thought Leythana was the only one who *didn't* go in swinging swords. But this prince from Cardon apparently tried his own hand at diplomacy."

"Cardon." She leans over and scans the passage. The tip of her curl brushes my bare wrist, and the lilac and apple blossom scent of her fills my nose. It's like a drink of water after nearly dying of thirst. "But isn't that where—"

She goes still, and the ghost of the story about the doomed Briar princess and the woman who broke her curse shivers be-tween us. Without thinking, I squeeze Aurora's wrist. She pulls away, but not before offering me a small grateful smile.

"It doesn't detail what he put forth in exchange for the staff," I say, clearing the hitch in my voice. "But whatever Leythana promised the Vila was obviously preferable."

Aurora bites her bottom lip as she does when she's thinking. "Maybe her dragon ships convinced them that she could keep the peace."

"Maybe. We'll never know now."

"Actually"—she indicates the shelves—"would you mind if I borrowed some other volumes? I'd like to see what I can find."

I laugh a little, wholly unsurprised that she wants to investigate the mystery, and pull a few texts off the shelf. "Take as many as you like. Here." I select one that I know contains information about the various creatures of Malterre. "You can read for yourself about the other members of court. I think you'll find that they weren't the monsters Briar portrayed them to be."

She accepts the books and hugs them to her chest. Her cheeks redden. "That story I told . . . about the monster. I was angry and—"

"Don't." I grasp her elbow. "I understand. And I was a complete idiot to think you would wake and immediately accept everything that's changed. That there wouldn't be . . . painful moments for you. But please believe me when I say that I'm so glad you're awake. That you're here."

We are still so close. She doesn't back away. And I let myself drink in every inch of her face. The curve of her cheek. The shape of her lips. The lines of her collarbones, and plane of her chest before it disappears beneath her neckline.

"Alyce." I will split apart at my name on those lips. "Thank you. For letting me grieve. I think I needed that ceremony more than I realized."

I nod. "It went well?"

"It did."

I want to ask more—want her to let me in like she would have done when we sat together in my Lair. But her eyes go glassy, and I can sense how exhausted she is. I don't resist when she pulls away and heads to the door.

"Thank you for these, too," she says just before she leaves. "I look forward to talking with you about them later. Over tea?"

Happiness fizzes in my veins. "Anytime you say."

• • •

"You won't believe the design of this weapon," Regan says as we walk together through the corridors the next day. "It fires *ten* flaming bolts. Malakar has outdone himself."

Callow warbles her appreciation from my shoulder, and I laugh. "It sounds like it."

An Imp gallops past with a plate of pastries, and I snag one before he rounds the corner.

"No time for that." Regan tugs me along. "He's in the gardens."

"There's always time for pastries," I say around a mouthful.

"In that case—" She snatches the rest from my hand and stuffs it into her mouth before I can stop her.

"That was mine!"

She grins, displaying a mouthful of bright pink filling. "Tomorrow you have to come to the practice yard. We're going to train with it, and several of the Demons have challenged me to duels. You won't want to miss out."

"Fine," I say. "But there had better be an entire tray of pastries waiting for me. A big tray."

Regan licks her lips and sticks out her hand. "Deal."

I shake on it. But I would have gone to the practice yard anyway. It's been ages since I've seen Regan spar, and she's stunningly good at it. We push through a side door and out into the courtyard. Malakar's voice rides the chilly breeze, and I expect him to be surrounded by a gaggle of Imps and other courtiers, all eager to watch him show off. But while he has drawn a crowd, there is one among them I did not anticipate.

Aurora stands in the center of a ring of onlookers, holding a crossbow.

"What on—" Regan starts.

I catch her arm and pull her to a halt with me, positioning us behind a statue so that we don't disturb them.

"You don't think she's going to fire that on us, do you?" Regan whispers.

"No." I'm reasonably sure. "But I'd like to see how she does."

Malakar stands close to Aurora, pointing out the various features of the bow. And it is a magnificent weapon, fashioned so that it appears as a roaring dragon. Like the other, it has a chamber that lights the bolts as they fire. But this one launches the shafts out of the dragon's open jaws, creating the illusion that the beast is breathing flame.

"Let this part rest on your shoulder," Malakar instructs, helping her lift the thing. "Aye, just like that. One hand goes here."

"Like this?" she asks.

"Aye. And be gentle-like. She's not going to run away from you." He corrects her form. "Now set your sights."

Aurora positions the weapon toward the target Malakar set up. Most of the crowd edges away from her, except for the Imps, who keep cartwheeling into the line of fire.

"Stop that!" Malakar scolds them with a growl. "It'll serve you right if she turns you into pincushions."

They giggle and dance away.

"Easy now, Princess." Malakar's typical gruffness is replaced with a patience that warms me through. "Just give that trigger a squeeze, and—"

There's the sound of a bowstring singing. A flurry of flaming bolts whizzes through the air and thunks into the target—directly in the center. After a moment of stunned silence, the crowd cheers.

"Aye!" Malakar laughs, clapping Aurora on the shoulder. "Well done. Like you were born to it."

Aurora lowers the bow. Her smile lights up the courtyard, and my very soul expands—seeing her so happy among the Dark Court.

"Well," Regan says. "She'll have won Malakar's undying admiration for that."

She will. The Goblin leader is already reloading the bow and challenging his own to beat Aurora's shot. She's still beaming, accepting congratulations from everyone around her.

"You should have a go," I say to Regan. "Show them how it's done."

She smiles at me, but there's a brittleness to it. "I'll wait until tomorrow," she says. "I've just remembered something else I need to do."

"I thought you—"

But she only waves at me and heads back to the palace.

For a while, I watch Aurora. Several others take turns with the bow, and she applauds and encourages them. Every fiber of my body wants to go to her. Bask in a sunlight that I have been denied these last hundred years.

But I stay back. Let her have this moment. And hope that one day—maybe even sooner than I think—we might enjoy another together.

CHAPTER TWENTY-TWO

*J*ust after dawn the next day, a sharp rapping at my window wakes me. Grumbling about the hour and the cold leaching through the stone, I kick off the blankets to find Callow hovering impatiently on the other side of the glass. As soon as I crank the panes open, she sails in with a fat mouse gripped in her talons and drops it at my feet with a proud chirrup. I yelp and hop away from the mess of entrails spattering from its gaping stomach.

"I told you not to bring me these." I toss the carcass back outside by the tail.

Callow clacks her beak, highly offended, and perches on the top of a dragon-headed bedpost.

"I mean it. No more. I don't care if your feelings are hurt."

She scolds me for being ungrateful and then sets to pruning her tawny wings. White fluff floats like snow onto the floor.

The bedchamber door swings wide. "Oh good, you're up." Regan sees Callow, the open window, and laughs. "What was it this time? Ferret?"

The dreary day is cold, and I wrap myself up in a fur-lined dressing gown. "Mouse. I swear, every time I toss one out, she brings me two in response."

"Maybe start ignoring them?" Regan heads to the wardrobe, moving faster than she has a right to at this time of the morning. "Or eating them. I think that's what she wants you to do."

Callow makes a noise that could only be interpreted as agreement.

"I'm not eating them." I tighten the sash on the gown. "And I'm not letting them rot on the floor. The chamber would reek."

The kestrel lifts her wing, examining her under-feathers.

"You can fuss about it later," Regan says, rummaging around.

"You're in a mood," I notice. "Is something wrong? I thought we were going to the practice yard."

She emerges and tosses me a particularly militant gown—a velvet that is the deep green of the Vila, with leather straps and gilded buckles down the bodice. "There's a rider."

I catch the garment. "A rider? Why haven't the sentries shot him down?"

"We tried. But he's from the High Court and his protections are too strong. And he's carrying a rowan wreath." She grins. "It seems the High King would like a parley."

The courtyard is packed. A Fae steed treads the air within a translucent orb of protection, the collar of gold-dipped laurel leaves and rowan branches wound around its neck—the Fae symbol for peace. And one we have never beheld in the Dark Court.

The Imps lash their barbed tails and launch one another into the air, attempting to reach the Etherian. Goblins and Demons line the battlements, firing arrows and crossbow bolts. His shield trembles but doesn't break.

"I don't give a Goblin's tit about your rowan!" Valmar shouts. His Imps cheer.

Instead of armor, the Fae rider wears a jacket of bark that appears to be molded from sheets of hammered gold. But it moves as fluidly as leather. His body appears cut from the trunk of a yew tree, like Regan's staff. Pale gray moss climbs over the backs of his knobby-boned hands and up the sides of his neck. He notices me. "Half-breed. Your court disregards the rules of war. A rider under rowan cannot be harmed."

Raucous laughter from the Goblins.

"You are under the mistaken impression that my court adheres to rules," I reply.

The Imps swing their clubs wildly, teeth bared. Another volley of arrows whistles from the battlements and bounces off the Etherian's shield.

He sneers. "Even your ancestors extended some semblance of courtesy in these circumstances."

A rotted apple arcs into the air and splatters into black sludge against the rider's protections. "A gift for the Fae," an Imp squeals. "Plenty more *courtesy* where that came from."

The rider's mount bucks. The Demons on the battlements do not lower their weapons.

"Then I shall make my visit brief. I have come at the behest of the High King, who requests an audience with the Crown Princess of Briar. In Etheria, of course."

Disbelief undulates through the crowd. And I try to disguise my own flare of shock.

"How did the Fae find out about her?" Regan bullies her way

to my side, voicing the very question that screams through my mind.

"I have no idea."

It's been over a month since Aurora woke. How did Oryn discover her? And why did he send a rider? There's another stir as Aurora herself maneuvers her way to the front of the crowd. Her hair is coiled on top of her head—like a crown.

"Princess." The Etherian dips his chin, which was more deference than I recall the lord ambassador Endlewild displaying for any mortal during *his* tenure at this palace. "The High King of the Fae bids me to convey his compliments and to inquire after your well-being and safety."

Murmurs churn like the angry sea.

"I am well enough," Aurora replies, polite but distant. The way she used to speak to her suitors. It makes my lips twitch up. But I'm still cautious. There are a hundred thousand ways this exchange could sour.

"A relief." The rider places one stick-fingered hand on his chest in what I assume is a gesture of blessing. "High King Oryn will be gladdened by the news."

"Will he?" Aurora tilts her head. "Why hasn't he come himself, then?"

The Fae steed rolls its shimmery wings.

"The High King has many matters to attend to," the envoy answers. "But you will recall Briar's alliance with the Fae before the Vila usurped your throne." Mortania swirls in her cave. "An alliance that, with your emergence, survives."

I suck in a breath. Damn that treaty. I haven't thought of it in years, and I never guessed Oryn would care about the agreement now that Briar is sacked. But he does. And my apprehension sharpens instantly to panic. After I saw Aurora with Malakar, after our exchange in my solar, I'd begun to hope that she might be warming to the Dark Court. But if Leythana's treaty is intact, that means Aurora has an army of Fae at her back. What will she do with it?

"Should we—" Regan starts.

"I have no alliance with Etheria." Aurora's words ring in the courtyard, eliciting a flurry of astonishment from the crowd. Relief and confusion collide inside me. "The Fae did nothing when the Briar Queens lost their sovereign rights to their husbands."

The jeweled sigil of the High Court on a circlet nested into the Etherian's leafy hair dazzles. "Rights those queens signed away willingly. A poor choice, but a choice nonetheless."

Aurora doesn't waver in the slightest. "The Fae also did nothing to aid their own kin—the Graces—when those poor creatures were being exploited by the humans in Briar."

"The Graces were merely gifted humans. A spoil earned by the mortal court during the War of the Fae, and therefore none of ours. We owed them nothing."

"And I think one day you will say that you owe me nothing," she smoothly returns. "Your interest in my 'well-being' is quite sudden. Where were you these last hundred years?"

The envoy strains to maintain his composure. His steed nickers, feeding off its rider's energy. "You were presumed dead, as was the rest of your family."

"*Presumed,*" Aurora echoes, folding her arms. "What an interesting word choice. But I've learned that Lord Endlewild himself softened my curse. I do not think he would have neglected to send word to the High King about that development. Therefore, I suspect that you possessed some idea that I lived this entire time. And that you chose to let me sleep."

The envoy . . . does *not* refute it. In fact, the orb on his staff blazes citrine, betraying his spike of frustration. Dragon's teeth, is Aurora correct? Were the Etherians always aware that she was alive? But then why didn't they fight for her after my siege? Regan is intrigued, looking from Aurora to the Fae envoy like a spectator at one of the Demons' games.

His bark-like jacket gleams. "Does so minute a detail matter? I am here because the High King wishes to offer his protection."

"In Etheria," Aurora says. "But, tell me—if I go with you, can I expect the same kind of protection he offered the Imps when they were captive in your courts?" The barb-tailed creatures shout, brandishing their weapons. "Or the citizens of Malterre, exiled from their homes because of your blight?"

My heart swells. She cares for them—for us.

"Enough." The orb on the envoy's staff swirls with power. "The High King will be most disappointed to learn that his generosity is wasted on you."

"I'm afraid I have not yet experienced *his* generosity." Sunlight glints off the buckles on Aurora's gown. She is straight-backed and fearless, and Leythana would be proud to see her. "Nor do I wish to, if it includes another century-long sleep."

The answering bellow of the court is deafening. Goblins shout all manner of curses, promising death and disembowelment and anything else their twisted minds can conjure up. Even from here, I can hear the creak of the Demons' bows as they nock their arrows.

A gilded laurel leaf falls from the steed's neck and drifts toward us. "I would not be so hasty to deny the blood oath your kinswoman earned."

"I deny nothing relating to Leythana," she says. "And if she knew what her *blood oath* wrought, she would break it herself. Relay this to your king: I will have none of your Fae bargains, full of traps and unseen costs. And I will not forget you the way you forgot me."

Shouts and taunts crash together in a cacophonous, jeering chorus. The Goblins stamp their boots on the flagstones, so loud that the Fae beast whinnies, and the rider has to jerk the reins to regain control. Some chant Aurora's name. Because, in this moment, they view her as one of us, firm and resolute against the Etherians. On *our* side.

The Fae envoy spurs his steed and wings away. Demons and Goblins fire arrows and hurl spears at his retreat. Aurora watches him go, utterly glorious, and then she turns to us. Her face is lit with triumph. I smile back, pride blazing inside me.

But then that euphoric feeling curdles.

Her smile is not for me. It's for Derek.

Aurora is instantly transformed into the princess of the Dark Court.

The Imps conjure up mountains of roasted game, including a peafowl whose emerald-and-violet train of feathers is promptly plucked and used to annoy the Demons. There's also a pie that frightens a Vila out of her wits when crows erupt from the crust as soon as it's cut. And the Imps must have learned of the parties of former Briar, for there are pyramids of gold-dipped pastries and fountains of peach-colored fizzy wine. A few of the Goblins pry down mounted Etherian heads and parade them around the throne room, smearing creamy filling over their gaping lips and pouring wine into their hollow mouths.

Regan sits beside me on the dais, her foot tapping along to the melody of the Goblins' playing. "Well, that was an unexpected turn of events."

Aurora is on the other side of the hall, speaking with Torin. Smoke curls from the Demon leader's skin in lazy tendrils, as it does when she's in a particularly good mood.

"Perhaps I was wrong about the princess after all." Regan selects a small cake from a passing tray. The Imps conjured it so that it looks like one of the ossified Etherian heads. And the icing is bright gold, so it appears that they're bleeding with each bite.

"I told you she just needed time," I say.

The dance ends, and one of the humans scuttles over to the princess and presents her with an arrangement of pastries topped with sugared miniature roses. It's Elspeth. She laughs at something Aurora says, but then the nearest Imp yanks Elspeth's hair and the whole tray goes flying. Typically, such a scene wouldn't trouble me. In fact, I've encouraged similar slights and humiliations when it comes to the servants. But this time . . .

"Do you ever feel bad about the way we treat the humans?"

The question surprises us both. I hide my embarrassment with a deep drink. The offending Imp claps his hands and cackles, but Aurora roundly scolds him until he picks up the cakes and hands the tray back to Elspeth.

"What we do with them has never concerned you before."

No. But the way Elspeth shrank from me in the library. She thought I would burn her mother's portrait simply for the thrill of hurting her.

She does not matter, Mortania insists.

But I can't rid myself of the shame. "I know. It's only . . . the Imps were abused in the Fae courts—tormented for the Etherians' enjoyment. Aren't we doing the same thing here with the mortals?"

"And what would you rather do?" Regan asks. "Give them rooms? Reinstate their titles? Should one of them hold a place at council?"

Each prospect is worse than the last. What would the humans do if we allowed them even a sliver of power? How would someone like Rose behave if my necklace wasn't keeping her in check? The possibilities are endless—and horrifying. Even so, the pleasure I used to experience when demeaning the former nobles has considerably paled.

"I don't want any of that," I say. "But I don't want to be like Oryn, either."

Regan squeezes my arm. "You couldn't be. The difference between Oryn and us is that we punish only those who deserve it."

She winks, but I can't return the sentiment. I scan the crowd, searching for Elspeth. She's disappeared somewhere. Instead, I catch sight of a hideous wig making its way across the room and toward Aurora. Derek again.

Dragon's teeth. I'd sternly instructed her Imps that Aurora was not to spend any time at all with the ship's boy. I didn't banish him from the revel. I want him to be able to see her and know that she doesn't care for him. But that *smile* in the courtyard.

"Since the sparring was canceled today, I suppose we'll have to pick it up tomorrow," Regan says. But I'm only half-listening. "You'll be there?"

"Of course."

A troupe of Imps tumbles away from their fellows and piles atop one another in front of the dais. In warbling, discordant tones, they belt out a hastily devised song about decapitated heads and plucked eyeballs, ending with a loud, lingering *Mistress Ni-mara*. But my answering applause is unenthusiastic, and I decide to handle the matter of the prowling ship's boy myself.

"Where are you going?" Regan asks at my back.

I mumble something in reply and keep walking. I've lost Derek in the sea of dancers. Imps giggle and tug at my arms, and I bat them gently away. Where has the damn boy gone?

"Looking for someone?"

A Vila couple spins past, and then I'm face-to-face with Rose. Glossy pink curls cascade in a flattering fashion over one of her bare shoulders, and her gown is of the same caliber as something she would have worn at a palace ball. The skirt is fashioned out of what appears to be pink butterfly wings, veined in gold. Matching ribbons crisscross up the bodice. The Imps must be more than satisfied with her elixirs.

"Are you enjoying yourself?" I mirror the Grace's sticky-sweet smirk. "Or do you miss the gaggle of men you had at your disposal?"

She fluffs her skirts. "As you can see, I'm getting on splendidly, all things considered. The princess and I both know that this is only a temporary arrangement."

"Are you certain of that? In case you failed to notice, Aurora snubbed the Fae envoy. There's absolutely no chance of your escaping to Etheria now."

One of the butterfly baubles dangling from her earlobes gleams. "Oh, I'm not worried about that. She'll come to her senses sooner or later. And I'll be more than ready when she does."

Anger fizzes in my fingertips. And I reach out to straighten her necklace. "Careful, Rose. You wouldn't want any mishaps to occur."

She narrows her gaze. The golden Grace powder limning her eyelids shimmers. "The only mishap in this realm is you."

I laugh. "Do you think your insults have any effect on me anymore? I'm not the Dark Grace."

"No? But what does *she* think you are?" Rose points behind us with her fan.

Aurora's Imps are vaulting onto one another's shoulders and flipping down again. She laughs at them and claps. One of them turns a stone into a pastry topped with a miniature crown and offers it to her on bended knee. And there is that ratty wig, far closer to her than it ought to be.

"Oh, they make a handsome couple, don't they?" She says at my shoulder. "What a touching romance. The man who lifted the lost princess's curse then stole her heart. The stuff of legends, is it not?"

Where my power dwells, Mortania stirs. I should have drained Rose's gift long ago. Let her go the way of Marigold and Laurel. I itch to do it now—dull those golden eyes and still that conniving tongue forever.

"Poor Malyce," Rose goes on. "Are you still in love with her? Did you think she would wake and run back to you?" She clicks her tongue, and I've half a mind to forgo my magic and rip it out of her mouth with my bare hands. "But how could she? How could she *ever* really love something like you?"

Some*thing*. The word lands like a hammer, just as it always used to. And then Aelfdene's voice rears its ugly head.

"It was not real."

No. I grind my teeth against the stinging in my eyes. And I will show Rose who's in charge of this court.

"Artesia," I bark out.

A nearby Vila peels herself away from her partner and bows in greeting.

I grip Rose's elbow and thrust her forward. "You've met our Grace? She craves a dance. In fact, she claimed that she could dance all night without ceasing. Could you accommodate her?"

Artesia grins, licking her lips. "Certainly, Mistress. It would be a pleasure."

Rose's perfect pink curls bounce as she's half-dragged away, the petrified butterflies sewn into the toes of her slippers flapping with each step. "No, I'm tired and—"

But the Vila is deaf to her protests, and Rose is soon swallowed in the throng.

And even though Derek is sitting with Aurora, and she is laughing at his inane jokes, I do not go to them. I slip away instead, into the chill of the night.

CHAPTER TWENTY-THREE

The gardens are empty. I stalk down the gravel paths, furious at Rose and Derek and especially myself. I am Mistress of the Dark Court. The most powerful Vila living. Why do I care about the human servants, or an idiotic ship's boy, or a vapid Grace?

Why indeed, pet?

Brittle branches and thorny vines snag in my hair and clothes. I send my magic out to meet theirs, and they shrivel away. Before I know it, I'm deep inside the garden, standing in front of a fountain I have not visited in a hundred years.

It is almost unrecognizable, the marble charred and blackened. The sculpted faces of the bathing maidens are smashed, some of their limbs missing. Under no circumstances could it spout water—or anything resembling liquid. But I close my eyes and imagine myself a century ago, angry and lonely and completely powerless against a realm that despised me for the very reasons it exploited my magic.

And now that realm is reduced to ash, but I can't help feeling that I am right back where I started. Anger presses against the inside of my skin. For a heart-stopping moment, I fear I will explode with it. That they will find me here, nothing but dust.

"I take it that this is still your preferred hiding place when something goes wrong at a party?"

The voice startles me into the present. I whirl. Moonlight glints on the copper-gold of Aurora's hair and drenches her luminous skin.

"I . . . didn't know anyone followed me." I tug at my dress.

"You were walking in that way that you do when you're furious about something."

"I don't have a walk like that," I say.

But she only arches an eyebrow. "Do you want to tell me what happened?"

And it's then that I fully comprehend that Aurora is here, not sitting with Derek, or gossiping with Rose. She chose me. Everything else becomes instantly unimportant.

"It doesn't matter," I say, letting my frustration slide from my shoulders.

"If you say so." Aurora shrugs and inspects the fountain. Something ripples across her expression. "Is this where we first met? The fountain you muddied up?"

"It is." A sudden shyness overcomes me. "I'm surprised you recognized it."

Aurora lets out a long breath, and I imagine that, like me, she is thinking of the person she was that long-ago night. "I see you still have a knack for ruining it."

She's teasing me. I feign outrage, pressing a hand to my chest. "You said you liked it better that way."

"Oh, I did." She laughs. "You should have seen the royal gardeners the next day. They were in a state for weeks."

I laugh with her, reveling in how familiar this is. How easy. I toy with a wandering vine, the stem smooth against my papery skin. "I saw you with Malakar and the others, shooting a crossbow. You're very good. Though I don't imagine you had much training in weaponry as Briar's princess."

"Mother would have had a fit if she'd been there." Her eyes sparkle in that mischievous way I adore. "But I rather enjoyed it. Not that I'd want to shoot at anything other than targets," she adds. "I'm relieved none of the Imps got in the way. I'm not sure how those little deviants survived in the Fae courts. They must have driven the Etherians mad."

"It's been a point of debate," I say.

Ravens trade their calls nearby. Aurora is quiet for a while, picking dead leaves from the nooks of the fountain and letting them crumble. "I'm glad you rescued them," she says at last. "No one should endure what they did. They deserve a home."

It's the first time she's acknowledged that I accomplished anything of value since she was cursed to sleep, and I'd like to believe it might mean she's beginning to trust the Dark Court. Maybe even trust *me*. But I'm too much of a coward to ask her outright. "Have you been reading any of the books I gave you?"

"I have," she says. "I've not discovered anything about Leythana or her negotiation with the Vila courts. But I have read about Malterre. You were right—the books present a very different version of its people than what Briar taught. Not that I'd read many of those texts."

No. The only books about the Vila were hidden away in the abandoned library. And even those were ridiculously one-sided.

"And have they . . . helped you to understand what I did? And why?"

It takes her a long time to answer. Wind groans in the branches. "I can understand your anger. And that you might have felt such a drastic response was necessary." Hope surges up from my toes. Then, "But, Alyce, that understanding doesn't bring anyone back. It doesn't change the fact that you've done to me and *my* home what Briar and the Fae did to yours."

Her words shudder through me, cruelly deflating any happiness. And the worst part is that I cannot entirely refute what Aurora says. That same fanged guilt that I experienced when I found out about the secret funeral sinks its teeth into my soul. Mortania writhes in the place where my magic lives.

Why should you feel guilt, pet? You were not the one to strike the first blow.

No, I wasn't. And I'd be willing to bet that Aurora would have razed some other realm if it meant protecting her own. Sometimes I wonder if she would have condoned the blight on Malterre during the first war if she'd been alive then. I draw myself up, recentering my focus where it always should be—on the Dark Court.

"You want me to say I regret what I did, but I don't." She flinches slightly, but I don't relent. "Your father, and Mistress Lavender, and everyone else—they pushed and pushed, until I finally pushed back. I will not apologize for that."

Night creatures chitter. "And I won't apologize for missing my family, even if they could be ruthless. Or for mourning the life I thought I was going to have."

My breath clouds in front of my face, the beauty of this night having shriveled as soon as it bloomed. Here we are, enemies again. "So where does that leave us?"

She picks at the chipped stone of the fountain. "I don't know."

A thousand thoughts war inside my mind. I want to tell her that I love her. That I hate her. That I'm angry with her for her constant judgment and criticism. That I'm sorry for her grief. But I say nothing. Eventually, Aurora's footsteps crunch back toward the palace. And I let them go.

Alone, and surrounded by the brittle and blackened foliage, the decaying statues and fountains, part of me misses how these gardens looked at Briar's height. It's late summer, and the sky should be sugared with stars, the air thick with the perfume of dozens of kinds of flowers. On a whim, I send my power out to find the thready magic of the curtain of bramble draped over the fountain and bid it curl away. And then I guide it to burrow into the ruined marble, discovering the firm heart of the stone itself, and re-form a half-crumbled maiden into a dragon's head. It's not like it used to be, but it holds its own sort of beauty.

And another idea wriggles its way out of the darkness.

Aurora and I are at a stalemate, each of us entrenched in the worlds we knew before. But what if there was a way to meet in the middle? To forge a path together, as we'd planned to do before everything went so horribly wrong.

I think I might know how to make that happen.

"Where were you this morning?" Regan asks as I take my place at the council table the next day. "You said you would come to the practice yard. I had a mountain of pastries waiting. We had to use them as target practice."

Dragon's teeth, I completely forgot. I'd been up the whole night planning and managed only a few hours of sleep in the early morning. "I'm sorry," I tell her, pouring out a cup of strong tea. "Next time?"

Her answering smile is forced. "Of course. But you did miss incredible feats of agility."

"I am sorry," I say again.

"No matter." She pushes a plate of cheese my way. "Here—you look like death."

I shoot her a glare but stuff a wedge into my mouth anyway.

"Enough dallying," Malakar says as he scoots his chair closer to the table. "It's time to discuss the siege of the High Court. My thought is—"

"Before we do that," I interrupt, steeling myself for what I'd spent a solid hour rehearsing last night. "I have something to present. Given what happened with Aurora and the envoy, I think we should do something for her."

A slightly confused silence follows.

"Already had a revel," Valmar comments, tail curling behind him.

"What I have in mind would be more formal," I explain. "A proper welcome."

"Such as?" Neve adds cream to her tea, stirring her spoon in a way I know she intends to be annoying. Silver scrapes against the china—and my nerves.

"I've learned from the Grace's reports that Aurora's birthday is coming soon," I say, doing my utmost best to keep my tone even and casual. "Humans enjoy birthdays. We should throw her a party. Celebrate her."

Unspoken questions hang thick above the table, like storm clouds lumbering in from the sea. I will not have much opportunity to sway them to my side.

"We all witnessed how she responded to the envoy," I go on. "She's been trying of late. Really trying."

Wind presses against the glass. The council members trade loaded glances.

"Mine do speak well of her," Valmar says around a mouthful of chocolate pastry, already selecting another.

"Aye." Malakar is playing with some trinket from the Court of Dreams—a glass ball with a galaxy of stars whirling inside the crystal—and it emits a musical sound as he rolls it back and forth on the table. "She handled the crossbow as easily as any of mine could. Quick learner."

"High praise," Neve drawls.

"It is that." Malakar puffs out his chest. "She even complimented the craftsmanship. Built the thing myself."

I smile into my goblet. The way to a Goblin's heart is through his weapons.

"I believe what Nimara actually proposes is that this party will serve as an invitation for the princess to become a full member of court," Torin says.

She looks to me with that keen amber gaze, and I nod in confirmation. My pulse speeds up, as I'm not sure what I'll do if they reject this idea.

"It can't hurt anything," I insist before it's immediately shot down. "In fact, her official induction to the Dark Court could help our position. Aurora would be a human ally and a former princess. There are a multitude of diplomatic tasks she could help us accomplish after the war. And she's more than proven that she isn't like the humans of former Briar."

Neve inspects her ironlike nails. "*Would* she choose to join us? A few pleasant encounters do not guarantee a lasting alliance."

She's picking this plan apart because it's mine. For all her talk about *my* disrespect, she's as bad as Rose. "If Aurora is trying, we should try. *That's* how alliances are guaranteed."

Torin lets out a sigh. "I admit, the princess has impressed me. I assumed she would spend the rest of her life in her rooms or continue treating us like we were vermin invading her palace. But"— she gestures at Valmar—"yours have taken a shine to her. And even my Demons claim she is a cunning partner in their games. And a graceful dancer. Of course, they say the same thing about the boy."

I have no desire to include *him* in this discussion.

"Aye," Valmar relents. "Suppose it cannot hurt to ask her."

Triumph buzzes in my veins.

"Then it's settled?" I ask. "We hold a surprise party to officially welcome Aurora into our midst."

The ensuing pause is not as uncomfortable as it was before.

Malakar thumps his fist on the table. "It's an excuse for another revel, if nothing else. Don't have to yank my tail for one of those."

I laugh and raise a toast. And I do not realize until much later that Regan is the only one of the council who said nothing at all.

CHAPTER TWENTY-FOUR

The Imps are enthusiastic when I solicit their help. Fae and others of magical blood do not celebrate birthdays, as few of us can guess exactly when we were born, which makes the party seem marvelously eccentric.

Though I explained to them about other parties given in former Briar, the roguish creatures have no interest in Grace-grown flowers, or pots of redolent incense, or live hummingbirds flitting like winged jewels among the guests. Instead, columns are dressed as ominous trees with scythelike arms draped in cobwebs. Brambles curl along what's left of the mezzanine. Vases teem with midnight-petaled irises and a species of orchid only the Imps could have summoned—with miniature leering faces in the centers. Ravens are captured and let loose in the ballroom, their laughing calls sinister and echoing.

The cake was the lone suggestion the Imps took to heart. It's so tall that the layers list to one side. At first, the Imps tried to stick fat tallow tapers in the tiers as decoration. Crimson, so that it looked as though the candles were dripping mortal blood. But I convinced them to switch to smaller versions magicked to appear as dragons with wicks on the talons of their wings and tails. The icing is a shade of lavender, to honor Aurora, and piped into clusters of roses.

The Imps' favorite aspect of the party is its secrecy. All day, Aurora's trio of companions kept her away from our work. Shortly after sunset, the court assembles in the ballroom. A Vila plucks at her skirt, which is comprised entirely of thin tangled roots. Blackened branches make up the bodice, reaching over her shoulders and fanning out into a high collar behind her head. Several Demons sport headdresses with long curving horns, or nests of tangled serpents. A Demon wears a dress accented with bones, so that it appears the wearer's spine and ribs are visible. I spot a cloak that gives the illusion of ghoulish faces pressed against the swaths of fabric. Even the Imps have donned gargoyle masks and elaborate hats made out of petrified bats. I'd asked them to conjure me a gown of onyx silk with a silver overlay. Gossamer wings float down from my shoulders. Will Aurora recognize it as being similar to the one I wore when we first met? My heart stammers.

Aurora's Imps can soon be heard charging down the corridor. One is riding her shoulders, vermilion fingers clamped over her face. Two others gambol in front, shouting at her to avoid bottomless pits and duck under soaring spears. She laughs and tickles the bottom of the Imp's feet, and he backflips onto the floor.

I'd instructed her keepers to make sure she dressed for this party, and they didn't disappoint. Her gown is a striking sapphire color, littered with innumerable constellations of winking silver gems. It's cut low in the front, and the skin exposed by the plunging neckline shimmers with opalescent powder. Like the night sky was crushed, stars and all, and she bathed in it. I struggle to keep from staring.

But her expression falls slack as she takes in the court. "What's all this?"

"Happy born-day!" an Imp shouts at the top of his lungs.

Aurora's brow rumples, the glow of the candles dancing in the coppery threads of her hair. "What?"

"Happy *birthday*," I correct, shaking my head. "All this is for *you*, Aurora."

"My . . . birthday?" she repeats. "You remembered?"

"How could I not?" I gesture around at the room. "The Imps have been setting it up all day."

Those nearest begin to prattle off the various tasks they completed, tails swishing as it devolves into a dispute over who did what. But Rose, who stands beside Aurora, sucks her teeth. Splotches of gold erupt on her chest and neck, and the pearls dangling from her towering headdress vibrate. Her own gift of elixirs will appear as an afterthought following this grand gesture. She plucks at the petals of a peony on her gown. I smile at her.

Aurora scans the chamber, and her attention doubles back—to Derek.

The Imps have stuffed him into a formal suit. But it's moth-eaten and more gray than black. A ratty foxtail hangs limply from behind his waist. And there's a sad-looking hat made from a swan on his head. With any luck, it will give him fleas.

I snag two goblets of wine and pass one to Aurora, positioning myself to block her view of the boy.

"To Aurora," I say, raising a toast. "Who told the High King where to shove his staff!"

The court roars with laughter. Aurora hides her blush in her goblet. But she's not angry. She's not glowering at me or storming off. And I begin to let myself hope that this evening might actually go as I intended.

The party is glorious. Demons and Vila take turns gliding Aurora across the floor, and the Imps present her with plate after plate of their delicacies, chittering excitedly when she approves of each macabre pastry or odd-colored dish. Even the Goblins gruffly offer the princess some of their jewels to mark the occasion— a brooch from the Court of Sea, made of coral and glass beads, which are filled with miniature swimming fish, and a necklace strung with the mesmerizing pearls of the Court of Dreams they claim can grant her pleasant dreams. For a short while, there are no ancient wars or thorny histories between us. My mood isn't even soured when Aurora dances with Derek. But I don't wait long before I let a pair of Imps know that I'd like to see our ship's boy catapult them into the vaulted ceiling. They pry him away from Aurora before the music changes.

"Was this what you envisioned?" Regan asks. She's been lounging in the chair beside mine all night. She didn't bother with any sort of costume, preferring her leathers.

"It is," I answer, a lightness in my chest that I hardly recognize.

"Perhaps, after this, you'll finally have time to visit the practice yard."

There's a stiffness in her voice, and I sit back and really look at her. Tight lines bracket her mouth. She taps her fingers against the armrest of the chair in an agitated tempo. It almost seems like—

"Are you angry with me?"

"No." But everything about her manner screams otherwise. "I just—I hardly see you anymore. You're distracted at council meetings, and you lock yourself away in your solar for hours on end. It wasn't like this before she woke."

Beneath Regan's frustration, I sense the tinge of jealousy. Guilt prickles at my conscience. The Vila leader risked her life to be here. She's become my closest friend. I don't know what I would do without her. I certainly wouldn't be here today.

"I'm sorry," I say, reaching for her. The bone spikes traveling her forearm press into my palm. "I haven't meant to ignore you or make you feel—I don't know—like you're not important. Because you are."

She slides me a quirk of a smile. "Yes. I am."

I laugh and swat at her, grateful that the tension between us is so easily smoothed. "Tell me whatever day you want me to be at the yard, and I'll be there. Or we can do something else. Whatever you want."

Regan sips her wine. "Whatever I want? Really?"

Something flutters in my belly at the glint in her green eyes. "That's what I said."

She swirls her glass, thoughtful, and is about to reply. But then—

"Alyce?"

I'd been so focused on my conversation with Regan that I hadn't noticed Aurora slip up the dais steps. She holds out her hand. There might as well be an entire world sitting in her palm.

"Would you like to dance with me?"

Yes, I want to dance. I want to do every imaginable thing with her. But all that manages to escape my lips is a throaty warble. Aurora laughs and pulls me with her into the crowd, and I barely register that I've left Regan far behind us.

"I'm not much of a dancer."

"Don't worry." Aurora positions one hand on my waist and interlocks the other with mine. How long has it been since I glimpsed my own papery green-veined skin next to her bronze-kissed cream? I think I will implode at the sensations her touch brings. The silken heat of her. I am drunk on it.

The dance—set to a sinuous, slightly melancholy tune—calls for one partner to lift the other into the air. I Shift the muscles in my arms and sweep her up. The tips of her burnished-gold curls brush my cheeks.

"You're a better dancer than you think," she says.

I stumble on the next turn and laugh. "You're just a good partner."

She catches me, one arm slung around my waist, and seamlessly adjusts us back into form. "You've far more skill than those men I was commanded to dance with on my other birthdays. There was one who smelled as though he half-drowned himself in cologne." Her nose scrunches. "I sneezed twice and Mother barred me from the library for a week in punishment."

Our palms touch. "The worst was the one who thought he only had to kiss you to marry you. He didn't understand he actually had to break your curse."

Aurora laughs, tipping her head back. The powder on her neck and chest sparkles. "Thank the Dragon none of them did break it. I'd have been miserable."

Does that mean she isn't miserable now? I'm almost too terri-

fied to ask. But I let myself be carried away by the music and dancing and closeness. "Are you sorry that ours did?"

She slows. I was a fool to bring that up.

We've drifted toward the edge of the chamber. A raven perches
on one of the branches of a decorated column, eyeing us warily.
"No. I'm not sorry."

My heart thumps, as if it would snap the tethers of its moor-
ings. And I know without a doubt that this is the perfect moment
for my next surprise.

"Will you come with me?" My grip tightens on her hand and
she doesn't pull away. "I want to show you something."

Outside, the stars are hidden behind scudding clouds, the dull
coin of the moon slipping in and out of view.

"What are we doing out here?" Aurora shivers. I should have
brought her a cloak.

"The Dark Court may not be Briar," I tell her. "But that doesn't
mean it is any less beautiful."

She begins to ask another question, but I let my power free. It
canters along the gravel paths. Green flames spring to life from
hidden candles, drenching the garden in an emerald, ethereal glow.
I couldn't revive the plants and did not commission the Imps to
conjure a facsimile of the place Aurora loved. Instead, with my
own power, I've constructed a reimagined garden. Vines are
twisted and molded to mimic animal-shaped topiaries. Stones are
re-formed into benches and statues. Rubies and sapphires and
opals glimmer like so many petals on barren bushes. The fountain
flows with the murky water of our long-ago meeting.

Aurora approaches it gingerly and drags one finger through the frothing mud.

"You did this for me?"

Her voice is gentle and low. It brims with amazement . . . and something else too fragile to name. She drifts along the rows of hedges. Touches an oily-skinned tree trunk and the lapis clusters of an imitation hydrangea bush. Gems tinkle in the breeze.

I risk a tentative step toward her. Another. She doesn't retreat, not even when I'm brave enough to trace the soft line of her forearm.

"You told me the books you read helped you to understand at least some of why I retaliated against Briar."

Aurora moves away from me, train sighing along the path. "Yes. Some."

"I've come to a similar understanding," I say. "About your grief. And how difficult things have been for you of late."

She pauses, her skin drenched in the green light of the candles. "What are you saying?"

I'd practiced this next part, pacing my chambers like an idiot, but it was not enough to settle my nerves now that the moment has arrived. "We might never fully understand or relate to each other. We'll never be able to go back to the people we used to be. But look at this garden." I indicate the black-branched topiaries and the muddied fountain. "It won't ever be the same, either. But that doesn't mean it's ruined, does it?"

Gems tinkle in the breeze. "It's lovely," she says.

"The Dark Court is no different," I press on before I lose my fragile courage. The next part is trickier. "Of course, you'll never be queen here. And if the throne is all you care about, then I suppose there's nothing left to say. But if you're willing, we could build something together. Better than it ever was before. A place we could both be proud to call home."

A nightbird calls nearby. The fountain gurgles.

"And Mortania?" Aurora asks, rubbing the spot on her arm where her curse mark used to rest. "Would it be her home, too? Even after what she did to me and my sisters?"

Branches click and clack in the wind, like the sound of that long-ago spinning wheel. Mortania rumbles in her cave. The music of the jeweled petals is discordant.

"I don't blame you for distrusting, or even hating Mortania." I pluck at my sleeves. "My own feelings when it comes to the ancient Vila are . . . complicated. When your second curse began, I was furious with her. There was even a brief instant in which I wanted to cleave her from myself, as I thought that might lift your curse. Like when we tried to locate her magic and destroy it."

The ancient Vila stirs. *But I made you what you are, pet.*

And I lean into the scent of steel and loam. "But whatever she did in the past, Mortania taught me how to use this power. And not just to whip up elixirs or cast a summoning. To use it for what *I* wanted, instead of letting others dictate or control my magic. And," I add carefully, "I think you might know something about how important that control was to me."

Moonlight glimmers on the constellations of gems sewn into her skirt. She touches the pearlescent petals of a hydrangea flower. "You know I do," she says softly. "But you cannot expect me to share your gratitude when it comes to Mortania."

"And you cannot ask me to erect a shrine to former Briar. Not when so many of my own were exiled because of those rulers." I wait. She doesn't fire back a retort. "I'm asking if we can accept the other person exactly where they are now and move forward."

Her amethyst eyes are like twin stars in the night. I would give anything to know what she is thinking. My heart beats harder, anticipating her answer.

"Nimara?" a voice calls, shattering the moment. Torin emerges from the palace. "We've been looking for you. It's time to present our gift to the princess."

CHAPTER TWENTY-FIVE

We rejoin the court, but every nerve of my body is aflame. I think Aurora might have been about to say she agreed. That we might *finally* be able to draw a line under everything that's happened and start again. If so, I hope her answer will not change in front of the court. And I sorely wish there had been time for me to warn her of what's about to happen now.

And if she rejects you, pet?

I shake the ancient Vila away.

Regan bangs the butt of her staff on the floor, calling the attention of the room. The Imps halt their upside-down swinging from the chandeliers, where they've been pelting the ravens with pastries. Goblins topple from the shoulders of their dancing partners. The Vila press closer. Derek's mangy swan hat appears at the cusp of the crowd.

Aurora stands next to me, her brow pinched in curiosity. My palms prickle. I really should have told her.

"Tonight we celebrate Aurora," I say to the court. The Imps cheer, and Aurora blushes. I pull the ring from my pocket and hold it out to her. It's an Imp creation, the dark garnet stone resembling a wilting rose with a tarnished crown in the center. Candlelight glimmers on the gold metal. "And as birthdays typically involve gifts, consider this our gift to you—a token of our friendship and acceptance. And a symbol of your place in the Dark Court."

Aurora inhales a sharp breath. But she doesn't reach for the ring.

"What does it mean?" she asks so that only I can hear.

"Just what I said in the garden," I whisper back. "A fresh start for us."

She pins me with that depthless gaze. "That's what you really want?"

"It's what I've wanted from the day you woke."

The moments stretch out, each one longer than the last. Imps creep forward, ears twitching. The Demons' shadows still, like ink frozen in the air. Aurora's lips part, forming the shape of—

"Wait!"

A desperate voice cuts through the crowd, and then Rose is fighting through the throng of Vila and Demons to reach the dais. Fury balls in my chest. What does she think she's doing?

"Highness." Rose trips on a step and lands hard. But it doesn't stop her. "There's something you should know—about *her*."

No. The Grace will not spoil everything. I don't wait for the necklace to react on its own. I call on the curse myself. Diamond thorns spear into Rose's neck. She crumples as her golden blood streams down her neck, staining the bodice of her gown.

"What's happening?" Aurora kneels to Rose's level. "What's wrong with your neck?"

"Mistress made the necklace do that once before," an Imp—one from Rose's chamber when I interrupted her crafting elixirs—provides. I curse under my breath.

"She did what?"

Damn that Grace. I'd expected Rose to be looking for loopholes that would allow her to evade the necklace's restrictions. I did not think *this* would be her strategy. And suddenly I wonder if Rose *wanted* me to find out about Aurora's birthday for exactly this purpose. She'd been biding her time, like a spider in its web.

Aurora wheels to me. "Are you doing this?"

Between her gurgles for breath, Rose emits a choked noise of confirmation.

"Remove the necklace." That tone I know well. The one Aurora used on the guards when they discovered us together in the abandoned library. The royal command of a princess.

She is not a princess, Mortania hisses. *Teach them their places. Finish the Grace.*

It would be so easy. Just a little more pressure from the necklace to sever Rose's windpipe, and then I would never be bothered with her again. But I cannot bring myself to do it. At my sullen command, the necklace falls from Rose's neck, metal and jewels clinking on the marble steps.

"So it *was* you," Aurora grinds out. "I should have guessed."

I draw myself up as best I can. "If the Grace was to be freed, then I needed to be certain she wouldn't betray us. The necklace kept her in line."

"Freed?" Aurora looks from Rose to me. "I thought she was housed in another part of the palace. That's what she told me."

This is worse than I could have imagined.

"She forced me to lie," Rose rasps. She's weeping, making insufferable little sniffling noises. "You've seen what the necklace would do if I dared speak out. There are more Graces in the dungeon. We've been there for decades. They call it the Garden, the twisted beasts."

The Goblins snarl at the insult, closing in. Malakar makes no move to intervene. The Vila take up their battle cry. The Imps flip from one perch to the next, tails thrashing. Some of the Demons dissolve into their shadow forms and slink like wraiths along the ceiling.

Aurora ignores the brewing danger. "There are other Graces? Imprisoned? What else has she forbidden you from telling me?"

So quick I almost miss it, Rose flashes a smirk in my direction. And then it hits me—she *has* been plotting. And the Garden is not the only secret she intends to expose.

Panic reaches its fingers through my veins. "Aurora—"

"It's your sleeping curse," Rose speaks over me, climbing the blood-slick steps on her hands and knees. "I was there the night Laurel and Endlewild softened it. Anyone could have woken you. Anyone but *Malyce*. All they had to do was kiss you."

Beneath the sounds of jostling Imps and the mutterings of the Goblins, a dull ringing starts in my ears. I should do something. *Say* something. But all I can do is stare. A storm of emotion crosses Aurora's face.

"You knew?" The question is low, but it smacks like thunder. "You knew how to wake me and you *let* me sleep? For a hundred years?"

"It's not that simple," I croak out.

She throws up her hands. "It never is with you."

"I tried everything to wake you!"

"Except, apparently, the one thing you knew would work."

"I thought you would forget about me. I couldn't let that happen."

"All this time I've been wracking my brain, trying to determine why Derek's kiss broke the curse. You knew all along, and you *lied* about it. And you're asking me for a fresh start?" Aurora's chest rises and falls in short bursts. "You could have woken me every day for a hundred years. But you wouldn't because you didn't trust that our love was strong enough to withstand any curse. Because you couldn't bear to see me with anyone else, even for an instant."

I open my mouth to argue back, then realize that an unnatural stillness has settled over the court. The chamber hums with it.

Torin is the first to speak. Her gown is fashioned out of what looks to be huge moth wings and a matching cape flutters in the draft. "Did she say your *love*?"

Curse everything to the bottom of the sea and back. Imps begin to chitter. The Vila murmur to one another, foreheads creased beneath their bone spikes.

"You were in love?" Malakar's ears lay flat between his horns. "With a member of the family who allied with the light Fae and destroyed Malterre?"

Aurora is glaring at me, expectant. But my lips refuse to work. My pulse thumps out a terrified rhythm. And, most of all, I'm painfully confused. The court was warming to Aurora, more so than I ever could have expected. They agreed to throw her this party. I thought—

That is not the same as their mistress being in love, Mortania supplies. *She will always be a symbol of those who sent you into exile. They will never truly accept her.*

Truly.

"It was not real," Aelfdene's sinister words echo in my mind. And this time I cannot convince myself in the least that he was wrong.

Tears threaten and I blink them back. Aurora waits with her arms folded, and I can practically see the line drawing between us. Carving itself into the marble stone of the dais. The court or her? But I cannot turn my back on this—on them.

I force steel into my spine. "The princess is sorely mistaken. We were friends, nothing more. Anything else would have been impossible."

For one horrible, endless moment, pain flares bright in Aurora's amethyst eyes. It spears through me as well, poison-tipped.

She plucks the ring from my grip and hurls it at me. It pings off my bodice and clatters against the marble, the sound like all of my ludicrous hopes shattering. And then she turns and bolts from the dais, the gems on her gown winking in the candlelight.

CHAPTER TWENTY-SIX

My first thought after Aurora leaves is that Rose must be dealt with. But the traitorous Grace slithered away like the snake she is. Her necklace shines in a pool of her golden blood, so she's free to run wherever she likes. She cannot get far, though. And I dispatch a few Imps to ferret her out.

If the rest of the court is upset at Aurora's rejection, they instantly forget it. The party returns to its riotous glory. I should be dancing with Aurora. Lighting the candles on her cake and teasing her about what her wish might be. Instead, one of the Imps somersaults from a chandelier and lands on the top tier of that cake. Frosting and sponge go flying, and everyone cheers. And it pains me more than I can say that they've so easily dismissed her. Mortania was correct. They could never love her. She was only ever a novelty.

Before anyone can speak to me, I stalk down the dais steps and fight my way through the press of bodies, into the cool of the night air.

• • •

In the garden, my enchanted candles are still glowing in their nooks. Shafts of moonlight manage to battle through the clouds and reflect off the jeweled flowers. Indignation pounds through my veins. Aurora *would* have chosen us tonight if Rose hadn't interrupted. When I find that wretched Grace I will . . .

A faint crunch of gravel reaches me through the other night sounds. And then a voice. I Shift my hearing to distinguish it. Derek's. And he isn't alone.

"How could she do that to me?" Aurora is more furious than I've ever heard her. I melt into the nearest shadowy space, detesting Derek more than ever. She chose *him* as a confidant? "Did she think I'd never find out that she let me sleep in a cage for a hundred years while she did . . . this?"

This. Aurora had been enthralled with the garden when I presented it. But now it's an ugly, monstrous thing.

You do not need her, pet.

"You've a right to be upset, but it didn't sound to me as though Nimara lied to harm you. Not on purpose."

"It doesn't matter," Aurora shoots back, exasperated. "I don't know her anymore. The Alyce from before was kind, underneath everything. They treated her so cruelly—the Graces, the Etherians, my own father. And I believed this whole time that she was still there, somewhere. But now, her brutality. Her . . . malice. I do not . . ."

Outraged tears prick against my eyelids. I dig my nails into the flesh of my palms to keep them back.

Derek moves closer to her. "You cannot stay here."

"This is my home. My realm." She hugs her arms to her body.

"I won't abandon the humans who have survived so far. You saw how they were at the funeral. They need me."

"But the Fae envoy said your alliance with the Etherians was intact. Think of the protection the High King could provide if you escaped."

The cry of a raven drifts from the ballroom.

"It's my decision. The Etherians are devious, despite their light magic."

"But what else can you do?" Derek strangles his hat in his hands. "You can't just—"

"Whatever I'm thinking is none of your concern. I will not be managed or manipulated."

A wind bullies through the garden and rattles the branches.

"Forgive me, I did not mean—"

"You did," she cuts him off. Not rudely, but with a finality that gives me immense satisfaction. "I explained to you about my suitors and my father. Every man in my life has thought me an object for their pleasure or amusement or power. I did not wake from a century's sleep to succumb to the whims of another."

Gravel scuffs. "I want to help you, though."

"I know you do." Her tone gentles. "And I'm grateful for your friendship."

Why couldn't he have drowned with the rest of his crew?

"I just . . . you call this land your home, but look at it. Nothing grows. There's no trade. Is it worth holding on when there's so little hope?"

"There's always hope." Green light lends a halo around her body. "And just because something is at its worst doesn't mean you should abandon it."

A chill runs down my spine. Does she mean that Briar is at its worst? Or me?

"Will you let them tear you apart, as I've seen them do to their prisoners?" He waves his swan hat toward the ballroom windows. "They cheered you when you snubbed the Etherian envoy, but you've drawn a line, Aurora. And you're on the wrong side of it."

"What would you suggest I do?" She wanders down the path. The garden flowers emit their strange music. "Run away on your ship—the planks of wood scattered on the seabed?"

Derek pauses and seems to debate his reply. "There's something I've wanted to tell you, but I never had the chance with your keepers about."

I sharpen my hearing and dare a half-step closer.

He twists the swan hat. A feather molts from its wing and floats away. "When I told you about my home—"

A beating splits the night, and a shadow swoops over the garden. Derek spins around and pushes Aurora behind him. But he has no weapon, absolutely nothing to defend them. And he will need it.

An Etherian rider treads the air above them.

In half a heartbeat, I'm leaping out of my hiding place. My bones crack as wings peel themselves from my spine. A wicked-tipped tail whips out behind me. Fingernails elongate into claws. I have never Shifted this abruptly, and I'm dizzy with it. Disoriented as my wings vault me into the air and the world shrinks below me.

The Fae warrior is not expecting me. His mount rears and whinnies in panic, but he regains his seat as I summon a bit of my enchanted fire from the garden and hurl it at him. The shot misses, careening over Briar in a green crackling ball.

Gilded shields spring up around him just before my next attack makes contact. It deflects, and stone explodes where my power connects with the wall of the palace. Half of a second-story balcony plummets toward the garden. Derek knocks Aurora out of the way just before the massive thing flattens a tree. One of the hollow black limbs is cleaved from the trunk and cartwheels into Derek's shoulder. He staggers to his knees. Rage gallops through my blood. That could have been Aurora.

Destroy him.

In two wingbeats, I am high above the Etherian. If my Vila magic will not touch him, I shall have to try another tactic. I tuck in my wings and dive, knowing I have only seconds before his shields reappear. The wind whistles in my ears. A blast of gold— his shields or his magic, I cannot tell—blinds me. But I am just fast enough. I slam into the Etherian's side, raking my claws across his body. The mount screams, flailing, and the Etherian tips off the saddle and plunges to the ground.

The commotion has called the others from the ballroom. The court spills into the garden, and the Etherian hits the ground with a sickening crunch. Miraculously, the fall doesn't kill him, and neither have the wounds my claws inflicted. His steed lands next to him, bucking and stomping its hooves in a futile attempt to protect its master. Demons are upon both in an instant, seizing the Fae's staff and binding him with ropes soaked in blight elixir. The mount is penned in by a ring of Goblins.

I Shift back to my natural form as soon as my heels touch the gravel, the short-lived battle fizzing in my veins. Derek is moaning and clutching his arm. And Aurora—

"You were spying on me. Again."

• • •

The tide of adrenaline in my blood begins to ebb. Night air kisses the bare skin exposed by the ripped fabric in the back of my gown. Someone drapes a cloak around my shoulders, but I feel nothing of its warmth. The betrayal in Aurora's expression, the same look she wore in the throne room barely an hour ago, is bone-deep.

Several Imps surround Derek and begin tending his injuries. They've removed his jacket, and the shoulder of his shirt is slick garnet. He cries out as they prod at the wound, and I hope they make it worse.

"Another lone rider." Malakar kicks the Fae warrior. Golden blood seeps from where my claws shredded his skin. "Where are the others, beast? Waiting for your signal? Come to tear our palace down?"

"The damage wasn't his," I say. "He didn't attack, the same as the battalion that brought the Shifters."

Torin points. "Look at his uniform."

Those nearest the Etherian begin to mutter. The jacket he wears seems to be fashioned out of a latticework of gnarled roots and knobby antlers. Twin horns spiral up from his shoulders and curve behind his back. The orb and laurel leaf sigil of the High Court is displayed on his chest, but this version differs slightly. Within that iridescent orb are two crossed arrows. The Fae symbol of the Hunt.

And that is why this creature's shields were strong enough to withstand my magic. Oryn's Hunt is comprised of the most vicious and feared of the High King's warriors, and the shock of seeing him here snuffs out all thoughts of the disastrous party.

"A member of the Hunt." I grant him a mocking bow. Mortania's loamy presence unspools through my limbs. "To what do we owe the honor? You're not under the protection of a rowan wreath. Has Oryn dispatched you on some clandestine mission?"

The Fae rider glowers in answer.

Valmar's tail flicks. "Maybe the piss-eyed king decided to take the princess whether she wants to go or not."

"If I desired the princess, she would be halfway to the High Court by now." The Etherian's accent is so much like Endlewild's—dry leaves rustling in a wind—that I startle. He resembles the Fae ambassador as well, with skin like the bark of an oak tree. Windswept, reedlike hair is tied back at his nape. A faint pattern of rust-colored moss covers one side of his angular face.

Regan jerks at the rope. Blood drips from beneath the prisoner's jacket and stains the gravel. "That must mean that you *desired* to be captured."

He only grins one of those unnerving Fae grins.

"What is your name?"

"Larkspur," he replies, but it's obviously not his true name.

"And you will not tell us your purpose?" I ask. "If you insist on being obstinate, we will only take you to our dungeons, where your Fae magic will drain out of you, drop by golden drop."

"You think I can be broken?" He sneers. "I am of the Hunt, half-breed."

Regan and the other Vila hiss, and my anger rises in stride with theirs. I gesture for Malakar to hand me Larkspur's staff, and let my fingertips play over the curves of the orb, where the Fae's gilt magic swirls in a tempest.

Larkspur flinches.

"Perhaps you will not go to the dungeons at all and will meet your end right here." I let my power tap lazily against the enchanted glass. "Or . . . you could swear to us. A warrior like yourself would be granted a place of honor in the Dark Court."

Sweat beads across Larkspur's brow and tracks down his high cheekbones. Blood weeps from the gashes on his torso. "There is no honor in tainting my blood."

Tainting. Mortania thrashes in the place where my magic lives, and I run one fingernail along the orb. Larkspur's back hunches.

But then a flicker of movement catches my attention. Aurora has pushed her way forward. She shakes her head once. And I can almost hear her telling me to relent. *"Be the Alyce from before,"* as she was saying to Derek.

But I have no interest in who that Alyce was, weak and ineffective. And I press my magic harder against the enchanted orb of the glass. Mortania whirls, urging me on.

"If this glass breaks, it will destroy both you and your magic. Even if you Marked a successor, it will not matter. Every piece of you will perish here. In the Dark Court."

A mix of rage and terror shines in his gilt eyes. It must be a rare sight to glimpse in a member of the Hunt. I drink it in, inhaling the scents of damp earth and charred steel.

"Tell me why you've come," I try again.

His mouth moves, but he doesn't answer my question. Instead, his attention travels to something over my shoulder.

"Theodoric. I summon you forth. Return from whence you came."

Confusion loosens my grip. "Theo—"

There's a clamor of bodies being toppled. Everyone is moving at once. The Fae rider's mount rears and whinnies, dispersing the Goblins with the thudding of its enormous hooves.

Seemingly out of thin air, Derek—*Derek*—vaults into the saddle and kicks the steed into the air. The Goblins bellow and hurl their tooth-studded clubs at him, but golden protections spring up immediately, blocking their assault. How is he managing that? He zigzags across the garden, keeping low.

"Aurora! Come with me!" Derek unfastens a rope from the saddle. "I'll pull you up!"

"Land!" I yell at him. "This instant—I command it!"

He should be yanked off the beast in the same manner as he was tossed across the library when he broke Aurora's curse. But nothing happens. Above us, Demon sentries nock their bows and fire. Others transform into their shadow forms and wend around Derek in their horrifying shapes. Any attempt to touch him slides away like rivulets of water. And my mind spins with the impossibility of this situation.

Aurora gapes at the scene before her, but she doesn't move. "I won't. I'm sorry."

"Please," Derek implores. "We must go now!"

"Get down from there!" I scream. Mortania's presence pounds like a drumbeat.

He doesn't even look at me.

Aurora backs away. "This is my home."

Derek's expression falters, but he does not repeat the request. He digs his heels into the steed's sides and starts to turn away.

"Wait, please! Take me with you!"

In the tumult, Rose emerges from whatever hole she's been hiding in and bullies her way through the clusters of Imps and Goblins. Hands reach for her, but she wildly fights them off. My magic leaps out of its cage, barreling toward the Grace. But I'm not quick enough.

Derek lassos the rope over his head and throws it down to her. Rose is barely able to secure it around her waist before the mortal reels her into his protective shield and bounds away, the shadow Demons chasing at their heels.

The Vila swarm the Fae prisoner. Hunt or not, he won't last the night. Malakar roars for his Goblins to follow him to the stables and pursue the boy. All I can do is stare in the direction that the steed went. We should hear the screams as Derek's blood begins to boil, and then perhaps the crunch of bone when he falls. But there is only the commotion of the courtyard.

And through it all, the rattling cackle of Fae laughter.

"What," Regan demands, delivering a vicious kick to Larkspur's wounds, "could possibly be funny?"

Larkspur does not react to the agony that must be searing through him. In fact, he appears to be thoroughly enjoying himself. "You will not call him back. Will not catch him. He belongs to the High King."

I stalk through the cluster of Imps and Demons. "What does that mean? Oryn does not concern himself with mortals, especially not a worthless ship's boy."

"That was no mere boy." His dagger-toothed grin stretches wider. "That was the prince of Ryna."

CHAPTER TWENTY-SEVEN

The Vila drag Larkspur to the dungeons, where I doubt he survives long, and the council convenes immediately in our chamber. Torin insists that Aurora join us as well, in case she has any clues to offer about the boy and his abrupt disappearance.

No, not a boy.

A prince.

Ryna. The name rolls around like a marble inside of my brain. I can still picture the first prince, the star-chosen prince, striding to the royal dais on the night he was meant to break Aurora's curse. All those years ago, the Ryna astrologers predicted that their prince's kiss would be the end to Aurora's curse. They were correct—just a hundred years too soon.

Let one Ryna prince go in order to have another wash up a century later. They're worse than the rodents Callow brings me.

"How did you not know of this?" Regan barks at Neve. "This is what you *do*, isn't it?"

Anyone else would be cowed beneath her fury, but the questions simply slide off the Shifter leader's unflappable façade. "Pieces of intelligence often come together swiftly and without warning. Would you like to try your hand at spying?"

Regan seethes and sits back in her chair, jerking her dagger from the sheath in her boot and drawing the blade through her fingertips. I can guess what else she'd like to do with it.

"Was Derek the 'missing piece' you said you were investigating?" Torin asks, calm and contemplative despite the events of the evening. It is a disposition I do not share.

"He was."

My temper rises. "You believed we had a prince in disguise in our midst, and you didn't think it was pertinent to tell us?"

"I did not want to risk the boy finding out that we suspected his identity until I was certain," Neve continues. The golden gems on her gown wink. "In Malterre, court leaders understood that some intelligence must be handled carefully. Shifters were granted considerable discretion to perform their duties. I expected this court to be of the same mind."

Her implication about my leadership—or lack thereof—slinks across the table. The shadows in the corners of the room seem to coil and uncoil, like those in the black tower.

"It's best you share these theories now," Regan says tightly, the bone spikes on her knuckles stretched pale around the hilt of her dagger.

Neve rearranges her skirts, taking her time in answering. "Shortly after the light Fae were caught lurking across the sea, my Starlings reported that one of the kingdoms, Ryna, had lost their prince. In my experience, princes are not typically misplaced. And as Ryna was largely—and suspiciously—indifferent about the matter, I instructed my Starlings to probe further. We could not locate the prince, but we did discover that his disappearance coincided with the shipwreck that brought us our *Derek*."

I taste the steel-loam of my power. "You've been sitting on this information for—"

"Patience, Mistress," Neve interrupts. She traces the veins of silver in the table. Torin nudges me. My blood pounds hot. "Even after learning of that intriguing coincidence of timing, I remained unconvinced that Derek was indeed the missing prince. For one thing, the Ryna prince's name was not Derek. And based off the last known sighting of the prince in his realm, there would not have been enough time for his journey here. Unless"—she pauses, her focus sweeping the table—"it had been a *Fae* ship that ferried him to our shores. And if it was a Fae ship, it would mean that Ryna—not Terault, where the boy claimed he was from—was in league with the Etherians. Larkspur's actions tonight all but confirmed their alliance."

Dragon's teeth. I marvel yet again at my own obliviousness when it came to the boy, the countless details I'd overlooked. Derek's dashing charm and his grace when he danced with Aurora. Even the way his hands had blistered when he was working in the stables. Not simply because the Imps had sabotaged his gloves, but because he was unaccustomed to hard labor. And then there was Derek's interest in government. His willingness to do "whatever was necessary" to reform his realm. But he was never a revolutionary. He was a member of the royal family. Mortania rumbles in her cave, and I clench my fists.

"But I'm still confused as to why the Fae are involved at all," Torin says. "Why would they care enough to send a royal in disguise? What could he have accomplished for them? He cannot have been immune to Nimara's binding curse."

"Aye." Valmar mutters into his wineglass. "Too many details. Makes my head ache."

Neve grants the Imp leader a look that suggests his thinking is not the only source of his pain. "We all know the Fae conduct their bargains with their words. And among those words are names. Their *true* names."

A low tempo of thunder rolls over the realm.

"But Derek isn't—"

Neve clicks her tongue. "Theodoric, Mistress."

Understanding swishes at the corners of my mind, but I can't fully grasp it. Regan's leathers creak as she leans forward in her chair.

"That name, the prince's, was the missing piece I was hunting here at the palace. And it was the reason he was able to evade your binding curse tonight. Oryn likely invoked a glamour magic to put a blessing on the boy. Theodoric is the Ryna prince, protected by the High King of the Fae. *Derek* is the ship's boy from Terault, bound to Nimara. When Larkspur spoke the boy's true name, he activated the first bond—the blessing from the High King that undermined your curse simply because the boy was no longer Derek."

"No." The word is more Mortania's than mine. She churns in her sea of wrath like a monster in the deep. "Oryn can't *do* that. He can't imbue that kind of power on a mortal."

"He did so with the Briar crown." I startle a little at the comment. It's from Aurora, who is standing by the wall of windows, studying the horizon. She's been so quiet I nearly forgot she was here. "Oryn's blessing is why no one else could wear it. The crown itself would have killed anyone who tried."

A memory flashes—of Queen Mariel in the throne room on the morning after Aurora and I spent our night in the library. She was brandishing her crown at her husband, daring him to wear it if he wanted to be sole ruler of Briar. Not even Tarkin, arrogant fool that he was, had been brave enough to touch the gilded wreath of bramble and thorn.

"Correct, Princess," Neve says. "It is much the same idea. Oryn's magic protected the boy in the same way it did the crown. Just a drop, which carried his blessing."

"But Derek wore my curse mark," I insist. "I saw it react on more than one occasion. He wasn't able to lie. I made direct inquiry into his life in Terault. He had siblings. He wanted to make sure his family survived. The mark would have burned him if he was false, and it would have killed him if he was plotting against me."

"But did he lie?" Neve tilts her head at me. "Or were his answers sufficiently vague to be considered true? He was, after all, a 'ship's boy' while he traveled on the Etherian's vessel. A ship that might indeed have sailed from Terault's shores instead of Ryna's. He may have had siblings. He cared for his family—you just never inquired whether they were royal."

The silty taste of my power cuts between my teeth, and I have to resist the urge to hurl my wineglass across the room. Regan spews a stream of curses.

"But why tonight?" Torin presses. "Why would Oryn free the prince now?"

"We do not know that the rider was sent to free the prince, or even why the prince was here to begin with," Neve replies. "Larkspur could have been dispatched to relay instruction to the boy from the High King. After all, he did not attack."

"We've never seen any others 'relaying' messages," Regan argues.

"That we know of."

The rain is picking up, glass groaning against the panes. The chamber buzzes with our shared frustration.

"So." The silver blade of Regan's dagger flashes in the candlelight. "We've had a prince under our roof for months without knowing it, secretly working with the High King of the Fae."

"And now he's gone back to that king." Valmar curses and pours yet another goblet of wine. "After learning the ins and outs of our court."

"I'll give the order for more sentries immediately," Torin says, and the fissures mapping her body undulate from scarlet to yellow. "And we need to start planning what to do when Malakar returns."

"Attack, is what," Valmar says. He picks up a marker and slams it down in the center of Oryn's domain. "Who knows what that mortal is telling Oryn."

"We cannot be too hasty," Torin cautions. "Defense should be our strategy, especially if what Larkspur did was deliberate. Part of a larger plan."

They begin volleying ideas back and forth, but I am not finished with Neve. "You kept this from us."

She doesn't even blink. "I have already explained my reasons."

"And I do not accept them."

Tension hums taut between us.

"Nimara," Torin interjects, "this is not—"

But I'm not interested in her opinion on this matter. "This is exactly why I don't trust Shifters. They lie and manipulate and keep information back." I point at Neve, signet ring glinting in the light. "She should go to the dungeons, where we can peel back her layers one by one. Find whatever lies are nesting in her rot."

Neve goes perfectly still. The rest of the table gapes at me in the thrumming silence. Even Valmar's ears lie flat.

"Nimara." Torin's tone is like flint. "That is no way to speak to a member of council. Neve is an integral member of this court. Apologize."

I do not. Will not. I grip the arms of my chair, pulse hammering in my palms.

"Spare me," Neve says. "Despite what our mistress thinks, I am not interested in *lies*. And I will take my leave, if no one objects."

No one does. The Shifter leader gathers her skirts and stalks from the room.

"That was unacceptable," Torin hisses when she's gone. I can almost feel the furious heat radiating from her body. But I don't care.

"You don't know them like I do," I say.

She sighs, smoke curling from the surface of her skin. "*You* do not know her at all. Nor, I expect, do you even want to."

I grind my teeth. Valmar clumsily tries to change the subject back to how we will respond to the High Court. But my attention travels to where Aurora stands by the windows. She might as well be made of stone, staring through the seamless glass, toward the second Ryna prince and the future she might have had. One she might wish she could reclaim.

CHAPTER TWENTY-EIGHT

The court disperses while we wait for Malakar's return. Sentries are doubled, and I walk the battlements until the cold drives me inside. But I cannot be still. A prince was right under my nose for months—Oryn's informant. But my rage toward him pales when compared to that for Neve.

I cannot believe the council will not recognize her for what she is—another, far more sinister version of Kal, every one of her actions tailored to suit her own agenda. But what *is* that agenda? Kal wanted me to become the physical embodiment of Mortania so that he could be reunited with his love. Is Neve colluding with the mortal realms? Is she thinking to wait until the war is over and become head of the Dark Court? The possibilities swirl through my mind until I'm dizzy with them.

Worry not, pet. We will take care of her.

Not soon enough.

Before I know it, I'm back in the abandoned library. I haven't been here since I wrecked it, and the unspent adrenaline in my veins begs me to do so again. But I resist. The satisfaction of destruction would be too fleeting to be worth the effort. It's strange to me that the same place can house both wonderful and terrible memories. Moonlight shines through the gap in the wall, and I remember the way its pallid silver glowed against Aurora's bare skin. There is the place where we slept, tangled together. Where she touched me with a tenderness that made me ache. Where she told me she loved me exactly the way I was. That she thought I was beautiful.

Emotion claws up my throat. She'll never look at me like that again.

That stupid, wretched prince. If only he hadn't come. If only Laurel hadn't lied.

But would you take any of it back? Mortania asks. *If you had to do it over again?*

I fold my arms over myself and walk to the gap in the wall. Bits of bramble and debris crunch and pop under my footsteps. Former Briar is wrapped in a misty, post-storm haze.

No. I wouldn't.

"I thought I'd find you up here." Regan picks her way through the mess to stand beside me. And I'm suddenly self-conscious.

"Are you here to scold me about Neve?"

"On the contrary," she says. "I'm beginning to understand your reasons for hesitancy regarding the Starlings."

At least someone does. Pages ride the salty wind blowing in from the sea. Their fluttering movement almost sounds like laughter, the same sort that hounded me every day when I lived in Lavender House. The laughter of the Graces and the nobles. I've built my realm upon their bones, and yet still I cannot outrun it.

"I take no pleasure in telling you I told you so." But I did tell her. "Why did you come looking for me if not because of what happened with the council?"

She picks up a ruined book. Dust motes glimmer in the air. "I want to talk about what happened at the party, with the princess."

That is the *last* thing I want to revisit. I try to cross to another part of the library, but Regan follows.

"She rejected you. You offered her a place here, and she threw it back in your face. Literally."

The memory surges, all claws and fangs.

"And what? You want *her* taken to the dungeons now?"

"I don't know. But she's not one of us. She made that perfectly clear tonight."

Mortania flickers in something like agreement, the scent of her power stinging in my nose. I rub at the ache in my temples. "She was confused. I lied to her, and—"

"And how many excuses will you make?" Regan's green eyes gleam like twin blades in the gloom. "You spend all your time thinking of how best to please her. Gifts and parties and grand gestures. And she doesn't even appreciate them!"

"You don't know that. In the garden, she—"

"I know that you love her."

I take a step back. "What? No. I said that she—"

"I know what you said." Her jaw works. "And I also know *you*. Even when you lie."

"But." Panic begins to set in. My breaths come fast and short. "When did you . . ."

She laughs a little, but it's not unkind. "From the first day I saw her. There was no other reason you would have kept her here. Or why you would have burned down a realm and spent decades trying to wake her."

I chew my lip, entirely exposed. And it kindles my anger. "I suppose I'm to have nothing of my own, then? I'm so predictable. Anyone could guess my secrets."

"That's what I'm trying to tell you—you don't need to have secrets from me. I crossed an ocean to be by your side. I see every part of you." Regan's touch trails along my forearm and up to my shoulder, raising gooseflesh in its wake. "Parts that others might consider wrong or evil, but which I wholly adore."

Confusion ripples through me. Regan . . . adores me? Not like that, I tell myself. It's not what she means. But then her lips are on mine, tasting of cool, wet earth. Of spice and charred leather. Of Vila, a taste I would know anywhere, though I've never encountered it before.

For a moment, I allow myself to melt into an embrace that is warm and inviting. Regan's strong, sinewy muscles are firm beneath her leathers, bone spikes like tiny mountain ranges along her shoulders and collarbones. She guides me backward, both of us landing in a chair, limbs tangling. I'd forgotten how good it feels to be desired. And Regan does desire me. I can feel it in the caress of her fingertips. The nipping of her teeth on my neck. And it would be so easy to let myself be swallowed by this—lose myself in the heat coursing between us.

But she is not Aurora.

"No," I say, gently pushing her back. "I cannot."

She looks at me, lips swollen from our kiss. Eyes shining. "Will you really shut me out? For her?"

I cannot hold her gaze. The hurt blazing within it threatens to undo me. And the worst part is that I *want* to love Regan like she wants me to. I want this stubborn heart in my chest to change, those chambers reserved for Aurora ossifying as if they had never been. But deep in my soul, deeper even than where Mortania dwells, I know that it will not. The kiss between Aurora and me broke one curse and began another. One I will carry until the day I die.

"I'm sorry," I whisper.

Regan clears her throat and straightens her jacket. "One day you will see what's in front of you. But I'm not your plaything. Or some consolation prize. I will not wait for you forever."

And then she's gone.

I spend the rest of the night huddled in the mess I made. Sleep comes in fits and starts, filled with distorted images of Aurora's outrage, and Derek bolting away on his steed, and Neve's conniving smirk. By the time dawn breaks, my very bones ache.

I start back to my rooms, hoping Malakar has returned—though I haven't heard any sentry blasts. My eyes are so tired that I have to Shift to keep from smacking into walls in the dank and cloistered corridors. But the distant glow of a candle is bright as it trickles through the crack in a semi-concealed door. I halt in my tracks. Hardly anyone else ventures this deep into the palace. I tiptoe closer, curiosity piqued, and position myself so that I can just peek through the slit in the panel. The room beyond is vacant and relieved of most of its furnishings, but someone is examining the remains of a tapestry.

Aurora.

The door hinges squeal, drawing her attention. And I freeze, caught.

"I— What are you doing here?" Even I cringe at the question, one spoken like a jailer.

Her candle flame flickers in the draft. The events of the last day have taken their toll. There's a weariness in her posture that does not suit her, and I worry again about the effects of the curse lifting. I should search Rose's room for the finished elixirs. Or perhaps see if another Grace in the Garden can accomplish the task.

"You of all people should know how good I am at evading my guards," Aurora replies. "They're sound sleepers."

She wants to be alone, certainly doesn't want me, but I can't convince my feet to reverse their course. And after the total disaster of last night, I crave her company. Which I realize is insane, seeing as most of the disaster occurred between us. But Aurora says nothing as I approach, only continues her inspection of the tapestry. The scene depicts Leythana. She stands at the helm of one of her legendary dragon ships, their flared and taloned wings repurposed into sails and wide jaws open at the bow in a jagged-toothed cry.

Aurora's fingertips brush against the threadbare embroidery. A few strands still glint.

"The Imps could repair it, if you like. It might not look exactly the same as you remember." They might decide Leythana looks better with horns. Or a wolf's maw.

"No. The damage is done." She picks at the fraying images, lingering over the dragon bowsprit. "You look a mess. What happened to you?"

Regan's kiss still burns on my lips. "I didn't sleep well."

The silence is oppressive, and I grapple for something—anything—to fill it. The only subject I can think of is the one I'd like to avoid entirely. But it looms like one of the Demons in their shadow forms. And I won't be able to outrun it forever.

"About what happened in the throne room," I begin, vainly

attempting to clear the awkwardness in my voice. "With Rose, and what I said to the court. I'd like to explain."

"Why? Your excuses will be as inadequate now as they were then."

I suppose I deserve that. "Please—"

"And I think," she interrupts, "deep down, that I always knew."

Wind whistles through the cracks in the walls.

"You . . . knew that anyone could break your curse?"

"No. But there never seemed to be anything special about Derek. Not in the way of curse-breaking anyway. He wasn't my true love."

Shivers race down my spine, and I dare let myself hope that the title still belongs to me.

"I knew there was something you were keeping from me," Aurora continues. "When Rose said what she did . . . it all made sense."

That Grace would be wise to never return here.

"Please understand that I—"

"Will you let me speak for once?" She waits until I nod. "When you broke my first curse, I was willing to sacrifice everything for you. I stood before my parents and named you as my future wife. Future queen, to rule beside me. I didn't care that you were the Dark Grace, or what the council would say, or even how the realm would react. You had the same opportunity to stand beside me last night, and you didn't take it. Worse, you lied about us— again."

I feel about the same size as the mice Callow brings me. "I'm sorry."

"I don't forgive you."

Tense, horrible silence descends on us again. Even Leythana, nearly indiscernible, seems to be glowering at me. But I cannot leave. I fear that if I do, we'll never speak again.

But I can't endure this oppressive quiet, either. I gesture at the tapestry. "Did you ever find out what she offered the Vila in exchange for Oryn's staff?"

It is an excruciatingly random question, and I think I hear her let out an annoyed breath.

"No," she answers tightly.

"I wish I had more books or papers to offer you," I blunder on. "I've always been curious about Leythana's early life. There isn't even anything left in the crypt, like the mementos of the other queens."

Aurora traces the stitching of a taloned, dragon-wing sail, which shines in the flickering candlelight. "It's a shame." Her shoulders soften in the slightest. "I want to know more, especially about the dragon ships. The palace was so stifling, and sometimes I yearned to just . . . fly away."

She still does. I can see the desire written on her face. And as much as it pains me that she would want to leave here—leave me—I have an idea.

"What if I could show you what that might have been like?"

"What do you mean?"

"You said you wanted to fly. I could help you."

Her brow rumples, but I can tell the thought tempts her. "I'm not a Shifter."

"No," I agree, grinning. "But I happen to know how to grant you wings."

CHAPTER TWENTY-NINE

Chaos is skeptical at first. As is Aurora. I can't blame her. The Fae beast towers over her head, and one of his massive hooves could crush her skull like a grape. But after some coaxing on my part, and perhaps because he realizes he'll get a reprieve from his pen, Chaos allows himself to be saddled and bridled.

I set the mounting block to one side of him for Aurora. She worries the edge of her cloak. "You're sure this is safe? Derek told me he's never managed to ride him."

"That's because the Ryna prince is incompetent—and Chaos hates him."

Chaos chuffs in what might be confirmation, and her lips twitch up.

"I'll be right beside you," I promise. "I won't let you fall. Well—not very far anyway."

She is so close that my breath catches. But then she gathers her skirts and steps onto the block. "You'd better not."

• • •

Chaos needs no encouragement to bolt into the gray morning. Aurora lets out a cry as his huge wings boost them into the air. I Shift and tear after them, worried that I've given the Fae steed too much freedom, and that—bond or not—he will attempt to flee with no thought of Aurora's weight on his back. But then she straightens, tossing her head back and letting the wind take her golden hair. Chaos is a streak of silver in the sky, his tail like that of a comet as he soars over Briar. A sound of pure delight leaves Aurora's lips as the realm shrinks below us, one I think I will remember until my last breath.

Callow, the clever kestrel, joins us almost as soon as we've left the stables. She sails alongside me, entertaining Aurora no end. My kestrel chirrups, challenging me to rolls and races as we typically do on these pleasure flights. But I'm careful to keep Aurora in sight, always close enough to dive and intercept her if Chaos takes a bad turn. But the steed is remarkably steady. He whinnies in unmistakable joy, letting Aurora steer him from one end of the shoreline to another. As her confidence increases, she bids him plummet and dip close enough to the steel-capped waves so that the tip of his wing sends freezing spray into her face. We loop over the Crimson Cliffs, high enough that she can almost touch the bellies of the clouds. It's Aurora who signals for us to come down. We land neatly on the cliffs outside Briar's main gates. Callow perches on my shoulder.

"Done already?"

Aurora slides from Chaos's back. Rivers of bronze and crimson race over his body as he folds in his wings. Aurora pats his flank. "Not at all. But I wanted to take in this view. And then let's head that way." She points east.

Callow warbles her agreement, earning a laugh.

"We'll have to be careful," I say, rubbing warmth into my limbs. The cold is like a blade this close to the sea. "Chaos isn't accustomed to so much exercise yet. I don't want him getting tired and falling out of the sky." The steed snorts in what is undoubtedly offense. "Another day I can show you—"

But she's stopped smiling, her attention fixed on a spot behind me. I turn and discover the black tower hobbling over the tops of trees. Dragon's teeth. I should have paid attention.

"I thought you would have destroyed it," she says quietly.

"I meant to." Too many times to count. "But it was the last place you were awake, and I . . . couldn't."

The sharp-edged memory of that night rises between us like a specter, and I hate it for spoiling this moment.

Aurora stalks toward the tree line.

"What are you— Wait!" I run after her, then remember Chaos and pivot back. Callow complains and flaps away. "It's not safe. The stone is unstable."

"Good," she calls back. "Let it fall."

"Aurora!"

She plunges ahead into the gnarled woods.

Given that I had to secure Chaos's reins to a sturdy enough tree, Aurora reaches the ancient oaken door well before I do. Her stubbornness knows no bounds. She kicks at the warped wood until it gives way, then plows into the sooty dimness without so much as a backward glance.

Another century of Briar's storms and the change in our climate should have toppled this structure, but the gaping hole in the side is only slightly wider. The stones are moldier and the stench of dead fish and rancid seaweed stronger. The banners are all but demolished, only scraps of fabric hanging from rotting beams. The graveyard of debris glistens with silt. I jump at every shadow, imagining the prisoner who dwelled here, bound by the light Fae. Mortania hisses.

Leave this place.

I'd like nothing more. But, as if spelled, Aurora makes for the stairs.

"Where are you going?"

"I want to see where it happened."

Callow grumbles, disliking this turn of events as much as I do. But I trudge up the brine-slick steps anyway. The door to my old room is just a shell now, eaten by storms and squalls. Cobwebs drape the corners. Decaying furnishings litter the floor. There's the corner where Kal bound me with his shadows while he Shifted into my shape and lured Aurora to the cursed spindle. The place where he fell, his bones long turned to dust. Callow flies to the window casing and ruffles her wings, yellow eyes keen and vicious.

A growl jolts me back to the present. Aurora charges across the room, toward the wobbling remains of the spinning wheel. Bits of curved wood sprawl in a haphazard arrangement around the stand. Aurora snatches up a jagged spoke and slams it against the wall. It splinters with a wet crunch. She hurls the pieces out the window and into the sea, upsetting Callow. Wrenches a leg free of the stand and stomps on it, sobbing.

"Aurora." I go to her. She slaps at me, but then all the pent-up energy pours out of her. Her knees buckle, and I stumble down with her, pressing her against me as tightly as I can. Her face rests in the curve of my neck, tears hot on my skin.

"I'm sorry," I say, over and over again. "I'm so sorry. About the party, and what I said. The curse. I never meant to hurt you."

She pushes back, her lavender gaze bright as jewels and sharp as glass. "Why did you do it, then? Why did you burn Briar and let me sleep? And I don't want to hear more excuses. Just the truth."

"I—" Everything I've told her in the past smashes together in my mind. I was protecting her. I was building a realm for us. But, in this moment, back where everything started, it all sounds hollow. "I was afraid," I say. "Kal coated the spindle with *my* magic, and you might have died because of me. And then they were going to make you look at me the way all of Briar had looked at me for my whole life, and that was even worse. It was miracle enough that I won your heart the first time. I never believed I would be able to win it a second."

Aurora blinks at me. I'm not even sure she's breathing. "Alyce. That's the first time I've heard your voice in a hundred years."

And then there's something else written on the lines of her face—something I never thought I'd glimpse again. She tips slightly forward. And then her lips brush against mine. It's the same feeling as when we broke the first curse—the world splitting in half and careening back together in a smear of light and color. I deepen the kiss, drinking her in, ravenous after so many years of being starved of her. She tastes of salty tears and sweet summer berries and the heady essence that is her. One of my hands tangles in the exquisite silk of her hair. The other slides down the curve of her body, moaning as I'm reintroduced to every rise and dip. Her own fingers travel down to the laces at the front of my dress, tugging them loose. My breath halts in anticipation of feeling her hands on my chest, the tiny explosions about to happen in my bloodstream as she explores hidden places.

But then Aurora rips herself away from me. It's like the sun being robbed from the sky.

"This is too much," she says, scooting back.

The absence of her touch is painful, my body reeling. But I force my trembling fingers to retie my laces. "I understand."

A long moment passes between us, the kiss still crackling like wildfire. We sit in the molten core, pretending it isn't burning around us. I lick my lips, tasting her.

Aurora picks at the rubble around us. And then her attention snags on something. She digs through a mound of crumbled wood and dirt and extracts a large ring. A fat sapphire is set within a wide golden band.

"My father's." She wipes the stone with her skirt. It dazzles in the shafts of sunlight. Refracted rainbows dance over her face. "The one you were supposed to curse."

She slips the ring onto her thumb. It's far too big, as Tarkin was a mountain of girth. "When I stole it from Father's wardrobe, I was so certain that we were on the verge of something bigger than the two of us. Monumental."

"So was I," I say, drawing my knees close to my body. "I had the same feeling when Regan and I decided to establish the Dark Court. Like we were forging an entirely new world."

Aurora doesn't comment, but her eyebrows lift subtly. And her silence is weighted with judgment. My hackles rise. "What? Do you not approve of what we did?"

"I didn't say that," she replies—too coolly.

"Yes, I think there's much you're not saying."

"Like what?"

The answer surfaces, ugly enough that it must be true. "Like you think *your* version of Briar, your reign, would be better than ours."

She points at me. "You just said that—not me."

"But you've thought it, haven't you?" Aurora fusses with the ring. I laugh, darkly. "And who exactly would have benefited from Queen Aurora's rule?"

Yes, pet. Mortania stirs. *Who indeed?*

"Everyone," she says, as if it is the most obvious statement in the world.

"Even me? What about *my* family? You pride yourself on standing before your parents and naming me as Briar's second queen. But would you have crowned me? And what of the tapestries celebrating dead Vila, those I passed every time I visited the palace? The trophies from the first war. Were you even going to take them down?"

"You think I would have been a tyrant, like my father?"

I lift a shoulder. "It's interesting that you won't directly answer the question."

"Why should I?" she fires back. "You've answered so few of mine, except with lies."

My blood hums. "Well, I'm sorry you don't find me as biddable as you used to, back when I was the Dark Grace and at your royal command. It's a pity your prince flew off. His lies were much easier for you to tolerate, weren't they? As were his kisses. Probably better than mine ever were."

Waves smash against the base of the tower.

Aurora gathers herself up and goes to the window, watching

the crows and vultures circle over the quicksilver sea. The fragile truce between us lies smoldering at our feet as soon as it formed, but I'm tired of tiptoeing through every interaction—desperate to please her when she is interested only in punishing me. When she ignores and dismisses everything Briar put me through.

"I don't know what I would have done," she says eventually.

It wounds me deeper than I'd like to admit. And a horrible thought oozes over my skull. That Regan was right. I've put Aurora on a pedestal. But we were always too different.

Yes, pet. Forget her.

"Perhaps you should have flown off with Prince Theodoric, then."

Aurora stiffens. Callow fixes me with a reproachful stare. And I sulk as waves hurl themselves against the base of the cliff, picking up brittle pieces of rubble and crushing them between my fingers.

"Do you love me?" The question is almost too low for me to hear.

I drop a scrap of wood. "How can you ask me that?"

She turns, backlit by the watery sunlight. "Because you haven't said it. Not once since I woke."

The sea heaves and my mind reels, riffling back through all the moments we've shared since her curse lifted. I must have said it. Even if I hadn't, she must *know* it.

"And now I'm worried," Aurora goes on, "that you don't love me anymore. That in the last hundred years, you became obsessed with the idea of me. And that is not the same as love."

Grackles trade their calls outside.

"But the garden, and—"

"I appreciated the garden," she says, and I think she means it.

"And when you gave Elspeth the book, and when you helped us hold the funeral for Briar—though I know you didn't understand our need for one. *That* is the Alyce who loved me. The Alyce I need."

My throat tightens. "You speak as though I'm a completely different person. That I woke up one morning and decided to seize Briar on a whim. But I had reason—*good* reason."

"And I know from watching my father that there is a right way and wrong way to use power."

"And who decides what that is?" I throw up my hands. "You? Are your intentions better—worthier—than mine because you're a princess and I'm what? A villain?"

"*You were never a villain to me,*" she'd said, years ago. But she does not repeat it now. She doesn't say anything at all.

Wind pushes in from the sea, salt-laced.

"Sometimes I think we could compare our wounds for the next century and still discover fresh ones."

A shudder runs through me. That's exactly what I'd thought about the war—how we don't heal because we like to bleed. But it's not how I want things to be between *us*. I sit down on a fallen beam. "And so we're just going to bicker for the rest of our lives?"

Callow mutters something that is unmistakably exasperation.

Aurora is quiet for a long time, tapping the ring against the casement. "When we were in the garden, you asked if I could start again."

I cross my arms. "And then you threw the ring in my face."

"Because I was furious with you. I still am. But . . ."

An eternity hangs in her pause.

She looks down at her father's ring. The jewel glimmers. "I'll never agree with the war and the violence. But I'm weary of this never-ending arguing and accusation. If we don't start working together now, we never will."

Mortania churns in the place where my magic lives. *She is manipulating you.*

My head begins to throb. My initial instinct is to trust the ancient Vila. But the way Aurora is looking at me . . .

"Alyce." Despite everything, my name on her lips turns my insides to hot wax. She reaches for me, and I'm pulled like the tide. Like she was to that cursed spinning wheel a hundred years ago. "I'm willing to try if you are."

Mortania vehemently objects, and a small part of me screams to heed her warning. But it doesn't matter. Nothing matters, save for the spark in Aurora's amethyst eyes. One of possibility.

"All right," I say. "Let's try."

CHAPTER THIRTY

The next day, another storm rolls in from the sea. Winds pound the palace and rain drips in through the cracks in the windows. The Demon sentries are doubled, but there's no sign of Malakar or his Goblins. Much of the court shelters in the throne room, their unease roiling in time with the punishing gales as the hours slog by. The Goblins cannot focus on their gambling. The Imps care nothing for pranks. Everyone huddles together in clusters, whispering.

"Do you think we've lost them?" I ask Torin. Even the Demon leader is unsettled. She fidgets with the loose threads on her sleeve and flinches at every fork of lightning.

"I do not know. The Fae steed was one of the Hunt's. It might have been faster than a typical mount. Malakar would not have given up the chase, no matter the risks."

Callow perches on the back of the throne. She bridles and chuffs, as if claiming that she wouldn't have given up, either. "We should send a scouting party after the storm passes."

Torin murmurs something in agreement and pulls at her pendant.

Across the room, Aurora is sitting with a circle of Imps around her, attempting to comfort them. I notice how Regan gives her a wide berth as she paces the perimeter of the chamber, flipping the serpent hilt of her dagger from hand to hand. The Vila leader and I haven't spoken since our kiss, and I feel more than a little guilty at having avoided her. Especially since I was kissing Aurora in the meantime, and making promises that would cause Regan to want to skin me alive.

Thunder claps. The doors of the throne room swing wide. I'm on my feet in an instant, Callow shrieking and flapping to my shoulder. Two Demon sentries stride through the clamor of the court, carrying something. No—a small body. A Goblin body.

"Found him outside the main gates," one of the Demons explains. The pair set their burden down gently at the base of the dais.

I recognize this Goblin. His black hair is matted to his head, which lolls to one side. His limbs are limp. Several other of his cadre hurry forward to tend him. The mossy green of his skin is waxy. Water from his drenched clothing pools around him.

"Is he . . ."

"Alive," the other sentry says. "He carried this." She holds out a plain burlap sack, crudely tied together and spotted with brown stains.

Dread slithers between my ribs. Callow's talons prick through the fabric of my gown.

Torin descends from her seat and accepts the bag from her sentry. She tugs at the rope and looks inside. There's a moment of charged silence as she pulls something from the bag—and then a roar like the keening of a wounded beast, so loud that small bits of mortar fall from the ceiling. The floor vibrates with the stomping of a hundred boots.

It takes my mind a moment to process what I'm seeing. Lightning brightens the angular features. The snubbed snout of a nose. The scaly hemlock-green skin and small horns poking through bristly curls.

Malakar.

His bloodshot Goblin eyes stare back at me, leaden and void. His lips are open in a final scream, teeth reduced to broken nubs. His head is mounted on a gilded plate like those served at royal dinners. Like the Goblin who was returned to us at the start of the war. The floor lists wildly and I stumble.

A folded parchment flutters from the plate. Regan snatches it up, then reads:

For your collection.

Like a stone dropped into water, the impact of the Etherians' message reverberates outward.

"Malakar!" a Goblin bellows. Renard, one of Malakar's closest warriors.

Torin slumps to the floor with the plate on her lap, tears hissing on her cheeks when they meet the molten grooves in her skin. The court is wailing, vowing vengeance and death and every other torture their minds can conjure. Regan raises her staff and leads the Vila in their battle cry. Mortania thrashes in the place where my magic lives.

And in the feral howling of the court, in the aching of my heart, I feel the first fissures in the vow I made to Aurora. It wouldn't matter if I tried or not. There will never be a way forward with the Etherians, not after this. Torin's philosopher was right. The hatred between us is in our blood. There's no scrubbing it out. And I'm not even sure I would if given the chance.

The unconscious Goblin survives.

His name is Clip. He's badly burned, half-drowned by the storm, and wounded, but he awakens the next day and insists he's well enough to debrief with the council.

"The Hunt was waiting for us." A mug of hot wine sits before him in the war room and his small form is cocooned in a thick blanket. Still, he trembles. "We chased the boy for ages—his steed was faster than any creature I've ever seen. But as soon as dawn broke, the others appeared. It was too late to turn back."

My gaze travels involuntarily to Malakar's painfully vacant seat.

"If the Hunt was skulking near our lands, why was there just one rider that night?" Valmar's hooked nose is swollen from weeping.

"A ruse, probably," Torin says. The grooves in her skin are dim with the shade of her grief. "They likely sent the rider to lure Nimara out, presuming she would pursue the boy herself, and then they planted themselves far enough away from the palace so that she couldn't summon reinforcements. Neve may know more when she returns."

The Shifter leader left us immediately after the debacle of our last council meeting, supposedly to glean information from her Starlings. But who knows what she's really up to.

The knots of my stomach cinch tighter. This is my fault. I should have fed Derek to the Goblins as soon as he set foot in our court. Should never have let Malakar and the others venture after him alone. Mortania's presence undulates in its cave.

"And the boy?" Regan is trying to be respectful, but the question is tinged with impatience.

Clip's snout quivers. "We was gaining on him. But then the Hunt—I never seen them coming. They popped up from no-wheres." He swallows. Fat tears track down his moss-green face and splash on the table. "I was behind, but Malakar and the oth-ers couldn't stop fast enough. Rode right into them. One of the Hunt caught me. Held me while . . . while they . . ." A thousand gruesome ends swarm within his choked silence. "After, they dropped me outside the gates with . . . Malakar."

Callow mutters from her perch on the back of my chair. And I swallow back another bout of tears with a deep drink of wine.

"There was nothing you could have done," Torin assures Clip. "Malakar would be relieved to know you live."

Valmar grunts his agreement. "And he would tell us we need to strike. Regan can lead the next campaign in his stead."

"And be intercepted by the Hunt or some other battalion?" Torin asks. "Oryn will expect such retaliation."

"I don't give a Goblin's tit about what the Fae king expects." The Imp leader climbs onto the table and rearranges the markers.

Clip wipes his snout with a corner of his blanket. "I want to go, too. Give 'em what they gave us and worse."

I study the boundaries of the High Court on the map. It's shielded by the strongest protections known to the Fae, and Oryn is squatting inside them like a toad, waiting for us to send armies so that he can return their heads on golden plates.

Anger crackles in my wrists. Mortania whirls, and the scent of charred steel and loam fills me up—the same as it did when I swept Tarkin's archers off the battlements and loosed my green fire on this palace. We do not have time for treaties or amicable resolutions.

"He's right." The attention of the table veers to me. "Caution has served us in the past, but that time is over. We stop sending piecemeal forces. One last battle to end it all. And then these lands will belong to the Dark Court alone."

Valmar and Clip cheer their approval. Torin studies me with that unreadable Demon expression, but she nods. And Regan looks at me like it's the first time she's seeing me in a long time. The corners of her lips curl up.

"Ours alone," she echoes.

The skin between my shoulder blades prickles. I try not to think of Aurora.

CHAPTER THIRTY-ONE

Malakar is laid to rest with a ceremony that rivals any other. The Goblins bury him in the palace crypt. Not alongside the effigies of the queens, of course. There is a special chamber they dug out years ago to bury their own, and they fill their leader's stone casket with piles of jewels and treasures, as well as weapons he designed. We feast in his honor through the next day, sharing stories that cause us all to laugh and weep in the same breath. I recount his arrival at court—Malakar and several other Goblins hid in barrels on a human ship, then commandeered the vessel and navigated to our shores. He'd stood on the prow as the ship pulled into the harbor and kneeled before me for the only instance I would allow him to do so.

As the memorial ends, the Goblins unanimously elect Renard as their leader. And the whole of the court is desperate in their cries for vengeance. A final stand against Oryn, so that none of us will ever fall victim to the Fae again. I give more blood than I've ever shed to the blight elixir in preparation. We trade plans and counterplans around the council chamber table as the inevitable battle takes shape.

My renewed vigor toward our cause is a balm to the hundred tiny rifts between myself and Regan. We've still not spoken of our kiss, and there's an unsettled energy between us when our heads are pressed close over the map of Etheria or when our hands brush, passing markers back and forth. But we're slowly finding our way back to each other, and I'm grateful for that.

I avoid Aurora entirely. She sends me notes from her chambers, asking for texts on various subjects or to speak with me. I comply with her requests but decline to visit. I'll speak with her later, when I can better explain myself. She'll understand.

And what if she does not?

I get my answer sooner than I anticipate. Aurora is waiting outside the great dragon doors before the next council meeting. She has a book in her arms and a look in her eyes that tells me she has plans of her own. Dragon's teeth.

"What are you doing here?" I ask, pulling her to the side.

"You gave me no choice." She shrugs. She's wearing a dress of dark green that might once have been satin. But the Imps have altered the fabric so that it appears rough and scaled, like the hide of a dragon. Talons curve out from each of her shoulders, securing a cape that is veined like wings. "You've not replied to my notes, so I decided I'd come to you—and the rest of the council, while I'm at it."

I let out a sigh. "I'm sorry. But you can't just show up here."

"Why not?" She raises an eyebrow in challenge. "Will you restrict my access to important meetings, the same as my father used to do? I thought we were going to try to work together."

"We are, but—"

"But what?"

I twist my signet ring, unable to think of anything helpful to say in my defense.

"Is that the princess?" Regan strides toward us, and I curse my terrible luck. "I didn't realize we would have the pleasure of your company today. But you're alone. Where are—"

"The Imps are otherwise occupied." Aurora lifts her chin. Her dragon wing cape flutters in the draft. "I let them know my wardrobe needed freshening."

"I see." Regan looks to me. "You invited her?"

"No," I admit, flustered. "I didn't know she was coming."

"Ah." Regan smiles, but it carries an edge of haughtiness. I'm not surprised. Aurora wasn't exactly polite at their last encounter, so I'm sure Regan is relishing this opportunity to return the favor. "Then I'm afraid whatever you planned on reading to us"—she gestures at the book—"will have to wait. Won't it, Nimara? Seeing as the princess is not a member of council."

Twin spots of pink bloom on Aurora's cheeks. She glares at me, plainly asking me to take her side. The others—Torin, Renard, and Neve, who has returned far sooner than I would have preferred—are making their way toward us. It would be so easy to tell Aurora to go. That I'll speak with her alone, later. But I *did* promise to try in the black tower. And I know how much it infuriated her when Tarkin barred her from all political matters. I don't want to be like him. Perhaps if Aurora sits in with us, she'll better understand why our attack against Oryn is our only option. And this could be an opportunity for her to smooth things over with the council after what happened at her party. They've been distracted since that night, but that won't last forever. Her rejection was too public to be ignored.

"I don't see the harm in hearing her out," I say.

A faint twinge in her jaw is the only sign of Regan's annoyance. She dips her chin. "Very well, then. This should be entertaining, at least."

She pushes her way through the dragon doors, boots clipping against the marble. Aurora follows me after her and grants me a grateful smile as a seventh seat is added to the war room table. But I'm not sure she quite understands what she's gotten herself into.

"Never thought a human would be among us," Renard comments, stuffing a healthy wedge of cheese into his mouth.

"And a *princess* at that," Neve adds. She winds the end of her tangerine-colored hair around one finger.

I deal her my most disdainful glower. The Shifter leader shouldn't be sitting here at all after what transpired with Derek. I pour out a glass of wine and nudge it in Aurora's direction. "What was it you wanted to present?"

"Aye," Valmar says. "Thought you made yourself clear at that party."

Aurora presses her lips together. I give her a subtle lift of my shoulder. If she wants to be here, she'll have to learn to handle them.

"I was angry that night," she begins. "But that doesn't mean I didn't appreciate your effort to include me. This"—she gestures toward the windows and the scene beyond—"may not be what I predicted for my future, but it's been an honor to get to know each of you. To hear your stories. An honor I'm ashamed to say that I likely would have missed if I'd been Briar's queen."

Her answer hums in the quiet. And I'm a little stunned that she allowed herself to be so vulnerable. The energy of the table softens. Pride beats out a rhythm in my chest.

The grooves of Torin's skin fade from amber to pale yellow. "You have our attention."

Aurora takes a steadying sip of wine and taps the cover of the book. It's one of the volumes I'd provided at her request. "I've been doing quite a bit of reading recently. And something that has always interested me about this current conflict is Oryn's refusal to invade Briar. His courts are falling, but he only engages when the battle is within his domain. Am I wrong?"

Regan crosses one leg over the other. "No. Besides the Shifters, we've had none of our own blood spilled on our lands."

"And has there been any communication from Oryn's side?"

"Nah," Valmar answers. "Just the envoy."

"An envoy dispatched decades into a war?" She looks around at us. "Doesn't that seem odd, even for the Fae?"

I'd never considered it much before. But yes. It does. I sit back in my chair. Even Regan's brow is pinched beneath her bone spikes. Neve leans forward. "And I suppose you have a theory to explain his disengagement?"

Aurora opens the book. "When he came for me, the envoy alluded to the Fae treaty with Leythana, which would have afforded protection for me should I have asked for it. In fact, it was protection Alyce and I were counting on when we planned the coup against my father."

"Yes," I confirm. "But Laurel told us that the Fae wouldn't intervene unless summoned."

"Exactly." She finds a page. "At the time, I thought the summoning was a Fae formality. But it's stronger than that. I believe that Oryn *can't* send forces unless the Briar Queen calls him."

Dragon's teeth. Is she right?

"And you didn't know this before?" Torin asks. "You were Briar's heir. Surely the treaty—"

Aurora laughs, but it's hollow. "I read the version of the treaty kept in Briar's royal library. It had been edited, no doubt, by some Briar King who was quite content to know that the Fae were powerless to overthrow him without his wife's consent. No king would have wanted his queen to understand the extent of her sovereign power. This"—she swivels the book toward us—"is probably closer to the real version of the treaty."

Regan snatches the book and scans the wording. "But it doesn't say that Oryn can't attack."

"Not explicitly. But as I've learned about the Fae, there can be more power in what *isn't* said. Here." She underlines a phrase with her fingertip. "*No mortal foot shall tread within the Fae courts, and none but the Crown may call the Crown.* I assumed it was some obscure phrasing to keep the mortals from pestering the Etherians. Oryn didn't want to be receiving petitions from the humans, and so only the heads of the realms could communicate."

"Sounds like Oryn," Valmar grumbles.

"But then I remembered how the High King used to ignore my father's letters. Any missive from Oryn was delivered directly to Endlewild, and then given to my mother—who of course immediately handed it over to him." I don't miss the bitterness in her words. If only Queen Mariel had possessed the courage to stand up to her husband. "I thought Oryn was just being haughty by excluding my father. But if strictly read, this treaty dictates that

Oryn could only communicate with the recognized Crown—the Briar *Queen*—and no one else. As there hasn't been a queen for the last century, Oryn was blocked by his own restrictions."

"But the envoy," Torin argues. "He communicated with you and he wasn't the High King."

"No, but he came at Oryn's *behest,* which must have been enough to allow for a message to be sent by proxy. And that's probably why the envoy wanted me to return with him to Etheria, where Oryn could speak with me himself and gain my permission to invade."

Her words sink into our skulls. I'm not sure anyone at the table is breathing.

"If this is accurate," Torin says slowly, "it is . . . interesting."

"It's more than interesting," Aurora says. "It's a weapon we didn't realize we had."

"Weapon?" Renard's ears prick.

"I know you're all convinced that we have to use Mortania's power to crush the High Court and the rest of the Fae. But it isn't Oryn we have to worry about—it's his power. Which is why we need to find a way to wrest control of that magic."

"And how would we do that?"

She folds her arms. "Aside from their latent magic, what is the source of Fae power?"

It takes a moment, but then comprehension dawns. A laugh punches up my throat. "Oryn's staff? What do you want to do—steal it?"

"It wouldn't be the first time the High King was robbed."

Long before the first war, a faction of Vila snuck into the High Court and snatched that staff right out from under Oryn's arrogant Fae nose. The theft sparked the Fae challenge, which earned

Leythana her Briar Crown. No wonder Aurora is attracted to the scheme.

"What's the point of stealing anything?" Renard growls the question. "We've enough blight elixir to blast the High Court to pieces, and—"

"Do you?" Aurora challenges. "Because it's my understanding that you have no idea what waits behind Oryn's protections. But if we succeed in stealing his staff, we can bring it here."

"Where Oryn can't attack," I say, pulse kicking up in anticipation. "We could hold it for another hundred years if we wanted to."

"And why would we want to?" Regan asks, inspecting the hilt of her dagger. "Let's use the staff to lure Oryn here and then finish him."

Valmar and Renard loudly voice their agreement.

But Aurora holds up her hand. "I understand the sentiment, but—"

"I'm not certain you do, Princess," Neve interrupts. "Shifters have been dropped on our doorstep in pieces. Malakar's head served to us on a platter. Do you expect us to sue for peace?"

Mortania writhes in the place where my magic lives, mirroring Neve's wrath. I grip the arms of my chair, bracing myself for this meeting's inevitable souring. Truthfully, I can't even argue with the Shifter leader. I want justice as much as the rest of them do. But I'd promised Aurora I would try.

"And how many more need to die?" There's no edge to Aurora's voice. Only cool calculation. "Will you be sated when Oryn's head is on the throne room wall? What about after, when there are no more Fae to conquer?"

I glance around at the others. None of us have ever spoken

about *after*. And it makes me wonder yet again about Torin's philosophy. The wounds we do not allow to heal.

"It would be easy to kill Oryn," Aurora goes on. "But think of the fate you *really* want for him. Do you desire him dead and buried, nothing but a severed head? Or alive and powerless, subject to the authority of the Dark Court?"

The question hits like an arrow striking home. The table goes perfectly still, and I imagine Oryn being unbreakably bound to us. Oryn, who murdered so many of ours, reduced to nothing but a shell of his former glory. For a fleeting instant, I'm almost sorry I killed Tarkin. It would be far sweeter to have him toiling away in the palace, watching me destroy everything he built up. Mortania whirls with pleasure.

"I like it," Torin says. The rivulets on her arms brighten and dim, scarlet to umber. "It means we trap the High King in his own turn of phrase. He'll never expect that we're capable of outsmarting him."

"Aye." Valmar's barbed tail swishes in a thoughtful tempo. "Could make him dance to our tune for a change—the way he'd made mine dance at his revels."

And just like that, Aurora has won them over. Myself included. Even Mortania thrums with something akin to appreciation.

I pour out a fresh goblet and raise a toast. "Let us make the High King of the Fae live out his days as a servant to the Dark Court."

Aurora lifts her own glass and smiles at me. And I know in my bones that this is not the last time we will sit here together. That this is the first day of a new beginning.

CHAPTER THIRTY-TWO

We spend the rest of the day and into the evening strategizing. In the end, it is decided that we'll go to the High Court with a small number. As powerful as my magic is, I'm not convinced it is capable of fully breaking Oryn's protections. But I think I can cause them to falter for long enough to let us through. Then Torin, Renard, and their regiments will position themselves around the border and divert the court's attention with the blight elixir, allowing Regan and I to infiltrate the palace and steal Oryn's staff.

But as meticulously as we've planned the details, there remain a thousand avenues for failure. Long after the council meeting, my mind buzzes with the unknowable variables. After sufficiently haunting the corridors, I find myself on the battlements, unable to let my mind rest. Callow keeps me company, and I'm grateful for the pressure of her feathered body. A fine mist begins to fall, like shards of ice. Only the Demons, with their molten fire blood, could endure sentry duty tonight.

"Here." A mug is thrust in front of me. "You'll freeze to death."

I blink in surprise. Aurora stands beside me. Callow mutters a greeting, relocating to roost on the ledge of a turret. Torchlight plays on Aurora's luminous skin.

"You're not tired?"

"I'm exhausted, as I'm sure you are. But I can't sleep."

The mulled wine steams in the chill. I wrap my hands around the cup to thaw my stiff fingers. A few sentries pass us and dip their chins.

"You were wonderful today," I tell her. "I had no idea you'd been reading so much and planning. I'm sorry that I . . ."

"Tried to order me back to my rooms?" She slides me a sideways glance.

I drink the wine. Spices burn down my throat and web outward. "I didn't mean to treat you like your father would have."

"I know," she says softly.

Wind whistles over the battlements.

"But I should have guessed you'd think of something so brilliant. I can't believe we missed it. All this time, and Oryn cannot attack us." I shake my head. "The reason for his reluctance has been staring us in the face."

A grin twitches at the corners of her lips. "I was rather proud of it."

"You should be." I nudge my shoulder against hers. "You put the first Briar Queens to shame. Your father had no idea of the strategist he housed under his roof."

Callow warbles in what I interpret as agreement.

"My father possessed little idea about a lot of things," Aurora says, and I don't miss the salt in her tone, the same as in the council chamber. "Neither did my mother. I never understood why she let my twenty-first birthday creep closer and closer. Why she let my sisters die. She should have figured out about the treaty. Called on Oryn long before we thought to do it."

Her knuckles are stretched white around her mug, and there's a deep-seated rage to her rigid posture. Without thinking, I pry one of her hands loose and hold it in mine. She doesn't pull away.

"Whatever happened, or didn't, I'm glad you're here now. I hope you understand how much it meant to the rest of the council to hear that you respect them. For so many in this court, Briar is a symbol of the fall of Malterre. No one in that room could have imagined that one of its princesses would support them."

Faraway thunder growls.

"I meant what I said." Aurora stares out at the bottomless black of the horizon. Torches snap in the wind. "And I hope that isn't the last council meeting I attend."

Her wish is so close to my own that fresh happiness shimmers in my blood.

"Oh, no. I'm fairly certain that after today they'll demand you join us. Torin, especially, was impressed."

"How could you tell?"

"Her veins turned bright yellow. That always happens when she admires something."

"Really?" Aurora's brow scrunches. "I'll have to pay more attention."

"I'm sure you'll be seeing it often."

She squeezes my hand, and I realize that this is the longest we've touched in a hundred years. A heat that has nothing to do with the wine blooms in my belly.

"You know I'm going with you to the High Court," she says.

The next press of wind cuts close. "Absolutely not. It's too dangerous."

She extracts herself from my grip and regards me with the same expression she wore in my Lair when she'd been determined to experiment with the summoning ritual. "Stealing Oryn's staff was my idea. And I will not stay here and watch the Imps cartwheel into themselves while the rest of you carry it out."

"But we haven't planned for—"

"Then adjust." She shrugs. "I'm going. If I have to hide myself in a weapons chest, you know I will."

Dragon's teeth, she can be so stubborn. I gulp down the rest of my wine. Moonlight paints the copper threads in her hair. "Fine. But you have to stay with me. No wandering off, doing Dragon knows what."

She waggles her eyebrows and doesn't even pretend to promise.

But instead of annoyance, a heady lightness expands through my limbs. I've missed her—missed this—so much.

"Thank you," I say.

"For what?"

Embarrassment nips at me. "For actually trying, like you said you would. When Malakar came back to us, I automatically assumed the only way forward was with violence. I didn't even consider another path, and I shut you out. But you didn't let me."

She finds my hand again. Her thumb traces circles over my knuckles. "Because I know you, Alyce. You can pretend to be Nimara all you like, but your heart is the same. You must promise me to keep trusting it, no matter what happens."

Aurora's lips look velvet-soft in the torchlight. And the sentries are away on their rounds. I wonder what would happen if I leaned in and—

"Here you are." Regan emerges from the shadows, and I jerk back from Aurora. Callow chuffs and rearranges herself. "I see you're not alone."

"No." I fuss with my mug. "Aurora and I were discussing the council meeting."

For the briefest instant, Regan's emerald eyes harden. But then she recovers. "That's exactly what I was coming to see you about."

"Then I'll go." Aurora turns.

I catch her arm. "You don't need to. Does she, Regan? We were all at the meeting."

Regan folds her arms. Bone spikes line the ridge of her forearms, visible through the slashes in her leathers. "We were," she says slowly. "But—"

The sound of a sentry's horn reverberates between us. Callow screeches and takes flight.

I peer over the battlements. All I can make out are the thick, churning clouds and the coin of the moon struggling to be seen. I sharpen my eyesight. There—a dull speck speeding toward us with the Etherian Mountains at its back.

"A rider!" I shout.

The three of us sprint down the winding stairs and back through the palace. The rest of the court streams out with us, calling for weapons and shields and vengeance as we stampede into the main courtyard. Regan commands her Vila into formation.

But when I scour the skies, I don't see a horde of Fae beasts with armored warriors. There's only the one. And its flight is haphazard, as if both steed and rider are drunk.

I dart through the crowd, toward the main palace gates, where the rider is making a clumsy descent. He's wounded. Badly, as is the mount. The beast lands heavily. The Fae rider somersaults from its back and rolls on the ground.

Vila flank me as we creep closer. At least a half-dozen arrows protrude from the steed's hindquarters. Bright amber blood seeps from the wounds at its neck. Its mane is snarled with debris and crusted with sweat and grime. And the Fae is much worse. He's wearing armor, but it's dented and covered in what looks like charred marks. He's unusually small for a Fae. Perhaps a female. Her limbs look short and stocky compared to the other Etherians I've encountered. Definitely not a member of the Hunt.

A Goblin races forward and pulls on the gilded helmet until he tumbles backward with it. Instantly I know why the rider does not resemble a typical Fae, and why his steed is riddled with wounds.

The rider is Derek.

Part III

The Vila are not a wicked race.

For all the slain princes and kings who failed the Fae challenge before me, it was a remarkably simple endeavor to request a parley with the purportedly malicious creatures.

Even easier to convince them to ally with me.

They will be angry, of course, when they learn the truth of our arrangement. I suppose there will be a price to pay for what I did to solicit their trust.

But it matters not. There was no alternative. What the Vila seek is unattainable. They would understand that eventually. And then it would be too late.

The hatred between the two realms is too deeply rooted to ever be mended. A weed choking a garden. It will continue until there is nothing left.

I must protect my realm against its blight.

—From the lost writings of Leythana, first Briar Queen. Age of the Rose, 20

CHAPTER THIRTY-THREE

For the second time, Derek—prince of Ryna—is bound and kneeling before my dais.

Regan and her Vila proposed hauling him straight to the dungeons, but the rest of the court wouldn't hear of it, especially the Imps. I think they imagined him as one of their own, or at least their most entertaining plaything, and therefore his escape was nothing short of betrayal. And the Goblins are sharpening their curved blades and cracking their bone whips and claiming the bits of his body they'd like to devour.

Derek slumps in his bindings. Several of his wounds need tending, but that is a privilege reserved for those who have not been hiding their identities and plotting against us. He received wrappings on only the worst of his gashes before this interrogation began. Even Aurora stands stone-faced at the foot of the dais.

"Well, well." The buzz of the court dulls. "You certainly seem to be making a habit of dramatic entrances, *Your Highness.*"

Laughter.

"What do you have to say for yourself? I suggest you do not waste our time with lies. There is much we know already, and my court is ravenous."

Spears and staffs bang against the marble, and Derek shades impossibly paler.

"You're right." His voice is hoarse. "I am Ryna's prince. The shipwreck that brought me here was staged as an attempt to disguise the fact that I was on a mission from the High King of the Fae."

The Vila prowl closer, and I know they ache to let their magic boil his blood. If I wasn't so interested in what he had to say, I would let them.

"What of your family?" Aurora demands. "Were they a fabrication as well?"

"No." He swallows. "My father is dying and, as both of my siblings succumbed to plague, I'm the last heir. You know what that's like."

Her icy expression thaws in the slightest. Meddlesome prince.

"We've guessed at how you circumvented my binding curse, with the blessing from the High King," I say, drawing his attention back to me. "But what we do not understand is *why* he would have wasted his magic on such an inept mortal. What did Oryn task you to do?"

Derek's jaw works like he doesn't want to answer. Several of the Goblins cry out that we should kill him and send his head back to the High Court on a golden plate, like Malakar's.

"Keep your secrets if it pleases you." Tendrils of smoke unspool from the surface of Torin's skin, signaling her temper. "But you will die with them. And I suspect there is a reason you fled the High Court."

Resignation settles over his features. "Some years ago, long before I was born, a Fae lord came to Ryna."

I exchange a look with Torin. We were aware that the Fae are visiting the mortal realms, but not that they've been doing so for decades. "What did they want?"

"They presented a bargain, similar to the one in place before the time of the Briar Queens. They needed someone to infiltrate these lands." He pauses. Reddens. "And to wake the sleeping princess."

A hush falls over the crowd. Aurora's fists ball at her sides. I share her anger. I knew there was a larger reason Derek had found himself in that library with his lips where they didn't belong. Mortania's presence canters through my limbs.

"You knew about me?" Aurora breathes. "All that about 'stumbling upon' me while I slept, and how you were 'just acting' when you kissed me. You were deceiving me. Manipulating me."

His flush deepens, a bright scarlet guilt. "Yes, I lied. I am sorry for that. But I had to intervene on behalf of my realm."

"*I would have done whatever was necessary,*" he'd said in the garden, what feels a lifetime ago.

"And what did the Fae promise you in return?" Aurora goes on. "My hand in marriage? Briar?"

"Both," he admits. Aurora lets out a rueful laugh. "The Fae said we would rule together, so as not to violate Leythana's treaty regarding the Briar Queens. But I would never have coerced you into marriage. The only relationship that I intended to form between us was a beneficial arrangement for our realms. Ryna needs money and Etherium, and Briar needs to rebuild. We could have helped each other."

"Until you decided to rule alone, as every other Briar King did."

"You must believe me. I wouldn't have . . ."

He strains against the ropes, and the sentries yank him back.

"No one cares," I say, waving my hand dismissively. The cracked jewel of my signet ring flashes. "But I admit that I'm puzzled. You clearly held up your end of this bargain. Aurora is awake. But *you* are rather far from being Briar's king."

Callow grumbles from her perch on the back of the throne.

"I'm not entirely sure what happened," he replies. "The Fae never specified when they would honor their side of the arrangement. But my guess is that their delay has to do with Aurora. After she woke, I suppose they assumed she would go to Etheria as soon as the opportunity presented itself. But she . . . didn't."

A smile tugs up the corners of my mouth, recalling how thoroughly Aurora had rejected Oryn's so-called generosity. The Imps and Goblins cheer.

"I'm sorry to hear I've dashed all your lofty aspirations," Aurora comments.

Derek slumps like a chastened child.

"Is that why the member of the Hunt came here?" Torin asks. "Was Larkspur relaying instruction to you regarding Aurora?"

"I don't know that, either," Derek says, as it appears he is woefully uninformed about most things. "The Fae never explained why they wanted me back at the High Court."

"How convenient." Regan flips her snake-handled dagger from one hand to the next, and I share her suspicion. "And how long before another member of the Hunt comes to collect you— *Theodoric?*" The Vila laugh, cold and cruel. "Or perhaps Ryna's army, charging in to rescue their prince?"

Derek studies the floor and says something I can't make out.

"Louder," I order.

One of the Vila prods him with the toe of his boot.

"No one is coming for me." There's pain in his voice, and it almost makes me feel sorry for him. Almost. "King Elias, when he returned from this land a century ago, refused to let any Ryna ships cross the sea for the Fae. He made his successor swear to remain out of the conflict, and every king after him—including my father—adhered to that command. No matter how dire the circumstances. I never understood why, and I judged it ridiculous to be so stubborn. Without Briar's trade, there was no future for my realm. And so much time had passed since King Elias's return that I presumed the tales of the monster were nothing but overinflated rumor." He pauses. "So I accepted the Fae challenge in secret."

Interesting—and foolish. Perhaps this is why Neve's Starlings reported that the Ryna prince was "missing," and that there seemed no inquiry into his whereabouts. The king wanted to keep his son's defiance concealed.

"I don't believe it," Regan declares. "There are far too many auspicious gaps in the prince's knowledge. If the Fae can stage one arrival, they can stage another. He's here for Oryn."

The boy doesn't shrink. "Kill me, then, if that's what you want. But think—why would Oryn send me back here, knowing that's what you would do? What sort of idiot would I be to agree, when I have no protection?"

"The tasty kind!" A Goblin raises his spear, the long handle decorated with stacked skulls.

"Then why," I ask over the tumult, "*are* you here?"

He meets my gaze without wavering. "Because it was a mistake to ally with the High King."

"Oooo a mistake?" Valmar leaps onto his seat, long ears pointed back. "Why's that? Was the crown the Etherians gave you not pretty enough? Had you no taste for their ambrosia wine?"

The Imps cackle, but Derek's expression hardens. And something scratches at the corners of my mind. I lean forward, signaling them to be quiet.

"The Etherians lied," he says.

More laughter.

"I'm afraid that's not possible, princeling." Neve's gown, which is rough and textured as if it is made of crushed-up gemstones, glimmers in the torchlight.

Blood from a cut on Derek's forehead tracks down the side of his face and he swipes it away with his bound hands. "Maybe they didn't lie like one of you could, but they tricked me. Tricked Ryna and all the other realms they visited."

"And this is a surprise to you, mortal?" Regan drawls. "What did you assume the light Fae did—grant wishes?"

But Aurora inches nearer. "What did they tell you?"

Gratitude shines warm umber in his eyes. "I accepted the Fae challenge to help Ryna. But after I escaped these lands and arrived in the High Court, I discovered that nothing I did for Oryn would have mattered."

"What do you mean?" Torin studies the prince closely. Beneath her iridescent sleeves, the grooves in her body pulse orange and gold and red.

"Oryn cannot come here himself. His treaty with Leythana prevents him from encroaching on these lands without invitation from its queen."

Aurora's attention flits to me.

"We guessed that might be what's happening," she says.

"And it's irrelevant." Regan waves her dagger as if the prince is no more than an annoying gnat.

"I assure you it is of the utmost importance," he says, with a firmness that intensifies my curiosity. "Oryn has spent the last century crafting a weapon. An enchantment. It was a last resort, should anything happen to Aurora. But after her rejection, he's decided to use it." He pauses. "It's a cage. No creature, human or otherwise, will be able to come here or leave. Ever again."

There's a moment of uncomfortable silence. And then a storm of interrogation. Derek winces against the onslaught. Mortania undulates in her den, her own dread bleeding through my limbs. She'd been trapped in a similar enchantment once before. Now we might all share that fate. All our work undone. Another home lost.

"Why would you come back here if you knew what Oryn intended? Do you have some reason to believe he won't trap you with us?"

"Because if I stayed with the light Fae, I might have avoided the cage, but Ryna would be lost. Once the enchantment takes hold, there will be no Etherium trade. No help for the mortal realms. The Fae care nothing for any of us."

Chatter rumbles around the throne room. And my mind spins with this information. I have no doubt Oryn would cast such an enchantment. But am I powerful enough to stop it? Is there time?

"You're offering quite a lot of information." Regan cocks her head and fingers the hilt of her blade. "But I find it hard to accept that the light Fae would confide all their plans to a mortal, prince or not."

"Aye." Valmar's tail thrashes. "Smells off to me."

"They did not confide in me," he says. The blossoms of blood on his shirt continue to widen. "Oryn granted me his blessing, but

I was hardly welcome in Etheria. The Fae ignored me, and I took advantage of that."

The same way he took advantage of us. Dragon's teeth, I knew I hated him. Callow ruffles her speckled wings.

"We shall have the Starlings investigate the matter," Torin determines. Neve dips her chin in acknowledgment. "And in the meantime?"

The court volleys a hundred suggestions as to what to do with the prince, each one nastier than the last. The Goblins are already goading him with the serrated tips of their spears. My first inclination is to let them do whatever they wish. Who cares if he survives the night? But the fear snarled on Derek's face—the blood still weeping from his wounds. I despise the prince, but I also believe he found himself caught in a web of the Etherians' making. That he chose poorly but for good reasons.

"Wait." I hold up a green-veined hand. "I can think of a better use for him." Imps complain, pulling faces at my spoiling their sport. "As the prince has been in Oryn's keeping, perhaps he knows something else of value. Something about the High King's staff."

"*Perhaps* he feeds us more lies and sends us to a waiting battalion," Regan retorts.

"If that's his ploy, he'll die for it. Oryn will not spare him. But if what he claims is accurate . . . stealing Oryn's staff may be the only way to prevent the Fae king from casting his enchantment."

Murmurs of grudging agreement.

"It seems I'm overruled." Regan grabs Derek by the collar of his shirt. "I rather hope you are lying, princeling. I'd quite like to see the yellow of your innards."

CHAPTER THIRTY-FOUR

For the entirety of the next day, the council interviews Derek in the war room. He tells us of ponds in Oryn's mountain palace, teeming with singing fish. Of the land that is veined with quicksilver rivers and mirror-smooth lakes and ambrosia groves with jewel-bright fruit that twinkle on their boughs like stars. The nymphs that can divine the future in the whorls of bark on a tree. The wish-granting pixies who live in the puckered buds of giant flowers. Details that have eluded Neve's Starlings since the beginning of the war. And the fact that *Derek* provides them only further fuels my suspicion of the Shifter leader.

Derek places a marker in the exact center of the High Court, where Oryn's mountain palace is said to climb far enough that it almost scrapes the translucent, domed ceiling of the court's shields. The tallest peak of the structure juts into the clouds like a spire, and countless others corkscrew their way down the sides. Tunnels and bridges lead from one section to the next, which house apartments and audience chambers and ballrooms. Derek, an insignificant human prince, was afforded only the cramped rooms that might have been reserved for servants. In his short tenure at Oryn's palace, he glimpsed just the massive, hollowed-out cavity that served as a throne room, as well as a few dining halls and libraries and many well-guarded doors. All the intelligence he provides was gleaned during gatherings in which the Fae spoke too freely among themselves.

I believe him.

I don't want to. I want some reason to push him off the Crimson Cliffs and remove him permanently from our lives. But he details the elaborate Fae costumes—the brooches made of clustered hummingbird nests set with pearls and headdresses sculpted from coral. The cavernous bark-walled halls and the hundred instances of magic he couldn't possibly fabricate with his pea-size brain. And his disdain toward Oryn is a fanged, wild thing—seething with the white-livid sourness of a deal gone wrong. Whatever was between the prince and the High King is over now.

But I still think he would betray us if he had the chance. So our captured prince is escorted to the cells after we've finished with him, and then we settle in for another long night spent in strategy and counterplans.

The court is restless. Neve has gone ahead to inform her Starlings of our plans. And there's a constant charge in the air, coupled with the sound of the Goblins hammering and sharpening their weapons. Of Imps gallivanting through the corridors, one atop the other's shoulders, calling for a hundred Etherian heads to be brought back as trophies. Of Demons whirling about in their shadow forms and Vila honing their magic on statues and other targets. Most will be staying here, with Valmar acting as head in my absence. Too large a party will only attract unwanted attention, and we must have the palace defended in case Oryn devises another loophole that allows him to attack.

On the night before we are to set out, I'm standing at the windows in my solar, observing the ruins of the districts and the black silken line of the sea. Callow, a warrior in her own right, hops from perch to perch, as ready as the rest of them to soar into battle. A cold draft leaches in through the open panes, laced with the scent of a storm. This night reminds me very much of another. In the black tower, when I'd waited for Laurel to bring me an item of the king's to curse. Just like then, I feel my fate—and everyone else's—hangs on what happens in the next hours.

And just like then, there's only one person I wish was beside me. Instead of fighting the impulse, I make my way to Aurora's rooms.

"May I come in?" I ask. It's late, but she's still in her gown when she answers the door. It's an Imp creation, an indigo deep enough that it's nearly black, with patterns of bramble and thorn embroidered into the satin.

She steps aside and allows me access. Piles of books teeter on tables and cushions. Her Imps are in various contorted sleeping positions—wedged into corners or curled beneath blankets, snoring with abandon.

"At least some of us are sleeping," I comment.

Aurora laughs softly and greets Callow, who, though not particularly in the mood to be touched, acknowledges her before flapping to a post on the back of a chair that looks like a dragon spreading its wings.

"Do you still want to come with us?" I ask. "Because you could change your mind."

"You know I won't." She stirs the embers in the grate. "This is my home. I will defend it in any way I can."

A warrior queen to her core. "You'll stay with me. No firing crossbows."

She shrugs, stubborn as ever. "We'll see."

I shake my head. One of the Imps mumbles and kicks in his sleep.

"You may not believe this, but I am sorry about what happened with Derek. I know it was a shock to learn he was the Ryna prince, but then to hear that he knew about you . . ."

She sets the poker down. "I felt like such a fool. I spent most of my life entertaining suitors. Learning the machinations of court. And yet he thoroughly deceived me. I should have seen through him."

I reach her for. "Don't. He deceived us all. If it's any comfort, I've given him the worst cell in the dungeon. And assigned Imps to keep him awake all night with whatever annoyances they devise."

A ghost of a smile flickers across her face.

"If you'd like a turn, I'm sure Renard would open the armory to you. You were very good with that crossbow."

"Alyce, that isn't funny."

But she's laughing again. One of the Imps snorts and turns over.

"I was joking," I say. Aurora arches an eyebrow. "Mostly."

"I'm actually glad you came tonight."

She selects one of her books and thumbs through it. The glow from the hearth catches in the threads of amber-gold in her hair. And I notice that there is absolutely no evidence of our late nights etched on her face. No dark circles or tired lines. "I take it Rose's elixirs are working. I'm glad she was able to finish them before she left us."

Aurora pauses. "Elixirs?"

"That's the whole reason I freed her from the Garden. I was worried that the curse lifting after you slept for so long would be too much of a shock to your body. That you might . . ." Shrivel and die overnight. "Well, Rose was supposed to be perfecting an elixir that would mitigate any negative effects."

Her brow furrows. "I've not seen an elixir in a century."

I step closer. Her appearance is exactly as it was when the Royal Graces were alive. "You're sure Rose hadn't been slipping it into your tea?"

"Is that what you told her to do?"

"No . . . it's just strange. I would expect you to have Faded at least a little."

"Let me Fade if I'm going to. I'm not interested in elixirs." Aurora raises a magnifying glass to a page crammed with spidery script. "I told you before, I've always wondered what's under this Grace magic."

For perhaps the only time in my life, I miss Rose. The screw of her lips at hearing that remark would be deliciously satisfying.

"Anyway, here." Aurora swivels her book toward me and taps a diagram. It's a text about Vila magic. The illustration beneath her fingertip details a pair of joined hands encircled by light and dark magic, representing the ritual that transforms a Fae into Vila. Blood is shed, hands are clasped, and both parties must command the alteration to happen. "What is this part talking about?"

I lean closer and inhale her scent of apple blossom. My heart flutters.

> Green and gold
> Gold and green
> A power which we've yet to see
> Ah, but ne'er will come the day
> When called a force unknown to Fae.

"Ah, that. It's bothered me, too. At first, I thought it had something to do with Fae turning their magic into that of Vila. But it says, 'a power which we've yet to see,' so that doesn't quite make sense. The Fae have always known about Vila power."

She frowns, thumbing the corner of the page. "And you don't have any other guesses?"

"I'm afraid not. So much of those old books remain a mystery to us. But maybe we'll discover more when we go to the High Court. After we have Oryn's staff, you can ask him anything you like."

I toss a dried beetle to Callow, who gobbles it out of the air and fixes me with her golden stare, waiting for another.

"Yes." Aurora sets the magnifying glass down. "About our mission. I want you to promise me that no matter what happens you'll stick to our plan."

The next beetle drops from my hand. Callow complains. "Is that your way of saying that you don't trust me?"

"I've always trusted you, Alyce. And I can see that you're genuinely trying to uphold the promise you made to me in the black tower. But when I was cursed the second time, you acted without me. *For* me. But without me. Please don't leave me behind again."

The fire crackles. "I never intended to leave you behind."

"I know that."

She catches my hand, thumb trailing along the hummingbird pulse at the underside of my wrist. The seconds tick by, punctuated by the bleary gibberish of the Imps. And I wait, breath held, hoping she will say something else—that she forgives me. That she's finally ready to accept me for who I am.

"I'll see you in the morning, then," she says instead, letting me go.

Disappointment swoops in my belly. I turn to gather Callow. But then, "Could I— Do you want company?" She stiffens. "Not like that. I just want to be here. With you. In case . . ."

It is the last time, I cannot bring myself to say.

She fusses with her sleeve.

"No," she replies. "Maybe one day. But tonight, I'd prefer to be alone."

I should just go. But I can't help the surge of anger that simmers behind my breastbone. Callow senses it and mutters. "Then you still do not forgive me."

It's a long time before she answers. "No, Alyce. But . . . I do want to."

My eyes sting. And I transfer Callow to my shoulder. She knocks her head against my cheek in what I gather is sympathy. *Want*—the word follows me down the corridor, heavy and loaded. It's a fraction of an inch closer than where we were on the night of her party. But it is not nearly enough. And I'm not sure it will ever be.

CHAPTER THIRTY-FIVE

Roughly a hundred Goblins, Vila, and Demons make up our small army. Renard argued for triple the number, but that would slow us down, and we already run the risk of being spotted by Fae scouts. Derek tells us that, by winged steed, the High Court is a day's journey from our own. But we have only about a dozen of those creatures ready. And so, amid a boisterous send-off of dancing Imps and pounding drums and trumpeting horns, our party sets out on foot.

It is the first time in years that I'm witnessing the damage our war has brought to the Etherian courts. We march through ambrosia groves that are nothing but skeletal trees and scorched earth. Pits steaming with foul miasma. Caves and wide hollowed-out tree trunks that might have been Etherian dwellings, shards of household trinkets stark against the charred debris. Fae corpses, their bodies decomposing as their latent magic vainly attempts to sprout silver-limbed saplings between their bones.

Regan is proud, pointing out various landmarks where her

Vila triumphed in battle. Goblins, clad in skeletal armor with skulls serving as epaulettes, swap war stories and crow their ballads. Mortania's presence swells in my body like an overinflated balloon. But this time it is an uncomfortable pressure. When we initially invaded Etherian lands, I was overwhelmingly convinced that they deserved to lose their home. That we deserved to take it. But here, among the wreckage our campaigns have wrought, all I feel is emptiness. I cannot say that I wholly regret the war—not with our blood-soaked history with the Etherians. But my restless thoughts keep circling back to what Torin said about hatred, passed down from generation to generation, neither side willing to let go. About the wounds we refuse to staunch. What *will* happen when the war is over and all of Etheria is a smoking ruin? Will it have been worth it? The cold wind, laced with the tang of sulfur, bites into my soul.

Aurora shares my disquiet. She rides Chaos, who is annoyed at being relegated to the ground, and nudges his sides whenever one of the Goblins' tales reaches her ears. Now and then, she'll look at me. And I see in her eyes the pledge she pulled from my lips, coupled with the whisper-thin thread of hope she spun when I asked about forgiveness.

"I do want to."

As dusk encroaches, we make camp. Aurora's tent is close to mine, but she prefers to sit with Derek and his Demon guard. All of the white-hot ire she harbored for the mortal prince seems to have melted away since his return, and it kindles my own frustration. Why can she forgive *his* transgressions and not mine? Why is what *he* did to save his people acceptable, and what I did isn't? It no longer seems to bother her at all that he plotted with the Fae to secure her hand in marriage.

"Careful." Regan settles beside me on the fallen trunk of a Fae tree. "If you keep staring at him like that, you might kill him. Not that I'd particularly mind his death, but then he wouldn't be able to help us navigate Oryn's palace." She passes me a stick with roasted meat on the end.

"This isn't vulture again, is it?" I did not enjoy my first taste of the creature.

"Grouse, I'm told."

I frown, doubting that very much, but nibble on the end anyway. Grease dribbles down my chin and I swipe it away. "We should have brought a couple of Imps with us."

Callow has graced me with at least half a dozen mice and snakes and other such tribute since we left the palace, and I have no inclination to eat those, either. She's off on one of her hunts now, and I cringe at the thought of waking to find my hand in a nest of splattered intestines.

"And have them pestering the Goblins with whatever hare-brained prank popped into their heads? I think it's better we eat vulture."

I'm not sure I agree. But I chew the stringy meat and study the fire. The nights are long, and I can't dispel the feeling that this last stand will end as Malakar's had—with all our heads on golden plates.

Trust in me, pet.

"Torin says we should reach the rendezvous point with Neve by tomorrow."

I nod and pull my cloak closer. This sort of cold makes the memory of our drafty palace feel like a warm blanket. From farther away, the sound of the Goblins' gravelly laughter echoes, laced with the song of steel being sharpened.

"You're not nervous, are you?" Regan asks carefully.

I gnaw off the last of the meat. It was definitely not grouse. "A little." I poke the fire with the end of my stick. The residue of fat pops.

"You'd be a fool if you weren't." The nickering of Fae steeds drifts from deeper in the camp. "But yours is the greatest power of this age. This time tomorrow, we'll have Oryn's staff."

Her encouragement should bolster my confidence, but I find myself fixated on something else Regan said: *this age*. "Do you remember Aelfdene?" I ask. "How he said the mountains would crumble?"

"Yes," she replies wryly, "and then he bit off his tongue. I'm not sure I trust that 'prophecy.' "

"But if it is true," I press, disregarding her sarcasm. "Do you think the new age he alluded to is ours?"

Wind stirs the fire, making sparks dance. "You don't?"

"Torin thinks it might mean a time without Vila or Fae because none of us will survive."

Regan stares at me, then pries my stick from my hand and sniffs the sharpened end. "You're right. No more vulture."

"It's not that." I snatch the stick back.

"Then what is it?"

"I don't know. During our early sieges, everything seemed so clear. We rescued the Imps, and the whole court was calling for revenge. But now . . ."

Shadows dance over Regan's features, stirred by the Demons weaving overhead. They've been taking shifts since we left Briar, cocooning us with their shroudlike forms in order to obscure our party from Fae scouts. If I listen closely enough, I can hear them whisper. It raises gooseflesh on my arms.

"I came looking for you last night."

My cheeks flame, and I dig my stick into the black silty earth at my feet. "I couldn't sleep, and I wandered."

"Nimara." She catches my wrist. "I can guess where you went. And I think it's probably the same reason you're having these thoughts now."

I yank my arm away. "You think I can't make up my own mind?"

"I think," she says slowly, "that the princess's waking has complicated matters."

"Complicated." My laugh clouds in front of my face. That's a good word to summarize the myriad of disasters that have occurred since Aurora opened her eyes.

Trust in me, pet, Mortania urges from her den. I wish it were that simple.

"Can I ask you something?" Firelight washes over Regan's rich brown skin. "When you're with her, is it easy?"

The question is harder to answer than I'd like to admit. I twist my signet ring, the bramble band rough against my finger. Aurora and I have had our arguments. Shouting matches, even. Hurts and betrayals. None of which could be remotely described as *easy.* But then I think of the look in her amethyst eyes when she came to thank me for the funeral. Her lips against mine. The way she said my name. "Is it supposed to be easy?"

Regan shrugs. "Maybe not. But look at how things are with us." Her hand crawls across the log to meet mine. Bone spikes atop my green-veined skin. My breath catches, as it did the very first time we touched. "That night in the library—didn't you feel something?"

A lump forms in my throat, and my lips tingle with the memory of the taste of her. How her body wrapped around mine, and what it felt to be *wanted*. "Yes. But—"

"Don't." She squeezes my hand. "Not again. Just think, please. Think about how you want things to be. How they *could* be, all the time, if you would let them. Will you?"

I should tell her no—that I cannot give away my heart when it belongs to another. But then a laugh resonates between us. My attention tracks over to Aurora, who is sitting close to Derek and helping him eat. And I wonder if there is a way back to what we were. If there was ever an *us* at all. Or if I'm pining away for something that never existed. Because Aelfdene was right.

"It was not real."

"All right," I hear myself say. "I will."

I sit at the fire for a long time after Regan goes to bed, knowing I won't get a wink of sleep after our talk. When the embers finally dim, I decide to visit Chaos where he's being tended with the other steeds. But then I notice that Derek is alone. My steps veer in his direction.

"This journey must be infuriatingly longer than your last," I say in greeting, "what with no Fae steed from the Hunt."

He's gnawing on a leathery strip of meat and coughs as I take a place opposite him. The Demon guards salute me from their posts. "I'm in much better shape for it."

"Are you?" His wounds are healing, but his bandages are still spotted scarlet with his blood. And there are angry welts on his wrists where the ropes are digging in.

"I'm conscious." He shrugs. "No one is shooting at me."

"Yet."

He laughs and then sobers when he realizes I'm not joking.

The Demons' shadows churn, blocking out the moon and stars. The rabble of our camp is beginning to dull. The sound of Goblins snoring floats toward us. "Briar seems to attract a slew of Ryna princes. First Elias. Now Derek, or Theodoric, or whatever your name is. An uncannily lucky sort, the lot of you."

"As I'm a pawn in two courts"—he pauses and counts on the fingers of one hand—"no, three courts, I can't say I agree. And I only half-lied about my name. Derek is what my mother and sister call me. It's short for Theodoric."

His true name, hidden in plain sight. "I really don't care."

The dwindling fire smokes in a gust of wind.

Derek tries to bite through the meat again but gives up and flings it away. "You met King Elias?"

"He wasn't a king then," I tell him. "Though he had ambitions of breaking Aurora's curse and becoming Briar's."

His brow rumples beneath his swoop of crow-feather hair. "I thought he didn't want to marry—"

"Were you there?"

He swallows his next remark. A log collapses and sparks skitter over the ground.

"You look like him," I admit grudgingly. "Same eyes. Unnerving dimples that make you look like a child."

He swipes the back of one bound hand over his mouth. "Did he seem mad? That's what our historians say was rumored, even after the stories about Briar were verified."

I should lie to him and tell him that the first Ryna prince was absolutely mad. And vile, and as much a tyrant as Tarkin. But for some reason I don't. "He was perfectly sane. He and Aurora—" I picture them during the celebration in which he kissed her. Her radiance. The care he took when touching her, requesting her permission instead of treating her like an object to be owned. "They were friendly. He was respectful."

The noises of the Fae steeds carry over the camp.

When Derek speaks, it's careful and measured. "I mean no harm to her. And I entertained no intention of forcing her to marry me or . . ." He shifts in his seat. "She's a good person. I want to help her if I can."

I note the way his voice goes huskier when he speaks of her. The slight upturn of his lips and the way his shoulders relax. I know the feeling well. And I don't like seeing it mirrored in someone else.

"If you care for her, let her go. She isn't yours."

The doltish boy doesn't even blink. "She isn't yours, either."

That night, the prince of Ryna finds his bed on the cold, muddy ground.

CHAPTER THIRTY-SIX

Torin's estimation is correct. By dusk the following day, our party pulls to a stop. The sky in the horizon isn't the charcoal gray of Malterre but a brilliant azure streaked with the tangerine and russet of sunset. Even from here, I can glimpse birds skating through the clouds—not the ominous night creatures of our lands, but graceful bright-feathered things. And the air is warmer, untouched by the eternal winter of Briar.

Before long, we can smell the Fae.

A faint hint of dewed grass and summer roses. If they could, our army would charge ahead and try to hack away at the High Court's protections with their spears and swords. But the memory of the murdered Starlings restrains them. We wait, hidden in the oil-skinned trees, not even daring to light a campfire lest we be discovered.

The hours crawl by, broken only by the howl of the wind and calling of owls and wolves. Demons wend and whirl overhead, patrolling our perimeter. Goblins ready their weapons, which must be deadly enough by now to slice through a Fae limb as easily as butter. The Vila huddle with Regan. And Chaos's impatient breath steams in the air. At long last, a blur of indigo and orange sails above us and perches neatly on a tree limb—Neve.

The Starling leader warbles out the tune she taught us to recognize. Mortania surges up in response, and her enthusiasm is contagious. The energy of our army swells.

"We'll be ready when the protections break," Torin says as I climb onto Chaos's back.

"You'll need to be," I tell her. "I'm not sure how long they'll be disarmed."

Or if they will falter at all.

Trust me, pet, Mortania's voice sighs between my bones.

"Be careful." Torin pats Chaos. "Take no unnecessary risks."

"And you," I say, pulling Aurora up behind me. "I want us all home and whole."

"Aye." Renard slaps the haunch of Regan's steed, which startles and rises into the air. "But let's give the Fae king a good show first."

His gravelly Goblin laughter reverberates in the stillness of the night. And as we join Regan and Derek in the sky, chasing the bright streak of Neve's body, I try to let myself be carried away by the adrenaline pumping in my veins. To ignore the foreboding tapping at the base of my skull—the memory of the last time I broke Fae protections in the black tower and everything that happened after.

• • •

The Shifter keeps a swift pace, Callow just behind her, flying high to avoid the teeth of the Fae's orblike protections. Beyond the borders of the decimated Court of Dreams, Oryn's domain unfurls. It's nothing like Briar used to be—the districts mapped out with poplar-lined streets and ornate structures. Instead, there are rolling fields carpeted with flowers drenched in starlight and rivers that appear as silver veins in the night.

And there, in the center of it all, is the High King's palace.

Derek and the Starlings had not been exaggerating. Like our own palace, this one appears to be constructed of the pink stone of the Etherian Mountains. But it's as if that stone erupted out of the ground itself. Oryn's stronghold dwarfs ours in every way. Hundreds of small buildings climb up the side of the mountain in a spiraling pattern, branching out in towers that are connected by bridges and staircases and covered walkways. The pointed spire at the top, studded with dazzling windows, pierces the clouds. But the most spectacular feature of all is the sparkling, gold-tinted liquid pouring out of archways and gates. It cascades over rooftops and rushes down sides. Froths at the base of the mountain, where it pools and then flows outward through the land.

"What the hell is that?" Regan calls, she and Derek slowing beside us.

"It's the magic," Derek answers. The Vila leader must have been careless in her flight, for the boy's brushed-copper face is rather green. And she obviously didn't allow him to touch her. He grips the saddle instead, his uneasiness clearly annoying the Fae steed. I smirk. "I told you, it's everywhere here. I think Oryn himself controls it somehow."

Dragon's teeth, he might be right. Each Fae court governs an aspect of the natural world, but Oryn's domain carries no such designation. It must be magic itself that he rules—Fae magic anyway. No wonder he's so arrogant.

The Starling leader treads the air directly above the spire of the palace. Callow circles over my head, and Chaos chuffs—silver-dusted wings beating out an impatient tempo. Oryn's protections shimmer far below us, as if the Fae realm is underwater. A late summer breeze brushes against our cheeks, tinged with the sweet scents of mountain laurel and peony.

"The High King's chambers are in the spire." Derek points.

Neve chirrups in confirmation.

"The rest of the Fae live"—he sweeps an arm over the sprawling palace—"everywhere else. The court could be a city unto itself. And there are refugees from the fallen courts in residence as well."

It looks as though triple the population of former Briar, Common District included, could be housed in the vastness of this stronghold. Derek briefly explains what he knows of the general layout: the location of the large cavernous chamber where the court would gather, and the area in which his own rooms were kept. Given the late hour, he thinks that most of the court has probably retired to their apartments, including the High King. Which makes the spire our target.

"And the staff?" I press. "Oryn will have the staff?"

The mount bobs and Derek teeters in the saddle. "I never saw him without it. The Fae are territorial about them. I don't think Oryn would have permitted even his best guards to handle it."

I'd feel better if that information were based off more than what the boy *thinks,* but there's nothing to do about it now. I roll my shoulders against the nerves fluttering in my belly and turn my attention to the dome of Oryn's protections. During his interrogation, Derek claimed that the protections simply dissolved to allow him through when he fled our court, which means they can be broken. I just have to determine the best way to do that.

Mortania strains inside her cave. I lean into the steadying pressure of Aurora's arms around my middle and inhale the familiar scent of her body. All we need is Oryn's staff. As long as I trust our plan, the rest will follow.

The limb of my magic lashes out with such force that I'm dizzy with it. Like the walls of Kal's shadowy cage, the protections around the High Court are solid. And they're charged, like lightning bolts woven together. As soon as my power makes contact with the barrier, heat jolts into my body, violent enough to shock. I let out a yelp and Aurora pulls me closer.

"Are you all right?"

"I can do it," I tell her as much as myself. I *must* do it.

Re-centering my focus, I try again. This time, my power hovers just above the glittering shields, mapping them out. Apprehension begins eating through my confidence.

They will kneel at our feet, Mortania whispers.

That voice. An anchor, as it had been when I Shifted and razed Briar.

Yes, pet.

Letting everything else fall away, I roll my power into itself and build it up. Forge an intent that is stronger even than the High King's abhorrence of my kind. I think of the first Vila, my namesake, banished by her own courts. Of Mortania, imprisoned in her medallion. Of my mother, driven into hiding and then killed. Of the vicious curl of Endlewild's lip when he visited me. The scent of charred steel and coppery loam scalds the back of my throat and I release my magic.

It cracks against the Fae protections with enough speed that our mounts are tossed backward. Aurora struggles to keep her seat. Regan yanks on the reins of her steed and pumps her fist, spurring me on. And Mortania—I taste the heady wine of her power steeped with mine.

Yes, pet. Yes.

Magic sizzles as my power sinks its hooks into the Fae enchantment. The Etherian magic pushes back with blistering heat, and I know I won't be able to hold it long. I burrow deeper, until I inhale the sharp smack of dewed grass and spring rain, the heart of the enchantment. With everything I have, I send my intent through the cord of my magic.

Break, I order. *Falter.*

Like the keening of some gargantuan beast, the protections begin to tremble. Mortania's power pounds in an intoxicating current through my blood. Yes. *This* is who I am—unstoppable.

Loud popping sounds begin to explode from below. Spooked, Regan's steed vaults higher. I push my commands harder. There's another groan, a deep, menacing rumble. And then—

The world goes white, as it had in the black tower when I freed Kal. A gust of wind like a sea squall sends our mounts kicking at the air.

"Now!" Regan shouts.

We plunge toward the High Court.

Aurora clings to me as we descend in a furious corkscrew. Callow's scream resounds from far away. The wind whistles against my eardrums, the mountainous Fae palace looming larger with each one of my iron-clad heartbeats. The spire, painted in moonlight, is perilously close. My magic leaps out of my body, ready to storm through the side of it. But it's hardly touched the glass and stone before Chaos bucks, screaming in alarm, and we begin to waver.

I can't see what's hit us, only the whooshing blur of towers and waterfalling Fae magic. Regan banks to meet me, and Derek gestures wildly at the palace. There—Fae warriors are lining a walkway. More appear in the windows and archways. Callow belts her war cry and goes after them. Arcs of gilded Fae magic crisscross the skies. I curse and command my power to wrap around me in a shield of green Vila magic as Chaos bolts in the other direction. Regan follows, but her own shields are weaker than mine. They collapse in an instant after a double attack slams into her. Her mount spins like a top. Dragon's teeth. They'll both be killed.

Aurora points. To our right, there's a large, wide window about the size of the stained-glass mosaic in our palace's ballroom. I don't hesitate. My power pummels into the glass. Shards soar in every direction. Regan avoids colliding with the palace wall just in time to sail after us, into the gaping opening.

Into the palace of the High King of the Fae.

Hooves spark against the floor as Chaos lands. Aurora and I are tossed from the saddle. Bone crunches where my shoulder meets a hard surface, and I flip from back to belly like a fish expelled from the sea. Agony throbs through every limb. Stars dance behind my eyelids. The sounds of bodies thumping and curses being hurled echo in the quiet. I taste my own loamy blood in my mouth.

Instinct pushes through the pain. *Get up. Move before they find you. Get the staff.*

I manage to roll onto one side and raise myself onto my elbow. The tendrils of darkness recede from my vision. Aurora is taking stock of her own injuries a few feet away. Regan is snarling at Derek, blaming him for the Fae sabotage. Colorful glass litters the floor. Moonlight spills in through the broken window, and I can just make out the shadowy curve of the walls. Hooves clop, and hot, chuffing breath brushes my cheek—Chaos. I don't see Callow.

The struggle to stand is like hauling myself through thick mud. But I use Chaos for support and force my muscles to obey. "Are you—"

The chamber blazes to life. The Fae steeds whinny in panic, both galloping out the broken window.

"Nimara," a deep voice resonates. "Welcome to my court."

CHAPTER THIRTY-SEVEN

Oryn, High King of the Fae, regards me with a contempt so pronounced I can feel it like a brand on my chest.

His identity is unmistakable. Though he's sitting, the length of his limbs suggests that he's taller and broader than most Fae. His golden gaze is stark against the grooved reddish-brown of his skin, which is like the bark of an ancient redwood tree. No such trees exist in Briar, but I've read about them. Some were said to be as thick around as a palace turret and as old as the land itself. A crown of tall alabaster branches rests atop Oryn's long moss-green curls and comes to a point at his forehead, where the jeweled sigil of the High Court is like a beacon in the light of the sea of candles.

Members of Oryn's court surround us in a wide ring, a living forest. I've never seen this many Fae gathered in one place. Their bodies appear cut from the trunks of peeling sycamores and delicate spotted birch and crimson-tinted mahogany. Their outfits would make even the richest nobles of former Briar fume with envy. Elaborate headdresses comprised of antlers and strung with blossoms that rebloom into varying shades and species every few moments. Entire gowns constructed of living butterflies. Capes that look as though they were spun by a thousand spiders, studded with gems as tiny as grains of sand. Rings set with real robin's eggs are stacked on knobby-boned fingers. One of them hatches before my eyes, and a miniature bird shakes off bits of shell and twitters away.

I will my racing heart to quell and slide a murderous glare at Derek. But the useless prince appears as shocked and terrified as we are. His face is chalky, the complete opposite of the pallor of a spy returning to his master. But if Derek didn't betray us, then how did Oryn know we were coming?

"I'm ashamed to find we are underdressed." I smooth my clothing, attempting to appear as though we intended to crash into the High King's audience chamber, and not like all of our carefully made plans are unravelling at our feet.

Fae laughter echoes in an eerie symphony of babbling water and rustling leaves. Dozens of staffs pulse with Fae power, glazing the room with gold.

The outside of the High King's palace might look like a mountain, but this cavernous chamber resembles more of a forest glen. The walls are covered in bark. Dripping candles nestle in small nooks and cavities. Songbirds take up residence in hollows, calling and answering in their ethereal language. Flowering vines of every color meander their way over branches and climb the boughs of the vaulted ceiling, petals glowing in undulating shades of opal and citrine and periwinkle.

Oryn himself lounges on his throne, a gargantuan stump with

a high back that bears an enormous crest of the High Court above his head. Roots snake their way from its base and through the chamber like tentacles. One winds around my ankle, and I have to restrain myself from flinching.

"It matters not what one wears to one's defeat," Oryn replies.

A half-dozen more roots slink from the throne and find Regan and Derek and Aurora. Regan growls and tries to hack her bindings away with a dagger, but it's pointless. My own power is depleted from the effort it took to break the shields and fend off the Fae attacks. Even if it weren't, we'd be overwhelmed in seconds if we attempted anything. Hulking Fae, their breastplates constructed of interlocking gilt branches and gauntlets of hammered-gold laurel leaves are stationed throughout the chamber. Mortania paces inside me like a caged tiger, and my very skin itches with the desire to set my magic free.

"You do not care for our hospitality," Oryn drawls on.

"The same sort of *hospitality* you demonstrated to ours?" Regan brandishes her dagger in his direction. I'm surprised she hasn't cut herself to try to use her own blood as a weapon. But that wouldn't be enough to save us now.

"Are you referring to the Shifters or the Goblins?" One of the High King's spindly fingered hands goes to his doublet, where a thick chain set with jeweled renderings of each emblem of the Fae courts is draped from shoulder to shoulder. My own signet ring burns on my finger. "In either case, I simply mirrored the treatment demonstrated by your own court. A custom I am eager to repeat when we welcome the rest of your paltry company. They should be arriving shortly, should they not?"

His implication slithers across the floor. Oryn knew about everyone—not just us. But I still can't figure out how.

Regan pokes her dagger at Derek, straining against her bonds. "I *knew* you were in league with the Fae. I will—"

He puts up his hands. "No, it wasn't—"

"Let the princeling be." Oryn waves their argument away. "He was of use to us, but his pathetic mortal brain is too feeble to comprehend precisely how. In fact, he judged himself very clever indeed, nosing about in places he did not belong. Cataloging our palace. But we allowed the boy to see only what we put before him. To learn the details we wished him to learn. And then to return to you."

Dragon's teeth. The High King has been plotting this for some time. My mind combs back over the last few weeks. Had this been why Larkspur was dispatched to free the prince? Oryn *wanted* Derek in the High Court. Wanted him to learn of the enchantment, then to use that information to spur us into attacking. Because the High King wanted us *here* all along. Derek bristles. I almost feel sorry for him.

"But this is a tiresome subject." Oryn rises. Fireflies swirl around him. One of the butterflies on a Fae's gown untethers itself from its fellows and floats to the High King's shoulder. "Let us come to the heart of the matter. Our bargain."

"Bargain?" I echo. "We have not come here to—"

"Alyce. Listen to him."

Aurora's tone pulls me up short. When Oryn revealed himself, she looked as frightened as we were. But now she sounds as though she knows what the High King is going to say next. As if she—but no. She couldn't have. Wouldn't have.

Roots skitter out of Oryn's path. Flowered vines unspool and drop from the ceiling, as if longing to be near him. "The real threat to our realm is not you, half-breed, but the power that resides within you. I have it under good authority that you would be willing to surrender that power. If that be true, perhaps we can come to an arrangement."

I round on Aurora. "Do you know about this?"

Her chin is high and her hair is coiled in a braid on top of her head, as it was when the Etherian envoy came—like a crown. "You told me that you'd thought of cleaving Mortania from your body. She was trapped in a medallion before. High King Oryn could cage her again, and this conflict would be over. You would be free."

Mortania snaps and sparks in her den.

"This isn't possible," I go on, reeling. "You *asked* Oryn to do this? But you rejected the envoy. Refused to parley with the High King."

Oryn extracts something from his doublet and holds it out for us to see. It's a flat silver disc, like a mirror, but the surface does not reflect this chamber. I see another room instead. "The princess did dismiss my messenger. But we initiated other avenues of communication. Tell her of our discussions, Princess. I enjoyed them well."

The vision in the glass registers. It's Aurora's bedchamber. "You've been watching her."

"I am not a voyeur, half-breed." Fireflies weave and wink around him. "We cannot craft these portals without invitation. You will find this mirror's twin in the princess's chambers, one that connects to mine. It was she who suggested this method."

I don't want to believe it, am desperate for Aurora to say he is lying. But she remains stubbornly silent. And pieces begin clicking into place. The books Aurora was reading about the first war and the Fae. The hours she spent strategizing, which I stupidly believed was for the benefit of the Dark Court. And then she'd wanted to be alone that last night. But not because she needed space. Because she was scheming with the High King.

I'm hardly able to think—to breathe—around my wrath.

"How *dare* you." I do not recognize my own voice. "You had no right to bargain anything on my behalf. None whatsoever."

Regan growls her agreement. If the roots weren't holding us in place, I'm not sure what she would do. Or if I would stop her.

"Can't you see that I'm protecting you, Alyce?" Aurora says. "Mortania cannot be allowed to—"

"So it's fine for *you* to decide what protection means?" A root winds higher up my calf and bites into my muscle. "It's fine for you to sacrifice *a piece of my very being* without my knowledge or consent?"

The ancient Vila whirls as if she will break free of the barrier of my skin.

"Mortania is corrupting your mind," she volleys back. "You're addicted to her power."

Oryn's court has clumped together. A Fae wearing a gown made of drooping wisteria blossoms licks her honeysuckle lips and leers.

"Have you stopped to think for one moment what they might do if I actually agreed to what you suggest? Chain me to the shadows in the black tower and wait for me to die, perhaps. You saw what they did to Malakar. What they did to the Vila in the first war."

"A war is what I'm trying to end!"

"And what of our plan? The plan you *begged* me not to abandon when something went wrong? Which, I might point out, is exactly what you are doing now."

Songbirds trade their tunes, but Aurora won't answer. The truth digs between my ribs. "Because that was never the plan," I say, numb. "You made it up to distract the council—and me. While you hatched your own plot with Oryn."

Fae laughter eddies around us. Laughter that is hauntingly similar to that which I endured as the Dark Grace. I clench my fists and forbid myself to hunch against it.

"I had to get you to come to Oryn's palace without the might of your army behind you. Otherwise, you never would have agreed. Neve said—"

"*Neve?*"

"Yes," she replies smoothly. "I needed her help to communicate with Oryn. And she was the only member of your court whom I trusted would see the value of this strategy."

I hate that Shifter. How long has she been colluding with the Fae?

Regan curses and tries to sever her bindings again. More roots coil around her legs and torso. Mortania howls and thrashes. All Aurora's talk of forgiveness. Of us finding our way back to each other. She was only using me. Some fragile, tender part of me dies.

A breeze wafts through the broken window behind us. Vines rustle. The opalescent light of the strange blossoms glows against Aurora's skin.

"I told you a long time ago, that I would be the queen Leythana was. That I would protect my realm. And whatever means I employed—the deception and manipulation"—she fixes me with a stone-hard glare—"I learned from you."

Her words are like a slap. Mortania churns, furious. The scent of molten steel and silty blood floods my lungs.

"There will be no bargain today," I grind out.

"I did not presume that there would be," Oryn replies, surveying us like we're a pair of Imps squabbling over a bad dice throw. That unnerving Fae laughter begins to swell again. "But I desired you both here so that the last princess of Briar can witness your death. One a century in the making."

Aurora cries out in protest. But had she really imagined this meeting would end any other way? The guards close in on us. The magic in Oryn's staff begins to pulse and spin. He aims at me.

A shrill screech slices through the chamber. A smear of tawny brown and white charges the High King. Callow. A heady mix of pride and terror beats in my chest. Oryn stumbles in alarm, ducking in a decidedly unkingly fashion as Callow pecks and claws at his face. His staff—the most powerful weapon in Etheria—clatters to the ground.

Now, pet!

I let my power free.

My magic pummels into the roots holding us, clamping on to their Fae magic in an instant. They scream and shrivel, blackened and burned husks wilting away. Regan leaps out of her bonds just before a gilded arc of magic slices through her middle. My power dives from one Fae guard to the next. Armor clangs as the massive creatures topple like felled trees. Oryn is still trying to fend off Callow's assault.

"Regan! The staff!"

The orb encased in its gnarled and knotted nest sputters on the ground. Regan bounds toward it and skids across the floor—a heartbeat too late. Oryn lands a blow to Callow's body. My bird is tossed to one side like a child's toy. Rage boils. He will pay for that. Oryn picks up his staff. Mortania's presence canters through my limbs, more potent than I've ever felt it. A scythe of the High King's power sweeps toward me.

Something careens into my side.

Glass shards pop under my feet as I struggle to get my bearings. Aurora is standing between me and the High King.

"Run!" I can barely hear her over the riot of magic.

But where is there to go?

Regan fights through the swarm of Fae, Callow tucked to her side. She grabs my arm and pulls me along. The rest of the court converges on us. Fae power ricochets off the walls and zigzags through the air like shooting stars. The wind tugs at us, reeling us toward the broken window. A familiar whinny echoes from below. I peer over the edge, catching the blot of a silvery-winged body. Chaos.

"Jump!" I shout at Regan.

"What?" She eyes the dizzying drop.

"Just do it!"

The Fae press closer, pointed teeth gnashing. Regan is not convinced. But the steed calls again, and then she spews a string of curses, secures Callow in her arms, and catapults herself into the void. I wait only long enough to see the quicksilver blur that is Chaos swoop beneath her and break her fall, then dive after them.

The wind snatches the air from my lungs. Shapes and colors bleed past in a nauseating whorl. I can't tell up from down, and I'm certain Oryn will get his wish and I'll be a splattered mess at the base of this mountain. But an instant later, wings erupt from my back. I cry out, body twisting in somersaults. My wings unfurl, snapping as they catch me.

I steady myself, streaking through the air like one of the Goblins' loosed crossbow bolts. Chaos huffs a greeting as I pull beside them, Regan clinging to both Callow and the steed's star-dusted mane as she throws up her shields and fends off attacks. Fae magic blasts through windows and archways. But that gilded power only bounces off my own green shield. And then the sparkling Fae palace is shrinking into a flicker of white-gold as we race back toward Briar.

Without Aurora.

CHAPTER THIRTY-EIGHT

We do not see Torin or the others as we sail across the edge of Oryn's domain, and their disappearance only fuels my fear. I hope that they sensed the trap and retreated, and that they were not intercepted by Oryn's forces and are currently imprisoned in a Fae dungeon. Because we do not have time to go back for them. Not when anything might be waiting for us at home.

It takes a full day of breathless flying before the silhouette of the Dark Court comes into view. Relief rushes through me when we cross the Etherian Mountain border, and I see that the palace appears undisturbed. There's no enchanted cage or battalion of armored Fae warriors. But then Regan points to the sea, where several specks skate across the horizon. My blade-sharp eyes home in. They're ships. Human ships, and they're moving faster than they ought to be, sails full-bellied despite the calm. I'm able to pick out a flicker of color atop one of the masts. Navy and bronze. The colors, I recall dully, of Ryna.

What would *they* be doing here? Clearly, the Ryna king's opinion on allying with the Fae has changed. Which means the ships are likely Etherian-made. Mortania's wrath sizzles across every nerve.

I drive myself harder and faster toward the ruined districts. At their Fae-gifted speed, the ships will reach Briar's shores by tomorrow. The court must be protected.

"Where are you going?" Regan shouts, struggling to keep up as I swerve away from the palace and toward the sea cliffs. Chaos whinnies.

"We have to slow them down!"

I pull to a stop, treading the air outside the main gates. Using both my Vila and Shifter magic after flying for a straight day is beyond difficult. But I lean into the fresh agony of betrayal Aurora inflicted in Oryn's audience chamber, letting the pain spur me on. My magic finds the black hearts of the oil-skinned trees, and I bid them climb toward the sky, melding together to create an impenetrable wall of bramble. Wicked thorns glint in the weak sunlight, as long as a human's arm and deadlier than a Goblin's sword, closing the Dark Court to the human invaders. It will buy us time—but not much.

The Demon sentries blow their horns from the battlements to announce our return. Exhaustion blunders my landing in the courtyard. Imps scatter in every direction. Callow hops from Regan's arms, mildly injured from her ordeal in the High Court, but whole.

Chaos's flank is lathered, his sides heaving. Regan slides from his back and stalks across the courtyard. Her whole body vibrates.

And then pain cracks across my cheek.

"I warned you."

The courtyard wobbles, made worse by the sudden onset of hunger and the overuse of my magic. One hand goes to my throbbing jaw. She . . . *hit* me.

"Damn you, Nimara! I warned you about her." Rage rolls from Regan in waves. "I told you not to trust her. But you didn't listen. Nothing else mattered to you—not even this home we have sacrificed everything to build. All you've ever cared about was the path to her fickle human heart."

I have never seen her so angry. In the century we've known each other, Regan and I have hardly ever quarreled. Not like this. And my chest aches with shame and remorse and a hundred other emotions. Because she is right. I should have suspected Aurora. Instead, I allowed our history to cloud my judgment. Let her endanger my court and bargain away my own power, all for the hope of some imaginary future together. The Imps around us begin to mutter, confusion wrinkling their ruddy faces. But no one dares to intervene.

"I lost my way," I say, cringing at the excuse.

Regan bends close. "And how many times did I try to tell you that? Or attempt to help you find your way back? You dismissed me, preferring *her* sugar-coated lies. The greatest power of an age"—she laughs darkly—"and it is wasted on you. You're too much of a coward to wield it properly."

Coward? A different kind of pain sings through me, sharp-edged and white-hot. I shove the Vila leader away. "Yes, she deceived me. But you've never understood what was between Aurora and me. Just because Pansy—"

"Don't you dare bring *her* into this," Regan bites back. She paces, the bone spikes on her knuckles stretching pale as her fists clench and unclench. "But at least I knew my sister. The princess was a stranger to you. I assumed that once the boy woke her, you'd see that she wasn't worth all your pining. That she was just like the other nobles when it came down to it. And no matter how many times she demonstrated . . ."

Her vitriol continues, but I've stopped listening. Something else snags in her words. "What do you mean, 'once *the boy* woke her'?" I interrupt. "Did you . . . did you know that Derek would kiss her?" And then, a far more lethal question. "Did you help him somehow?"

Regan wheels to me, indignant, but I detect the hint of panic in her emerald eyes. "How could you ask me that? The boy knew about the princess before he set foot in the Dark Court. He came here specifically to wake her."

"But he didn't know where she was," I counter. "He spouted that story about seeing the opening to the library while training steeds, but it always smelled rotten to me." At the expression on Regan's face, her lack of outright denial, a horrible certainty crackles like frost over my skin, replacing the bruising ache in my face. "You did help him, didn't you?"

She is not daft enough to refute my accusation, and I didn't know it was possible to feel the sort of anguish that pulses through me. Regan is my friend. Almost more than that. I can still imagine the press of her lips against mine. Lips that had been lying every day for Dragon knows how long. Are my instincts so skewed that I am blind to deceit?

"All those times when you claimed Aurora would be welcome," I say softly. "Invited her to court. None of it was real."

"You were obsessed," Regan says at last. "She was some . . . *goddess* to you. I needed you to understand that she was mortal. With *mortal* desires that didn't include you. If she'd woken and been as you said—accepting and open-minded—I would have been happy to have her in the Dark Court. But she *wasn't*, Nimara. And she never will be. She proved that today."

The air is too thin, and there isn't enough of it. "How did you even know how to wake her? I never told you."

She rubs her thumb over the gleaming scales of her twisted snake ring. "I paid a visit to the Graces in the Garden," she admits. "The one you freed—Rose, or whatever—was happy to inform me of the princess and her curse in exchange for a decent meal."

Rose? But that means the Grace knew that Aurora was alive well before I presented her with the necklace. She'd likely been plotting how to reach the princess, and I'd played right into her hands. Of course I did.

"And Derek?" I swallow down the lump of embarrassment in my throat. "How did he get to Aurora? He never said anything about your assistance."

"A Vila trick to lure prey," she says. And she does not look remorseful in the least. "A few drops of the boy's blood on a stone I dropped in the library. It called to him until he ventured near enough."

So he *had* been drawn to the library, just as he claimed.

"The kiss was luck, or so I assumed," Regan goes on. "I didn't think the boy would be able to resist her. That he'd hack apart the bramble enclosure with his bare hands if he had to. But I had no idea that the Fae had already told him what to do."

My head is spinning. "You punish me for falling for Aurora's traps when you have set just as many of your own. I thought you were my closest friend, but you've been manipulating me—far more than she ever did."

A memory of the game we shared together surfaces, when Aurora claimed Regan was exactly like the duplicitous courtiers from Briar. I should have listened.

"I am your friend," Regan snaps. "I'm your *family*. And sometimes family has to do what's best, even when it hurts. You think what I did was worse than what just happened in Oryn's court? The princess went behind your back to the High King. Demanded that you give away your power, so that *she* could keep hers. She does not care for you, Nimara."

Shared ire wafts and wends between us. Callow shrieks, and Chaos chuffs and thumps a foot. But I can think of nothing to say in return. As furious as I am with Regan . . . she isn't entirely wrong.

Movement ripples from the fringes of the courtyard.

"Nimara." Valmar hurries toward us, oblivious to the simmering tension in the air. "Where are Torin and the others? Oryn's staff?"

Regan answers without ever taking her murderous glare from mine. "We had to leave them behind. It was sabotage."

The Imp leader's tail begins to twitch.

"Aye. That explains the human ships the sentries spotted." He fires off a litany of orders to his nearest Imps, who bound away in a chittering cloud. "Who was it betrayed us? The boy?"

"It was Neve," I answer, unwilling to say Aurora's name. Regan, mercifully, stays silent on the matter. My temples ache with unspent adrenaline.

Valmar's long ears lie back. "Neve? Are you certain? She hates the Fae king as much as the rest of us."

"Obviously not," I say. "Have the sentries keep a watch for her. I want her captured and brought before me if she dares to show her face."

And then I stalk away, leaving Regan seething behind me.

Valmar and the others spring into action. Sentries are doubled, and the remaining Goblins begin handing out weapons and arming themselves with vials of blight elixir. The rest of Regan's Vila coat their own blood over arrows and sword edges—anything that might give us an advantage in the battle to come. Again I pray that Torin and Renard and the rest are safe. That they hadn't gone charging into the High Court after me, assuming I'd been captured. I want to send a party to rescue them, but we cannot spare anyone. Even so, if anything happens to them, I'll never forgive myself.

Having expended an enormous amount of my magic during our flight and in erecting the wall of bramble at the main gates, I'm all but banished to my rooms to rest. I shovel down as much food as the Imps can conjure, but sleep eludes me. There's a constant hum in the air, anxiety and bloodlust mixed together. I pace my rooms, so restless that, despite her injuries, Callow demands to be let out into the night. I don't blame her. My anger at both Regan and Aurora is like the sea during a storm, one I also yearn to escape. How could I have been so careless—again? Each of them knew exactly how to lure me in. How to use my love as a weapon. And I allowed them to do it.

Still, my traitorous mind wanders to Aurora.

What happened after we left? Is she in a Fae dungeon right

now? Dead? It shouldn't matter. But my wretched, wasted heart pulses out her name anyway.

At some point, I sink into a fitful slumber. Dreams creep through my brain like sharp-footed spiders. Sometimes I see Torin and the others, their small party overwhelmed by Etherians and slaughtered. Other times, the tale Regan told me of her past comes to life—villagers bludgeoning her to death. And then Aurora, standing beside the High King as she orders my execution with a flick of her royal wrist. Her laughter is brittle and cruel. It winds around me until all I can do is scream and scream.

I jolt into consciousness. The bedclothes cling to my sweat-drenched skin. A shadow curves in the light of the dying embers in the hearth. I'm still half inside my nightmare and believe it might be Kal come back to torment me. No—that Shifter is dead. But another is very much alive.

I scramble to my feet. "Neve."

CHAPTER THIRTY-NINE

The Shifter turns slowly. She's wearing a gown that might have been spun from shadow, layers of gossamer ebony fabric fastened to a high collar, which causes her to blend into the dim surroundings.

"Nimara."

I should have posted guards. Shouldn't have let Callow out on her hunt, even though the kestrel was stubbornly adamant. I pull on a dressing gown and cinch it tight. "You're either very brave or very stupid to come here. I know about Oryn and Aurora. Their secret mirrors."

End her, Mortania growls from her den. But I want to know why first.

Neve lifts a delicate shoulder. Her skin is pearly and rough. "Ah yes. I suppose you shouldn't be surprised. Such duplicity is what you always expected of me, isn't it?"

I blink. "Is that why you did it? Some kind of petty revenge?"

"Petty?" She bares her pointed teeth. "You have undermined

and humiliated me in front of this court for years. If I had sought revenge, it would have been well-earned."

"Humiliated?"

"Do not insult my intelligence by denying it." She prowls closer. "When the Imps and Demons and Vila hobbled into this court from whatever holes they'd been hiding in, they were showered with revels and gifts. But I hardly received a welcome before I was dispatched on 'official duties.' My rooms were given away—in my absence—to a mortal princess. You, mistress of this court, barely participated in the Shifter funeral. And they were your *kin*, Nimara."

Something recoils inside me. "I'm not a full Shifter. Not like—"

"Who?" Her eyes glitter. "The Shifter in the black tower?"

I flinch. That corner of my past is not a secret at court, but Neve and I have never spoken of Kal. I didn't much see the point. She probably would have defended him.

"Do you suppose that I'm not *acutely* aware of how you compare me to him? That you detest me and all the Shifters because of his betrayal?" Her breath comes in short bursts. "But I feel sorry for you, Nimara. You don't hate us. You hate yourself."

The ancient Vila whirls in rage. "You know nothing about me."

"Yes, and that's the way you prefer it, isn't it? You hide yourself behind your Vila magic, going so far as to adopt the name of the first Vila. But how did you take this realm? How did you escape the High Court, or bring down a member of Oryn's Hunt? With your *Shifter* magic. You ignore an entire part of yourself until it's convenient to do otherwise. Worse—you're ashamed of it. But why are you ashamed?"

"Because I don't want to be like you!" The answer is out of my mouth before I can pull it back. It rings around us. Neve stares at me, every muscle tensed. And now that I've started, I can't stop. "Kal was horrible. He tried to turn me into someone else. He took *everything* from me, and I never guessed who he really was until it was too late. You've given me no reason to believe you'd be any different than he was."

A long moment passes. An ember in the hearth pops.

"And have I given any reason for you to believe I would be the *same?*"

The question stings. But I shove the guilt away. "You betrayed me."

"You gave me good reason to do so."

"So you colluded with Aurora and sent me to the High Court in the hopes that I would lose my power? That was my punishment?"

She waves me off. "I would have *punished* you long ago, if that was what I had in mind."

"Then why?" I press. "You must have known what Aurora wanted."

Neve is quiet for a moment. "When the princess came to me, she seemed to assume that Oryn would be able to peel Mortania from your bones, as if the Vila were a second skin. But he could not have done so—not without killing you. And, as I said, I could have accomplished that myself." Her dark eyes sparkle in the firelight. "So yes, I did know what she desired. But what *she* did not understand is that her plan would never have worked as she imagined. Even if Oryn could have done what she hoped, you would never have agreed to give up your power. However, her temporary alliance with the High King *did* provide the most direct access to him. It was an advantage I could not ignore. And that is why I agreed to help her."

"I don't believe you," I seethe. "You would have told the council."

"And if I had?" she asks, toying with the edge of one of her long shapeless sleeves. "The council would have been furious at the princess's treachery. Somehow, I doubt they would have been able to hide their feelings."

I fidget with the sash of my dressing gown. I certainly wouldn't have been able to hide anything. And then our connection to Oryn might have been severed. But I'm not letting Neve off the hook that easily. "You let us walk into a room full of armed Fae. We were nearly killed in that palace."

She frowns. "I was not aware there would be so many."

I fold my arms. "Perhaps that's the sort of information we could have discovered if you'd presented the plan to the rest of us."

Annoyance flashes in her gaze. "As I've said, some information must be handled carefully. You needed to focus on the plan to rob Oryn of his staff—not some silly notion of the princess's. And there was always going to be a fight in the High Court. Or did you assume Oryn would politely pass you the most powerful weapon in Etheria?"

"A fight was why we brought an army with us."

"An army that would have been a match for the whole of the High Court?" she asks archly, and embarrassment climbs up my neck. We'd taken such a small number. "If anything went wrong, you would have been overwhelmed, though it was clear no one else wanted to recognize that danger. I listened in to a good many of the princess's talks with Oryn. She made sure the High King was expecting you. She requested a private audience. I assumed Oryn agreed and I judged that it would be a simple matter for you to swoop in, acquire the staff, and make for home. It was better than having you root around the Fae palace with only the boy for assistance."

I laugh. "Oh, Oryn was absolutely expecting us. His archers tried to shoot us down. And then he bound us with roots, and I couldn't move, much less—"

"You could Shift," she says, tilting her head at me. "Did you?"

The question catches me off-guard. No, I hadn't. Not until we left the palace. And *why* hadn't I? I could have summoned claws to rip apart the vines holding us. Or altered my body to merely step out of them. Could have done a hundred things—become the beast that razed Briar.

"*You ignore an entire part of yourself until it's convenient to do otherwise,*" she'd accused. But I don't want to examine that thought now.

"I . . ." I fumble. "I was exhausted. I barely possessed the strength to get us home."

Neve sniffs. "Yes, flying here from the High Court in only a day sounds like your magic was extremely fatigued."

She's insufferable. Frustrated, I stalk over to a sideboard, pour out a goblet of wine, and drain the contents in one gulp.

"It doesn't matter what power I used. We didn't get the staff— which we might have done, if you'd been honest—and now our army is likely captured. I'm sure they'll thank you for your si- lence."

"I will not allow anything to happen to them," she says. "Sev- eral of my Starlings were at the ready. They will do everything in their power to get the others home safely."

Had that been why we didn't see Torin and Renard? I hope so.

"And where were those Starlings in the High King's audience

chamber?" I ask. "Did you instruct them to let me rot in a Fae cell? Did you care at all?"

"I only would have left you there for a night or two." She grins, those predator's teeth gleaming in the gloom. But I scowl at her, and she sobers. "Of course I care. What bothers me most is that you cannot seem to comprehend that. Worse, that your low opinion of me is contagious."

"That's ridiculous."

"Is it?" She throws up her hands. "I am practically a ghost in these halls. Hardly anyone outside the council speaks to me, or even looks at me. Why do you think the Starlings never accompany me to court?"

"They have business—"

"Because I do not want to subject them to this sort of treatment!"

Something about her tone, about the expression on her face, rattles me to my very core. Her shoulders are slightly hunched, like a wounded animal's. It's a posture I recognize from my years in Lavender House, where I was feared and despised because of my magic. And an overwhelming rush of clarity overcomes me. Could Neve feel that way, too? Like an outsider in her own home?

The taste of the wine is sticky-sour. Is this what I burned down Briar to become?

Ignore her, pet. Mortania stirs in her cave. But I cannot.

"Then why have you stayed at all?" I ask quietly.

Dying embers wink behind the grate.

"For the same reason that I have endured every veiled insult, barbed comment, or dismissal of my advice," she says. "Because however you may view me, I believe in what you have founded. A home for us. Even though I cannot—"

She stops short and stares at the fire. I don't think I've ever seen a flush paint her cheeks.

"Cannot what?"

"Do you think it coincidental that I chose to stay in Torin's rooms after mine were gifted to the princess?" The question is nearly lost beneath the sound of the wind pressing against the walls. "That I'm so often found in her company?"

"You're friends. There's nothing—" But then I comprehend the look she is giving me. Dragon's teeth, I'm an idiot. "You're lovers."

She nods. And I curse my own stupidity. This is why Neve was so worried about our army being overwhelmed in the High Court. Because Torin was with us. She was protecting *her*.

"But why didn't you say? There's no shame in it."

Neve barks a rueful laugh. "Because we were worried how you would treat Torin if you knew."

And I am more than an idiot. I'm . . . cruel.

"Neve, I-I didn't realize about the two of you or . . . any of it. Torin warned me about the shadows of my past, and I—" I'm rambling and stop myself. "I'm sorry."

The seconds drag on.

"Torin has a rather annoying habit of being right, doesn't she?"

It takes me a moment to register the joke. I laugh, and Neve joins me. And it is the first time we have *ever* done so together. A weight is lifted from my shoulders, one I've been carrying for far longer than I knew.

"But I suspect that I am not the only member of court with a secret relationship."

The lightness of the moment evaporates. But I do not sense

that Neve is condemning me or even that she disapproves. "Is it so obvious that everyone knows?"

"I cannot speak to that," she says, not unkindly. "The only reason I guessed of your involvement with the princess is because she came to me with her plan. She, too, was concerned about the shadows of your past. And she would not have risked my revealing her betrayal unless she genuinely cared for you."

My heart thumps against my breastbone. Mortania whirls.

Listen not.

"What shadows did Aurora mean?"

Neve doesn't answer right away. She stirs the fire, coaxing a flame. "What did the Shifter in the black tower tell you of Mortania?"

It's an odd question. Mortania herself buzzes like a hornet, urging me to banish the Shifter from my rooms. But curiosity has already sunk its teeth into my brain. "He said they were in love, but they couldn't be together. And her retaliation against her own court is what started the first war."

"And do you believe him?"

I'd never had cause to doubt it. "You don't?"

"I believe that the story he told you was his perception of truth," Neve replies. "But reality, in my experience, is never so uncomplicated. If they were star-crossed lovers, why didn't they run away? After all, your own parents were Shifter and Vila. They obviously found it possible to be together without inciting violence."

Her assessment carries an uncomfortable note of truth. I squirm against it. "What does this matter now?"

"You speak of the traps the Shifter laid for you, and I'm not excusing anything he did. But have you ever considered the snares Mortania set for *him*?" The fire lengthens the angles of her face. "Her 'love' could have merely been a way for her to coerce the Shifter into sparking a war she desired for her own reasons. And then, when her plan soured, she found herself conveniently locked up with the one person who would toil for centuries in order to free her."

Is that what had happened? Unwelcome memories are dredged up from that night. Kal's shadows banished forever. His hungry, rictus smile. The popping sound his magic made as it sputtered out for good. And Mortania, spurring me to kill him. At the time, I thought perhaps the years of bitterness had hardened whatever was left of her heart. But had there ever been affection between Kal and Mortania? Or had she poisoned his mind and then discarded him as soon as he was no longer valuable?

Do not heed her, pet. She despises our kind. Pressure squeezes between my temples.

"The princess," Neve continues, "worried the same fate would befall you. That you were losing yourself without realizing it. And that fear was the reason behind her misguided attempt to remove your power."

I shudder, but I am nowhere near ready to forgive Aurora. "You should go. And keep out of sight. The palace is under the impression that you're in league with the Etherians."

"I suppose I deserve that," she allows with a sigh. "But there's something else you need to know. Oryn is here."

"Here?" My pulse kicks up, and I hurry to the window. The night is dark. "I don't see anything. He couldn't have followed us so quickly, and we would have seen them cross the mountains. I haven't heard the sentries, or—"

"You don't judge the High King of the Fae capable of masking himself?" She asks behind me. "That Oryn could not call on the winds to hasten his progress?"

Of course he could. I wheel around to face her. "Where is he, then? He cannot set foot on these lands."

"There is only one place he could muster where our magic cannot harm him." The sleeves of her gown billow softly in the draft. "The black tower. It was a Fae enchantment that bound the Shifter prisoner there for many centuries. The magic seeped into the stones."

I shake my head. "I broke that enchantment ages ago."

"There cannot be much of it left," she agrees. "But enough for Oryn to make his final stand, if he is swift enough."

And he will be. Which means I'll need to be faster and far deadlier. I'm already reaching for my clothes. Thinking of how best to approach the tower and whom I might need to take with me. But then another thought lands in my mind.

If Oryn is in the black tower, Aurora might very well be with him.

CHAPTER FORTY

The brambles at the main gates part at my command.

Beneath my shroud of invisibility, it's nothing to slip past the Fae guards flanking the entrance to the tower. In the end, I decided to come alone. It was better for Neve to keep hidden for the time being, and Oryn would immediately see our army coming if we began traipsing across the districts. I need to determine what we're up against before we do anything drastic. And especially, I think with a stab of guilt, if he has Aurora.

Forget her, pet, Mortania urges.

I wish I could.

Inside the tower, water drips against the stones. The sea pounds the cliff face. The ghosts of my past sigh in every inky corner. Those of my present, the High King and a few other armored Fae, are huddled around a table spread with maps and markers. It's not unlike a scene from Tarkin's war room. Now that I think of it, Oryn and Tarkin are not entirely dissimilar. Both of them considered themselves masters of their own universes. And both greatly underestimated me.

I sharpen my hearing in order to pick up their conversation.

"The humans will take the land siege. Ours from above."

"The boy?"

"Missing," the Etherian answers with a grimace. "Apparently there was some scuffle when depositing him on his ship. And he may have acquired a steed."

"Find him," Oryn commands. "I do not care whether he survives, so long as we have a body to return to the mortal king. Our bargain regarding the prince's return must be fulfilled."

Had that been why the Ryna king agreed to send ships—whatever army he could scrounge up in exchange for his son? The Fae got the better half of that arrangement. I tiptoe behind the stump of a column. The scent of brine and rotting seaweed mingle with the floral essence of light Fae magic. Pallid moonlight glints off Oryn's armor, which is a stunning display of interwoven gilded branches and chain mail that resembles a curtain of ivy leaves. The jeweled sigils of the seven Fae courts are embedded on his breastplate. And his cloak is fashioned out of the same material as the envoy's leathers, hammered gold bark that billows in the night.

"Is the Marked one safe?"

"Indeed, My King. He and his battalion are heavily guarded."

"Keep him watched. We know not what surprises the Vila may have in store."

Murmurs of agreement. So Oryn brought his heir with him, which means he must be slightly worried that he'll die here. Good. Another figure pads down the stairs. I press farther into the shadows.

"Ah. The Grace." Oryn's lip curls.

"You summoned me?" Rose is dressed in a Fae creation of bark-patterned trousers and a jacket seemingly comprised of supple branches, adorned with gilt-and-bronze leaves. Her pink hair is braided and pinned at the back of her head. A fresh wave of fury consumes me at the sight of her. How clever she must deem herself, having manipulated me into releasing her from the Garden. The same as when she would inflict her petty cruelties when I was the Dark Grace of Lavender House.

You are not that creature anymore, Mortania rumbles.

No. I am not.

"There is one final item I require before we enact the enchantment," Oryn says. "The Briar crown. Do you know where it might be found?"

The crown? It's a strange request. I would assume that Oryn considered the gilded wreath of bramble and thorn as nothing but a human trinket, far beneath his notice.

Rose adjusts the collar of her jacket, overlaid with something fine and shimmery, like a spider's web. "I've not seen it in a century, High King. It may well have been lost in the mongrel's siege."

Mongrel. I flinch reflexively, wishing that I'd not been persuaded to remove Rose's necklace.

"She proves more useless every day," one of Oryn's Fae mocks with a sneer.

Rose stiffens. "I am sorry to disappoint you. But perhaps I am not the best person to ask."

"Whom do you suggest in your stead?" Oryn sets down his marker.

"The princess, of course. She's the one who would care most about such an object."

My heart thumps against my breastbone, blood flashing hot, then cold. Aurora *is* here.

The High King's moss-green curls stir in the sea breeze. "Fetch her, then."

Rose nods then strides back up the stairs, boots clipping on the stone. Voices drift from the upper story, and then—

Torchlight shines on Aurora's bronze-kissed skin as she descends into the chamber, still luminous even though it's marred with the evidence of her journey. Threads of crimson-gold glimmer in the mess of windswept braids coiled beneath her hood. Her hands are bound in front of her. The sight of a cut on her cheek threatens to undo my Shift.

She betrayed you, Mortania fumes.

She did. Unforgivably. But in this moment, damn my feckless heart, I want to go to her. Burn this cursed tower to the ground and fly away with Aurora in my arms.

"Princess." Oryn's spurs, fashioned like pairs of thistles, jangle as he nears her. "I seek the Briar crown. The Grace informs me that you may be aware of its location."

Anyone else would be cowed and trembling, but Aurora regards Oryn as if *he* is the prisoner. "The crown is no business of yours. It belongs to Leythana's heirs. And I haven't seen it in a hundred years."

The squawking laughter of grackles bounces off the curved walls of the chamber. Oryn inhales deeply. "You lie."

She only shrugs and blinks innocently back at him. "Can you prove that?"

A low warning hiss emanates from the other Fae. Spindly fingered hands go to gem-encrusted blade hilts, and the High King's guards stomp forward. Six orbs begin to pulse from gold to amber. Light flashes across the wreaths of laurel leaves on their helmets.

"Perhaps the mortal princess will feel more inclined to honesty without a hand, High King." One of the others, a Fae wearing epaulettes fashioned like screaming eagles, unsheathes a knife from his belt. "We can present it to the boy to fulfill our bargain. That is what he desired, was it not? Her hand?"

Laughter, like branches clicking together.

No. They will not harm her.

Let them keep her, Mortania orders. Her presence fizzes in my fingertips. *She cares nothing for you.*

A pounding starts in my head. But then the circle of Fae surrounding Aurora tightens. Before I've fully realized what I'm doing, I'm sprinting across the tower, my Vila magic pummeling into the first Fae it lands on.

The guard roars as my power weaves past his ribs and squeezes his insides. I leave him on his knees and aim for another.

Oryn bangs his staff on the floor, his signature stoicism fracturing. "What is this? What is happening?"

Waves hurl themselves against the base of the cliff.

"It must be Malyce!" Rose shouts above the tumult. I should have dispensed with her first. "Hurry—the princess. It's the only way to stop her."

I spin in Aurora's direction, preparing to catch her around the waist and vault out the gaping side of the tower. A dangerous, insane ploy—but it's the only chance we have. I'm too slow. One of the Fae guards seizes Aurora, his bark-handled dagger pressed to her neck hard enough that a thin line of crimson blood dribbles onto her collarbone.

"Stop this!" Rose shouts, attention roving in search of me. "Show yourself, Malyce. Unless you want her to die."

It will be the Grace who dies, I think, my magic poised to strike. Oryn's Fae sport various states of injury and outrage. The tips of the High King's crown gleam, menacing as spears. I can end this battle here, before it begins. But then I see the pleading in Aurora's expression—the way her lips might form the shape of my name. And I am unmoored.

Mortania's presence thrums. *Leave now, or you will face a far worse fate than a medallion.*

Wind howls through the chamber. My very bones ache, as if I will split right down the middle. But I resist the ancient Vila's urging, skin prickling as my Shift falls away.

"Ah." Rose smiles at me, saccharine. "There she is."

One of the hulking Fae guards moves to bind my wrists.

"Leave her," Oryn instructs. The sigils of his fallen courts glare at me from his breastplate. "We have her chains here." He indicates Aurora. "If the creature Shifts, if she tries to lash out at us with that abominable power, it will be the princess who suffers."

Every fiber of my being wants to attack anyway, or to flee. But I am rooted to the spot, attention fixed on Aurora's head, where something is glimmering.

In the scuffle, Aurora's hood has fallen around her shoulders, and her braids have loosened, exposing something beneath. I bite my bottom lip to keep from uttering a curse. Where had she found *that*?

"Don't worry, Malyce." Rose straightens a bronze leaf on her sleeve. "We'll take good care of her. You, perhaps not. But the princess—" Her whole body goes rigid. "Dragon's teeth."

"What is it now?" Oryn demands.

Rose points, and my stomach sinks. She noticed it, too. "The crown, High King. She's wearing it."

The Fae who is holding Aurora glances down. His knife moves from her throat and takes two swipes at her braids. Thick chunks of copper-gold hair flutter to the floor, revealing the gilded wreath of bramble and thorn.

Low Fae laughter—like the first greeting of thunder—winds around us, cresting to a peak that makes my blood boil. Aurora juts out her chin, defiant as ever, but I can sense the current of fear that must be threading through her veins.

"Ah, Princess." Oryn smiles, all sharp teeth and menace. "You never fail to amuse me."

A wave shatters below.

"Shall I?" Rose reaches for the crown, greedy snake that she is, but Oryn stops her.

"Leave it."

A few of the Fae exchange uncertain murmurs.

"Is that wise, High King?" one ventures.

"She will not wear it long." The leaves of his chain mail chime as he moves. "I should like for this so-called queen to watch her realm crumble."

Stars leap and spin within the orb of the High King's staff, bathing the room in gold. In the shimmery haze, Aurora is like a statue come to life—like Leythana's outside the main gates of Briar. But she is not Leythana.

We are both prisoners.

CHAPTER FORTY-ONE

We're kept under guard until dawn, one of the Fae always close enough to reach for Aurora if I misbehave. Rose was dispatched shortly after my failed attack—something about completing the High King's business. Every muscle aches to fight back. Dig for each heart of Fae power and squeeze until there's nothing left. A taste of metal and blood coats my tongue, Mortania wilder than Chaos in his worst temper, far more so than I've ever sensed her. But if anything should happen to Aurora . . .

You should not care.

But I do.

That does not mean that I forgive her. I am *furious* with her. She let me believe we could find our way back to each other when all she really wanted to do was hand me over to the High King. Extinguish my power. But I cannot stop looking at her where she sits on the other side of the tower. Cannot stop wondering what she's thinking as she stares out the gap in the wall. After an eternity, her gaze tracks to mine, and my heart crashes against my ribs like the waves against the cliff below. I wish I could scream at her. Hold her. And I search her expression for some hint that she's sorry. That she's realized she made a mistake. But those amethyst eyes are closer akin to the churning sea—angry and frigid and deadly. I do not dare look at her again.

As the sun begins to rise, Briar shrouded in the shades of the gray dawn, we're marched up the piecemeal staircase to the very top of the black tower. Three of the Fae whistle, calling their steeds and galloping off toward the ships behind us. And I notice a faint beating that I ascribe to the tempo of waves and the gales buffeting the tower. But it's a different rhythm altogether, punctuated by barely perceptible whinnying. Oryn's army. I can't see them, but they're here, perhaps hovering just above the sea.

"Another member of your ilk dwelled in this place some years past." Oryn's hammered-bark cloak shimmers as it swells behind him.

"Dwelled?" I reply. "You mean the Shifter you chained here in shadow?"

"It was a fitting punishment, the Shifter and his mate imprisoned together. Close enough to hear the screams of the fallen. To understand the full extent of their defeat."

Defeat. My mind wanders back to the conversation I had with Neve, and her suggestion that Kal had been a pawn in a larger game. Since that awful night when Aurora was cursed again, I'd painted the Shifter as a monster. But how much had he done out of desperation because he believed he was right? And what does that say about everything *I've* done? Can the death and destruction be wholly justified? Mortania is eerily silent.

"We'll see if you don't share a similar fate by day's end, Oryn."

The jewel on his forehead glimmers. "The day has much in store for us both, half-breed. And I am not the one held captive by my enemies."

Oryn's staff taps against stone as he moves away. Aurora and I are alone, save for the Fae guards behind us. It's the closest we've been since Oryn's audience chamber, and my skin tingles with the urge to touch her. I curse myself for the weakness and ball my hands into fists.

"Your new allies handle you poorly," I observe, low enough so that they won't hear.

"They aren't my allies," she mutters back.

"Illicit talks and intricate conspiracies." I huff out a laugh. It clouds in front of my face. "No, those don't sound like the sort of things allies do together. Call him off if you're no longer on good terms."

Her jaw sets. "I tried."

I blink, and a wisp of hope flutters in my chest. "You did?"

"It may surprise you to learn that I do *not* want my realm locked within an enchanted cage."

"Then why is Oryn still here? Doesn't he need your permission to invade?"

Aurora's shorn locks stir in the icy sea-salted wind. It carries her scent—apple blossom and cool water. And that endless craving I feel for her is both sated and intensified at once.

"Apparently, my summons cannot be rescinded once given." She swallows. "I thought I'd been so careful, but he . . ."

Crows wheel overhead, trading their calls.

"You're not the first to fall victim to Oryn's trickery," I say, gentler than before. "Fae bargains are unpredictable. Which is why I never expected you to make one."

Her dirt-smudged face at last turns to me. "I lied to you about Oryn because I knew if Mortania guessed my plans, she would influence you to abandon them. And I was right. As soon as the details came to light, you changed course—even though you promised to trust me."

The ancient Vila swirls with displeasure.

"Promises don't count when they're made under false pretenses," I fire back. "What of the trust I placed in *you*? I thought you really wanted to build something together. But you just wanted me to be powerless."

"I never wanted that."

The scent of steel and loam lands on my tongue. "No? Then why was Oryn prepared to strip me of my magic while you were secretly wearing your crown?" She opens her mouth to reply, but I cut her off. "Don't trouble yourself. That crown is the only thing you've ever cared about. Even if we had been wed, *you* would have been queen, and I your consort. My power at *your* disposal."

"Are you finished?"

I'm not. But I chew my lips and don't say anything else. The nickering of the Fae steeds floats up from below.

"This crown is the only thing I have left of my life before," Aurora says. "You want me to forget Briar. Forget *who* I am. Well, I cannot. I will not. Not for you, nor anyone else."

Mortania roils in her den, and my palms ache from where I've been digging my nails into my flesh. "Was any of it real?"

For the briefest instant, hurt flickers across her expression. And then it glazes over, colder than a frigid sea. She studies the horizon, refusing to reply. It is answer enough.

"Your plan wouldn't have worked," I say, angry tears stinging on my dry lips. "Oryn would have had to kill me to remove her. Trap *me* in some medallion along with her. Did you know that? Would it have mattered?"

The next gust of wind grabs at us both. But Aurora gives nothing away. And I'm honestly not sure what I expected her to say. Or which answer would have hurt me worse.

The sun finally heaves itself over the horizon line. A dull orange dawn bleeds through the realm. Mist billows across the land and climbs over the bramble barrier at the main gates. The human ships are even with the Crimson Cliffs. A horn sounds and my heart beats harder. The lights of the palace begin to glow, like rows of eyes watching. I should be there.

And then an explosion reverberates from the direction of the palace. Panic spears through me, and I try to Shift my eyesight to determine what it is, but I'm out of range. Another blast echoes. The Fae king is smiling. His moss-green curls dance around the antlers of his crown.

"What's happening?" Aurora tries to inch closer to the edge of the tower, but her guard hauls her back.

"Patience, Princess." He combs his sticklike fingers through her uneven locks.

I count three more explosions, one rumbling into the next, before something much nearer the black tower catches my attention.

Hooded figures are hurrying from Briar's main gates. At least two dozen. Oryn doesn't seem alarmed and doesn't call for the party to be intercepted. They scurry through the clumps of skeletal trees, heads bent, and file swiftly into the tower.

"Who is that?" They're too small to be Fae. And how did they get past the bramble barrier? Footsteps clatter up the stairs and one of the cloaked figures emerges.

It's Rose, returned from whatever errand the High King assigned to her. Her clothes are mud-stained and there's ash on her face.

"I take it your strategy was effective," Oryn says.

"Oh, yes." Rose sweeps him a curtsy, pleased with herself. "The tunnels served our purpose beautifully."

The tunnels. That's why my brambles didn't stop them. I curse my own stupidity. Rose must have learned of them when she attended the funeral.

"What have you done?" I breathe.

"As His Majesty requested," she answers, beaming at Oryn. "I've helped rid the world of the Vila scum. Everything was accomplished exactly as you bid, High King."

"And the runes?"

"Awaiting your command."

"What is she talking about?" I stalk forward, but then Aurora's guard clamps his sinewy arm around her shoulders.

"Hold your temper, half-breed. Lest your princess lose her head."

I snarl at him. Oryn hasn't moved. He stares toward Briar, the jewels on his breastplate glimmering in the sunrise. Fae steeds chuff and whicker behind us. It's then that I see it. Smoke curls up from the palace in sooty tendrils. The explosions.

I whirl back to Rose. Beneath the grime, her cheeks are smeared with a golden flush of exhilaration. "You did this."

"You think you're the only one among us capable of formulating a plan, Malyce? Maybe you shouldn't have kept us locked in a dungeon for a hundred years if you wanted to inspire loyalty."

Us. And suddenly I know who the others were—the Graces, escaped from the Garden. "The Goblins—"

"Were all busy preparing for the Fae siege. The keys were hanging on a peg." She laughs again. "It was too easy, really."

Dragon's teeth, Valmar. He must have assumed that playing jailer to a couple dozen caged Graces was a waste of time given the current situation.

"Rose, how could you?" The pain in Aurora's voice is palpable. "My home. *Our* home."

"It isn't our home anymore," she replies, adjusting her jacket. "They took it from us. Honestly, Highness, I did you a favor. The war is all but won now. You won't have to deal with *that*"—she jerks her chin at me—"for much longer."

Mortania strains beneath my skin. I have no one to blame for this but myself. I knew Rose would cause trouble if I let her out. But I'd wanted to please Aurora.

Show them what you can do.

But the risk is still too great.

Rose gathers her composure and addresses the High King. "The others are waiting downstairs. Shall I tell them you'll come?"

"For what purpose?"

That brilliant Grace smile hitches. "For . . . our reward. I hate to seem impatient, but with the battle coming, we're all anxious to—"

"Reward? Is the destruction of these creatures not enough to satisfy you?"

"It is, of course." Rose brushes a stray pink curl out of her eyes. "But you did promise . . ."

The orb of Oryn's staff pulses. "What did I promise?"

"You said we would be full Fae. That you would turn us."

Ships' bells clang in the distance.

"I assure you, *Grace*." The word is flung like an insult. "I made no such agreement. For if I did, I would be bound to honor it."

Every muscle in Rose's body coils. "You said—"

"I said . . ." He advances on her, spurs singing. His companions angle themselves closer. "That you would have the life of a Fae. *That* is what we agreed."

"The life of a Fae, precisely . . ."

"And you will be permitted to live within my court, an honor no Grace before you has ever attained. You already know that if you do not spend your gift, you will enjoy a long existence. It is sufficient. It is what we agreed."

"But . . ." Bright honey splotches erupt on Rose's chest and neck.

Understanding dawns in my mind. Like the Briar King during the first war, Rose was clumsy with her words. She assumed she was bargaining for power. A staff, probably. A title and prestige among the Fae. But Oryn would never grant her any of that. Would never deign to consider her an equal. Should she ever live in Etheria, the only status Rose would claim would be the same as mine used to be in Briar—of a half-breed. An outcast. I'd laugh if the situation weren't so tragic.

"If you dislike our arrangement, you may release me from my vow." His leafy eyebrows rise in challenge.

I can almost glimpse the storm brewing beneath Rose's skin, like the Demons before they change into their shadow forms.

"I do not release you," Rose grinds out. "And I demand that you—"

A deafening blow roars around us. I'm knocked to my knees. The tower sways, listing to one side. The High King scrambles for his staff. Stone crunches and pops.

A sharp whistle pierces the ringing in my ears and reels my attention to the right. Regan and another Vila are straddled on our flying steeds, pouches of blight elixir held in each hand.

"Come on!" she yells. How did she know I was here? "Now, Nimara!"

My steps are drunken as the tower pitches, but I make it to the edge of the roof. Regan is waving wildly, urging me on.

But Aurora.

Leave her!

I turn around and search for her amid the Fae. They're crowding protectively around the High King. I don't see her—

A high whinny cuts through the chaos, coupled with wing-beats. Another Fae steed soars over the tower and loops back. But it's not an armored Fae rider perched on the saddle—it's Derek. Damn that mortal. Where has he been hiding? He shouts Aurora's name, and she emerges from behind a guard. The prince swoops around the tower.

"Jump!" He banks the steed as close to the wall as he dares.

Aurora throws a last look over her shoulder. Our eyes meet, the seconds slowing and thudding against my eardrums. And then she vaults over the side of the tower and into Derek's waiting arms. The steed pivots and bounds toward the ships on the horizon.

Oryn staggers to his feet, staff in hand. Before he has the chance to attack, I leap over the edge of the tower, Shifting as I fall. A pair of wings peels from my spine and I'm carried away. Behind me, Regan and the other Vila toss the last pouches of explosives at the tower, then send two arrows after them.

There's a final blast. And then the black tower, and everyone in it, is buried in a mountain of ash and rock.

CHAPTER FORTY-TWO

Regan and the other Vila pull even with me a short distance away from the smoldering wreckage. My heart is still slamming against my ribs. Derek and Aurora are nothing but a speck speeding toward the human ships.

"How did you know I was here?"

A familiar warble answers. Callow. She lands on my shoulder and knocks her head against mine.

The other Vila smirks. "Damn bird was haunting the courtyard. Wouldn't give us any peace until we followed her. I think you have to eat a raw mouse to thank her."

I owe my kestrel much more.

"And there was the boy," she adds.

"Derek?" I ask, startled.

The Vila dips her chin in confirmation. "He showed up in the night to tell us Oryn had set up his camp at the tower. Between his information and Callow, we could guess where you had gone."

Derek is . . . helping us? The Fae guard said he'd stolen a steed, but I would never have guessed he'd go to the palace. His human fleet is still waiting with the Fae army, poised to attack. What could the boy be . . .

"And suppose you went to the tower to confront the High King? *Alone?*" Regan looks at me like I'm an Imp she discovered in her wardrobe.

Like a rogue wave, the argument from before smashes between us. Callow, sensing the change in my energy, screeches.

"I don't have to explain myself," I say to the Vila leader, ignoring the confusion scrawled on her companion's face. "I received intelligence from Neve and acted on it."

"Neve? You trusted her after everything that happened?"

A spiteful retort builds behind my teeth. But it won't do any good to spar with Regan now. Briefly, and more to the other Vila, I explain the last hours—why Oryn was able to muster at the tower, his wanting the Briar crown, and how Rose snuck back into the palace and released the other Graces.

"The High King has planted something, then." Regan angles her steed toward the Grace District, where smoke streams into the low clouds and creeps through the graveyard of buildings.

"He must have," I say. "If it's magic, I might be able to undo it."

"We'd best hope so."

The Fae beast snorts.

"But why would Oryn have wanted the Briar crown at all?" the other Vila asks.

"Who knows?" I gesture at the fallen tower. "In any case, he doesn't have it now."

"Yes, because the princess does." Regan spits Aurora's title in what I know is a deliberate attempt to goad me. But I don't possess the will or energy to respond. Oryn's army is beginning to stir, word undoubtedly spreading about what transpired at the tower.

"I'm going back," I say.

Regan clicks her tongue and wheels her mount toward the cliffs. "I'll see what can be done about the human fleet."

The first punches of cannon fire reverberate from the ships. Regan's steed whinnies, its wings beating harder. A cloud of ash still hovers over the black tower. And the severity of the looming danger at last registers. It pulls me up short. We have no idea what the next hours will bring.

"Regan, wait," I call.

She motions for the other Vila to fly ahead. Her brow furrows. "What is it?"

I fly nearer. "Whatever else has happened—thank you. If you hadn't come . . ."

The fire in her emerald gaze dulls. Her shoulders soften. "I told you before. I would cross the sea a hundred times over to be by your side."

Emotion tightens my throat. I'm still angry with her. Still wounded by her betrayal. But I reach for her anyway, my green-veined skin juxtaposed with her rich brown bone spikes. A Vila. Just like me.

"Don't die," I say, my voice rough. "We aren't finished fighting."

She barks a laugh, kicks at the sides of the Fae steed, and hurtles toward the Crimson Cliffs.

A battle has begun in earnest by the time I make it back to the palace. And I'm relatively certain Oryn is still alive. Were he dead, his power would have transferred immediately to his heir, which—given the depth of the High King's magic—is an event I doubt we could have overlooked. The Fae certainly behave as though nothing has changed. They flood our skies on their steeds, laying siege for the first time in a hundred years. Demons swirl over the realm in their shadow forms, boasting the nightmarish shapes of deadly wolves and spear-toothed monsters. Imps and Goblins take cover in the skeletal buildings of the districts, loosing arrows and firing crossbows. Golden scythes of power lash the skies. Fae bodies clad in woven-branch armor look like falling stars as they're toppled from their mounts.

Valmar is upon me as soon as I land. "Nimara! The palace is aflame."

Callow flaps to the ground but stays close. Goblins and Imps stampede through the courtyard, some of them hauling sloshing buckets of water and others brandishing weapons. An Imp hurries up to me with a breastplate made of bones. I motion her away. The weight of it would be too cumbersome.

"How bad is the fire?"

Valmar scrubs the back of his neck. "It's chewing through the palace like no fire ought. Mine are working as fast as they can, but nothing touches it."

"Valmar!" An Imp scurries up, pudgy vermilion cheeks darkened with soot. "We found more of 'em."

"Where?" he demands.

"Most of 'em in the back corridors. Glowing, they was."

"More of what?"

The Imp's long ears twitch. "Drawings, Mistress. Strange like. Found 'em painted in hidden corners and such. Don't know who put 'em there or why they all lit up."

"Drawings." I kneel to the Imp's level. "What do they look like?"

"Like the symbol of the piss-eyed king." He cups his fingers together in an imitation of the laurel leaves curving around an orb. "All of 'em gold."

Those have to be the runes Rose told Oryn she and the other Graces drew. How they were able to skulk through the palace undetected, I'll never know. Oryn must have given them some charm or the like for concealment. And he'll probably be completing his enchantment as soon as he digs himself out of the rubble of the tower. Which means we need to work quickly.

I'm about to instruct the Imp to show me what he found, when the clamor of wingbeats gusts around us. Callow screeches a warning and several beasts sail overhead, but they're not Fae. These are more akin to a griffin I saw illustrated in a storybook, with huge taloned feet and scales instead of feathers. One swoops into the courtyard and—my breath catches.

"Torin!" I'm crushing her in an embrace before her feet have fully reached the ground. "You survived. We looked for you, but couldn't—"

"We had help," she assures me, and pats the griffin creature's flank. "Meet one of Neve's Starlings. Merkin here, and his compatriots, warned us of the Fae warriors lying in wait at the border. We turned back before the protections were even broken. The Demons hid us until it was safe to start for home."

Mortania hums with disquiet. *The Shifters are not to be trusted.*

My initial instinct is to agree, and I feel myself take a reflexive step backward. But I stop. Neve obviously hadn't been lying when she said she had her Starlings waiting. She'd made sure everyone got home safely. No matter what Mortania says, I've treated the Shifters like enemies for too long. Shame climbs up my neck.

"Thank you," I say to the Starling.

Merkin paws at the flagstones and chuffs.

"I take it the plan to steal the High King's staff failed," Torin guesses, eyeing the battle.

I almost laugh. "There was never any plan to do that, at least not as Aurora presented it."

"So I've been told." Torin nods in Merkin's direction. The grooves traversing her limbs fade from amber to pale yellow. "Honestly, I have no idea what Neve was thinking, keeping a scheme like that from me. She was in completely over her head."

There's something in Torin's tone. A possessiveness regarding the Shifter leader that I intimately understand. And I scold myself again for the hundred details I missed over the years. "Her motivation is clear enough."

"What could possibly have—"

I grant the Demon leader a wry smile. "Neve wanted us in and out of the High Court as quickly as possible. She didn't want our forces involved at all—forces *you* were leading."

Shock blooms in the Demon leader's amber gaze. The fissures on her skin flare a bright red, such that I have never seen her wear before. "Oh. She . . . told you."

"She did. And I owe you an apology," I say, the shame from my earlier exchange with Neve hitting me all over again. "I shouldn't have caused you to feel like you had to keep something like that a secret." I turn my attention to Merkin. "Or caused Neve—or any of the Shifters—to feel like outsiders in their own home."

Merkin bows his head. And Torin tugs at her onyx pendant. "Where is Neve now?"

"I don't know." Smoke pours steadily from the open windows of the palace and chugs through the main door. "When we got back, I . . . sort of blamed her for what happened at the High Court. She's keeping a low profile for now."

Torin sighs. "We'll sort it out."

"And Renard?" Valmar asks. I'd almost forgotten he was there.

"He flew ahead to corral his Goblins. I'll do the same with my Demons." Torin accepts a ladleful of water from an Imp. "By the way, how did you manage to persuade the humans to fight for us? I know it wasn't Regan's doing."

I stare at her.

"Humans fighting for us?" Valmar grunts. "Did you drink the ambrosia wine in the High Court?"

The ladle splashes into the bucket. Torin wipes her mouth. "We flew past the fleet on our way here. You don't know?"

"I know Derek came to warn Regan and the others about the High King. But last I saw, the mortals' cannons were firing at *our* shores."

Torin swings onto Merkin's back and hauls Valmar up behind her. "See for yourself."

I'm back in the air in an instant, Callow beside me. The Ryna ships are minuscule next to the Crimson Cliffs. I sharpen my eyesight until I can see the white puffs of the cannon shots. Guns that are no longer aimed at Briar or at the Vila darting about on their steeds but at the light Fae warriors.

"I assumed you made some sort of pact," Torin calls.

I deny this emphatically. A harpoon is launched from the deck of a ship and impales a Fae steed. Both mount and rider spiral into the sea.

Torin says something else, but I'm distracted by a deadly crunch of wood. One of the Ryna ships rocks back and forth in a dangerous rhythm, and then the bow and stern begin rising simultaneously. Dragon's teeth. The hull is splitting in half like a cracked egg. A cheer goes up, one that sounds unmistakably like the Vila war cry.

Regan.

If the humans have switched to our side, why is she still attacking them? And then another, far more terrifying thought takes root:

Aurora is on one of those ships. Maybe even that one.

Valmar is still shouting my name as I tear toward the wreck.

The smoke from the palace fires rolls in a gritty tide across the Grace District. It burns in my lungs and blurs my vision as I cut through it, Callow beside me, dodging arcs of golden Fae power and armored riders. Goblins appear in the windows of decrepit manors and Grace houses, hurling bone-tipped spears soaked in Vila blood. Demons prowl above them, hardly discernible from the noxious smoke. I spot one in the shape of a gargantuan sea creature, its eyes like orange embers. It swallows a mount and rider whole. The Fae steed screams in terror as the darkness engulfs him, and then goes eerily silent. Sinister laughter echoes as the Fae warrior cartwheels like a ragdoll to the ground below, her staff extinguished.

I'm almost to the main gates when a rider intercepts me. I veer out of his way and a heartbeat later hear his cry of anguish as a Goblin's raven-feathered arrow impales him in the throat. He slumps in the saddle, gilded helmet lolling as his steed gallops away on the wind. I urge my wings faster.

The Ryna ship is already underwater when I land at the edge of the Crimson Cliffs. Regan's steed spots Callow and nickers.

"What are you doing away from the palace?" Drying Fae blood splatters her leathers and the bone spikes along her forehead.

I gulp down air and point. "Why did you sink that ship?"

"I told you I would keep the humans back."

"But they're helping us! They're firing at the Fae. I saw them harpoon one of the steeds."

"And?" Her mount begins to dance and she reins it in. "They're still our enemies, Nimara. Maybe their plan is to eliminate both us and the Fae, then claim these lands for themselves."

The wails of the drowning sailors float up from below.

"They have less than a dozen ships, and not nearly enough force to conquer two armies."

She shrugs. "Greedy and stupid, then."

"Regan—"

"*Enough*. I know why you're here. For her. You think she's on one of those ships. If she is, it's her choice. She didn't choose you, and she never has. Not once."

Listen well, pet.

The wind whips around us, ruffling the Fae beast's gold-dusted feathers. Callow's talons dig into my shoulder. Ships rock and pitch on the choppy current.

"This isn't about her. We have to keep Oryn from casting his enchantment, and if the humans can help us do that—"

"Then stop Oryn," she replies. "Use your power for the Dark Court instead of distracting yourself with people who don't matter."

Yes, pet. Use me.

"It's not that simple."

"And why not? The humans have absolutely nothing to do

with us." Regan jerks her chin at the turmoil below. "She's drawn a line. You cannot be on both sides of it. And I'm tired of giving myself to someone who would throw away everything we've built for some mortal princess. I came here for you. I *love* you." Her eyes shine.

"Regan, I . . ."

"*Think* before you choose her again."

The cold air stings in my lungs. Wood smashes as a ship collides with a rock at the base of the cliffs. The roving dots that are sailors hurry from bow to stern, lassoing ropes out to try to reel in the survivors of the sunken ship. Cannons boom. Destroying the fleet would be so easy—the same as when I peeled up the docks in the harbor a hundred years ago. Mortania's presence floods my veins, thrumming through every limb.

And then a flicker of gold catches my attention. I sharpen my eyesight until I can see clearly. Aurora. She's standing at the prow of the ship, the Briar crown gleaming on her head.

As if she can feel my gaze, she turns. That connection between us hums.

"Damn you, Nimara." Regan nudges her steed closer. "You're not some whimpering half-Vila anymore. You are Mistress of the Dark Court. And if you will not do what is necessary, I will do it for you."

Before I can utter a word to stop her, the Vila leader spurs her mount and takes a flying leap over the cliffside.

CHAPTER FORTY-THREE

The other Vila assume I've come to join their fight against the Ryna fleet. They raise their fists, my name mingling with the punches of cannon shot. Some of the Fae riders notice me as well and abruptly change course, staffs sparking. I let my power loose, and it jumps from one Etherian to the next, repelling attacks. Callow joins me, rending faces and slicing steeds with her talons. Fae plummet into the sea. Mortania cackles.

But dispensing with these threats slows me down. By the time I reach Aurora's ship, Regan is poised above the mast, too high up to be touched by their guns or harpoons.

"Stop!"

Her steed rears. "I vowed to protect you—protect our home—at all costs. And I will show you what it means to keep a promise."

Regan's steed snorts and bucks, feeding off her energy. She stares down, brow pinched in concentration. The sea groans and heaves. The Ryna ship begins to wobble, more like a toy than a warship. And then, to my complete shock, the water directly behind the ship begins to rise. It's as if a string is attached to the whitecaps, reeled upward by an invisible hand until a massive, lethal wave looms. Droplets fly from its inky surface and fleck my cheeks. Fins and tentacles puncture the wall of water and then vanish. This is powerful magic.

"Regan!"

Sweat pours down her face and her eyes are fever-bright. The wave climbs higher, level with the cliffs themselves. The ship will be capsized. I have to stop her myself.

I bid my power unfurl and find Regan's before it's too late. But for the first time since I learned how to use it, my magic resists. I can feel it pulsing inside me, but it won't budge.

Mortania.

This is for the best. Her voice winds through my skull in oily ribbons.

No. I reach for my magic. Claw for it. The ancient Vila blocks every attempt. And I am so stunned that I nearly lose control of my Shift and fall out of the sky. All these years, I considered Mortania an integral part of me. A mentor, even. Whatever she'd done in the past, she was the one who guided me to take control of my magic. Harness my rage and wield it like a weapon against Briar. She shouldn't be able to restrict the use of my power. But she is. And the full truth of the last years trembles through me. I'd terribly misjudged the ancient Vila. Mortania has been hiding. Casting herself as a vague and barely present spirit. Waiting, just like Kal waited, until the moment was exactly right.

Mortania's sinister laughter echoes in the deepest part of my soul. *We are one and the same now, pet. There is no untangling us. Fighting it will make things harder on yourself.*

White-hot panic rises in stride with Regan's wave. If I cannot use my magic, I cannot prevent this. But no—I will not lose Regan. And I will not let Aurora be drowned.

I charge toward the ship.

Regan anticipates me. A jet of water erupts in my path. I swerve to the right only to pull up short in front of another, then another. Not even Callow is quick enough to dodge them.

"Regan, please!" I shout above the roar of the sea.

Through the veil of salty mist, her eyes lock with mine. And in their emerald depths I glimpse the sadness buried in her core. The years she endured before she came to Briar, driven into hiding. Her mother's death. Her sister's disloyalty. Mine. An elixir more potent than any I could have concocted as the Dark Grace. A cold certainty spreads like rivers of ice through my veins. Regan came here for Nimara, but that isn't who I really am. It never was.

Regan appears to realize that, too. She raises her fist, the silver snake ring on her hand shining in the sun, and bellows a war cry. The wave begins to vibrate, like a beast readying for a strike. And then—

A howl of agony reverberates between the spears of water. Regan clutches her chest and curls into herself. It's her power. Regan's intent was strong enough to summon the wave, but she's only half-Vila, and there was never enough magic to maintain it. The tether inside her snapped like a too-taut string.

No. Not like this.

Her name wrenches from my lips, but Regan can't hear me. Her body goes slack. Without her magic to guide it, the wave shudders, and then begins to collapse back into itself.

Regan falls with it.

She slides from the saddle, and her steed whinnies and rushes away. Several other Vila streak toward us in an attempt to rescue their leader. I tuck in my wings and dive, but I'm not fast enough. Regan somersaults, head over feet, and disappears into the sea in a splash of white froth.

My first instinct is to plunge in after her, but I wouldn't survive it. The Ryna fleet bobs like a cork in the wave's wake. Vila howl Regan's name.

"Alyce!"

My attention jerks back to the ship. Aurora is braced against the railing. The sea absorbs the shock of the slamming wave like a blow. The Vila scatter. Aurora's ship is flung toward the cliffs at an impossible speed. I dart after it, muscles rebelling as I Shift in my arms.

Just as the hull of the ship crushes against the cliff face, I scoop Aurora up and catapult into the sky.

We skid onto the cliffs and roll apart, bruised and drenched. All I can see is Regan's body as it was swallowed by the waves, her face contorted as her magic guttered out. The air is too thin. My hacking coughs turn into sobs. My fingers dig into the loamy earth, desperate for something solid to hold on to. Desperate to change what just happened, even though I know it wouldn't have mattered. Regan made her choice. And I made mine.

Callow lands near me and brushes her wings against my cheek.

"I'm so sorry, Alyce." Aurora's voice penetrates the fog of my grief.

Without thinking, I reach for her. Her arms come around me, and I let myself cry into her chest. Clutch at her. She holds on to me just as tightly. Strokes my hair, and murmurs comforting things

I can't make out. And when I've finally caught my breath, I look up at her. She's blurry through my tears. The pad of her thumb skims the ridge of my cheekbone.

"You saved me," she says.

I let out a breathless laugh. "Of course I did. I love you. I don't know how to do anything else *but* love you." I scoot away from her, hugging my knees to myself. "I wish I did."

"Do you mean that?"

"Yes." I swipe my arm over my face, skin stinging with salt. "No. I don't know. And it doesn't matter now, does it? Not after everything that's happened."

Aurora doesn't answer. She pushes herself to stand and watches the tumult of the sea below. A few Vila are still patrolling the area where Regan vanished. The rest of the Ryna fleet is struggling to stay afloat in the repercussions of the wave. Several of the ships have tipped over, and one is completely capsized, its barnacled hull sticking out of the water like a whale breaching. The one that carried Aurora is nothing but scraps of wood. I shudder, imagining her broken bones at the bottom of the sea. Right next to Regan's.

"Leythana lied."

Aurora's voice brings me back into the moment. "Leythana . . . lied?"

"That book," she replies, "where you read about how there was another realm that tried to negotiate with the Vila. We didn't know what they offered or why the Vila allied with Leythana instead. But I found out."

I get up, wincing at the aches in my muscles. "Is it really important right now?"

The battle rages around us.

Aurora continues as if it isn't. "I discovered some of Leythana's writings, locked away in the royal crypt. It's where I found this." She picks up the crown from where it tumbled from her head. The wreath of bramble and thorn glimmers in the sunlight.

I frown. One of the humans must have taken it there to honor Mariel. They'd hidden it well, too, for I never saw it.

"There wasn't anything left of Leythana's. I told you already that I checked."

"There wasn't anything behind her *effigy*," she says. "Not like with the other queens. No special gowns or other tribute. But I found a loose brick far in the back of the crypt. The writings must have been stashed there long before your siege."

"Dragon's teeth," I mutter. If I'd lived at the palace for another century, I never would have thought to go scrabbling about prying bricks out of the walls of that dank place. "What writings?"

"Leythana's journal entries, some of them from before she was queen. A few were from her time on her fleet of dragon ships. Others during the Fae challenge."

I step closer, curiosity piqued. "The Fae challenge? And she wrote about how she convinced the Vila to surrender Oryn's staff?"

"Yes. She offered the Vila a weapon or something. It wasn't explicitly clear," she says. "And that's not what's important. Leythana *lied*. She told the Vila she would get them this weapon. She made them trust her. And then she never followed through."

"Are you sure? Maybe she just couldn't forge the weapon or—"

"No," Aurora interrupts. "Leythana knew she would never get it. But she lied to the Vila in order to persuade them to give up

Oryn's staff. So that she could win the challenge and become queen."

It hums between us, burying the sounds of the fighting. I have no idea what to say. What to think. "Why are you telling me this?"

"Because when I found what she did, I was shocked. Angry. My whole life, I'd idolized Leythana. But she built her reign on deception."

My hand twitches, wanting to reach for her. But I force myself to hold back.

"And then I thought, what did it matter? Leythana wasn't re-membered for her deceit, but for all of the other things she accom-plished. I could be, too. The ends would justify the means." Like Regan said. The crown glimmers in the sunlight. "And that's why I went to Oryn. Why I lied to lure you to the High Court. I thought that if Mortania was somehow gone, things would return to how they used to be. And that everything I'd done would be worth it."

I stare at her. "But at the black tower, you said—"

"I was angry. And I wanted to hurt you the way you hurt me." She exhales a long breath. "But you were right. We can't go back. And I was asking you to give up a piece of yourself. To change into someone who *I* wanted you to be." She shakes her head. "I don't want you to be powerless. I don't want you to be anyone other than who you are."

The salt-laced air burns in my lungs. "Are you sure?"

She nods, tears leaking from her eyes. I close the distance be-tween us and trace the silver trails on her cheeks, warm and wet against my fingertips.

"I love you," I say. "I might not have said it, but—"

"I know. And I love you, Alyce." She pulls me closer. "Always."

It does not soothe all of the wounds we've inflicted on each other. It does not make anything right. But it is the truth.

My heart thuds away in my chest. Mortania whirls in her den, warning me that this is another trap. Another ploy to get me to lower my defenses. But I believe Aurora. Her face tips nearer. Even covered in the dirt from the last days, she is beautiful.

A whinny pierces between us. We break apart to see a Fae steed hurtling out of the confusion and toward the cliffs. Aurora points. "It's Chaos!"

It is. Last I checked, he'd been taken to the stables to rest after our journey home. Callow warbles a greeting at the sight of her friend. One of the Vila must have been brave enough to saddle him for the battle. But it's not a Vila riding him now. It's Derek. I thought he was on the Ryna ships—and likely dead now . . .

Clods of dirt fly from beneath Chaos's massive hooves as he lands. Derek swings from the saddle and reaches Aurora in two strides. "You're alive. I thought—"

I bully myself between them and shove him back. "You *thought* you'd dump Aurora on a ship while you escaped. What are you doing riding my steed?"

Callow settles on my shoulder. I slide a suspicious glance at Chaos, who tosses his head in what might be an apology.

The prince swipes his sea-slick hair out of his face. Cuts mar his handsome face, seemingly his only injury. "I left Aurora on the ship because that was the safest place I could find. And then I returned to the palace to offer my assistance. By the time the sentries signaled to us about the wave, my steed had been taken. Chaos was the only one left. I had to get back here."

It's exactly the sort of irritatingly heroic endeavor I would expect from this prince. I cross my arms and raise an eyebrow at Chaos. "You didn't think it better to buck him into the sea?"

"Alyce." Aurora nudges me in the ribs.

I don't apologize. "Why is your fleet firing at the Etherians anyway?"

He grins at that. "The ships are Fae, as my father sent what was left of his army to Oryn in exchange for my safe return. But we decided to give them a taste of their own medicine—*misdirection*. We feigned an alliance until the fighting started."

That's . . . a clever plan. Much to my annoyance, some of my anger at the boy ebbs. "And why would you do that? Did you miss the Imps?"

"Not because of them. Because of Oryn." He gestures in the direction of the fallen black tower. "Rulers like him are the reason wars exist in the first place. Setting rigid borders and hoarding power when it could help others. That enchanted cage he plans to cast is the perfect example. I don't want to live in a world that's so . . . senseless."

Senseless. The word carries an uncomfortable resonance. I look out at the fighting. The Dark Court pitted against the Fae. Shifters returned to us in pieces. Malakar. The Fae heads on the throne room walls. We initiated this war for revenge—and there is much I do not regret—but what will be left at the end? Are we forcing the Fae prophecy to come to pass, hacking away at one another until there's nothing left?

"Well," I say, attempting to disguise the gruffness in my voice. "I don't see how your fleet is going to make much of a difference at the bottom of the sea."

"Alyce," Aurora chides again.

"But thank you," I relent. "For keeping her safe. And for helping us. I know you're the reason Regan came to my rescue at the black tower."

And why I'm still alive, I don't say. I wouldn't want to give the boy too much credit.

He looks at me like I've grown horns. "You're welcome."

Chaos chuffs, like the boy should show more appreciation for my praise. And he should. It will likely be the last time he receives it.

"And what are we to do now?"

The palace still burns. Clouds of charcoal smoke chug across the districts, laced with the cries of the Fae steeds, and the dying, and the song of steel on steel.

"We have to end this some way." Aurora turns the crown around in her hands.

"There seems an obvious solution." Derek waves toward me. "Can't you blast the Etherians to pieces or something?"

"Not at the moment. Mortania blocked me after I tried to keep Regan from releasing that wave." I reach for my magic, but it's still locked within whatever prison Mortania devised. I can almost feel her pacing inside it. "I can't use my Vila magic at all. And I probably won't even be able to manage a decent Shift now that her power isn't bolstering those abilities."

"Decent?" Aurora laughs. "Alyce, you pulled me from a sinking ship and hauled me through the air like I weighed nothing at all. I would call that decent."

She has a point, and it sounds a lot like what Neve said in my chamber, about my having flown back to the Dark Court in a single day without tiring. All this time, I assumed Mortania amplified all of my magic. That *she* was the reason I grew wings and claws on the day of my siege—and every other instance after. But if that were true, I wouldn't have been able to pull Aurora from the ship after the ancient Vila blocked my power. And for the first time I wonder—*What if Mortania only provided the confidence I needed to Shift? If I never actually needed her at all?*

"Dragon's teeth," I mutter.

The ancient Vila had far more control over me than I ever realized. Neve was right; I've been ignoring a whole part of myself. Despising it even, out of ill-founded prejudice.

"We might still have a chance," I say, an idea taking swift shape in my mind. One that is dangerous and reckless and the last thing I will probably ever do. "Oryn is going to try to recast his enchantment. We have to get to him before that happens."

Chaos rolls his shimmery wings and snorts.

"Oryn?" Derek asks. "We have no idea where he is—or if he's even alive."

"He is," I insist, still convinced that I couldn't miss something as monumental as the High King's death. "And he must be at the black tower. Whatever remains of it is the only thing that can protect him from our latent magic. And that," I take a deep breath, "is where I'm going to challenge him to a duel."

A wave smashes against the base of the cliff. Aurora gapes at me. "You can't. Your Vila power is blocked and he'll—"

"He'll be too arrogant to refuse," I say. "And my Shifter power is perfectly fine. It's what saved Regan and me from the High Court, and you from the ship. It will help us now."

It will NOT. Mortania thrashes inside the place where she's hoarding my magic. But I ignore her.

"You could be hurt," Aurora argues. "Killed. Can't you just make yourself invisible and fly in and snatch the staff?"

It means more to me than I can say that she cares. "It will be too difficult for me to fly *and* remain invisible. He'll see me coming. And if he agrees to a duel, his guards won't be able to intervene. All I need to do is grab Oryn's staff during the fight, as I should have done at the palace. After that, I can fly away with it. Hold it hostage, as was the original plan."

Derek scrubs the back of his neck. "There seems . . . a lot of ways this could go wrong."

"Are you worried about me?" I ask, arching an eyebrow. He only frowns, clearly unsure how to respond. "What other option do we have?"

As if to illustrate, brine-soaked wind gusts in from the sea, carrying the wails of the sailors, along with the commotion of the Vila and the Fae. The sea moans and wood splinters. Another explosion sounds from closer to the palace.

Aurora sighs. "Fine. But don't you dare try to convince me to go back to the palace. I'm coming with you."

"That's ridiculous," I say. "There's nothing for you to do and—"

"I'm going," she repeats, in that tone I know so well. "Besides, I'll be riding Chaos, and he'll take me wherever I wish. So you couldn't stop me if you wanted to."

The steed thumps his foot in what could only pass for affirmation, and I curse their stubbornness.

Derek grumbles something about death wishes. But he adjusts Chaos's saddle. Aurora goes back to the edge of the cliff. Her skirts whip in the wind.

"You'll watch her, won't you?" I ask Derek quietly, nodding toward Aurora. "You won't let anything happen to her should this go wrong?"

He doles out one of those lopsided smiles. "I was about to ask the same of you."

A strange feeling of warmth spreads through me. It tugs at the corners of my lips. Derek notices, and his brown eyes sparkle. I scowl at him. "You, on the other hand, are another matter. Should Oryn decide to feast on your entrails, I'll not lift a finger to stop him."

Derek laughs. And to my utter surprise, I join him.

But I still hate him.

CHAPTER FORTY-FOUR

It takes enormous effort to convince Callow to leave my side—she's just as adamant about accompanying me as Aurora, but I can't bear to have anything happen to her. Eventually, the kestrel understands and retreats toward the palace. Aurora and Derek pile onto Chaos's back, and the three of us soar over the landscape, past the fighting, and toward the remains of the black tower. I'm proven right—there's a formation of Fae riders assembled above the smoldering rubble. And there, evidently unscathed by the tower's demise, is Oryn, his hammered-bark cloak flapping as he surveys the battle in the districts.

The Fae riders lower themselves as we land. Derek dismounts and lifts Aurora down. Chaos flicks his shimmering tail, staying close.

Upon further inspection, the High King of the Fae is not entirely intact. A few of the Fae sigils are missing from his breastplate, which is dented and coated with ash. Several antlers on his crown are jaggedly broken. His own Fae blood tracks in glistening rivulets down the rough umber of his redwood face. Good.

"Ah, the mortal prince returns." Oryn continues to observe the districts, as if he couldn't care less where we'd gone or why we've returned together. "Here I'd thought you'd be retreating with whatever men you could manage to scrounge from the sea, given that your plan to overtake my army has so disastrously failed."

Derek shades slightly pink, evidently mortified. It's an expression he's likely had plenty of opportunity to wear in his brief lifetime. Aurora glares around like she wants to murder everyone. I'm quite proud of her.

"Though I suppose some congratulations are in order," Oryn continues, bored. "Those are Etherian ships you managed to sink. A difficult feat to accomplish."

The branch-clacking, rushing-water sound of Fae laughter eddies.

"And you, half-breed." Oryn at last directs his gilded attention to me, pinning me like I'm a specimen on a board. "I am surprised to discover you among your enemies."

"They're not my enemies," I say firmly.

"But they have each betrayed you in their turn." He points his staff between Aurora and Derek, its orb glittering. "Is your memory so short that you have forgotten the fickle nature of mortal alliances?"

Despite how I try to deflect it, the jab lands as intended. And for the first time since the Crimson Cliffs, I doubt this plan. Even doubt Aurora. Did she mean what she said about wanting me to be myself? Could she actually respect my power, or will she turn on me again? Mortania seizes on the opening.

Choose me, pet. And I will release your power. Then nothing can stop you.

I can almost feel it happening, like a lock unclicking in the den where my magic dwells, promising exquisite relief. But then I shake myself free of the ancient Vila's talons. I have no idea what it would mean to "choose" her. If I yielded, could she take over my body? My mind? Would she *become* me somehow, devour me—like when I cursed that mirror in the black tower and my appearance morphed from that of the Dark Grace into Mortania's? I will not let her.

"And what of your own alliances?" I say to the High King. "I met Aelfdene. He told me how poorly you treated him, and I suspect many of the Fae boast similar tales. You're not a leader. You're obsessed with yourself. Worse than King Tarkin ever was."

Oryn's nostrils flare, anger flashing ocher in his eyes. But he instantly recovers. "The opinion of a dead half-Vila matters naught."

From a sheath at his waist, the High King retrieves a small dagger. I assume he's going to aim it at me, and brace myself to Shift. For this fight to finally begin, with or without a formal challenge. But he slashes one of his knob-knuckled fingers instead, then crouches, drawing his shimmery golden blood on the stone in a pattern I can't decipher. "I judge it fitting that our journey should end here, on the ruins of this ancient tower. The bards of the Court of Dreams could not have penned a better tale."

One of the Fae riders lets out a long, low whistle, and the others within earshot begin to disperse. The whistle carries, one Etherian to the next, and soon they're fleeing the Districts in droves. But why? Oryn tilts his staff to the ground. His Fae power sparks and swirls inside its orb. The glass touches the stone where the High King shed his blood, and a spear of golden light erupts.

The wreckage of the black tower begins to quaver. Small rocks ping down the side. Sparkling Fae magic spills over the cracks and crevices in waterfalls, like at Oryn's palace in the High Court. It sizzles as it hits the barren earth and veins outward, toward Briar's gates.

The enchantment.

This is how Oryn plans to use the runes the Imps found throughout the palace. They're all connected—tiny pieces of Fae magic the High King is now activating with his very blood.

Oryn's power corkscrews up the wall of bramble at Briar's main gates. Cries of confusion and outrage swell as it canters through the districts and toward the palace. When it reaches the runes, the cage will form. And then Oryn will likely kill us all before he escapes with his Fae, leaving the Dark Court imprisoned forever.

Use me, Mortania urges. *It will be the end of everything if you do not.*

Pressure pounds between my temples, but still I resist the ancient Vila. We do things my way now.

"High King," I shout. "I have a bargain for you."

Oryn halts. Glances at me over his shoulder. But his magic continues to flow into Briar. "What could I possibly desire from you?"

"My power," I rush on. "You said yourself that if I were to surrender it, there would be no need . . ."

He narrows his gaze. "You expect me to believe you are willing to do so?"

"No. But I am willing to prove myself. Let us have a duel—end this war here and now."

With my luck, he will likely scoff and finish his enchantment. But his interest shows in the creases of his redwood brow. The flow of his power thins and then stops altogether. Triumph flashes through me. I knew he wouldn't be able to resist.

"Have you shed your coward's skin after all this time, half-breed? Even though we have your princess in our keeping?" At his signal, the riders gather around Aurora. And I have to restrain myself from reacting. But he will not harm her. Not when he knows how to use her against me. "You speak with some confidence. But I am the lord of all Fae. The master of light magic. Do you truly dare to take on the might of Etheria?"

I force a grin, though my heart is hammering. "If you're afraid of me, just say so."

This is where I expect him to lash out at me. But he steps nearer, his staff tapping on the stone. "Something is changed about you."

Dragon's teeth. Deep in her den, Mortania whirls.

The High King inhales deeply, as he did in the black tower when he accused Aurora of lying about the Briar crown. It must have something to do with his latent magic—some power of detection. Because then he laughs, long and rolling and cruel. "It is your Vila power. Trapped, somehow. I see the princess received her wish after all."

His guards join him, jeering down at me. I grit my teeth and lift my chin. "This has nothing to do with Aurora. Only the two of us. The bargain stands—whoever wins this duel, wins the war."

"Ah, but I should decline." His curls dance in the wind. "It would not be sporting to quash so feeble a creature."

Feeble. The word scrapes against my pride. Mortania writhes and seethes, demanding to be released. But still, she will not let me reach into the place where my magic lives. And I will not bow to her whims.

But you will lose, pet, she growls.

Maybe the battle. But not myself. Never again. "If I am so feeble, then make quick work of me. Or are you worried that your reign will come to an end? Aelfdene also told me about the prophecy."

His guards look confused. But Oryn knows exactly what I'm talking about. He slams his staff on the stone. Sparks of golden stars erupt from its orb. "I accept. You were always going to die today."

I sketch a mocking bow, daring one last look at Aurora. A single tear tracks down her face, perhaps understanding that this may be the last we see of each other. I try to shake that thought away. Focus on the power I will need to win this.

A familiar cry resonates above me. Callow, the stubborn bird. I should have known she wouldn't stay away long. The kestrel belts her war cry, the same one that echoed over Briar during our first siege, when we flew side by side through the curling green smoke. Us against the whole realm. I smile at the memory. And then I Shift.

Wings flare out from between my shoulder blades, nails elongating to claws. My kestrel and I descend on the High King as one. I dodge his first blow easily, an arc of power aimed at my middle. It leaves a crater in the cliffside. Callow darts around the High King, clawing at his neck and shoulders, and pecking at his pointed Fae ears. Bark-like Fae flesh rips and tears. He curses and swats her away, but his grip on his staff is firm.

Mortania roars and threatens, but I will not yield to her.

Another blast misses me by a hair's breadth. The next grazes my arm. I spin like a top through the air as molten fire sears through me, and green Vila blood wells from the wound.

Callow shrieks. Oryn readies his next attack. His damaged breastplate slides down one side of his chest, exposing his shoulder. I charge him and swipe at just the right moment. Gilded Fae blood spurts from the gashes my claws leave behind and weeps from twin slashes on the backs of his legs. Oryn's knees hit the stone, but only briefly. He swings at me and his staff connects with my stomach, too quickly for me to attempt to wrench it away from him. Pain erupts on my torso, the same as when Endlewild gifted me the burn that became my crescent-moon scar. I'm flung backward like a leaf on the wind.

"Alyce, look out!"

Oryn's power hurtles toward me, aimed directly at my heart. I swerve out of the way just in time to see it cleave a gnarled tree in two. I pump my wings, rising higher as the cold sea air sears in my throat. After the events of the last days, I'm exhausted. A tingling begins in my bones as my Shift weakens. The muscles of my back quiver, struggling to hold up my wings. But my Shifter power hinges on my own confidence. I refuse to let it falter.

"Concede defeat," Oryn calls up at me, "and perhaps I will permit you to live. Take you back to my domain as a trophy."

Just another good hit. The right one, and he will fall, the staff with him. The magic in its orb builds. I focus on my Shift and count my thudding heartbeats. Right after he—

Gilded power barrels past me. There's a shrill peal of pain. One I'd know anywhere.

A blot of tawny feathers spirals to the earth.

"Callow!" I tear after her, unthinking.

She thumps to the ground, her wings splayed out. I land heavily and trip over an exposed root, wrenching my ankle, and crash to my knees beside my bird. Callow's body is limp. Lifeless. If there's a heartbeat, I cannot find it.

Anger rises, stronger and far deadlier than the wave Regan summoned. I turn back to Oryn. Blood oozes from the wound at his shoulder and the scratches on his face. There will be much more of it before this is done. Forgetting my exhaustion and my own injuries, forgetting that he is the High King of the Fae, I charge toward Oryn.

His power hits me squarely in the chest.

My back collides with rock. Stars parade across my vision. My wings sputter out, and my claws retract.

It is not too late, Mortania's voice is distorted. *Choose me, and I will—*

A furious whinny breaks through my thoughts. Motion blurs above me, and I force my fuzzy vision to focus. What on—

Chaos's massive shadow engulfs me, his mane sparkling in the sunlight. And on his back, the Briar crown like a beacon, is Aurora.

"I command you to stop," she shouts, "in the name of Etheria!"

There's a moment of quiet. I expect the Fae to laugh. For Oryn to take aim at Aurora, and I'm horrified because I do not think I could save her. But to my complete astonishment, the High King goes entirely still.

His riders are incensed, gnashing their teeth and brandishing their staffs.

"Stay back," Aurora orders.

And incredibly, the High King motions for them to heed. They sneer but retreat.

"Aurora," I rasp. Every muscle in my body throbs. "What are you doing?"

She sits taller in the saddle. "It is his true name. Etheria."

Waves crash below.

"And who," Oryn grinds out, "divulged that particular piece of information?"

I practically have to scrape my jaw from the ground.

"You did," she answers. Chaos bobs on the wind.

"I most certainly did not."

"Not directly, nor intentionally," she allows. "But I've had quite a lesson on how to read between the words of the Fae. You are the High King of the Fae, their only ruler in recorded history. All magic stems from your court. You said Alyce is nothing against the 'might of Etheria.' Because you *are* Etheria."

The seconds stretch out long and thick. How many times had I uttered the word? It's been written and sung and whispered since the dawn of Briar and before. But it's never, I realize, been used as a name for Oryn himself. It's been hidden in plain sight.

"High King," a rider calls, "the princess lies."

He pays them no mind. Only bares his pointed Fae teeth, as enraged as any snared beast who judged themselves too clever to be caught. "And what shall you do with my name, Princess?"

Chaos rolls his wings, breath steaming in the air. "I imagine you do not want such knowledge to spread. Do what you will with your guard." She flicks a gesture at the riders. "And I will vow to keep your secret. Alyce and Derek will do the same. But in exchange, you will—"

Something whistles past the side of my face. There's a wet, fleshy *thunk* and then a howling like I've never heard reverberates against my eardrums. It's coming . . . from Oryn. Because there's an arrow shaft protruding from his eye socket. Blood pours down his cheek and neck.

Footsteps pound up the side of the tower, and I angle my wasted body to see who could possibly have—

"Rose?"

There's a bow in her hands and a quiver slung across her back. My mind reels. I thought she died when the tower collapsed. Where did she come from? When did she learn to shoot?

The Fae riders are just as dumbstruck. Time itself seems to slow, the sounds of the distant battle and the steeds' wingbeats are syrupy and distorted. But then everything lurches into motion.

"Where is Terrill?" one shouts. "Find him!"

In unison, the Fae guards yank the reins of their steeds and race back toward the districts. They must be going in search of Oryn's heir, which means they believe the High King is going to die. But in their haste, they've forgotten one detail—Oryn's staff has fallen, undefended, at his feet.

The Grace tosses aside her weapon. Oryn moans and clutches his face. Armor chimes and clanks as his knees meet stone.

Rose kicks at him until he falls to his side. "Transfer your power to me!"

Dragon's teeth, she's lost her senses. Aurora lands hastily, clambers off Chaos's saddle, and sprints toward us with Derek.

"Rose, stop," I attempt. "He cannot—"

"He can. There's still time to Mark me. I will be High Queen of the Fae!"

Even with an arrow sunk in his eye, the High King rattles out a laugh. "You think I would ever name you as my heir? You are half-human. Unworthy of such a boon."

"In the name of Etheria, I command it!"

Oryn hisses. "It matters not what name you invoke. Even if I Marked you, you would not survive it."

She kicks him again. "Do it now, or I will make sure your magic dies with you."

"Try," Oryn croaks.

Rose growls. She gives up on the High King and reaches for the twisted birch of his staff instead.

"Rose, wait—" I want to tell her about Aelfdene, and how the magic must choose to bind itself to hers. But she will not listen.

"Shut up, Malyce. I know what I'm doing." She taps at the orb, then turns the staff one way and then the next, searching for something. "There must be another way to—"

Rose stops. Sniffs. I smell it, too—the stench of burning flesh.

Tendrils of golden smoke twist up from where Rose's hands are clamped around the birch wood. She drops it. Glass clatters against stone, but the orb remains intact.

"What . . . what's happening?" Rose slumps, gaping at her upturned palms. Dark veins web out over her fingers and steadily work their way up her forearms. "What is this?"

"Did you assume I would be so careless as to forgo protection? After the Vila robbed me of that staff?" Oryn wheezes. "Rash, vain creature. None but the High King can wield that weapon."

That's why the riders left it behind. None would dare to touch it.

A fresh spike of horror jolts through me as Rose's fingers

crumble to ash and fall off her hands. Flakes of grayed skin swirl away on the wind. The poison climbs in a grotesque lattice up her arms and across her chest. It weaves around her neck and along her jaw.

"Make it stop," she whimpers, thrusting her mangled arm in my direction. "Please. You helped me before."

When she'd cut herself while taking bloodrot and nearly bled to death in her own parlor. But this is vastly different. Her left arm is gone now, her shoulder disintegrating. I shake myself out of my stupor and go to her. "I want to, please believe me. But I cannot. I'm sorry."

"I wanted—" She gasps. Tears streak through the grime on her face. "I only wanted . . ."

But I know. Power. She wanted power. And watching her, I realize that this is what Mortania was doing to me for the last hundred years. Eating me away bit by bit, so subtly that I did not even notice.

I did nothing you did not invite me to do, pet.

And I shiver because I cannot entirely deny that.

I hold on to Rose for as long as I can. The end is swift and eerily soundless. I sit with the Grace's remains staining my clothes. A single pink strand of hair glimmers on my skirt. I pick it up, and it dances in the breeze. Even an hour ago, I would have been glad to see Rose dead. But all I feel now is emptiness.

A low exhale rattles behind me.

"Alyce." Aurora stands over the High King. Blood still gushes from the wound in his eye, but his chest is still.

Wisps of gold begin to unspool from the orb of Oryn's staff and snake toward the High King. I drag myself closer. I've witnessed hundreds of Fae meet their deaths in my throne room but never like this. The threads of gilded power knot themselves together and congeal in a tight ball over Oryn's corpse. It pulses once, then darts upward like a fallen star returning to the skies. Hovers for a heartbeat.

And then plunges into the Briar crown.

CHAPTER FORTY-FIVE

The last princess of Briar staggers with the impact.

I take her by the shoulders, steadying her. "Are you all right?"

"I—" She blinks, dazed. "I think so. What was that?"

The Briar crown blazes with light.

"I don't know." Nothing about these last moments makes any sense.

A low warble reaches my ears. Callow. I half-bound, half–fall down the side of the tower and sprint to where she lay in a heap after Oryn's attack. My heart swells. She's alive. Stunned and wounded but nipping at my fingers and able to weakly flap her wings. I press her to my chest and she nudges her head against the underside of my chin.

"I told you to stay at the palace."

She mutters something that is unmistakably a retort.

"Here you are, filthy beast." A Fae rider soars up from below the cliffs. She angles her staff toward me. I curl protectively over Callow.

"NO!"

Wind pummels into me. The Fae warrior is shoved backward, her steed bucking and whinnying in panic as it's sent somersaulting over the sea. A wall of shimmering, translucent gold launches up from the ground and arches in a dome over our heads. Callow bridles in alarm. Aurora stands on the rubble behind us, palms held out and chest heaving.

"Is that . . . a shield?" I ask. "Did you summon it?"

"No—I couldn't have. I'm mortal. I don't have powers or . . ."

Several other Fae riders converge, but their magic pings harmlessly off the barrier. Even the sounds of the battle raging in the districts are muffled.

"It's definitely a shield," Derek says.

But Aurora *is* mortal. How could she . . .

Oryn's power. It's an impossible answer, but the only one that fits. We'd all witnessed the High King's magic dive into the wreath of bramble and thorn. But the only reason Oryn's magic would have found the crown is because it was Marked, and it couldn't have been. The Fae don't Mark objects, do they? Even if it somehow was, it doesn't explain why Aurora— Dragon's teeth.

"The Briar crown," I say to Aurora. "When Oryn blessed it, it was more than just the crown. It was Leythana herself, wasn't it?"

Aurora blinks at me, still a bit dazed. "Yes. Leythana's entire line was blessed. That's why all the queens bore daughters—the Fae magic in Oryn's blood."

Fae magic passed from princess to princess. And just like that, the final piece of this puzzle clicks into place. I suddenly understand why Aurora never felt the effects of her curse lifting after a century of sleep. Why Oryn sent an envoy to fetch her when she woke, and why he wanted the Briar crown before he cast his enchantment. Why he'd traipsed realm to realm since my siege, seeking a champion to wake Aurora and remove her from our influence.

I stare at the gilded circlet, comprehension stitching itself together. And then a laugh punches up my throat and rings around us. Before long, I'm doubled over.

"What's wrong with you?" Aurora gives me a slight shake.

"I wish Oryn were alive. He'd be furious."

"Alyce," she repeats. "What are you—"

"The High King used his own blood to bless that crown. Which means he *Marked* it—and Leythana's descendants along with it." I pause to let that sink in. "Oryn named them all as among his possible successors."

Aurora plucks the thing from her head. "He couldn't have. He *wouldn't* have."

"Oh, I'm sure he never thought his power would *choose* to bind itself to a mortal over some other Fae he Marked. But it did." I laugh again, recalling what Aelfdene said about how Oryn hated to be proven wrong. "It came to you. Aurora, you're the High Queen of the Fae."

Deep in her den, Mortania emits a low, rumbling growl. Chaos nickers at another pair of Etherian riders who try unsuccessfully to blast the shield apart.

Aurora's knuckles are white around the crown. She gapes at it like it might transform into a beast and devour her whole. "I don't want it. I've seen what people do for this kind of power. Rose went practically mad to achieve it."

"Power cannot make someone wicked," I tell her, having learned that lesson the hard way. "I used to believe it could, like with the Shifters. But I was wrong."

Shame cuts between my teeth. I'd assumed the worst of Neve and her Starlings, all because of Kal. And look at the pain my own prejudice had wrought. Another formation of riders attempts to descend upon us, and they are batted away like ragdolls. Chaos swishes his tail in a decidedly satisfied tempo.

"The Fae magic chooses where it resides?" Derek asks, still surveying the fighting through the glimmering border of the enchantment.

"Yes," I say. "We learned that from the High Lord of the Court of Dreams. Oryn could have Marked a hundred heirs, but the magic itself would select its next home."

He looks back at Aurora. "There must be a very good reason it came to you."

The prince has a point. Aelfdene was selected as High Lord, though his brother was the stronger Fae. Had the magic seen something in Aelfdene? Had Oryn's seen something in Aurora?

"What if Oryn's magic somehow understood that another ruler like him would be ruinous?" I ask slowly. "If it chose you because you're different?"

Aurora shakes her head. "I'm not, I—"

"I think," I say, "that the very reason you're afraid is because you are the right choice. You're *supposed* to do this."

"How can I?" She gestures at the battle, exasperated. "I cannot stop this. There's no possible way to negotiate or sue for peace. It's just this endless cycle of tearing one another apart. Nothing will change it."

I squeeze her hand, wishing I had something useful to offer her.

"You don't know that," Derek attempts. "If you try . . ."

But the rest of what he says is lost to me. I'm focused on Aurora's hand in mine. There's a gold flush to her skin, thanks to

Oryn's power tingeing her blood, the shade made all the brighter by my green-veined paleness. And the sight of the colors together ignites something in my mind.

Green and gold . . .

The mysterious poem from the Vila book. And that first verse crashes into the next.

Green and gold
Gold and green
A power which we've yet to see
Ah, but ne'er will come the day
When called a force unknown to Fae.

It means nothing, Mortania insists. But I know better than to listen.

"*A force unknown,*" I say out loud.

"What?" Aurora asks.

I'd interrupted Derek, and he frowns at me, offended.

"Do you remember the poem?" I ask. "About the green and gold . . . and the power?"

Her brow scrunches. "I think so. But what—"

"When you said Leythana lied about the weapon she promised the Vila," I hurry on before the idea flits away. "What if *that* force, from the poem, was the weapon?"

Aurora bites her bottom lip as she does when she's thinking. "I don't understand. The weapon didn't exist."

"Which is why Leythana vowed to forge it." It's like a veil being lifted. "And I don't think it was a weapon at all, but an entirely new kind of magic. *A power which we've yet to see,*" I recite. "It could mean a fusion of green and gold—Etherian and Vila magic. Which could be why the Vila stole Oryn's staff in the first place. They wanted to create the magic themselves. But they couldn't use Etherian power—"

"And so Leythana promised to convince him to cooperate," Aurora says softly. The clang of battle resonates through the shield. "But she knew he would never agree. And she didn't care. She wanted the throne. After she was crowned, the Vila couldn't do anything about it."

Another detail falls into place. "Maybe they could. All those stories from before the first war—about the Vila sneaking into mortal lands and stealing children and raising havoc. It was all retaliation because Leythana failed to honor her word."

"Dragon's teeth," Aurora mutters. "You could be right."

"If she is," Derek says, scrubbing the back of his neck, "might that power be something that could help us now?"

I hadn't thought that far. And though I have no doubt that a blend of light and dark magic would be formidable, it doesn't exist.

And it never could. Mortania thrashes. My mind swarms with her commentary about humans and Fae. The hundred lines drawn and crossed. The thousand knives sunk into one another's backs.

Once, I would have listened. Deemed such a power impossible. But an idea blooms, opening like a long-ago Briar rose. The very thing that has hindered such a power might be the key to creating it.

"There's something we can try," I say to Aurora before I lose my nerve. "The ritual to turn a Fae into a Vila hinges on desire, specifically the Etherian's rejection of their power. But if we *both* concentrated on melding the powers instead of turning them, it could work."

Like Torin's version of how the first Vila was created. Not by force, but by choice.

It would kill you, Mortania seethes.

Maybe. Or maybe that's just what she wants me to think. Because to forge this power would be the end of her, I can sense it in my bones. She could not survive in a world where light and dark magic existed in harmony. Where the cycle of hatred finally ceased.

"Could?" Derek asks, and I don't appreciate his tone.

"It is a risk," I allow.

A foolish and deadly one, Mortania supplies.

The whinny of a Fae steed leaches through our shield. Another, much larger, formation of Fae riders approaches. Chaos rears and flares his massive silver-dusted wings.

"All right, Alyce," Aurora says at last. "I trust you."

There's only one obstacle: I'll need to access my Vila power, where Mortania is stubbornly squatting inside her cave. She laughs, the sound warping against my skull.

If the High King of the Fae could not destroy me, you certainly will not.

Aurora reads my expression. "What is it?"

"Mortania. She's still preventing me from—"

"She cannot prevent you from anything." Aurora places her palm on my sternum, and I can feel the heat of her through my gown. "It has always been your power. Never hers. And I'm sorry I didn't see that."

She lies, Mortania snarls, surging like a maelstrom. *It is my power. And you have only ever been a vessel to house it.*

My head throbs violently enough that I fear it will split in half.

Pushing past the ancient Vila's wrath seems impossible. But so did breaking the protections around Kal's shadow chains a century ago. So did building the Dark Court. And so did earning the love of a princess.

That does not mean—

But I ignore her and concentrate, finding my way to the place where my power lives. Mortania bucks and roils, hurling every vile name she can at me. And part of me wants to laugh at how quickly she has pivoted from flattery to insults. How easy it was to distract me with praise. I may have become Mistress of the Dark Court, but inside, part of me was always the Dark Grace, hungry for acceptance. I examine the cracked jewel of my signet ring and its band of bramble and thorn. I thought embracing my power meant destroying everything that stood in my way. It might have once. But now it's time for a different course.

Like a glass shattering, the barrier blocking my power yields. I'm amazed at how immediately it disintegrates. How thoroughly I convinced myself that Mortania was in control. Magic floods through me. I gasp, staggering a little as the smell of woodsmoke and loam fills my nostrils and coats my tongue. Mortania is furious. Her presence smolders in my belly, and I know she'll waste no time in attempting to block me again.

Without letting myself think about how disastrously this could fail, I snag Derek's dagger from the sheath at his belt. He protests, and Callow chases him back.

"Now," I say to Aurora.

She offers her hand. I draw three quick, neat slits on her palm. Her red human blood wells, and I think I see speckles of gold— Oryn's magic. No. *Her* magic.

And then I slash my own palm and clasp our hands together,

human and Vila and light Fae magic all mingling. Intentionally. Willingly. Defying all obstacles and history.

Gold-and-green light erupts from our joined grip, and an invisible energy throws me back. Aurora stumbles. But we hold on to each other. Mortania is deafening. An overwhelming rage explodes from the place where my magic lives. I grind my teeth against it.

"Is it working?" Aurora shouts.

I'm not sure. Something is happening, with the way that Mortania is howling inside my skull. But I don't know if it's enough. Aurora pulls me closer.

"What are you doing?"

Her other hand cups the back of my neck. "Our kiss broke a centuries-long curse. It is the strongest magic I know and capable of anything."

And before I fully comprehend what is happening, her lips brush mine, soft at first, and then harder. Hungrier. I cling to her, our joined hands pressed tightly between us as we drink each other in, cocooned in this swirling tempest of green-and-gold light. *Choosing* each other.

Behind my breastbone, my magic strains as though it is fracturing. Perhaps it is. Perhaps there's no way to untangle myself from Mortania, and this ritual will indeed kill me. The thought doesn't frighten me as much as it probably should. I focus on Aurora. The wine-sweet taste of her mouth and the silken fire of her skin beneath my touch.

"I love you, Alyce," she says against my lips.

No matter what happens next, it is enough. It will always be enough.

With a final, desperate shrilling, Mortania's voice splinters and fades into nothing. The light shatters and dissolves, and Aurora's golden shield with it. In their absence, the wind knifes between us and the sea cracks waves against the cliff face. Aurora releases me, and I let out a gasp at the sight of her. The Briar crown is now threaded through with bits of green—emerald thorns and jade roses and hemlock vines. Dark and light magic melded together.

"It worked," she says. Even her violet eyes have altered. Slivers of gold and green, like shards of gemstones, dance within their depths. "It didn't hurt you, did it?"

I take stock of myself. There's no pain that I can tell. No cuts or bruises. And my magic feels the same as it ever did. "I'm fine."

"And Mortania?"

There's a strange emptiness where the Vila used to live, my mind unnaturally quiet. "Gone."

Just as I knew she would be.

"I'm sorry," Aurora says.

"You're not." I smirk. She smiles back. "And neither am I. You were right—I never needed her."

She reaches for me, and I revel in how her hand feels in mine. Her hummingbird pulse beating through her skin.

A throat clears behind us. Derek, interrupting us as always. "And what are we going to do now?"

Aurora looks back toward the districts. The line of Fae warriors has re-formed and is charging toward us.

"I don't know. I'm not sure how it works."

"You used your power once before," I remind her, though the shield has dissolved.

"But I—"

"Trust yourself," I say. "The same as you asked of me."

At first, she frowns, doubt tingeing the striking color of her eyes.

But then she inhales a steadying breath. And in a voice that could only come from Leythana's heir, she shouts, "STOP!"

A ripple of gold-and-green power radiates from Aurora and canters outward. Each time it touches a Fae or Goblin or Demon or Vila, the creature freezes. The magic roves across the districts, the palace, and beyond. I can only gawp in amazement.

The clamor of the battle drains away. Even the wind and the sea subside. But then, like the stirring of some legendary beast, the Etherian Mountains begin to rumble.

CHAPTER FORTY-SIX

The quaking is terrifying, far stronger than when we broke Aurora's curse. Bone deep.

The Fae steeds bolt in every direction, their riders scrambling to keep their seats. Terror that Aurora's power is too much forks through me. That the earth is about to cleave open and swallow us whole. Because the rose-tinged mountains—the huge, eternal beasts I've known my whole life—crack like eggs from peak to base. From the yawning holes of their rupture, an avalanche roars toward Briar, rock and debris and a choking cloud of dust. At the palace, Tarkin's war room leans dangerously to one side. A spire topples from its tower.

Aurora grabs for my arm and points. "Is that . . . ?"

A pink lustrous powder flows down the mountainside. Etherium. It gushes over the palace and into the streets of Briar. Slams into the main gates and the barrier I summoned, which promptly wilts and allows the tide of Etherium to gallop toward us. I scoop

Callow up, and we clamber onto the wreckage of the black tower. Chaos whinnies in alarm and lifts off the ground, treading the air. Etherium pools around the rubble and begins to waterfall into the sea. Dragon's teeth. Our dark magic didn't taint the mineral after all. I had no idea there was this much of the stuff inside the mountains.

"What in the world caused that?" Derek crouches and pinches some of the Etherium into his palm, then releases the twinkling grains into the wind.

Aelfdene's voice drifts back to me from very far away.

"A new age will begin when the Etherian Mountains crumble."

The prophecy wasn't about me—or even the Dark Court—after all.

"Her." I smile at Aurora.

"I didn't tell the mountains to fall," she says, numb.

"No. But I expect your magic hinges on intent, the same as any Vila. You wanted the fighting to stop, and it did. You wanted a union between both realms, and the Etherian Mountains have been a hindrance to that union for—forever. And so they fell."

Derek startles at something behind us. "What in the name of . . ."

I sharpen my eyesight and scan the Grace District. Goblins and Vila climb out of the rock and Etherium. The Imps have already started packing the crushed mineral like snow and chucking it at one another. But then I notice something else. The trees nearest the main gates, which had morphed into sickly oil-skinned things since my siege, are . . . changing.

Ribbons of healthy bark wind up from the exposed and gnarled roots. Green leaves sprout from blackened scythe-like arms. Bushes bud and flower, producing blossoms the color of pale peony and deepest indigo. Climbing vines, some with bright green leaves and others with wicked-tipped thorns, hesitantly prod their way through dissolving mortar and holes in the stone.

"It must be the Etherium," Aurora says, watching the powder pour in every direction from the empty shells of the mountains. As it spills into the sea, the liquid steel of the water is threaded with currents of the flawless aquamarine it boasted at Briar's height. A breeze tinged with hints of honeysuckle and rose brushes our cheeks, warmer than I've felt in decades.

"Maybe," I say. "But Etherian magic can't undo ours. This is something else. A world of light and darkness—just like your magic."

And part of me wonders, if I had known about this power before, would I have wanted to create it? Would it have righted all of Briar's wrongs? Healed the wounds carved into my soul? I don't know. And it doesn't matter. I can't go back and choose that other path.

"We need to go to the palace," I say.

Aurora lets out a long breath. "I don't even know how to begin to tell them what happened."

Apprehension needles between my ribs when I think of how the Fae will absorb this news, and that's nothing compared to the Dark Court. Just because this power exists doesn't mean they will understand its value. But I don't let the fear consume me, as I would have done in the past.

"We'll figure it out," I promise Aurora. "And I might know the perfect way to make our entrance."

Exhaustion eats away at my control, but I manage to Shift the muscles in my back, firming them up, then add girth to my torso. Wings the size of a ship's sail fan out from my spine, taloned and scaled—an exact replica of a pair on one of Leythana's dragons. Derek whistles and hops onto Chaos's saddle. Aurora hooks her arms and legs around me, and I kick into the air. I Shift in my lungs and give the best, loudest roar I can muster as we sail over the districts.

I can't see her, but I know that she is smiling as the three of us make our way to the palace, her head held high and the Briar crown sparkling as we soar into the dawn of this new age—one many generations in the making—together.

Hours later, Aurora stands beside me in the main courtyard of the palace. The survivors of this final battle crowd around us, some of them hanging out of the upper story windows or climbing on one another's backs to get a good look. The light Fae have not dismounted, their steeds bobbing slightly in the current of wind. The human servants have ventured out of the palace, still alive, I assume, because my magic is now melded with Aurora's. I notice that the marks on their forearms are puckered and pink. Any direct connection between us is severed. And I find that I'm surprisingly relieved that I don't have control over them anymore, the way Briar once controlled me. I wonder if the lack of our bond means the humans will retain their immortality, or if their years have resumed as if they've woken from a century-long sleep. Time will tell, I suppose. Derek is here, with the men the Vila plucked from the sea. He grants me an encouraging smile, and I grudgingly nod back.

"Are you responsible for the death of the High King?" one of the Fae riders calls down to Aurora. Icy contempt wafts from the throng of their steeds.

"Not directly," she answers.

My heart clenches, picturing Rose's body dissolving away on the wind.

"But you do carry his magic," another snarls. "I can smell it on you."

Rumblings and mutterings, from both the Dark Court and the Fae. Aurora doesn't so much as flinch. "I do. Which means I am now your queen, and you will not address me with your typical disrespect."

Several riders hiss. But their oath must extend to more than just Oryn, to the magic of Etheria itself. For at last, they dip their chins.

"*She* carries Oryn's magic?" Armor clanks as the crowd parts for Torin. "The High King's power chose a mortal host? But she couldn't have been Marked."

I gesture to the crown. "We think he Marked her when he blessed the Briar Queens with his protection. Leythana's descendants have always carried a piece of Oryn's power."

"But . . . that's incredible." The fissures in Torin's body change from scarlet to pale yellow in a contemplative rhythm. "Why would the High King have risked such a—"

"It was not a risk," a Fae rider interrupts. "The blessing on the queens meant naught. No human would be capable of wielding the High King's power."

Anger snaps in my chest. I open my mouth to argue back, teach this Fae his place, but Aurora raises a hand for silence.

"As you can see"—she indicates the mountains—"I am more than capable. Would you like further demonstration?"

The Etherian glowers, and the Fae steeds nicker, sensing the fury of their riders. But none are brave—or foolish—enough to challenge her.

"And what does this mean for us?" Renard demands. "Nimara?"

I expected this moment would come, but I'm no better prepared for it. And a strange part of me misses Mortania. Normally, she would grant me some encouraging words to fuel my confidence. But I suppose I must rely on myself, as I should have done all along.

"Nimara is dead." The words are sticky. An undercurrent of confusion snakes through the members of the Dark Court. "She's been dead for centuries. I thought that by adopting her name, I would emulate her power. That I needed to be some kind of symbol. But I never needed to be anyone but myself."

A lightness expands in my chest as I realize how much I mean what I've said. The court accepts it with low grunts and uncertain chatter. Callow is nearby, and I wish she would perch on my shoulder, a familiar pressure against the wave of disquiet.

"Doesn't matter." Renard's snout wriggles. "You're still Mistress of the Dark Court. We don't have to listen to this mortal-turned-Fae or whatever she is."

Several of his Goblins voice their agreement. And another pang of fear knocks through me. That Torin's philosopher was correct, and this cycle of hate is never-ending. But no—if Aurora and I could choose each other after everything, these courts can find common ground.

"She's not Fae," I say. "And she's not mortal anymore. Aurora's power is a blend of light and dark magic. Do you see what it means for us—all of us—that these powers could come together?"

Renard grunts. "Don't see anything but crumbled mountains."

"Exactly," Aurora says, pointing to the mess of stone and Etherium. "Those mountains represent a fallen barrier. An end to the era when there were Fae and Vila and mortal courts. And do you know what brought them down? What forged this power?" She pauses. Vila and Demons trade glances. "Love."

The word ripples through the courtyard. My breath comes faster.

"Love—" Torin angles her staff between me and Aurora. "*Your* love?"

I look back at Aurora, into the amethyst of her gaze, flecked with green and gold. And I don't know how I ever could have been so foolish as to claim I did not love her. How I could have become so lost that I could not find my way back to her. Find my way home.

"Yes," I say. "I have always loved her."

A tear splashes onto Aurora's cheekbone. I want to kiss it away.

"Well . . ." An Imp's tinny voice rises above the low chatter. I brace myself for whatever is going to come next—anger, outrage, rejection. The night of Aurora's birthday party all over again. The barb-tailed creature scratches beneath his chin. "We love her, too, Mistress."

"Aye," another chimes in, displaying his daggerlike teeth. "Love all her bits and pieces. Skin and bones."

It is a slightly concerning show of affection, but I sense that it's genuine. And others begin to nod, gruffly admitting their feelings.

"You never said so," Aurora exclaims.

"Didn't think we was supposed to," the Imp replies with a shrug. "But we don't make tasties for just anyone, you know."

"Aye, and your gowns. Took extra care with those."

"And we didn't cut off any of your hair, though we could have."

"Or pull your teeth. Wanted some of those, I did."

They've become suddenly shy, toeing the ground with their long ears twitching. Aurora laughs. "It is an honor to have earned your affection. You've long held mine."

I think I see the Imps blush, though it's hard to tell with the crimson hue of their skin. But not everyone is satisfied with the day's developments.

"What then? This special power means that we should call you queen?" Renard demands. His Goblins stamp their disapproval. The Fae hiss down at him.

Aurora lifts her chin. I remember the day that she woke, when she declared that this was her palace and her realm—and how disastrously that had gone. But she does not repeat that speech. Instead, she takes the crown from her head. Sunlight, gloriously bright, dazzles on the bramble and thorn.

"For so many years, I thought I would be Briar's queen. That it was my destiny," she says. "But now . . ." Her attention roves over the crowd—the battle-weary Dark Court, and the timid servants, and the haughty Fae. "I've learned in my time here that there are many different kinds of destiny. And that even those people whom we admire most are not always who they present themselves to be."

I'm not sure where she's going with this. My heart kicks in my chest.

"That just because I wear a crown doesn't mean I'm owed anything. Or that I have the right to say what's mine." She swallows. "Therefore, I cannot ask any of you to call me queen."

Confusion trickles through the courtyard. Even Renard lowers his spear, warty brow pinched. And the Fae steeds bob up and down on the current of wind.

"You will abdicate?" one asks, hopeful.

Callow mutters a warning. And I resist the urge to make an example of this rider. He knows full well that there's no way Aurora could simply surrender her power. She'd have to die to give it up.

Aurora is quiet for several moments. "How many of you despised Oryn?"

The question surprises them. But even with Oryn rotting, they do not go so far as to voice their opinions. The truth leaks from their expressions, showing itself in tight lips and nickering mounts. I recall Aelfdene's story about how he was never supposed to be the High Lord of the Court of Dreams, and how Oryn despised him because of it.

"Go on—answer," Aurora presses. "He cannot punish you now."

"The High King," one finally speaks. "Could be a demanding master."

"And you did not rebel?" Aurora asks. "Oryn kept his throne for thousands of years."

"Our magic," the Fae goes on, "was bound to his. We could not defy him without . . . consequence."

Oh. Perhaps *this* is why so many Fae abandoned Etheria for the Vila courts. Changing their magic was the only way to escape Oryn's reach. A strange sympathy twists through me, one I never thought to feel for the Fae.

"Then I am sorry for you," Aurora says. Her focus drifts to the tight clumps of human servants. "And I'm sorry for everything that happened in Briar. The injustices and prejudices and inequality. It was my home, but it was far from perfect. And I understand that, for so many of you"—she indicates several nearby Imps and Vila—"it was a realm that drove you into exile. Destroyed your traditions and lands and families. We have all caused one another pain. But perhaps today—at long last—we stop."

Against all odds, something begins to poke its head up through the mess of confusion and resentment and fear. Hope. It's no more than a glimmer, but I lean into it.

"If I have learned anything from the Dark Court, it is that every voice deserves to be heard. Too many in Briar were silenced. And I expect it was no different under Oryn. But we can change that." She holds up her crown. "I propose that we share this symbol. We keep the existing council and add placements for the Fae and the humans. Let there be no more sides. No more rulers. We build a new court, the Briar Court, where all are welcome."

I hold my breath. Terrified that, in spite of everything, they will still reject her. That it's all been for nothing. But then a change creeps over the audience like a rising dawn. Miraculously, I hear two words begin to pulse in time with my heartbeat.

Briar Court. Briar Court.

Derek starts it, pressing his fist over his heart. His men follow suit. Then the human servants. The Imps. Torin. The Goblins, including Renard. The Demons and Vila. Even the Fae are no longer looking at Aurora like they're trying to determine the best way to kill her in her sleep. Some go so far as to lower their steeds and raise their staffs in salute. And soon the courtyard is ringing with the syllables. The sound of the Fae prophecy come to life, crumbled mountains and all.

Pride surges up from the tips of my toes and tingles in the roots of my hair. But it is bittersweet. I wish Regan were here. How would her life have been different if there had been a place like this for her?

Perhaps sensing my emotion, Aurora twines her fingers with mine. I hold on to her as tightly as I can. A princess and a Vila. But no, that's not the case anymore.

We are equals now.

CHAPTER FORTY-SEVEN

There is feasting and dancing. The Etherian heads are pried from the walls and burned in a ceremony headed by the light Fae. And then the court puts together its first official act—a joint coronation of the council leaders of Briar.

The throne room is a marvel, a cross between the glittering natural beauty of Etheria, Briar's opulence, and the sinister elegance of the Dark Court. The Imps outdid themselves. The center aisle is lined with silver-limbed trees, whose branches crest in an arch over our heads. Ravens and hummingbirds flit among Briar roses sporting shades of deepest indigo and sparkling gold and shimmery opal. Jewel-eyed dragons roar down at us from eaves. Another lounges, balanced on the railing of the mezzanine. The chamber is lit with orbs that could have come from the Court of Dreams, with clusters of stars casting a surreal glow to the proceedings.

When the time comes, I walk with the other leaders of this re-formed council, down the aisle, and toward the dais. Take my place on one of the seven seats. The thrones of the Dark Court, with their broken Fae staffs, have been replaced in favor of chairs representing each clan. The Goblins' is, naturally, decorated with an array of weapons. Aurora's with the spread wings of a dragon. Mine with an assortment of intertwined Vila crests. In the center, at my specific request, is the seal of the twisted serpents. Regan's. So that, in a way, she is here with me.

We'd called it a coronation, but there aren't any crowns. Instead, a representative from each clan presents their elected council member with an identical ring. It's fashioned from the gilded wreath of the Briar crown itself. Melted down and molded so that, while it looks like a crown, the tips are pointed toward our wrists—signifying that there will never be any single ruler of this land again. Along the band, jewels glimmer in the light. I press my fingertip into the sharp facets of the deep green emerald that represents the Vila.

Of course, the days since the final battle and founding of the Briar Court have not been entirely harmonious. The Etherians did not take kindly to the Imps' pranks, and more than one Fae retaliated by compelling the creatures to dance for hours on end. The Goblins must be repeatedly reminded not to use the mortals for target practice. And I've had to intervene in countless squabbles between the turned Fae and their former brethren. But it will all smooth in time. Probably.

"Are you all right?" Aurora whispers beside me during the feast. "You have that look on your face."

"Yes, I'm fine." I attempt a smile.

She's not entirely convinced. But the wrinkles on her forehead smooth, and her attention drifts back to the festivities. Though I try to lose myself in the dancing and celebration, I can't help but feel that something is missing. A deep gash in my soul that is impossible to staunch. I cannot tell if it's my grief for Regan, or melancholy over the dissolution of the Dark Court, or simply exhaustion.

Eventually, pretending to be happy is too great an effort. I slip into the shadows and disappear to the old wings of the palace.

Callow meets me in the old library. I wander through the wreckage, the ghost of my former self trailing behind me. I leaf through what remains of the books I'd scoured for the answer to Aurora's curse, questioning yet again what might have happened if I'd been brave enough to let her wake sooner. Would we be here today? Does it matter?

A breeze filters in through the gap in the wall, fluttering the brittle parchment. I pull another from a fallen shelf. A geography text. Its spine is broken, but its pages are filled with faded maps. It's the kind of book I would have devoured a hundred years ago, insatiably curious about what lay beyond Briar's borders. But that curiosity waned after founding the Dark Court. My gaze travels out the gap and over Briar, toward the sea.

"I thought I might find you here."

Aurora picks her way through the room, lit only by the taper she carries. The brambles guarding the door have shriveled to husks. Callow chirrups a greeting, swooping down from her place on top of a bookshelf. Aurora laughs and takes a piece of dried meat from her pocket.

"Weren't you enjoying the celebration? When I left, you were dancing with Derek."

She nudges me. "Don't say his name like that. I thought you two were coming around."

"*Slightly.*" But I smirk. "Will he be going home soon?"

"As soon as we can ready a ship. He's accepted the position we offered—ambassador to the human realms."

I thumb the corner of the book. "Fitting. That's what you planned for his great-great-grandfather or whoever, wasn't it?"

She raises an eyebrow. "You remember that?"

"Of course." I shrug. "I detested that prince, too."

Aurora laughs. "You know, you're not as hard-hearted as you'd like people to believe."

I press a hand to my chest. "Don't say things like that."

She nudges me again. And I wish she would stand closer.

"But why are you up here alone?" Aurora asks, inspecting some of the books. "Don't lie and say nothing is bothering you. I know better. Are you angry or disappointed? I would understand if part of you misses being Mistress of the Dark Court."

"Maybe a little—but that's not it." There's still a hollowness where Mortania's presence dwelled, like a phantom limb. Sometimes I feel the urge to break things simply to watch them burn.

Yes, pet, I imagine I hear on the whine of the wind.

"Then what?"

"I miss Regan," I say. "I wish that she could see the world we worked so hard to build. Even though I'm not sure she would have accepted it."

Night creatures trade their calls outside.

"I'm sorry you lost your friend," she says. And I know that she means it. "But I sense there's more than that. Does it . . . have anything to do with us?"

Callow lands on my shoulder. And I voice the question that has been plaguing my heart since the moment her curse lifted. "Is there an us?"

She twists her ring. The jewels flash in the moonlight. "I love you, Alyce. I do. But, beyond that . . . I just don't know."

A chill wind sweeps through the gap in the wall. I wrap my arms around myself. "I'm not sure I do, either."

She tries to smile, but it's a flimsy thing. "Is that because of what happened at Oryn's court? What I did?"

"Not entirely." Stars glitter overhead, uncannily bright now that they're not perpetually shrouded by thick clouds. "It's not even about you. Except . . . there will always be a part of me that is wicked. A darkness. And I'm not ashamed of it. But I'm worried you're waiting to see if I will change. I won't."

She sighs. Picks up a broken statuette of a dragon and traces its cracked wing. "That's not what I'm waiting for. Though I can't say that I'm not still angry, and hurt, over what happened to Briar. That I don't still mourn everyone I lost." She pauses. "Most of all, I just need to take a breath. Figure out who I am now that it's all over."

It's a fair answer, if a painful one. And I realize, hearing her say it out loud, that perhaps a breath is what I need, too. Space to sort out these conflicting feelings. The geography text is open on a nearby table, detailed maps staring out at me. All those realms I never explored. But they are more than ink and paper.

"I'm leaving," I say before I can stop myself.

"What?" The dragon falls with a thump. "Because of what I said? I didn't mean—"

"No. Not because of that." I pick up the book. Imagine what life is like within the borders of the other realms. "Briar is all I've ever known. First as the Dark Grace, and then as Nimara. I need to know who Alyce is away from all of this."

Away from you, I don't say. Because that's not what I want. But it might be what I need—what we both need.

Tears shine in her eyes, amplifying the slivers of gold and green. "I don't want you to go."

A month ago, I probably would have murdered someone to hear her say that. But now, a single question forms in my mind. "But why do you want me to *stay*?"

It hangs in the air, her silence heavy enough that I know this is the right course. Even though it threatens to break me apart.

"I've been thinking," I go on, to distract myself, "when the Vila and Demons and all the rest started coming to the Dark Court, they brought such horrible stories with them. I've heard about people who would collect Goblins like trophies. Villages like the one where Regan's mother was killed. Neve's Shifters were always searching for our kind in the realms across the sea, rescuing them. But we didn't put enough focus on the effort. This court could."

Aurora toys with the laces on her bodice. "And I suppose you want to be the one to do it?"

Yes. The desire races across every fiber of my being, stronger than I knew it was. "I want to do more with my power than turn candle flames green or give horns to mice."

Aurora smiles softly at the memory of our time in the Lair.

"Imagine if Regan never had to endure all the hardships of her life," I say. "I have to go—for her. And for me."

It's a long time before Aurora says anything. I don't need her permission to leave. But I'd like to have her support.

Finally, she nods. "Perhaps you're right."

I don't want to be right. I want to stay here and live the life I imagined for us. But that life was burned away when I seized Briar. And now we must make another.

"When will you go?"

"As soon as it can be arranged, I suppose."

"And will you—" There's a roughness to her voice. "Will you stay away forever?"

I wish I could tell her I'd be back. That our love would always reel me home. But I tell her the truth instead. "I don't know."

It wounds us both. She makes to leave, and I don't call after her. But just before she reaches the door, she turns back. "I've been thinking, too. About the protections Endlewild and Laurel put on my curse."

"What about them?"

"What if Laurel didn't lie?" She asks, coming closer. "What if she *did* attempt to alter my memories of you. But she couldn't. Because our love was too strong. There wasn't anything capable of harming it like that."

I turn this over in my mind. Aelfdene had said that true love was a farce. There was a time when I might have believed him. I still may. "Do you think that kind of love really exists?"

Instead of an answer, Aurora presses her lips to mine. I taste summer berries and sugared pastry and something else that is inexplicably her. Her hands go around my neck, drawing me closer. I drink her in, savoring every second.

And then she breaks off. "I suppose we'll see."

My lips still tingle, long after I'm alone.

· · ·

The Briar Court stages a raucous send-off for me. The Imps present me with countless bags of food, and the Goblins with more weapons than I can possibly need—or carry. My pockets are bulging with scraps of paper—names of friends and family members believed to be in hiding, and I promise to do everything I can to bring them home.

"You're sure about this?" Torin asks in the courtyard before I depart. I've just deflected another pack of wailing Imps.

"Don't you start," I groan. "You voted with the council to make me special ambassador."

The title had been Aurora's idea, and I'm grateful that she's shown such support for what I've decided to do. But she isn't here this morning. My chest aches with her absence, but I understand. We haven't seen much of each other since the library. It's probably better that way.

"I did." The grooves in her skin pulse orange. "I've just . . . never known the Dark Court without you. It will be odd not seeing that bird around."

From her perch on my shoulder, Callow warbles.

Torin tugs at her pendant. I still her hand, her fire-laced skin warm in the cool morning. "I have to go. For Regan and all the others."

"Indeed." Neve saunters from the palace. I had a time of convincing the Goblins not to gut her when she finally emerged after the last battle. But they eventually accepted that whatever happened with Oryn didn't matter. Neve is one of us. She always will be. "Mine will be in touch after you send word of your location. They'll arrange transport for whatever refugees you discover."

"Thank you," I say, meaning it. "And not just for that. You've done so much for me, when I didn't deserve it."

Neve deals me one of her cool Shifter smiles. "A debt must be paid."

"And what do you want? Your rooms back?"

I meant it as a joke, but her expression remains serious. "Do not forget us."

The answer surprises me so much that I cannot speak. And then, on an insane impulse, I throw my arms around the Shifter leader. It's like embracing a statue at first—but then her hands tentatively pat my back.

"I'm sorry," I say into her hair. "For not seeing you."

"Yes, well." She extracts herself. "I didn't always behave in the most becoming manner toward you, either."

I shrug. "I'm sure it won't be the last time."

She glares at me, but there's a spark of amusement in her eyes.

Someone clears their throat behind me. "You'd best be going if you want enough daylight for the crossing."

Derek has led Chaos into the courtyard. Saddlebags are strapped in place, and Callow flaps from my shoulder in favor of his haunches. He snorts a greeting and paws at the flagstones.

"Anxious to be rid of me?" I cross my arms.

"Yes," he says, so blunt about it that a laugh punches up my throat.

He kneels to help me into the saddle. But I place a hand on his shoulder. "You'll take care of her, won't you?"

Derek flashes me that lopsided grin, his eyes a warm umber in the morning sun. "She doesn't need my help, does she?"

An annoying emotion expands in my chest. "I'm going to miss tormenting you."

"And I you, Nimara."

"Call me Alyce."

I make to heave myself into the saddle, but Neve stops me. "Are you really going to ride that creature out of here?"

"What do you mean? The journey is long, and—"

"And you flew from the High Court to this palace in a day. We have discussed this already. Do not ignore your strengths." She jerks her chin toward the crowd. "Let them see you in all your glory."

Her eyes glitter, and I grin back at her. Yes. Without a second thought, I command taloned wings to rip through the fabric of my shirt and lift me into the sky. A tail elongates through the base of my spine. Chaos vaults with me into the air, mane streaming in the breeze like the tail of a comet.

And as we rise higher, over the palace, I let out a roar.

It's a sound like I've never made. A battle cry and a farewell all at once. The crowd below is in a frenzy as I circle the palace, waving and shouting. Even the light Fae look on, stoic as ever. I complete several laps with Callow and Chaos at my sides as the Imps pile atop one another and cheer. Goblins raise their spears and stomp their feet. Vila pump their fists and some of the Demons trail me in their shadow forms.

My attention snags on the endless blue of the horizon line. How long had I stared at it as the Dark Grace, desperate to know what lay beyond? It's time to find out.

I steer toward the sea. But as we round the last turret, a figure materializes, pressed against the balcony railing, her golden hair whipping around her face. She lifts one hand, beckoning me or waving me on, I can't tell which. But my keen eyes detect the sorrow etched in the lines of her form. The resolve. The love. A love that broke a curse, not once, but twice.

I roar a final time—for her. Aurora. Perhaps not destined to be queen, but certainly to bring about the dawn of her namesake.

And then the last shadow Demon melts away, and the palace shrinks into nothing.

EPILOGUE

"It's been hours. Are you certain she's coming?"

The Vila's gaze travels up and down the rocky shoreline, forehead pinched above the bone spikes studding her eyebrows.

"Don't be silly," the other answers. "Of course she's coming. Alyce wouldn't drag us all this way for nothing."

But it's obvious that she's trying to convince herself as well as her companion. She strangles her cloak in her fists, emerald eyes bright in the waning afternoon sun.

"She's coming," I assure them both. Callow chirrups from her perch on my shoulder.

Though I can't blame them for their apprehension. It's been a hundred years since I first set foot on these shores, but fear of my kind is alive and well. Despite the progress of the last decades, there will always be those who remain hungry to string up a Vila or a Shifter simply for the crime of existing. Not that I haven't dispensed with plenty of them over the last decades. Months ago,

I liberated a dozen Vila who were caged in a nobleman's manor. He was attempting to craft his own version of elixirs with their blood. What I'd done to that nobleman does not bear repeating, but suffice it to say that I have found *many* opportunities to utilize my magic on this side of the sea.

"Briar," the first Vila says, interrupting my thoughts. "It's really what everyone claims it to be?"

This is likely the hundredth time she's asked me about our court. But I am patient. "It is everything I promised and more," I tell her. "You'll not be turned away. I promise."

They nod, still nervous. Few of those I rescue believe that their lives can be free of the fear that has seeped into the marrow of their bones. And I've met too many to count. Goblins living under bridges and demanding tolls be paid, a bounty on their warty heads. Imps mistaken for forest spirits with their pranks, trapped and kept as household pets. I'd discovered these two Vila only weeks ago, living in a dank and frigid mountain cave. They would have died of starvation if hunters hadn't found them first. But they'll never have to worry about that again.

The council opened Briar's borders as soon as the realm was stable. Governorships were established in the outer provinces, formerly the Fae courts. Their merchants cross the sea to sell Fae-made sails that can never tear and seeds that never fail to bloom. Not weapons, though—nothing that might be used to start another fruitless war.

"But what about—" The Vila plucks at her jacket.

"You'll be safe," I say before another of her countless doubts resurfaces. Chaos—who has been snuffling for nonexistent plants to eat among the jagged rocks—snorts in what can only be affirmation.

But I understand the Vila's concern. Early on, there was talk in the mortal realms of laying siege to Briar. I'd heard the babble from under the hood of my cloak while passing through cities and towns. Realms that, despite their poverty, yearned to lay claim to the magic threading Briar. But then word trickled in of how Aurora's power ruptured the mountains. How all the creatures of magical blood banded together. Rumors of invasion ceased after that.

Callow repositions herself and warbles a warning.

"There!" One of the Vila points.

A shape soars closer, a falcon. But as it descends in front of us, its wings morph into arms, talons into legs, and its fierce eyes and beak into a face I've come to know very well indeed.

"Neve." I fish an apple out of my bag and hand it to her.

As promised, the Shifter initiated our communication within a year after I left Briar. She and her network of Starlings are now primarily responsible for providing refugees with a swift journey across the sea.

"How are things at court?" I ask.

She wipes apple juice from her lips. "Well. Torin and the others say hello. And *she* sends her regards."

Warmth blooms in my chest, as it always does, no matter how much time has passed. Even so, my memories of Aurora are bittersweet. Derek may not have captured Aurora's hand, but some did find their way to her heart. I've heard plenty of talk of courtiers whom I suspect are closer than friends. It used to bother me, learning that she'd taken a lover. That someone else was so intimately close to her. But, eventually, I came to understand that I didn't want her to be alone forever. She deserves happiness. And I admit that I haven't always been alone, either.

"You're the Shifter?" One of the Vila steps hesitantly forward. She's too thin, despite the food I've shoved at them these last weeks.

"I am." Neve dips her chin. "An arduous journey lies ahead of us. Let's waste no time. There's a camp a few hours from here where we'll pass the night." She glances at me. "I expect I'll hear from you before long?"

"Yes. There are rumors of a pack of Imps wandering south of here. I'll let you know when they're ready."

Neve groans and flings away her apple core. Chaos swishes his tail in interest. "Wonderful. The palace certainly needs more of those deviants."

I laugh, missing the creatures and their endless supply of pastries and fashion. The years of merchant's food, dried meats, and Callow's tribute cannot compare. Perhaps I'll keep the Imps with me for a time when I find them.

Without further delay, Neve Shifts into a winged beast, broad enough for both Vila to sit on her back. They embrace me, quickly and fiercely, before clambering onto her haunches, and then the trio rises into the air.

I watch the sunset-painted waves of the horizon until the chill of the night bites beneath my cloak and urges me on.

Some weeks later, while I'm in pursuit of the Imps, a branch creaks nearby. Callow chirrups, announcing her return, and flaps to my shoulder. Chaos thumps his back hoof in greeting.

"Well," I say to the kestrel. "What have you brought me?"

There's a scroll of parchment tied to her body—a missive from court, addressed to the special ambassador.

I am not the only ambassador on this side of the sea. The council deemed it more appropriate that a human should deal with the mortal rulers, which is fine with me. I have no patience for such relationships. The idea of tailoring my every word and action to suit some pompous monarch is nothing short of nauseating.

Derek was the first to serve as liaison to the humans. I encountered him a few times during my journeys. He became the king of Ryna before long and helped to bring wealth and prosperity back to his realm. And he was honored by the Briar Court when he died in his sleep at the age of ninety-seven. I did not attend, but I heard that he was buried with a locket around his neck, one that contained a curl of burnished-gold hair.

I thumb the gilt edge of the parchment. It's an invitation.

The Briar Court is pleased to announce the hundredth anniversary of its founding.

Festivities will be held within the month.

All are welcome to share in the realm's joy.

Another century gone. I can scarcely believe it, the years having drained away like grains of sand in an hourglass. And never once have I returned to Briar. There didn't seem much point. Neve tells me everything I need to know about court. And I receive letters—news relayed in a looping script that conveys a warm, if formal, tone. It's always been enough.

But then I turn the parchment over.

Alyce, I can almost hear Aurora's voice through the ink, *come home.*

My heart snags. Because I know that she doesn't mean the palace. Or even the court. She means *home.* To her.

Could I? No. There's been too much, and I'm happy with my life.

But then I close my eyes, imagining her scent carried on the breeze. The silken heat of Aurora's lips against mine on the night the world came crashing down around us. The quaking of the room, and of my very bones. The look in her eyes when she realized.

You broke the curse.

Perhaps, finally, it is time to break another.

ACKNOWLEDGMENTS

Authors always joke that their second book almost kills them. Reader, it is not a joke. There were many, many times when I worried this book was too much. When I lost my way and my hold on the story and its characters. And I think it's important for authors to be transparent about that—we don't always have the perfectly crafted story in our minds. But in the end, Alyce—in her surly fashion—came back to me. This is the book that was waiting to be found. Of course, if you disagree, feel free to imagine your own ending for our Alyce. Stories, after all, vary greatly depending on who's telling them.

Navigating this book would have been impossible without my incredible U.S. and UK editors, Tricia Narwani and Sam Bradbury. Thank you for your unending patience when it came to reading drafts and the gold mine of advice you offered (even when I went on tangents about hummingbirds). I would not have found the heart of this book without you, and I'm so grateful you pushed me to write the story Alyce deserves.

To my fierce champion of an agent, Laura Crockett. Thank you for talking me off the ledge while I stalked the aisles of that obnoxious store, and never doubting that I could do this. You're part agent, part therapist, part superfan, and mostly magician. And I am incredibly lucky you plucked me from the slush.

Thank you to all of my friends and family who helped and encouraged me during the writing of this sequel. To my parents and brothers, who were as excited about each step of this process as I was. To every person who bought my book just because they knew me—your support means more than I can say.

Ashley, the Dark Court was born during our high school obsessions with *Labyrinth*. I wish we could pack up and go there right now. And Bentley. You are such a cool person. I'm so proud of you, and now the whole world knows. I can't wait to watch you grow. We love you.

Chloe Gong, Tasha Suri, and Kaylynn Flanders, I have so enjoyed our commiserating, celebratory, and often snarky DMs. I'm so excited to read more of your books.

Tom, Kristin, and Liam, the stars that aligned to lead us to your backyard are the luckiest I know. I found my way through this book in that thin place. Kristin, thank you for being the biggest cheerleader ever. Tom, especially, thank you for shining a light I didn't know I needed. Liam, here it is in print, so it must be true—you can't see the way yet, but you will do incredible things. And most of all to Fitz. You cannot read, but you are just as great as Callow.

Thank you to the whole team at Del Rey, for prioritizing this duology and my villainous Alyce, and for championing this book with more passion than I could have dreamed. Whether it was gorgeous covers, generous giveaways, or once-in-a-lifetime opportunities, I've been a very lucky author to have found my home with you. Thank you also to the team at Barnes & Noble, who have welcomed both me and these books with open arms. Teenage Heather would lose her mind if she knew her favorite place in the world would one day house her books.

Thank you to every librarian, bookseller, and reader who loved this series and pushed it into other people's hands. Laynie (@thelaynierose) and Sammie (@booksdogsandcoffee), you have made my debut year especially amazing. Readers, I cannot tell you how grateful I am for you. Thank you for ushering me into the world of authorhood with your praise, fan art, videos, and overall squee. I do not quite feel worthy.

And lastly, as always, my biggest thanks to Lindsey. In so many ways, my life was cursed before I knew you. Thank you for lifting it. Thank you for your unending patience, your insistence that I celebrate every moment, your support when I'm angry with imaginary people. I'm writing it here so that you can't argue back— I am the lucky one.

ABOUT THE AUTHOR

Heather Walter is a native Southerner who hates the heat. A graduate of the University of Texas at Austin, she is both a former English teacher and a current librarian. Perhaps it is because she's surrounded by stories that she began writing them. At any given moment, you can find her plotting.

heatherrwalter.com
Twitter: @heatherrwalter5
Instagram: @heatherrwalter5
TikTok: @heatherrwalter5

ABOUT THE TYPE

This book was set in Sabon, a typeface designed by the well-known German typographer Jan Tschichold (1902–74). Sabon's design is based upon the original letter forms of sixteenth-century French type designer Claude Garamond and was created specifically to be used for three sources: foundry type for hand composition, Linotype, and Monotype. Tschichold named his typeface for the famous Frankfurt typefounder Jacques Sabon (c. 1520–80).